THE WOLF AND THE BUFFALO

Also by Elmer Kelton from the TCU Press

ELMER KELTON

The Wolf and the Buffalo

Introduction by Elmer Kelton
Afterword by Lawrence Clayton

TCU Press
Fort Worth, Texas

The Wolf and the Buffalo
by Elmer Kelton

The Texas Tradition Series: Number Five
James Ward Lee, Series Editor

Copyright © 1980 by Elmer Kelton
Afterword copyright © 1986 by TCU Press

First published by Doubleday and Company, Inc. in 1980

Library of Congress Cataloging-in-Publication Data
Kelton, Elmer.
The wolf and the buffalo.

(Number five in the Texas tradition series)
1. United States. Army—Afro-American troops—History—Fiction. 2.
United States. Army. Cavalry, 10th—History—Fiction. 3. Comanche
Indians—Fiction.
I. Title. II. Series: Texas tradition series; no. 5.
PS3561.E3975W6 1986   813´.54   85-20814
ISBN 978-0-87565-059-3 (pbk.; alk. paper)

TCU Press
P. O. Box 298300
Fort Worth, Texas 76129
817.257.7822
http://www.prs.tcu.edu

To order books: 800.826.8911

Cover painting by Burl Washington

Dedicated to the memory of friends
who never came home from *our* war.
They will be forever young.

Dick Allen
Billy Allman
Norman Dean Brunette
Herman Crawford
Lee Irvine
Edwin Wright

Introduction

OLD UNCLE HENRY MOORE, a longtime farmer who had worked on the Texas and Pacific Railroad in the early days of West Texas settlement, told me years ago that he thought a lot of people vitally important to the West's development were sadly overlooked in its literature.

He thought the cowboy and the rancher probably deserved the good press they received, but the gambler and the gunfighter, the saloon crowd and the outlaw were vastly overplayed. Neglected, he contended, were the dirt farmer, the merchant, the freighter, the carpenter, the teacher and the preacher. Those, he said, were the builders.

He did not mention the black soldier, but he could have. Only in recent years has the black soldier's role in the Indian wars begun to be given the recognition it deserves. Generations of Texas history students learned about the frontier picketline of military posts guarding the western fringe of settlement, but seldom was the point made to them that a substantial number of the soldiers were black.

The black trooper's service on the frontier was fraught with ironies. In general, the people whose interests he protected had little regard for him, and little gratitude. Indeed, in one instance black soldiers rode a Texas stagecoach as guards but had to walk back. The coach's owner—a Yankee, incidentally—accepted them as guards but not as passengers. Colonel William R. Shafter, always demanding of his buffalo soldiers but protective of their rights, forcefully put an end to that discrimination, though it earned him a reprimand and a mark on his military record.

In essence it was the black trooper's role to take the land away from the red man so the white man could have it. The soldier had little to gain personally except in terms of his military career. He was not encouraged to remain in the community when his service was completed, much less to become a landowner or businessman.

Relations between black soldiers and the local citizenry were usually strained, to say the least. Fort Concho and neighboring Saint Angela, later San Angelo, had one major race riot and a number of lesser confrontations arising out of mutual dislike. When the last black troops marched away to the west, one of San Angelo's pioneer settlers declared it to be the happiest day in the town's history. The soldiers probably considered it a happy day for themselves as well.

From the army's viewpoint, black soldiers offered both advantages and handicaps. An advantage was that as former slaves they were used to accepting orders without question. No matter how primitive and difficult their military living conditions might be, they were better than most of the buffalo soldiers had ever known. The desertion rate among blacks at the time was far lower than among white soldiers.

Disadvantages included an almost universal illiteracy among the first generation of black troopers. As slaves, few had been encouraged to learn to read and write, or even allowed to. In the early years it was difficult to get most black soldiers to take serious personal initiative, for in their previous condition of servitude they had been discouraged from doing so.

Black units tended to receive the poorest of equipment, the poorest of horses. White officers in black units often shared the discrimination exerted upon their men, for they were looked down upon by their peers in white units. Promotions came a bit easier in black regiments because fewer officers chose to serve in them and competition was less keen. However, a promotion's price could be severe in terms of an officer's prestige outside of his own unit.

••

The Wolf and the Buffalo is the only one of my novels written at someone else's suggestion. The publishers wanted a novel about the black cavalry in the West, and I agreed to the subject because I was already somewhat familiar with the history of Fort Concho, long a headquarters for the black Tenth Cavalry. I approached the project with some trepidation, feeling that it would have been more appropriate for the story to be told by a black writer.

Having risen no higher in rank than Pfc. in World War II, I thought I could relate in many aspects to the private soldier on the frontier. It was my intention from the beginning to tell the story from the viewpoint of a private, as far down in the ranks as it was possible to be. The few fictional works I had read on the subject were written as seen by a white officer, not from the ground-level view of the black enlisted man like Gideon Ledbetter, who ate the dust and took the abuse and rode until his rump was raw.

That was one of the few points which proceeded according to original plan. My intention was to bring in the Indian character, Gray Horse Running, only in a minor way to serve as a counterpoint to the soldier's experience. But Gray Horse would not let me get away with it.

People who have not tried to write fiction never seem to understand how a character can grab a story and run off in directions of his own, sometimes against the writer's wishes. They argue that the characters belong to the writer, who should be able to make them do whatever he wants. It does not work that way. Strong characters take on a life and a will of their own. It behooves the writer to give them a loose rein and allow them to follow their true nature. If he tries to force them back into his preconceived mold, the results too often seem artificial, lacking in spontaneity and even in plausibility.

Gray Horse kept expanding his role, rivaling the attention given to Gideon. He forced me to take a deeper and more compassionate look at his tragic situation. His way of life was collapsing with an awesome suddenness. He was being failed by the mystical protective spirits around whom his entire existence revolved.

I found myself writing two stories about two men whose lives were moving in contrary directions. Gideon, the former slave, was on the ascent, gradually acquiring confidence and self-esteem. Gray Horse, the Comanche, was losing his faith and his spiritual power as his people were being overrun by a force they could not withstand.

Throughout the story the two men cross trails but never become aware of each other as individual human beings. This is as it would have been. To the Indian, the buffalo soldier was simply another white man whose face happened to be black. To the black soldier, the Indian was the same deadly enemy he appeared to the whites. In retrospect it is evident that the former slaves and the Indians had much in common. It would be tempting to visualize their forming an alliance. But in history it seldom happened. An occasional escaped slave found sanctuary among Indians, but most often such runaways found only further enslavement or, more likely, sudden death. Neither slave nor Indian seemed to recognize the potential common bond.

In the end there simply was no way for the white man and the horse Indian of the plains to co-exist and share the land in any type of equality. Their vastly different cultures would have kept them eternally in conflict. The white man was acquisitive and sedentary. The nomadic plains Indian lived by the hunt and by warfare. Only through combat with his enemies did a man earn honor in the eyes of his people. Disarmed, unhorsed, the youth was robbed of his ancient rites of passage and the older warrior left impotent.

As for the black soldier, he gave his service and sometimes his life without gaining much recognition or honor. But at least it was a step up from slavery, a step toward the eventual recognition of his people as an integral part of the country he served.

There are no real villains in *The Wolf and the Buffalo*. I tried to keep the treatment even-handed and present the various opposing forces as products of their era, their traditions and their circumstances. It is unfair to judge past generations by the standards of our own time, any more than we would like to be judged by whatever standards may exist a hundred years from now. If, for instance, we are to condemn our forefathers for wresting the land from the Comanches, we must also condemn the Comanches for having taken it from the Apaches, and the Apaches for having taken it from even earlier dwellers.

Covetousness is not a trait of any one race. It is a trait of mankind.

Elmer Kelton
San Angelo, Texas

THE WOLF AND THE BUFFALO

One

LESSER MEN HAD invented the name the world knew them by: *Comanche*. Individual bands might be designated as the Buffalo Eaters or the Antelopes or the Honey Eaters, but the tribe itself had no name among its members. It needed none. They referred to themselves simply as *the* People, the true human beings, superior to all others and most favored by the spirits.

Gray Horse Running, one of the Comanche, trembled expectantly as first dawn touched the two mountains with fire. Up there, perhaps still sleeping, waited whatever spirit was to give him his medicine, his spiritual power for a life as a warrior and a man of the People.

He was in his eighteenth summer, and he had prepared a long time. Now he and the spirit would meet, face to face.

Out of the gently rolling plains of western Texas, a hundred miles beyond permanent white settlement, the dual promontories known on military maps as the Double Mountains pushed up like two ships adrift on a vast green sea of prairie grass. Many white men knew of them, but few had seen them. Randolph Marcy had mapped them in his exploration of 1849. Even earlier, angry Texas frontiersmen, seeking vengeance for a Comanche raid deep into their new settlements, had followed a trail carelessly left by retreating warriors who thought they were safe in their own homeland. Not far from here the *tejanos* had fallen upon a large village, leaving it a bloody, smoking ruin. But these penetrations had been rare. Even now, though watchful by their nature, the Comanches felt relatively secure in the shadow of these twin relics from an earlier geologic age, landmarks long a guide for buffalo-hunting bands making their way across this vast prairie.

A few miles to the south, the red-bottomed Double Mountain Fork of the Brazos River snaked sluggishly southeastward to join the Salt Fork and the Clear Fork, forming one great river that meandered down through old Texas settlements—Washington-on-the-Brazos, San Felipe—to spill its muddy waters into the Gulf of Mexico at Matagorda Bay. That was a land shut off forever from the restless Comanche but still remembered in stories the old men told of giants who had ridden their war ponies into the salty Gulf, snatching hapless *tejanos* from their boats and spilling their blood into the foaming water.

Summer had narrowed the river to a ribbon, its waters evil with salts and gyp. This band of the People had divided and strung their tepees along a pair of small creeks fed by sometime springs south and a little east of the mountains. The great horse herd ranged by day under a loose guard of young boys on the broad grassy slope reaching upward from the fork's south bank. The horses were brought together for closer guard by night. The Kiowas had been the People's allies for many years, and there was no fear of theft from that quarter. But to the west and southwest roamed the wily Apaches, blood enemies from so far back in time that no one knew why. Occasionally they foraged this far onto the plains in search of meat and horses and Comanche scalps to win acclaim in their scattered *rancherías* in those far, arid mountains to which the determined Comanches had long since driven them.

All summer Gray Horse Running had stood his turn at guarding the herd, but last night he had been freed that he could prepare to seek his medicine. At the direction of the medicine man, Comes Down from the Mountain, he had bathed in the creek so he could present himself clean in body and soul to whatever spirits might await him. He had smoked a bone pipe and had the shaman sing over him and paint his face and chest with symbols and colors. As dawn streaked yellow and orange through flat, low clouds to the east, he walked alone toward the nearest of the mountains. He was clad only in long-tasseled moccasins and a deerskin breechclout dyed a blood red. A long-faced dog trailed after him, endangering the sacred mission. Should the dog profane the vigil site—and it almost certainly would—all might be lost. One of the darker spirits might put a spell over Gray Horse. He hurled a rock and struck the dog a glancing blow along a bony hip. Howling in pain, the cur turned back toward camp, tail between its legs. Gray Horse had no wish to kill it, for it was a favorite of his younger brothers. But he would if he had to. The medicine was too important to risk for a dog.

He looked back a minute upon the quiet camp, upon the row of buffalo-hide tepees fronting the creek, all facing east. Smoke was rising through some of the wind flaps, between the upper ends of the long poles that formed the conical shapes. He smelled cooking meat on the faint cool breeze from the east, and it stirred him to hunger. But he was not to eat today, nor probably for the three days that would follow. To find a beneficent spirit that would guide his life, a young man was required to fast as many as four days and nights in a solitary place where neither he nor the spirits would be disturbed by human activity. Sometime before the four days were over, if he were fortunate, he would receive a sign; perhaps a clear and unquestioned visitation, perhaps only a brief and ephemeral wisp of sound or shadow.

Other plains tribes had well-defined group religions and elaborate ceremonies, honed to precision by long generations of tradition. They often regarded the Comanche as atheist, but this was not so. Gray Horse's nomadic people, so often on the move, so often divided for months at a time into small family groups or warrior parties, had no organized religion, no central church, no priest. But they believed in a Sure-Enough Father who lived beyond the sun. Each person talked with Him in his own way. The world was ruled by a variety of diverse spirits, some benevolent, some neutral, some dark and evil. Each man sought his own alliances with the supernatural, trying to obtain the blessings of one or more guardian powers that would guide and protect him.

Until a young man had at least the beginnings of his personal medicine—some sign of approval by a good spirit—it was not wise for him to venture upon the war trail. He would be a risk to himself and to those who rode with him. No matter what his other skills might be, he had no real stature in the band until he had proven himself in war. Gray Horse had chafed a long time, rebuffed in his efforts to go on a raid. He had proven himself worthy otherwise. By his tenth summer, he was known as a superior horseman and had earned the name he now carried. Three times he had joined the buffalo hunt and had pleased his family by good work with the shortbow. But he had not been accepted for a war party because he had not acquired power. He would not be considered a whole man until he had counted coup, and if his guiding spirit was a strong one, had taken scalps of the enemy.

There were many enemies to choose from.

Three times before, he had tried for power and had failed. This time he felt certain he would find what he sought, because to the People the number *four* had a spiritual significance. He carried a buffalo robe, a bone pipe and a plain bullhide shield without decoration. He had been weeks in preparing the shield, using the heaviest hide from shoulders of buffalo bulls he himself had killed, stretching it in several thicknesses over a convex frame of willow wood, packing buffalo hair tightly between the layers to absorb the impact of arrow or bullet. He hoped a spirit might show him how it should be decorated to give it more protective power. Spirits often provided this service.

He studied the mountains intently as he walked toward them. They were the highest places for a day's ride or more in any direction. The spirits would surely seek out the high points.

After an hour's walk he stopped and spread the robe on the ground. He packed sumac into the bone pipe, fired a twist of dry grass with his flint and lighted up, trying to put out of his mind any thoughts except of his quest and the careful instructions the medicine man had given him. He took six long puffs and blew smoke in each of the six directions, up, down, east, south, west and north. Smoke was a messenger, carrying the word of his coming. He sent it to the four winds, to his father beyond the sun and to his mother the earth. The shaman had told him to perform the ritual four times on the way to his vigil.

After his second smoke he saw a flash of movement ahead of him. From a distance the deceptive terrain appeared smooth, but it was cut by gullies, and on gravelly ridges numerous stunted junipers clung stubbornly to the shallow soil where the taller and better grasses could not sustain themselves. He saw a gray wolf scouting for rabbits or kangaroo rats or whatever else it might flush from hiding. The young man's heartbeat quickened. Traditions drilled into him from boyhood had conditioned him to watch for portentous signs.

The Comanche had much respect for the wolf and rarely killed it. It was a great hunter, and a man fortunate enough to acquire the wolf medicine would be a great hunter, too. The wolf was crafty and shrewd. It was accepted as fact among the People that a wolf could not be killed by guns—only by an arrow. If he observed all its rules, a warrior who had the wolf medicine could ride safely into the thickest of the battle, and the bullets would roll off of his body as harmlessly as the rain.

Gray Horse set out to follow the wolf at a respectful distance, far enough not to be in its way or to spoil its hunting, for he had no wish to make it angry and cause it to withhold its medicine. For a time the wolf zigzagged across the prairie in its search. It stopped on a ridge and looked back. He had heard old men say that wolves had spoken to them in voices as clear as that of a brother. He listened, but the wolf said nothing—or if it spoke, the distance was too great. Gray Horse stood a while after the wolf went over the ridge and out of sight. When it did not reappear, he walked toward the point where he had last seen it. It was gone. All he found was four tracks in a small patch of coarse sand—four of the biggest wolf tracks he had ever seen. He knelt and touched his fingers to one, hoping he might feel the power in it. He noted that there were not three tracks, not five—but four. That in itself was a favorable sign. Perhaps the wolf had spoken to him in a way of its own. Time and the vigil would tell him.

He paused a third time at the foot of the mountain, pulling grass burrs from his bare shins and spreading the buffalo robe among the boulders. Before he lighted the pipe, he looked up at the mountain and knew it was taller, more formidable than he had supposed. The day's heat was beginning to bear hard upon him. Sweat ran down his body, streaking the medicine man's paint.

The climb was difficult, for the sides were often steep and the gravel was treacherous underfoot. Several times he started to slide and found nothing to grab. The shield and the buffalo robe complicated his problem, but they were essential. Though his copper body was lean and hard and muscular and his lungs were strong, he found himself stopping frequently for breath, looking both ahead and behind him, always disappointed at how far he still had to go. His growling stomach reminded him that he had not eaten. Deep breaths were like the cutting edge of a knife to his dry throat.

The mountainside was reddish two thirds of the way up, then turned grayer. He wondered if there might be some supernatural explanation for the difference in color. Perhaps one set of spirits had built the bottom part and another had finished the mountain. He had heard legends of the earth's turning red where brave men had fought and died. Perhaps in the long-forgotten past, when men walked instead of riding horseback, there had been a battle on this mountainside and brave fighters had fallen. Or perhaps not even men at all, but the spirits themselves at war. The thought made him shiver. He had heard of stranger things.

The notion stayed with him as he climbed. What if the battle had been between good and bad spirits, and the bad spirits had won? What if they still controlled the mountain? The shaman's incantations and his paints had been designed partly to attract a good spirit and partly to ward away the evil, but after all, the the shaman was only a man.

Gray Horse remembered a cousin who had died on his quest for medicine. No one had spoken his name in two years, for the name was supposed to die with him. This boy had carried the protection of a shaman, but it had not been enough. The medicine of the malevolent spirits was stronger. On the fifth day, his searching family found his body swollen and black. The dark spirits had somehow deceived and distracted the lad and had sent a rattlesnake to bite him. The shaman said the boy probably had not followed his instructions faithfully and had nullified the protective medicine. He was known to be careless.

Gray Horse was almost to the top when the loose gravel slipped beneath his moccasins. He slid on his stomach, moving faster as he went down. The sharp rocks gouged and ripped at him. He lost the shield and he would have lost the robe, had he not tied it across his back. He slammed his left leg against a boulder and stopped. The pain was sharp and, for a moment, almost overwhelming. Half numb, he turned slowly and carefully onto his side, anxious not to slide again. The leg throbbed and burned. He seemed unable to move it. If it was broken, he would probably die on this mountain; no one was likely to come looking for him before the fifth day. Fear threatened to smother him. In defense he started singing an incantation the shaman had taught him, a song to draw benevolent spirits. His heart, racing at first, began to slow. He managed to sit up. He was able to feel the leg with both hands and assure himself that the bone was not broken. But his stomach and his legs were lacerated. In his left knee, where he had struck the sharp edge of the boulder, he found a deep gash, bleeding strongly. If the bleeding continued it would surely weaken him. He would never complete the climb, nor would he likely get back down to the foot of the mountain by himself. He inched his way carefully to a small patch of short, dry grass. Pulling it up by handfuls, he wadded it tightly and pressed it against the wound. It took a while, but he stopped the bleeding.

He felt a chill, then a long spell of nausea. He sensed that the longer he stayed here, the less likely that he could finish the climb. Soreness and stiffness were sure to set in. Painfully he dragged himself upward, inches at a time. He came to the shield and hung it on his left arm, as he knew he should have done before. He resumed the climb, pausing often to rest. After a terribly long time he dragged himself over the rimrock to the top.

There he looked westward across a flat mesa. A sudden strong wind struck him hard in the face. It was a warm wind—almost hot—but it was good against his sweating body. He struggled to his feet and gloried in the force of that healing wind. The pain ebbed. This wind had come to him as a friend. Some malicious spirit had tried to stop him, but his stern will had bested it, and he stood on top. The signs were favorable. He spread the blanket and smoked the fourth time.

By tradition, the Comanche looked to the east for good things. Gray Horse sat on the edge of the rimrock and faced eastward, settling down for what he knew would be a long and lonely watch. The cut knee had begun a rhythmic throbbing, but it had probably been given to test him. His uncle or his real father would have paid it no attention. His pride was troubled that he could not ignore the insistent pain. He tried to force his mind to important matters, to the quest.

He had been taught that a true vision seldom came quickly—not the first time. For most young men of hardy constitution, it rarely came before the fourth day or night, when hunger had banished all minor affairs. Only then was a novice properly receptive, ready to see and hear and accept the true significance of subtle and fleeting things. He thought about the good warriors he had known and tried to visualize how the power must first have come to them. It was something he had to surmise, for the most part, because few men were willing to talk at length about the experience lest sharing of the knowledge diminish the medicine. Not even his uncle—who had been father to him since his eighth summer—had told him everything about his own.

"When you are ready, you will be shown all you need to know," Black Robe had said.

Gray Horse sat with the afternoon sun hot upon his bare back. He tried to concentrate only on spirits and on the songs the medicine man had given him, but his youthful mind wandered as his gaze fastened upon the distant village. He remembered his previous vigils and his disappointment. Other men younger than he had been accepted to ride away with good warriors and strike the *tejano* settlements or to take the long and ancient war trail deep into Mexico, but he had been left with the women.

He had long worried that his true father's ghost might be troubled about his failure. As far back as he could remember, he had followed a difficult pattern. The memory was still vivid. No

one in the band had been more skillful at relieving his enemies of
their horses than his father. The Comanche did not regard this as
stealing. The concept of theft was applied only when something
was taken from one of the People. To appropriate property
claimed by an enemy was not only honorable, but a duty. Many
times Gray Horse's father had stolen into an enemy camp and
had taken horses tethered to Ute tepees or Apache wickiups or
tied to a white man's picket line. That carried more honor than
simply killing an enemy and then catching his loose horse. Other
warriors had been eager to follow him because his raids were
usually successful; they yielded many horses and many coups.
He could take his pick among good men. Seldom did he come
back into camp with his face painted black and his horse's tail
cut short because he had lost a man. Never did he leave a dead
companion's body to be mutilated and dishonored by the enemy,
condemning the soul to oblivion.

Then came a time when it was deemed necessary to carry
punishment to the Apache for an atrocity committed against a
small Comanche camp. It was a matter of vengeance, blood for
blood. Gray Horse's father had assumed the unquestioned leadership, and for this mission of honor he had taken an eagle-feather
bonnet never worn before in battle. The Comanches attacked
boldly but found the Apache force strong. Some warriors pulled
back, afraid that their medicine was weak. Gray Horse's father
stepped down from his war pony and plunged the point of his
lance into the ground, a sign that from that spot he would not
retreat. He cried for the others to rally. But the enemy swept
over him as he chanted a medicine song. To their credit, his
comrades did not leave him on the field to be scalped and hacked
and robbed of the afterlife. Two bold men riding abreast had
leaned down from their running horses and lifted him up between them, carrying him away to be buried with honor.

Gray Horse had been haunted ever since by the remembered
fear, by the wild lamentations spreading through camp as the
riders straggled in by ones and twos with blackened faces.
Shrieking her grief, his mother had hacked short her black hair
and had slashed herself until she fainted from loss of blood.

On its way home, the beaten war party had chanced upon a

small hunting group of Apaches and had vented their terrible wrath, killing every man, woman and child except one young girl, whom they passed from one warrior to another, dishonoring, through her, all of her people. When she was brought into camp, Gray Horse's relatives, their blood hot for vengeance, fell upon her and hacked her to pieces.

There was no question of mercy or pity. This was the way war had always been fought. No wrong could be done to an enemy, and the face of an enemy was the same whether it was man, woman or child.

The responsibility for the family had passed to the next oldest brother, Black Robe. The following spring, he had led eager young fighters into an Apache camp from which not one male over twelve summers had escaped. Among the trophies recovered was the blood-stained warbonnet. After that, following ancient custom, he had taken his oldest brother's widow to wife, though he already had a younger one of his own. He had taken Gray Horse and his brother and sister as his children, and their status in his eyes and in the family was the same as if they had been born to him. Gray Horse regarded him as his father and his cousins as his brothers and sisters. So it had always been among the People; it was the only way they had survived the ages. All kindred blood was family. The man who would let family suffer while he could ride and hunt and fight was of low degree.

Ebbing day stretched the shadow of the mountain across a long bench beneath him, then eastward to gentle the rough breaks and blend them into the rolling prairie. He was surprised to see a thin old buffalo bull out there, grazing alone, probably chased from its harem of cows by a younger bull in the constant struggle for prairie supremacy. He wondered how this aged bull had strayed so near the camp without one of the sharp-eyed hunters finding it. They surely would, sooner or later.

A movement on the bench caught his eye. Two wolves paced across it. The larger—a male—was probably the one he had seen on his way to the mountain. "Brother wolf!" he shouted. "I am up here." The big wolf gave no sign of hearing or, if he heard, that the boy was of any interest to him. Chances were that the pair had a den down there and were feeding young—if they

were real wolves. If they were spirit wolves, they knew well
enough of his presence. He sang the shaman's song so they
would know that he was ready to receive any message.

Night came, dark and lonely. He looked a long while toward
the village. He smoked again, following the form passed down
from the distant time when the People had been part of the
Shoshone, living a hard and precarious existence in the edge of
the great mountains somewhere to the north. Gray Horse was
aware from legends that once, before the horse, the People had
roamed and hunted afoot, the women carrying their possessions
from camp to camp on their backs and on small travois dragged
by their dogs, while the men carried only their weapons and
remained on constant guard. Their enemies were many. The
People had owned little because weight was a burden. Hunting
had been difficult, especially for buffalo. A man's personal medicine had been of extreme importance, for the whole world
seemed set against him; his only allies were the rest of the People, and whatever kindly spirits he might invoke to generosity.

Following the shaman's instructions, Gray Horse spread the
buffalo robe and lay upon it, then pulled it over his head. He lay
awake listening to the night wind crying across the mesa, to the
crickets, to the birds that hid by day but came out at night to
sing in praise of the moon. He faced east, that dawn might not
catch him asleep and unaware. He had to be awake for the rising
sun to give him its warmth and power.

He did not sleep well. Though he had been taught not to fear,
fear of another failure was with him. The gash on his knee
burned with growing intensity. He rose up once and heard a surprised snort from some animal. He was startled but not frightened. He knew of no animal likely to harm him here.

He was sitting up waiting long before color came to the eastern sky. He smoked and took all the power the rising sun would
give him. His knee was stiff. The edges of the gash were beginning to puff and redden. When he had performed the rituals he
began a slow and limping exploration, looking for something that
might heal the wound. Horse or buffalo dung would be best, but
he found none on the mesa. He came upon a prickly pear plant.
Gingerly, avoiding the bigger thorns, he cut away several of the

pear pads, impaled them on a stick and carried them back to his waiting place on the rimrock. Using a sharp-edged flint knife, he sliced a pad open, laid it across the gash as a poultice and tied it in place with a soft leather string. Though he had cut away the large thorns, his fingertips were pierced by the tiny ones, most no larger than a human hair but wickedly sharp and persistent. Some unkind spirit had armed the prickly pear with many weapons for self-defense, as it had done with the mesquite and many forms of brush, and the other kinds of cactus. All these plants were useful, but all extracted a payment. The tiny thorns would bedevil him for days, taking their small revenge.

His mouth was dry. His stomach ached from hunger. Doggedly he forced his mind to concentrate upon the powers he needed. He looked down on the bench, hoping for a glimpse of the wolves. He also looked for the old buffalo but did not see it, either. Though his uncle-father had talked little about it for fear of weakening the gift, Gray Horse knew that his uncle had once received the medicine of a young buffalo bull. It had been useful to him as a hunter and good for his family. But his true father had had the medicine of the eagle, enabling him to see what lay beyond the vision of other men. It had given him fierceness in attack, valor and great strength. Gray Horse had always believed that his father could not have been killed had someone in the band not inadvertently violated a taboo and weakened the medicine.

The day was long and quiet, and no vision came. Perhaps tomorrow—but more likely on the fourth day.

In the afternoon he removed the pear pad and found its pulp drained almost dry, but there was yet much fever in the wound. He split a fresh pad and applied it. The whole leg was swelling and becoming sore to the touch.

Night came, and the loneliness. He looked down toward the village, picturing his family singing or listening to his uncle-father tell of his war adventures, stories the children knew by heart but always wanted to hear again, glorying in the stealth and skill and bravery they bespoke, the challenge they presented to the boys. He let some of the stories run through his mind, tales of havoc wrought upon the Apache and the Ute, tales of raids into the Texas settlements for horses, for cattle to drive onto the plains and trade to the Mexican Comancheros, for scalps and for female captives to ease the burden of work upon the People's own women as well as to provide exotic diversion for the warriors who owned them. His uncle-father had once brought back a pale-skinned, blue-eyed and skinny creature who whimpered at every task the women set her to and whimpered most when his uncle forced her under his robe. There had been no resentment among the wives, for a good provider was entitled to his amusements. His uncle-father had finally traded the woman for two horses and a gray mule, confident that he had the best of the deal.

Gray Horse had always enjoyed most those stories of the great war trail into Mexico, for these were epics of distance and time and richly varied experiences. These raids had begun soon after the People had first acquired the horse from the Spanish and had learned how to exploit this great god-dog for war. The new and almost unlimited mobility had made no distance too great, no territory impenetrable to men whose medicine was good and their daring sufficient to the test. Down across the plains to the deep and salty Pecos the warriors would ride, pausing for sweet cold water at the great springs west of the river, then striking out again across the awesome desert and the great dry mountains to the wide river the Mexicans called the Bravo. Far to the south lay large villages and *haciendas* rich in mules and horses. Here a diligent warrior could obtain scalps enough and glory enough. Here could be captured all the women and pliable children the People might want to help in the work, to offset the low birth rate among their own, and to add to the number of a man's wives without the cost of the horses he would have to give the women's fathers if all were from the People. Over the years, Black Robe had told him, the great remudas of captured horses and mules being driven north had worn deep trails on both sides of the Bravo and all the way to the Pecos. The Pecos was a treacherous and unfriendly place; there the captured horses drank their fill of bad water after a long dry drive, and many lay down on the banks and died. Here also was a place of tears for the captive women and children, for at this place the warrior bands often split, dividing the newly acquired slaves with little regard to whether mothers and children remained properly paired. One did not leave mares and colts together for a lifetime.

He smoked and lay down for the second night. The leg troubled him, but exhaustion and the increasing weakness from thirst and hunger made sleep come despite the pain. Next morning—the start of his third day—he was down to the last pear pad. He tried to walk back for a fresh supply but found the gashed leg so swollen and painful he made only a few hobbling steps. Fear teased him, fear he would not be able to make his way back to the village even if the vision came, fear he might die here from this fevered wound as his cousin had died from snakebite. He dragged himself back to the robe.

Through the day his eyesight blurred. His tongue was swelling from thirst, and he could not plainly sing the songs the shaman had given him. He felt a great heat, not all from the relentless sun. He lay on the robe, drifting in and out of sleep, or unconsciousness.

Once, just at dusk, he awoke to some kind of noise. He saw—or thought he saw—the two wolves pursuing the old buffalo. It had somehow hurt one foreleg and was trying to run on the other three. It kept falling on the rough ground, the wolves darting in and slashing at its hind legs while it swung its great black head about and tried to gore them. He could hear the angry bellowing, could see the blood trailing from its nose. He wondered, later, how he could see all this clearly when everything else was masked by a swirling haze. In his lucid moments, he reasoned that this was somehow meant as a message. He saw the old bull go down, bleeding slowly to death while the wolves fed on his living flesh.

This much was proven: the wolf medicine was stronger than that of the buffalo.

He slept awhile and found darkness had come. Sitting up, he struggled a long time trying to light the pipe. He had no thought of giving up, for none of the ritual should be left undone. He trembled from fever, his leg afire. He managed to finish the smoking before consciousness left him.

He awoke in the night and heard thunder. Opening his eyes,

he saw distant lightning. Uneasiness came quickly. The People feared few things they could see, but they feared the storm because its power and fury were beyond their control or comprehension. The fever was strong, the robe hot. Sleep would not come again. He thought he heard his name. He roused a little, listening. It came again—less a sound than a feeling. He heard no audible words, not a spoken language such as the People used among themselves; but someone or something was reaching his mind with a message. It was as if there were a transfer of thought from some other mind directly into his, silent but clearly understandable. He sat up, blinking at the lightning, trying to answer but finding his tongue swollen. He could not speak. Yet somehow he felt that his desperate thoughts were understood.

In the flashes of lightning, a great form took shape in the darkness before him. Clearly, on the rimrock, he saw the great wolf. It was larger now than it had been before, larger than any horse he had ever seen, larger even than a tepee. It seemed to move around him in a circle, from south around to the north and back to the starting place, as a man customarily did upon entering someone else's lodge. Its steps were silent. It seemed to look directly into his eyes, telling him not to be afraid, for it had come to help a brother. It lowered its head and licked his wounded leg as a dog might do. Somehow the pain started draining away. In its mouth the wolf picked up the unfinished shield he had brought, shook it a few times and dropped it before Gray Horse. On it he clearly saw the four wolf tracks he had seen that day in the dry sand—except now they were the red of fresh blood, stark against a field of black divided by the zigzag track of lightning like those streaks now splitting the sky. From its edges flared a mixture of feathers from birds of four kinds: the eagle for its soaring majesty, the crow for its impudence and adroitness at theft, the roadrunner for its fleetness on the ground and the raw nerve which led it to attack even the rattlesnake, and the hawk for being fiercely protective of its nest against all enemies. From the bottom of the shield hung the tail of a buffalo. The wolf told Gray Horse to follow its ways in all important things, and he would have a medicine no man could defeat. He told him of the things he must do and the things he must not, that the medicine remain strong. Then—as quietly and quickly as it had come—the wolf was gone.

When Gray Horse awoke, a cold rain was pelting his uncovered body. Where he had been fevered, he awakened to a chill. He drew the robe around him, but it was wet and cold. He was startled by the suddenness of his awakening and surprised that daylight had come. He huddled shivering, trying to drive the clouds from his mind.

The vision came back to him in memory as vivid and sharp as when he had seen it. To his joy, he found that he could remember every detail. This had been no fleeting dream, quickly gone like a wisp of smoke on the wind. It had been a true vision, all the shaman had told him to expect and more. He looked around quickly, seeking visible proof to substantiate what he had seen—perhaps tracks of the great wolf. The rain had washed the ground clean; the tracks were gone. The shield! It would show the wolf tracks in red, and the lightning and the feathers. He stood up in alarm, fearing that the wind had carried it away. That shield was a vital part of his medicine. He could not lose it.

He saw it lying beside a bush twenty long paces away. He limped quickly to it and grabbed it up, wiping mud from it onto the wet robe. At first glance he was disappointed, for it showed no red wolf tracks, no zigzag lightning, no feathers. Slowly the realization came that the wolf had not transformed it for him but simply had shown him how he was to paint and decorate it for himself.

It occurred to him that he was walking, though with a limp. Yesterday he had hardly been able to move about. The leg was less swollen, less angry. Somehow in the night he had lost the pear pad that had been bound to the wound.

He would never be able to tell the details of the vision. Some skeptic would say the wolf had existed only in his fevered mind, that the sensation of its licking his wound had been only the first falling of the rain. But he knew better. Along the hard edge of the shield, where he had stretched bull hide around a willow frame, he found deep scratches that had not been in it before.

Tooth marks. In at least two places the tooth impressions were plain. They had been left by a wolf. Not the great wolf of the vision, but a wolf of normal size—one of those from down on the bench. It had been here during the night and had tried to chew through the flint-hard hide.

A chill came, not born of the rain. The wolf spirit *had* left a sign—one that would remain with him as long as he lived and carried this shield.

He slaked his thirst from rainwater collected in a concave stone, taking modest amounts each time and going back until he was satisfied. He was weak from hunger. He thought of the buffalo bull. If that had not all been a fevered dream, he knew where it lay at the foot of the mountain. When the rain stopped, he slowly and carefully made his way down, carrying the pipe and the robe and the shield.

He was not surprised when he found the slain bull stretched out as he had seen it in its final throes. A ravenous hunger took charge of him. Everything was wet. He could not build a fire and roast any meat; he would have to eat it raw. The bull had already stiffened, the body cold. At another time Gray Horse would have been repelled, but now he was too hungry to turn away from even spoiled meat. He split open the bull's belly and reached for the intestines. In the buffalo slaughter, the People enjoyed eating these raw. He drew a length of cold gut between his fingers to squeeze out the partially digested grass, then stuffed it into his mouth. He gagged at the off flavor but managed to get it down. In light of the vision, he had no doubt that the wolves had made this kill as much for him as for themselves.

His first hunger sated, he drank again from a shallow hole caught full of rainwater.

In the vision he had seen a buffalo tail hanging from his shield. He cut off the bull's tail high against the rump, splitting it partway down to make two strings by which he could tie it. He cut away excess cartilage and fastened the tail securely in the lacing which held the several thicknesses of hide against the framework. This, then, was another gift of the wolf.

About to leave, he looked back speculatively at the carcass. This old bull just possibly might yield up one more piece of medicine. Gray Horse dragged out the paunch, split it open and poked into its smelly contents until he found a ball of hair not quite as large as his fist. This hair, which the buffalo had ingested during a lifetime of licking its own heavy coat, would not pass through its digestive process but instead was captured in the stomach and worked itself into a hard round ball. These were often found in deer, and even in the white man's cattle. These hairballs were widely regarded as having medicinal value.

This one, Gray Horse was sure, would have stronger than ordinary medicine because it was a gift from the wolves which had given him so much more.

He would need a medicine bag in which to keep the hairball. He split the bull's stiffened scrotum, cutting the hide away from the testicles and scraping off the flesh. He put the hair ball into it, gathered up his belongings, turned to stare at the mountain in a moment of reverence, then limped toward the village.

He had come away from there a boy, incomplete and searching for the guidance that would point the direction of his life. He was returning a man, confident of his destiny. He possessed what he had hoped for: the medicine of the wolf.

Two

THE LAST TIME Gideon Ledbetter had heard the chant of an auctioneer, one article of merchandise had been himself, body and
soul. Now they were selling Old Colonel Hayworth—not his
body, perhaps, but certainly his soul.

Gideon remembered little from that other time except being
frightened, tightly gripping his mother's trembling hand. Now
he stood a bit short of six feet tall and was acknowledged one of
the strongest men on the Hayworth plantation, but he still felt
that old, remembered uneasiness. He quivered, listening to the
rise and fall of a resonant voice droning strange words that made
a peculiar rhythm but carried little meaning except an occasional
intelligible figure.

"And now, you farmers," the auctioneer shouted across a half-
moon cluster of two hundred people standing in the long, sloped
front yard below the big white house, "we have here a good
spring wagon—Studebaker—somewhat experienced but still capable of carrying a crop of cotton to the gin. Who'll bid me
twenty, make it twenty, I said twenty, got the twenty, somebody make it twenty-five. . . ." From there the voice lapsed
into gibberish that meant no more to Gideon than the Cajun
French he often heard on this Louisiana delta. He took it for

granted that the white people understood it, as they seemed to understand the French. At least, they appeared to be having themselves a right good holiday, picking over the lifetime accumulations of someone else.

Old Colonel sat to one side of the auctioneer's makeshift stand in a straight-backed, cane-bottomed chair fetched down from his front veranda. The appellation "colonel" was honorary. During the war he had commanded a company of local militia, old men, boys and cripples. They had never been called upon to do anything except drill. His spine was as straight as a ramrod, both his hands firmly gripping a black cane whose tip he had pressed two inches into the soft ground. Each stroke of the auctioneer's hammer was wiping him out, a piece at a time. The sprawling fields and the big white house were already gone; the parish government had confiscated them for taxes. Gone were the Negro houses and the barns, the thoroughbred horses, the orchard, the fine stand of cotton now setting its blooms toward a summer's crop. Going now was the farm machinery and the rolling stock. Sooner or later they would even sell the chair out from under Old Colonel. He would leave here owning but one black carriage, one horse to pull it, and whatever clothing and personal belongings he could put into it and carry away.

That, and the stubborn Hayworth pride he would take to the grave.

Gideon's dark eyes clouded with sorrow as he watched two sweating black men who served as the auctioneer's helpers, bringing up the tall grandfather clock he had listened to as a boy, marveling that it always knew when time came for fat Aunt Ella to feed Old Colonel and Old Missus. He glanced at Big Ella and the other plantation help standing in the shade of a moss-strewn oak a respectful distance to one side of the white crowd which pressed in to bid or to watch in morbid curiosity the last small symbols of the Hayworth fortune passing into strangers' hands.

"It's the carpetbaggers and the scalawags," Ella had angrily told Gideon a few nights ago. "They runnin' the government now. They sees a farm they wants, they just sets the taxes so high to where there can't nobody pay them. They keeps shakin' the tree, and when the apple falls they grabs it. Black boy steals a pig, they flogs him. Carpetbagger steals a farm, they just smiles and says, 'Help yourself to another while you're at it,' like it was a piece of mince pie."

They had sure got Colonel Hayworth's plantation.

Looking at the white-haired patriarch, rigid as if he had been carved from hickory, Gideon sensed that a great tide of tears was building behind those stern, ungiving blue eyes. But nobody was going to see them; nobody was going to shame Old Colonel. He would die where he sat before he would let those people see the torment of his soul.

Hayworth held his ground until they began selling off precious things which had belonged to Old Missus—her fine china, her powderbox, her small collection of modest jewelry. He pushed up on his cane and strode toward the house. Gideon pulled away from the small group of house help and field hands, pushing his long legs to catch up to the old man. He waited until the noise of the crowd and the auctioneer were well behind him before he called.

"Colonel? Colonel, sir?"

Hayworth stopped, but he did not turn. He waited for Gideon to come past him and face around.

"I was wonderin', sir, if you got any special work you want me to be doin'? You didn't tell nobody what you wanted us to do."

Almost as far back as he could remember, he had been asking Old Colonel what to do. Hayworth had never encouraged his slaves—or after the war, his hired help—to think for themselves. In the first instance, he had never considered them capable; in the second, it was dangerous to let the serving class be self-sufficient. Only so long as they were heavily dependent would they remain manageable.

The old man blinked. Gideon found himself unable to look into those sharp and blistering eyes. He looked at the ground, as he had been trained to do since boyhood.

Hayworth spat an oath, at which he was uncommonly good. "Work? Damn you, boy, haven't you got it through your woolly head that I've no longer got any work for you to do?

I've got no place for you to do it. They've taken it all away from me!" The voice was strained and thin, on the edge of breaking.

Gideon mumbled, "I'm sorry." Hayworth's hands flexed on the curve of the cane. Gideon braced himself, half expecting the old man to strike him across the shoulders with it.

But Hayworth spoke again, his voice softer. Now it was Old Colonel who stared at the ground. One vagrant tear rolled down the leathered cheek and lost itself in the carefully combed gray whiskers. "I didn't mean to speak so sharply to you, Gideon. You meant me nothin' but good; I know that." The colonel lifted his chin, staring at the white-columned old house built by his father in better times. "When that spectacle down yonder is over, and all the vultures have taken their loot and gone, I wish you'd get Jimbo to hitch my good sorrel pacer to the carriage and bring it up to the house. And I wish you'd bring all the people, all my good old hands. I'll have a few words to say before I take my leave of this place."

"Yes, sir, Colonel." Gideon stepped aside and watched in silence as the old man resumed his determined stride toward the front steps and the wide, vine-shaded veranda.

Gideon had not always been sure how he felt about Old Colonel, who was a changeable man of unpredictable moods. The same hand which administered the cane could sometimes be gentle. The eyes that flashed with an unreasoning fury could sometimes sparkle with laughter and even soften paternalistically. The man's sadness pressed heavily on Gideon as he walked to the barn.

He heard someone running up behind him and saw Jimbo, the head groom, the only man on the place Old Colonel trusted to take care of his prized thoroughbreds. Jimbo had literally grown up in the stables. He spoke two languages, English and horse. He usually spoke with a laugh.

"What you fixin' to do, Gid?"

Gideon told him of the colonel's order. Jimbo nodded. "I washed the carriage this mornin'. Shined it like it was a new silver dollar. Soaped and oiled all the harness and groomed Big Red like he ain't been slicked up in a long, long time. I figured Old Colonel would want to leave this place in high style."

It bothered Gideon that Jimbo seemed to take the situation for granted. Gideon had never quite accepted it. He had kept hoping Old Colonel would find a way out of this trouble as he had worked through and survived other difficult times. Gideon had been taught that the Lord would find a way to smite the transgressor, and he had held to a stolid faith that the Lord would smite the thieves who had stolen Old Colonel's farm. Only now had that faith begun to crumble. Gideon walked up to the gentle sorrel and rubbed a firm hand along the strong neck, down to the muscular shoulder. He summoned courage to speak the doubt he had suppressed for days. He and Jimbo had been friends since boyhood. They had shared a bachelor cabin on slave row since both had been considered old enough. Gideon had always been able to speak his mind to Jimbo.

"I don't know what's goin' to become of us."

Jimbo shrugged. "We'll take care of ourselves, is what. Old Colonel can't do it no more."

Gideon kept rubbing the sorrel's neck, letting his mind run free over things unthinkable before. After freedom, he had studied awhile about leaving Old Colonel. The law had given him the right. But Gideon knew little of what lay beyond this farm. The outer fences had more or less been his own outer limits, except for a dusty little cotton town three miles up the road. He had only the vaguest notions of any other existence. Life was not easy here, but it was familiar. He had stayed, trading freedom for the comfort of knowing what to expect most of the time.

Gideon had never been devious. His thoughts usually showed plainly in his face. "I'm scared, Jimbo."

"There's other places, Gid, better than this one. There's other farms we can live on."

"They ain't home."

"They will be, when we get there."

The sun was low behind the big house when Jimbo brought the carriage around. Gideon loaded Old Colonel's few cases and a trunk, and a couple of boxes of goods belonging to Big Ella.

Of all the hands and servants, only she would be going with Old Colonel. Only she knew how to cook the things he liked in a way that wouldn't rile his touchy stomach. Gideon doubted that the old master would speak of it, for dependency on others wounded his pride, but he was going to live with a daughter and a son-in-law in Baton Rouge. The son-in-law was an attorney. Louisiana had become an open gold mine to lawyers in these unhappy days of political turmoil since the war.

When Old Colonel came out onto the veranda, plantation men and the black womenfolk straightened to attention. Hats were removed and held in black hands. The subservient attitudes of slave times had not been put aside. His solemn gaze slowly moved from one face to the next until it had made the round. "Old friends . . . ," he said, and his voice pinched. He stopped, looking past the people while he swallowed and regained control. "I realize I've not always acted as if I considered you my friends, but I did—even in the old times." The voice thinned again. He gritted his teeth and gripped his black cane. "The new owners will be here tomorrow. I have no wish to see them, so I take my departure now. I tried to persuade them to keep all the old help, but they want to be rid of you because they are afraid you will remain loyal to me instead of to them. I confess that this thought brings me comfort. I only regret that it means a hardship to *you*. You-all have served me well, and my lady in her time. I wish I could have served you better." He blinked, his eyes on Gideon. "On the floor in the parlor you'll find a box with some envelopes. Go fetch it for me, please."

Gideon could not remember that Old Colonel had ever said *please* to him before. He paused a moment in the parlor, unable to accept its empty look, the floors bare of furniture, the shelves denuded of keepsakes and books. The feeling was that of suddenly finding himself in the midst of a graveyard. Stooping to pick up the box, he saw that each envelope bore handwriting. In slave times it had been forbidden for him to learn to read or write, and in later years he had somehow been too busy to consider correcting the situation.

Tears rolled down Big Ella's round ebony face. Gideon ached at the probability of being parted from her forever. His own mother had taken down during one of the fever epidemics and had died the third year after Old Colonel had brought her and Gideon to this place. The task of looking after Gideon and pointing him in useful directions was left to Ella, in addition to her kitchen and general house duties. She had alternately switched him and loved him, as the occasion demanded. The loving always lasted longer than the switching.

Hayworth drew the first envelope from the box. "I would like to have done better by you, but this country has been turned over to thieves who rob with a pen instead of a gun. The best I can do is to write a recommendation for each of you. Take these letters with you. They may help you get work. You'll each find a few dollars in your envelope. It isn't much, but they didn't leave me much."

With each envelope went a handshake. Gideon watched in wonder; it was the first time he could remember ever seeing Old Colonel shake a black hand. Done, Hayworth moved slowly across the veranda, stopping at the edge. "Go through the house and take anything you want. Take everything out of the cabins because everything's yours. I don't care to see anything left for those carrion eaters except the bare walls. If I still had a young man's nerve, I would not leave them even that. I would burn this place to the ground!"

Gideon helped him into the carriage, then stepped up to pat the sorrel's neck one last time.

Old Colonel beckoned to him. "Gideon, I hope you'll keep Jimbo with you wherever you go. He's a good boy, but he needs watchin' after."

Gideon nodded solemnly. "I'll do that, sir."

"And, Gideon . . . watch out for yourself. You're a good boy, too, but you have one failin' that could get you killed. You've got a stubborn streak that makes you say what comes into your mind sometimes when you should keep silent. I've put up with it because I know you. Folks that don't know you, they may not stand for it."

"I'll try to be careful, sir."

Big Ella saved Gideon for the last good-bye. Her cheeks were wet as she threw her big soft arms around him and pulled his head down. "You, boy, you remember the godly things old Ella has taught you, and don't you do nothin' to shame me, you hear?"

"I hear you, Aunt Ella," Gideon said tightly. He was crying, something a man his size was never supposed to do.

Jimbo helped her into the back of the carriage, behind Old Colonel. When the carriage moved away, some of the field hands and the women hurried into the house to quarrel over the pitiful leavings. Gideon stood at the bottom step, watching the blurred image of the carriage disappearing down the lane. Ella waved her hand as long as he could see her. Old Colonel never turned to look back.

The dust had settled before Gideon moved, his envelope in his hand. He could feel coins. Jimbo had opened his, and his strong teeth shone like ivory. "How much did you get, Gid?"

"I don't know. I ain't looked."

"I got twenty dollars. I believe to my soul that's more money than ever I seen at one time."

Gideon didn't understand how Jimbo could smile, even if he did have twenty dollars. Didn't he know they were homeless? Didn't he know they were about to be set out upon the road like two unwanted pups hauled a long way off and dumped? He said as much.

Jimbo only shrugged. "That ain't till tomorrow. I'll worry when I see the sun rise." He looked up at the high columns. "You ever sleep in the big house?"

Gideon nodded. "Sure, after my mama died. Aunt Ella kept me in a little room off of the kitchen till she said I was too growed to be stayin' with a woman. That's when they put me and you together."

Jimbo said, "I been on this farm all my life, and I ain't never slept in this house. I ain't even *been* in the house except when Old Colonel called me up here to save hisself some steps." His eyes sparkled with wickedness. "I got a notion to sleep in here tonight, Gid. Ain't no white folks to say we can't."

Gideon saw no fun in it and said so. "We'd have to sleep on the floor. We still got good beds out in the cabin."

"Floor'll do. I just want to be able to remember the rest of my life that I got to sleep in the big house."

Before his trouble, Old Colonel would have whipped them off the place if he had known such a thought had entered their heads. Now, Gideon supposed, he wouldn't care.

Even if he did care, he was gone.

They gathered their few belongings out of the cabin. Gideon had a worn-out carpetbag Aunt Ella had given him. He supposed it might have belonged to Old Colonel a long time ago, or to one of the Hayworths before him. Its colors had faded to a dull and lifeless rust and brown. Jimbo had never had anyone to give him a carpetbag. He rolled up his clothes and few personal belongings in his blankets, tying the ends with cotton rope. They fixed themselves a bite of supper. At dusk they took a final look at the little frame shack.

Jimbo said, "We ain't leavin' much, come right down to it. You could pitch a dog through the cracks in the walls."

"But they was *our* walls."

"They was Old Colonel's walls. He just let us have the borry of them long's we done his work."

Gideon said nothing. He knew if the Good Lord were to smile on Old Colonel and put everything back like it had been before the trouble, Gideon would consent to look at the cracks in those walls the rest of his life. He might not always be happy here, but he would feel secure. He wouldn't have to worry about what he was going to do tomorrow. Old Colonel would always tell him, or somebody else would.

They walked up to the big house. Gideon had an odd feeling that about the time he laid his hand on the doorknob, Old Colonel would holler to know what the hell he was doing there. Jimbo started for the back door, as had been his habit when duty called him to the place. Gideon caught his arm. "The front door, Jimbo. If we're goin' to do it atall, we'll walk right in the front door like we was company come."

The cavernous old house seemed even bigger now for having been stripped of its furniture and fixings. The wallpaper had light spots where pictures had hung, where tables and chairs and shelves had stood against the walls in one place for years upon years. The overall effect was more sad than scary. Though he had never really been a part of it, Gideon sensed that happy lives had been lived in this place. It seemed vastly wrong that this house was about to pass into the hands of people who knew nothing and cared nothing about those who had left their marks and something of their souls here.

Jimbo asked, "Which room did Old Colonel sleep in?"

Gideon pointed to the broad staircase. "Up yonder."

"That's where I'm fixin' to sleep tonight. What about you?"

Gideon shrugged. "One floor's about as hard as another."

Not so much as a lamp had been left. Gideon had not thought to bring a candle. He stood by the window through which the Hayworths had often looked down upon the big front yard, upon the oak-lined lane which led in from the town road.

Jimbo stood at another window. "Yonder's the barns and the stables and all. I never knowed Old Colonel could stand up here and watch just about everything I done. No wonder he give me so much hell sometimes." His face went solemn. "Reckon what them Yankee folks is goin' to do with my horses? You reckon they'll take care of them, or you reckon maybe they'll turn them out and let them starve down? Or maybe sell them to pull a cotton wagon?"

Gideon figured they would do whatever looked like it would fetch the most money. "It ain't your concern no more, Jimbo."

"Them's good horses. I hate to think of somebody mistreatin' them." For the first time Gideon saw in Jimbo's eyes a reflection of the sadness he had felt all day himself. It took something special to touch Jimbo.

Horses were always special.

The two young men lay in silence on the floor, staring into the darkness. Down on cabin row an abandoned dog set up a howl. Another picked it up, and then another. Gideon listened for Jimbo's familiar snore but didn't hear it. Jimbo was lying awake, too.

Before sunup Gideon carried the food sack down to the kitchen and stoked a fire in the big wooden range. There was no pot, so he boiled coffee in a can and mixed batter for hoecakes.

These he cooked on the flat top of the stove itself. By the time they were ready, Jimbo was there, staring blankly at the range.

Jimbo lied, "That was fun, sleepin' in Old Colonel's room."

"Sure was," Gideon lied back.

In silence they ate a skimpy breakfast which leaned heavily to the coffee for strength. Neither man looked at the other. They gathered and rolled their blankets and moved out onto the veranda.

As he blinked into the rising sun, Gideon saw a carriage pull up, with two white men sitting in it. They were as surprised to see the two black men coming out of the big house as Gideon and Jimbo were to see them there. The taller of the men pointed a finger at Gideon. "Boy, you stop right there!"

Fear clutched at Gideon's throat. Caught—where they weren't supposed to be. The situation summoned up a dread that went as far back as he could remember.

The man demanded, "What're you boys doing, coming out of that house? What're you trying to carry away?"

Gideon managed a few words. "Nothin', sir, only what's ours. Just a few clothes is about all."

The voice was imperious. "Open everything on the ground. Let's see what you have."

Gideon and Jimbo were slow to comply. The man jerked the whip from its stock and lashed it across both men's shoulders. "When I tell you to move, I mean *move*—and be damned quick about it!"

The other man was pointing a pistol. Gideon's heart hammered. Never had anyone ever pointed a firearm at him. He spilled the contents of his carpetbag on the ground. He untied his little roll of two blankets. Jimbo had unrolled his blankets and dumped his clothes out.

The men were not satisfied. "Your pockets," the tall one demanded. "Turn your pockets inside out."

Gideon did, taking care not to lose the silver coins and the five-dollar gold piece Old Colonel had given him in the envelope.

The sharp voice demanded, "Is that money you've got in your hand?"

"It's mine," Gideon said defensively. When the man flexed the whip, Gideon opened his hand to show him.

The short man said, "Probably found it in the house. Niggers don't come by that kind of money honestly."

Gideon realized they meant to take it from him. He clasped his hand and held it behind him. "Old Colonel hisself give me this money, sir."

The short man held the pistol at arm's length, pointed straight at Gideon. "I'll give you something too, boy, if you don't hand that money here to me."

Fear clamped Gideon's throat. They would kill him without hesitation and without regret as an example to others. He opened his hand but nervously spilled the coins.

"Pick them up!" commanded the short man with the pistol.

Gideon gathered the silver. For a minute he could not find the gold piece; it was too much the color of the road. He realized the white men could not see it either. Agonizing in his loss, he handed over the other coins.

Jimbo was slow in giving up his money. The tall man laid the lash across his shoulders and head until tears ran down Jimbo's face. On his left cheek, they mixed with blood from a whip cut.

The tall man took Jimbo's money. "I own this place now, and I own everything on it. If you boys are ever seen here again I'll have you shot on sight. Do you understand that?"

Neither Gideon nor Jimbo summoned voice to answer. The short man grinned coldly and fired a shot into the ground between them. That frightened the horses and almost spilled him out of the carriage. The shot set a dozen dogs to barking down on cabin row. They came running out, some of them, to see what was happening and to challenge the intrusion. The tall man pointed. "Birchfield, this place is overrun with nigger dogs. I want you to shoot every mongrel you see."

As a lanky gray dog ran up, barking at the carriage, Birchfield fired a bullet into its ribs, just up from the flanks. The dog howled and dragged itself off by its forelegs. Birchfield ignored its plight and aimed at a second dog, killing it instantly. The rest scattered.

The carriage rolled on down to the stables. The two men didn't bother to look back at the Negroes they had whipped. A job done right didn't have to be done twice.

Jimbo had taken the worst beating. He sat on the ground, sobbing a little. Gideon grimaced, looking at the mixture of blood and tears on a face meant only to smile. He felt his anger rising, not just for himself but for Jimbo and for all the others left homeless by those men and the legal thievery they stood for. He watched the two white men striding into the stables to inspect their property. He clenched his fists, wanting to strike out against them but not knowing how. He looked up at the big house, wishing Old Colonel were still here; he would know how.

The house! The idea burst upon him full-grown and complete, with a startling suddenness. He was not accustomed to making decisions on his own, or even initiating ideas of any real account. Old Colonel had always taken charge. The enormity of the notion made him tremble. His voice was unsteady. "Jimbo, Old Colonel told us if he had a young man's nerve he'd of burnt the place down so them people couldn't have it. You remember him sayin' that?"

Jimbo nodded dully, not yet comprehending.

Gideon's anger swelled. "*We're* young men."

Jimbo's eyes went wide. "You sayin' we're fixin' to burn the big house down?"

"To the ground!"

Jimbo wrestled with his doubts, but his outrage quickly won. Whatever Gideon wanted to do had always been all right. He dusted his britches. The tears had stopped. "How we goin' to do it, Gid?"

Old Colonel had always kept a barrel of coal oil in the back yard to service smaller cans used for filling lamps, for starting fires in the big kitchen and in the several fireplaces that warmed the house in winter.

Gideon said, "Let's gather up our stuff and skin around to the back." He kept looking cautiously toward the stables until he passed behind the screen of shrubbery and flowers. He pushed against the wooden barrel to test its weight. "Between us two, I believe we can carry it." He dropped his bundle and carpetbag where he could pick them up in a hurry. He paused to plot their escape route across the cow pasture and out the back side of the plantation, where the moss-hung timber was thickest.

He motioned for Jimbo to grasp the barrel with him. Together they picked it up, carrying it up the rear steps and into the kitchen. Gideon kicked the spigot open with the toe of his old boot. As the coal oil flowed, he pointed with his chin. "Around the walls. If we get the walls to goin', I expect the rest will burn easy."

They carried the barrel through the rooms of the ground floor, spilling a continuous stream along the outer walls. They had made three-quarters of the distance when the flow thinned to a tiny trickle and then to vagrant drops. They set the barrel down where it had emptied. Gideon started back for the kitchen, Jimbo only a step behind him and looking apprehensively over his shoulder. Beside the kitchen range was a small black shovel used to remove ashes. Gideon picked it up. He slid a round iron stove lid aside and scooped up a shovelful of glowing coals left from breakfast.

"You skin out the door, Jimbo."

He gave Jimbo time to clear the steps, then pitched the embers into the puddle of coal oil. For a second or two he did not think they would take hold. Then flames shot up with the suddenness of quail flushed from cover. The fire licked its way along the trail Gideon and Jimbo had made into the next room.

Gideon cleared the back steps two at a time, going down. He grabbed up his carpetbag and rolled blankets, jerking his head. "Light out a-runnin'. They catch us, they'll shoot us like they shot them dogs!"

Jimbo stayed ahead of Gideon until they pulled up for breath beyond the cow-pasture fence. Shoulders heaving, they looked back on smoke—gray and black and brown, all mixed—climbing above the treetops.

Breathing heavily, Jimbo licked his dry lips and grinned. "We done it. Old Colonel'd be proud if he knowed what we done for him."

Gideon could not find it in himself to take pleasure. He looked at the smoke in sadness and anger and regret. "We didn't just do it for him, Jimbo. We done it for *us*."

They stayed to the back roads and took roundance on the town, for the new owners of the Hayworth lands might be searching for them. They trotted some of the time. A mile past town they were overtaken by a gray-haired old black man carrying two turning plows in a wagon. He offered them a ride, and they took it gratefully. As the sun reached midpoint, he said, "Dinnertime. Ain't got much in the way of vittles, but you boys is welcome to share what they is."

He had spoken truthfully. He had part of a loaf of bread and a small piece of cold hamhock. In a jug he had what Gideon assumed to be water until he uncorked it and found it to be corn whisky of the rankest kind. Jimbo found no fault in it.

Gideon unwrapped what little food they had brought from the plantation and added it to the bit the old man had put before them.

"Well," the aged farmer said, "the Lord will not smite us for our gluttony."

When he reached the gate where he was to turn in he suggested that Gideon and Jimbo might find work with his *master*. Many of the older people had never gotten over the use of the word. But Gideon feared they were too near the Hayworth place. Jimbo liked to talk. Sooner or later he was bound to tell what they had done. That kind of story would spread, for the black people would glory in it. Inevitably it would spread beyond black ears to white.

"We thank you kindly, uncle," Gideon said to the old man, "but we expect we'll just keep on travelin' for a while."

Bad memories twisted the farmer's wrinkles into a frown. "If I was a younger man, I'd like as not just leave this old wagon settin' here and go with you boys. I taken me a notion to travel once, like you're doin', only them days it wasn't allowed. Went a long ways before the slave catchers got me. Taken two months for my back to heal to where I could even lay on it of a night.

"You boys ain't been away from home before, so you don't know what to expect. I'll just tell you one thing: don't be ashamed to take a kindness anywhere it's offered to you. You won't see many."

The two young men watched the wagon skirt the turnrows of a cotton field and disappear behind a stand of young corn. Gideon could read Jimbo's thoughts. One word of encouragement would send Jimbo running after it. Gideon said, "Our feet are rested. We better be usin' them."

They walked all afternoon, passing through farming country that looked much the same as the place where he had spent his life. But it was not the same; the people were different. The men and women hoeing the fields were strangers to him, and he had never been at ease among strangers. Melancholy settled over him. He teetered dangerously along the edge of a fear that he sensed could turn to panic if he loosened his grip. He leaned defensively toward the whistling Jimbo, who kept picking up a rock and sailing it down the road. When he reached the spot where it had landed, he would pick it up and sail it again.

Toward sundown, Jimbo mentioned feeling hungry. Gideon could not muster the nerve to walk up to white folks' houses and ask for food. Just before dark he saw a black woman standing in front of a mean box shanty, calling her children to supper. There, he thought, they might find kindred souls.

He saw no kindness in her face. She retreated beyond the door, ready to slam it in an instant. The dancing flicker of a lighted pine knot made her shadow bob and weave on the smoothly swept ground in front of the cabin. Gideon took off his soft hat and bowed the way he had been taught from boyhood to approach his betters. "Evenin', lady."

She moved one foot distrustfully farther back inside the house, her hand on the edge of the door. "What you-all want here?"

"We're lookin' for work, and we run fresh out of anything to eat. We was wonderin' if after you've fed your younguns you might have a little somethin' left over?"

Her eyes narrowed. "You got money to pay?"

All Gideon had was his five-dollar gold piece—the one those carpetbaggers hadn't seen him drop on the ground. Jimbo didn't even have that. "No, ma'am. But we'd be proud to do some work to pay for what you give us."

"Tramps!" she said brittlely. "We can't hardly even feed our own, and you tramps come in on us ever blessed day to beg or steal even the little bit we got. Git now, do you hear me? Git!"

Gideon argued, "We ain't no tramps. We're a-huntin' for work."

"Everybody's huntin' work," she said.

A man appeared behind the woman and moved her out of the way. He was so large that he blocked off most of the light from the pine knot. "My woman spoke out plain. She told you to git. So git, or I'll *git* you!"

Chilled, Gideon backed off, then turned and walked to the road again, his head down. He did not have the nerve to walk up to another house after that rebuff. Jimbo didn't volunteer. They rolled their blankets in the grass and lay down hungry.

Gideon didn't sleep much. The ground was hard, and he was unfamiliar with sleeping in the open. In his mind he kept reliving the harsh day just past and borrowing from those he feared lay ahead. At dawn he threw back his blanket. He saw Jimbo lying awake, looking at him. Jimbo asked, "You as hungry as I am?"

Gideon nodded miserably. "I expect so."

"I been hearin' a rooster crow over yonder. Where there's a rooster, there's chickens."

"You studyin' on goin' and stealin'?"

"Not stealin', just borryin'. We ever come this way again, we'll pay them back."

"I don't want to do no stealin'."

"Then you just wait right here. I won't be gone long." Jimbo laid his blanket aside, climbed over a sagging rail fence and stooped low, disappearing into the undergrowth that surrounded a small field. In a little while, he returned carrying his hat in his hands. He motioned for Gideon to take it before he climbed the fence again. The hat held almost a dozen eggs.

Gideon said, "I didn't hear no commotion."

"I been borryin' eggs off of Old Colonel for many a year. We better get on down the road a piece before we do any cookin'."

Gideon hoped for much but expected little. He was not surprised. The day brought them nothing but rejections. It was a while before Gideon began to suspect that the swollen whip mark on Jimbo's face was an extra liability when they already had more than enough.

They had come to a cotton field where a dozen black men hoed weeds under the silent supervision of a white farmer. Hats in their hands, the two walked hopefully across the soft earth between the rows. A mean-looking black dog growled until the man told it to hush. Gideon announced that they were looking for work. The farmer eyed them critically, especially Jimbo. "Where you boys come from?"

Gideon told him they had worked all their lives for old Colonel Hayworth. The farmer seemed to know the name, but he frowned in suspicion. "If you quit him, you'd probably quit me, too, about the time I needed you most."

Gideon tried to explain that Old Colonel had lost the plantation, but the farmer didn't seem to be paying them much mind. He was staring at Jimbo. "Where'd you get that mark, boy? You been fightin'? Last thing I need around here is a fightin' nigger."

Gideon tried to explain, but the farmer put no stock in his story. "If it *is* a whip mark, then I expect you done somethin' to deserve the whippin'. No use me addin' to the grief I already got. You boys git yourselves on down the road."

Gideon argued that it wasn't what it looked like, and they were good, hard workers, both of them. But the man had had his say. He spoke to the black dog. "Sic 'em, Satan!"

Gideon and Jimbo ran all the way to the road, slapping their hats at the black dog snarling and biting at their heels. The farmer finally called him back. They kept trotting until they were well away, lest the dog take a notion to trail after them. Stopping for breath, Gideon found that the sharp teeth had ripped a hole in the lower left leg of his trousers. A thin seam of blood showed why he felt a burning.

It struck Jimbo funny. "That first hundred yards, Gid, I believe you'd of taken a lead on Old Colonel's good sorrel pacer."

Gideon failed to see the humor, but he supposed that was because the dog had devoted most of its attention to him and little to Jimbo. The inequity of the punishment only added to his anger. Sometimes Jimbo's cheerfulness was the balm of Gilead. Other times, it was salt on a raw sore.

They tried a few more farms that day. They weren't chased by any more dogs, but they weren't hired to work, either. One ragged white farmer, little better off than most of the black laborers, took pity enough to give them the leftovers from his family's supper. But he must have had a flock of hungry young-uns, because the leavings were meager and plain. About dark Gideon and Jimbo found an abandoned cabin from which all the windows had been removed and much of the roof was gone. Though they could see stars through wide gaps in the shingles, and the rotten wooden floor was even harder than the ground, it seemed somehow more civilized and fitting to sleep here than out on the open road.

They set out walking with no breakfast except a long drink of water from the old cistern. They were rebuffed at the first farm where they stopped, and Gideon had a sinking feeling that this had set the pattern for the day.

About midafternoon they came alongside an open pasture from which most of the timber had been cut years before, letting sunshine in upon the succulent grass. Scattered across the pasture were many thoroughbred mares, most of them trailing colts. Jimbo's tired shoulders straightened. "Gid, I wisht you'd looky there."

A couple of colts, one a brown and the other a chestnut sorrel, trotted up to the rail fence in ear-pointing curiosity. When Jimbo spoke, the colts hoisted their tails and loped away, one of them pitching a little and breaking wind. They stopped thirty yards into the pasture and turned, taking another look at the travelers. They ran again, moving well past the two men and then cutting back to the fence. There they stopped and playfully poked their heads over the top rail like children. Jimbo laughed.

Gideon had always been able to take horses or leave them alone. He could ride with a modest competence but had never shared Jimbo's eagerness or natural affinity. Old Colonel had always bragged that Jimbo rode like an Indian. Gideon didn't know. He had never seen an Indian.

Jimbo had forgotten about weariness. He was walking rapidly, almost in a trot, beckoning for Gideon to hurry. "This is the place, Gid. I'll work here if they don't even pay me for it."

You'll stay by yourself if you do, Gideon thought darkly, knowing Jimbo was likely to blurt out that offer before even hearing what the boss-man had to say.

Jimbo didn't wait to reach the gate. He climbed over the fence and cut across to the road. Gideon had to trot to keep pace with him. As they approached the barns he saw rising dust and heard shouts and running horses. He observed a carriage with a pair of brown horses hitched to it. Saddled horses were tied to a fence. He blinked in surprise at the sight of a blue-uniformed soldier slouching against the carriage, half asleep. That soldier was black.

Gideon's mouth dropped open. He had heard about black Yankee soldiers, but he had never seen one. Old Colonel had called them an abomination. Gideon was not sure what the term meant, but he assumed it was bad because Hayworth used it like a cussword.

Jimbo had never let caution restrain him when he wanted something. "Hey, soldier, how's a dark-complected gentleman get one of them pretty suits?"

The soldier stiffened. "You stay back away from the captain's carriage."

Jimbo cocked his head toward the commotion on the other side of the barns. "What they doin' back yonder?"

"It's army business and ain't none of yours."

"I hear horses runnin'. I believe I'll just go look." It never occurred to Jimbo that the soldier might try to stop him, and if it occurred to the soldier, the notion quickly died. Both Jimbo and Gideon were taller and broader in the shoulders. The soldier said sternly, "I told you. If they take a horsewhip to you, don't come blamin' me."

Gideon followed the fast-walking Jimbo around the barn toward the racket. Climbing up on a plank fence, he saw several horses running excitedly back and forth in a pen. In the center, two uniformed black soldiers and a couple of black farmhands had a young bay horse at the end of a rope and were trying to girth up a small military saddle while the horse shied and kicked in fright. The blue uniforms were sadly grayed by dust. Near the barn stood a tall white man in a uniform and a middle-aged, chunky man in the worn clothing of a planter, chewing worriedly on an unlighted cigar.

When the saddle was secure, the farmhands held the nervous horse while a soldier cautiously stuck his left foot into the steel stirrup and tried to swing aboard. The horse fought and pawed. The soldier managed to take a seat, and the other men stepped out of the way. Bawling in frightened displeasure, the horse dropped its head and crow-hopped around the pen. The soldier bounced, the daylight widening between rump and saddle. In a moment, he sailed to earth in an undignified scramble of arms and legs.

Jimbo laughed. The officer glanced up at him, then shouted to another soldier, "You try him, Roberson."

The planter bit down on his cigar. Gideon assumed that the man was trying to sell these young horses to the army officer, and that the show out there was not helping his chances.

The bay made even shorter work of the second soldier. Jimbo laughed and slapped his hand against his knee.

The officer glanced again at Jimbo, resentment in his sharp eyes. "That one of your boys, Mr. Cooper?"

The planter shook his head, surprised. "No. I thought they was with *you*." He cut his eyes to Jimbo. "You, boy, what you doin' here? You get down off of that fence and away from here before I take a whip to you."

Jimbo said, "Didn't go to cause offense, sir. Me and Gid, we just come here to see if we might get us a job helpin' you with your horses, sir."

"I already got more help than I need. A lot more. Get along."

"I was the boss horse handler for old Colonel Hayworth, sir."

"You don't look like any horseman to me." The planter took a couple of long strides toward the fence, his face darkening. "I told you . . ."

The officer raised his hand. "Just a minute, Mr. Cooper." He studied Jimbo critically. "You laughed at those boys of mine. Do you think you could do any better?"

Jimbo smiled. "Sir, them boys don't know how to talk to that horse."

"And you do?"

"I believe so, sir."

"Talk is cheap. Get out there and show us."

Jimbo climbed down into the pen. He flashed Gideon a look of total confidence and walked to where Cooper's men held the fidgeting, pawing bay. He touched his hand to the reins and said, "You-all just back off a ways. Let me have him."

"He'll bust you like an egg," one of the dusty soldiers said.

"Me and him is fixin' to be friends."

Jimbo started talking softly. Gideon couldn't hear the words and knew they didn't matter. It was his tone that counted. He was talking and subtly reaching out, letting the pony get a good look at him and his black hand before he took another step. The bay trembled and started to paw at him. Jimbo stood his ground and somehow seemed to talk the horse out of it. In a minute he had his hand on the dark neck and was rubbing from cheek to throat and down to foreshoulder, talking all the while. He rubbed and patted and cajoled, and the horse seemed to calm. Jimbo brought the reins up carefully, passed them over the suspicious ears and rubbed again, first the neck and then the shoulder. He raised his left foot slowly and deliberately until he fitted it into the stirrup. He let the horse feel his weight tentatively while he leaned against him, still patting, rubbing, talking. When he swung into the saddle, the horse was startled only momentarily. It stood trembling, back slightly humped. Jimbo leaned forward a little, letting the horse know the feel of his gentle hand along the neck, letting it hear the soft and reassuring tone of his voice.

He put the horse into a walk, then into a trot. Its back was still arched, and the steps were uncertain and threatening, but the horse did not pitch. Around and around Jimbo rode. The horse gradually let down its back. Its steps took on confidence. Much of the fear and all of the threat disappeared. Jimbo rode him directly up to the officer.

"There he is, sir. They ain't no mean in this horse."

The officer stared in silence.

The planter Cooper was smiling around his unlighted cigar. "Boy, I believe you said somethin' about lookin' for a job."

"Me and Gid yonder. We come together."

The officer found his voice. "What's your name, boy?"

"Jimbo."

"Just Jimbo? Nothing else?"

"Jimbo's all they ever told me, sir."

"Jimbo, can you do that with all horses?"

"Some takes longer than others. But, yes, sir, horses and me have always got along pretty good."

"Mr. Cooper here seems on the point of offering you a job. But I might be able to offer you a better one. Did you ever think about being a soldier?"

This time it was Jimbo who was surprised, and Gideon, too. "No, sir, such a thing never entered my thinkin'."

"I am stationed in New Orleans. Besides buying remounts, I am also charged with the responsibility of helping recruit good men for two regiments of colored cavalry. Would you be interested?"

Jimbo stepped cautiously down from the saddle and patted the bay on the neck. "You mean you want me to be a Yankee soldier?"

"Not Yankee—that's all over and done with. Just American. We're all Americans again. The life is interesting, the food is regular, and a private soldier is paid thirteen dollars a month."

Jimbo looked at Gideon, his lips forming the words, "Thirteen dollars." That was more than anybody would pay for farm labor. Aloud he asked, "Would I have me one of them pretty blue suits?"

"Everybody wears a uniform."

"And I'd get to ride horses every day?"

"I believe I can promise you that. You would be given some basic training in New Orleans, then be sent West as a replacement for one of the colored cavalry regiments."

"West?" Gideon felt a chill. The word had an ominous feel, a sense of strangeness, conjuring up visions of a distant and vaguely frightening land of wild animals and wild men. He had heard talk. Since the war, many of the white folks had drifted

West looking for a place to piece broken lives back together. Most had never been seen again.

The officer seemed to sense Gideon's foreboding. "You'll like the West. It's a new land, fresh and unspoiled, big and open and fine. A land of opportunity for everybody. How much opportunity will you ever find here? You're a slave here, or almost one. But out West, black or white, every man is a *man*."

Gideon looked at the ground. "It might be awful easy out there to be a *dead* man."

"Wild exaggerations. More men are killed in knife fights in New Orleans in a month than are killed out West in a year. And yellow fever! Do you know how many people die here when yellow fever sweeps this country?"

Gideon had a fair notion. His mother had died of it.

"Yellow fever is unknown out there. It's the healthiest place in the world for a young and active man. Fresh air, sunshine, three solid meals every day. And think of the money! Thirteen dollars a month. If you're frugal you can save just about all of that. In a few years you'll have enough to buy a farm or set yourself up in a good business anywhere you want to."

Gideon was tempted, but doubts remained.

The officer saw that Jimbo was already convinced. "Jimbo, as long as you're joining the army anyway, I'd like to have you try out the rest of the horses Mr. Cooper wants to sell us."

Cooper had listened sullenly, knowing he was being euchred out of a potential horse handler. But the pain was allayed by the improved probability of selling the army these horses and getting his hands on some good solid Union silver.

Gideon knew how the conversation would end. He could tell by Jimbo's eagerness in doing the captain's bidding. But he had a nagging suspicion that the captain had not fully answered his questions.

"Sir," he asked cautiously, "what about the Indians?"

The officer smiled. "Young fellow, I've known men who've spent years in the West and have never *seen* an Indian."

Three

GRAY HORSE RUNNING was so intent upon the deer that he almost missed seeing the soldiers until it was too late. He dropped upon his belly, his heart pounding in surprise. He raised his head slowly to peer above the heavy growth of seeded-out grass stems and to wonder at the first soldiers he had ever seen. Their faces were black—all but one. White men with black skins. He had heard of such things but had been skeptical.

These, then, were what the experienced warriors had been calling *buffalo soldiers*—the darkness of their faces and the short, kinky hair that somehow brought to mind the topknot of the buffalo. He lay transfixed in wonder as the riders came ever closer to him, driving a large number of loose horses.

Gray Horse was on the homeward leg of his first genuine raiding trip. After coming down from the mountain he had tried to convince the warriors that he had indeed found his medicine. His cousin, Bear That Turns to Fight, doubted it and said so. Bear had held a grudge against him since a day years ago when Gray Horse had beaten him badly in a horse race. More or less on probation, Gray Horse had been permitted to go on a couple of long cattle drives, but it had been left to experienced raiders actually to take the *tejano* cattle. Gray Horse had been obliged to

wait a safe distance behind and then help only with the menial
chore of driving the stolen longhorns to Yellow House Canyon
on the high plains. There the Comanchero traders of New Mexico waited to take them for guns and powder and flint and tobacco. After two of these dusty and uninspiring ventures, Eagle
Feather had finally decided to take a chance on Gray Horse. A
hardy veteran of many lucrative expeditions, Eagle Feather had
led a party of ten to see what booty they might find lying
around in the western Texas settlements. He had traversed that
country many times and knew its major landmarks. He knew
where good horses were to be had, and he knew the rough country where trailing would be difficult even for the Rangers. He
had told Gray Horse that the soldiers were always to be watched
and never to be attacked except when they could be taken by
surprise. They had the disadvantage of being slow to get started.
And unless they had the aid of good trackers such as the
Tonkawa scouts or the dark-skinned Seminoles, they were usually not hard to shake off of a trail. They were not implacable
like Texas Rangers—men always angry and always ready to
travel. Eagle Feather said that the Rangers were savages.

Traveling light, eating little and drinking water sparingly, the
warriors had left the rolling plains, crossed over the Colorado
and Concho rivers and had moved into the hilly live-oak country
which once had been a favored hunting ground for the People.
Now white settlers were crowding it with their towns and farms
and ranches, plowing up the grass and planting all manner of
weak and tasteless foods not half so nourishing as the buffalo.
The Comanche had never had much regard for the planter tribes
such as the Wichitas. The white men chased out or killed out the
buffalo and replaced them with spotted cattle whose flesh was
far less satisfying. They ribboned the country with wagon tracks
that brought ever more of the white-faced, blue-eyed spoilers.
Gray Horse had been hearing of that beautiful hill country all
his life, the home range of the People's Penateka band. It filled
him with resentment that he was not privileged to see it free as
his father had. The People had won it by right of conquest a
hundred years and more ago, driving out the Apache just as the
Apache earlier had driven out other tribes. It was the People's

great hunting ground, paid for in blood. No one else had the right to be there.

Ten men could hardly drive out all the settlers, but they had exacted a price from them for their perfidy. Late one night, in a show of daring, Eagle Feather had led the party into one of the villages. There Gray Horse saw for the first time the peculiar stone and wooden houses of the *tejanos*, cumbersome structures that a man could not pick up and move as the People could move their tepees. He wondered what the white men did when the rain failed and they needed to move with the grass. What did the white man do with his women when the changing moon brought their bleeding days? Among the People, a woman had to remove herself from her family during this period and stay alone where her sickness would not contaminate her man or his food or his medicine. For this purpose, Comanche women had tepees of their own in which they could wait out that annoying time, then bathe and cleanse themselves thoroughly before they rejoined the group to take up their normal routine. He saw no such separate places for the white women unless they be those tiny huts behind each large house. Perhaps those were large enough for white women, but Comanche women would have complained bitterly.

He thought it would be easy to invade the houses and kill their occupants, but Eagle Feather advised against it. One shot would rouse the village, and they would have to leave without as many horses as they could acquire by remaining quiet. Gray Horse crept up to the window of one building and stared in curiosity at men sitting beside tables, drinking what he surmised to be the make-crazy water he had heard about, playing some sort of game with little flat squares they held in their hands or laid down in a pile. Some seemed to be quarreling among themselves, but he could judge only by the tone, not the words. He marveled at their hairy faces, their hairy arms. They reminded him more of some strange animal than of men. They seemed, too, to be wearing a lot of clothes for the summertime.

One of the warriors tapped him on the shoulder and beckoned him away from that curious place. He pointed to several horses tied to a rail in front of the building. Gray Horse moved in

quietly, afoot, cut the reins and led the horses away in a slow
walk, making little sound on the soft, hoof-scuffed street. He
noted that the horses bore leather saddles much different from
the rawhide kind the People fashioned for themselves and even
different from those of the Mexican Comancheros. These appeared heavy and cumbersome, too much weight for a horse to
carry under pursuit. He wondered if everything the white man
owned was as unnecessarily heavy as his houses and his saddles.

Eagle Feather complimented Gray Horse on his stealth. Gray
Horse accepted the honor, but he knew where the power came
from; he had been granted the silent cunning of the wolf.

Resenting Gray Horse's accomplishment, Bear discovered
horses in an adobe corral behind a house. The settler evidently
was wise to the ways of Indians, for the only gate was beside the
house, near an open window where he could hear anyone moving it. But Eagle Feather had another strategy. He took a long
rawhide string, tied a rock in one end and quietly dropped it
over the adobe wall on the side farthest from the house. With
the rock acting as a counterweight, he began sawing through the
mud blocks with the rawhide. A chunky warrior named Terrapin made a similar cut a double arm's span away. Gray Horse
helped them remove the cut blocks, leaving an opening for the
animals to come through. Eagle Feather went in after them,
bringing them out quietly to join the others already captured.

By daylight the raiding party was miles from the *tejano* village
with more than a hundred horses and mules. Not a shot had been
fired. Bear complained that they had passed up a good opportunity to take scalps with a minimum of inconvenience, but Eagle
Feather counseled that horses should be the first consideration.
To Gray Horse, that seemed to exalt material gain over princi-
ple, but he kept the thought to himself.

Scalps had come—eventually—though Gray Horse had not
been privileged to take any. Scouting along their back trail, Terrapin found three men following the tracks. He took half the
party in a long circle backward while Gray Horse and the others
kept the herd moving. The Indians came up behind the trackers
and took them by surprise. They brought up three more horses

and three fresh scalps. Here were three *tejanos* who would never kill another Indian, never plow up another good prairie.

The raiding party went up by way of the big fort where three Concho rivers joined together. Eagle Feather said if the soldiers were careless, the warriors might add some army mounts to their remuda. To Gray Horse's disappointment, Eagle Feather left him with two other inexperienced young men to continue driving the herd north while seven reconnoitered the post. They had remained hidden in the pecan timber all day, watching, and had made a quiet sortie in the dark but had not been able to take any horses. There were too many buffalo soldiers.

Gray Horse took some silent satisfaction in their failure, especially Bear's vocal disappointment. If they had allowed him to go, his wolf instincts might have made the venture a success. Even if he had not been able to take any horses, he wanted very much to see those buffalo soldiers, to see if they had horns like the buffalo or merely the buffalo's color and hair.

They were a day's journey north and east of that fort now, on their way to another post named Griffin, where Eagle Feather hoped they might find the soldiers more careless. The warriors' horses had grown weary, and the men had had little time to rest or to eat. They had camped in breaks near the reddish Colorado River, which Gray Horse remembered crossing on the way down. The horses taken from the white settlements were turned out to graze under guard in a small valley where the grass was good. The first-timers including Gray Horse were sent out in opposite directions in search of fresh meat, their obligation to the seasoned men.

He had seen two white-tailed does at a distance, had tied his pony in a thicket to keep it out of sight, and had started a slow, careful stalking on the downwind side, trying to get close enough to put an arrow into the fattest of the pair. He had been almost within range when one doe had suddenly lifted her head from her grazing, glanced at something on the upwind side and bounded into the scrub timber. Only then had Gray Horse seen the soldiers.

He lay still, trying to keep a grip on himself when it seemed they were going to ride directly over him. He was at the edge of a small clump of scrub oaks. He began crawling backward without raising his body. He kept his head up just enough to see over the grass, to keep his eyes on the oncoming riders and their large string of driven horses. To his relief, he saw they would miss the trees by a small margin. He took a rough count of the soldiers. There were about as many as the fingers on both of his hands twice over. All were black but one. Some did not ride particularly well; they bounced in the small saddles and appeared very uncomfortable.

The white-faced man he gave only a glance, but the black white men fascinated him. He found it difficult to believe the color was real. Perhaps it was painted on for some religious or military reason. Or perhaps these men had spent their lives in the sun and had been burned so dark that the color was taken for black. Beneath those blue clothes, he thought, their skin was probably white like that of the one man who rode to the side of the others, with them and yet not one of them.

His heart skipped as his eyes seemed to lock on to those of a black soldier. The man was staring straight at him. Gray Horse stared back, expecting the trooper to shout an alarm. His hand tightened on his bow. His wolf medicine would have to be strong if all these soldiers charged down upon him.

To his relief, the blue-clad soldier said nothing to the men around him, though for a long time he kept watching the place where Gray Horse lay. Gray Horse studied the face. It was beardless and smooth, but he could make no judgment about the soldier's age. The dark faces all looked the same except for variations in beards and mustaches.

The soldiers passed on by him, except for one straggler who had stepped down to relieve himself and was slow to catch up. Temptation began to rise in Gray Horse. It would be easy to drive an arrow through this lone trooper. He could satisfy his curiosity about whether the color would rub off. The other men were far ahead. Unless this one made some dying outcry, or one of the others happened to look back, they probably would be unaware for a time that anything was amiss.

But Gray Horse knew he might not catch the soldier's mount. His own was tied a long walk from here. The soldiers would never let him reach it afoot. It was no gain to take a soldier's scalp if he gave up his own in payment. The life of an enemy was nothing, but the life of one of the People was not lightly to be thrown away, even in battle.

The loose horses had numbered something short of a hundred, not as many as Eagle Feather had grazing about his camp on the river. Almost immediately Gray Horse began plotting to get away with them—or at least a part of them. It came to him that these soldiers would soon reach the river, not far from the camp where the warriors were taking their rest. The soldiers were moving slowly, walking their horses. Once they were beyond sight of him, he could mount up, make a wide circle and reach the river ahead of them.

The plan was already forming in his mind, though he did not know whether the others would accept it. It seemed logical that the soldiers would spread the horses up and down the river to drink. If three or four warriors made a feint on one side, they might draw most of the soldiers away in pursuit. The others then could sweep down from the opposite direction and run off part or all of the horse herd.

The straggling black soldier disappeared over a low hill, never knowing how nearly he had come to losing life and hair. Gray Horse rose and sprinted briskly to the thicket where he had left his pony.

Cousin Bear would have to hold silent tonight.

Gideon Ledbetter's heart was in his throat. He would almost bet Old Colonel's five-dollar gold piece he had seen an Indian in the clump of oaks. But he wiped his sweating hands on the blue legs of the uniform and said nothing. Various recruits had been seeing wild Indians ever since they had left New Orleans, and especially since they had ridden out of Fort Sill, Indian Territory, on their way south to drop reinforcements and horses at the Texas forts. Last night an excitable Mississippian named Culley, helping guard the picket line, had fired at what he thought was an Indian. This morning the lieutenant had found a fresh bullet hole oozing sap from a live oak. Other troopers including Jimbo had rawhided the recruit unmercifully all day. Gideon did not intend to give a false alarm and be made a fool of, though hair tickled at the back of his neck.

He was jumpy like most of the others who rode through this strange and formidable land for the first time. It was wild and beautiful and awesome, bigger than he had imagined the whole world to be. Uneasiness had gnawed at him since they had left the last of the old towns and entered the wilderness, proceeding westward on horseback across the Indian Nations on their way to Fort Sill. That place, in the heart of the reservations, was headquarters for Colonel Benjamin H. Grierson and the black Tenth Cavalry. From there, just east of the Wichita Mountains and the land set aside for the "wild" tribes, the tall, scar-faced but basically gentle Grierson commanded detachments scattered more than two hundred miles south, all the way to the confluence of the three Concho rivers.

Near Sill was headquarters of the Indian agency, a tiny island in a hostile sea. Gideon had not yet recovered from the stifling dread of his first Indians on beef-issue day. He had sensed their hatred as they stared at the passing troops. In another time, another place, they would gladly have impaled him on a lance. These Indians were prisoners of war—even slaves, in a sense. Having been a slave much of his life he thought he should understand their feelings. But he had been unprepared for the hostility, the raw hate in dark and flinty eyes, the deep resentment at being reduced to dependence.

They both fascinated and frightened him, their seeming wildness a violent contrast to the well-ordered world of his own limited experience. They were like this land they lived in, alien to anything he had ever known or imagined. The immensity of this country, the almost incomprehensible distances, seemed overpowering to him, fearsome yet strangely exhilarating. Most days of his life he had not traveled more than a mile from cabin row. A three-mile trip to town was an event that required preparation. Some days here they had ridden ten or twelve times that, dropping off men at unfinished Fort Richardson on the banks of crooked Lost Creek, at primitive Fort Griffin standing like a sentinel atop a flat hill above the Clear Fork of the Brazos. He had never been able to shake the sense of being watched by hidden, hostile eyes. Other recruits had the same obsession, for they had talked about it. He had not spoken of his; he felt ashamed. He was both envious and resentful of Jimbo's calm, his ability to whistle obliviously when Gideon was sure they were about to be fallen upon and massacred by savage men in feathers and breechclouts.

Gideon's uneasiness was deepened by a conviction that if they ever fell into a battle with the Indians he would not even know enough about his weapon to defend himself. The army had provided Spencer rifles in basic training, but only once had it issued ammunition for practice. The white officers explained that the service was short of funds. The recruits were encouraged to practice marksmanship all they wanted, but they had to do it with empty rifles.

In training Gideon had not been allowed a chance to fire more than half a dozen live rounds, and not one had struck the bull's-eye. Two rounds had misfired. The cartridges were old, left over from the rebellion. Good enough for black recruits, he had heard one officer say. Damn niggers couldn't hit anything anyway. They could buy ammunition for themselves, an officer had commented, if they felt they needed more practice. But Gideon had found that the recruiting captain had not told him everything. He had not mentioned that the army was going to mark down almost a hundred dollars against him for his first issue of clothing. At thirteen dollars a month, it was going to take him a right smart while to have any money in the first place. On top of that, he had to pay the army laundresses to do his washing.

He had kept in mind what the captain had told him about being able to save his money and buy a farm. From what he had seen so far he would have a long gray beard before he had a hundred dollars.

The recruiter had not lied about riding horseback and getting a lot of fresh air. Gideon's rump was toughening now, but at first he was rubbed so raw that the saddle was agony. He had slept few nights beneath a roof. They had paused at Fort Sill barely long enough for the clerks to read the list of recruits and arbitrarily allot them to the various posts. It seemed to him that the officers devoted more time and attention to the division of the horses. The best mounts had been left at Fort Sill, since those officers had the authority to make the selection. Officers at Richardson had made the next cut and those at Griffin a third. Fort Concho would have to accept these eighty-odd picked-over remnants.

One consolation helped make up for many disappointments. So far they had not split him and Jimbo. Jimbo was Gideon's only remaining hold on the reality of the past, Jimbo and the five-dollar gold piece. The plantation, Old Colonel, Aunt Ella . . . those seemed already unreal, obscured in the haze of memory by the harsh demands of this totally different life, this unimaginable land.

Jimbo rode beside him, whistling a plantation work song, as unconcerned as if he were exercising one of Old Colonel's horses on a nice flat road beside a cotton field in full blossom. He had taken easily to this army life. His handy way with horses had won favorable attention from officers wherever he had stayed long enough for them to observe him at his work.

Gideon studied the young white officer who rode alongside the troopers, just distant enough to show he was in charge. Lieutenant Hollander was on his way back to Concho after leave to his old home in the East. He had been at the corrals the evening that Gideon and Jimbo and the others had arrived at Sill. Quickly discerning that Jimbo had more than average talent with horses, Hollander had seen to it that this talent was not displayed to the Sill officers. Being placed in charge of the recruits as they were scattered among the posts to the south, he had marked Jimbo down as his personal orderly.

"Don't you be doing any showing off when we get to Concho, boy," he had said. "I can win some money on you before they catch on. I'll give you a cut."

Jimbo had seen no objection to that, but he had insisted that he and Gideon stay together. Hollander had been true to his word.

Gideon had tried to figure out the lieutenant, comparing him to white folks back home. Hollander seemed troubled. At Fort Griffin when the officers meant to take all the good horses for themselves, Hollander had come near blows with another lieutenant. Only a captain's intervention had prevented a fight. Naturally enough, the captain had sided with his own lieutenant in the division of mounts. Outranked, Hollander had gotten drunk that night. He and the Griffin lieutenant had settled their differences behind the stables, in the moonlight. Hollander had won the fight but not the war. He was still left with the snide horses.

"It doesn't matter," he had laughed dryly as they left Griffin, heading south down the military road toward Concho. "The Indians will probably get them all anyway."

If the rest of the horses were as unmanageable as the brown Gideon was riding, the army at Fort Concho was in trouble, he thought. He was glad they moved mostly at a walk, for the brown trotted roughly enough to jar a man's innards loose. And it seemed to follow its own inclinations rather than those of its rider. He had what Jimbo called an iron jaw; he responded poorly to the bit. When Gideon tried to rein him to the right, the brown was as likely to go to the left out of pure contrariness. Gideon wondered if there might be a little mule blood in him.

Hollander touched spurs to his dark sorrel horse and rode to the front of the detail. "That's the Colorado River down there. We'll water the horses and rest them awhile. Keep your eyes open."

A chill came to Gideon's stomach as Hollander slipped his carbine from its scabbard and laid it across his lap. Hollander shouted, "Don't let those horses scatter too much on the river; just give them room enough to drink." He motioned for the men to spread out.

Gideon's mouth was dry, and he wanted to get a drink before the horses muddied the water. But he saw that the river carried a strong tinge of red; nature hadn't waited on the horses. Downstream, he watched ruefully as most of the horses waded right out into the water in a great splashing and threshing that roiled the mud and deepened the red. He was thinking he was too late for a good clean drink.

A loud shout jarred him. He glanced west first, toward the

other soldiers and the horses. Most of the men were looking in his direction and beyond him, milling in excitement.

Jerking his head around, he saw a stir of color and movement, horses running straight toward him. Indians!

For a moment he sat twisted in the saddle, numb. The breath stopped in his throat. He felt as much as heard an arrow whisper past him. The soldiers began firing. He realized he was between them and the Indians, and most were no better marksmen than he was. He counted three Indians racing toward him. No—four, waving feathered shields, loosing arrows, yelping like dogs hot on a scent.

Gideon managed to bring up his carbine and squeeze the trigger. The recoil slammed the butt hard against his shoulder, and through the puff of black smoke he had no idea if he had hit anything. In a second, he took another count. All four were still coming.

The firing behind him threw his horse into a panic. It ran away from the gunfire, toward the Indians. Gideon hauled frantically on the reins, trying to stop him, to turn him, to do any damn thing. The horse kept running, carrying him headlong toward those four feathered, shouting, surprised Indians.

Gideon's heart swelled to bursting. An insistent roaring in his head blocked out all other sound. His mouth was open, and he was either shouting or screaming; he didn't know which. He raised the carbine and fired again. The Indians suddenly spread out, startled by the unexpected sight of a lone soldier charging directly into them.

One held his ground. The next two or three seconds seemed to stretch into an hour. Gideon saw the young face painted in lightning streaks, the black eyes wide in exhilaration. He saw the stone-tipped war club in the warrior's outthrust hand. As he brought the Spencer up and sighted over the barrel, he saw the painted shield swing around, rimmed with feathers that seemed to fan out in the wind. It was painted black except for a jagged streak slashed across it and for four red spots like animal tracks. Beneath it hung some sort of a brush. No, the tail of an animal.

As Gideon squeezed the trigger the shield dropped a little and he saw the face again. He saw the eyes, wild with excitement.

The hammer fell silently. The cartridge failed.

The two horsemen slammed together. Gideon grabbed at the saddle to keep from losing it, and he dropped the carbine. He saw the war club streaking at him. Instinctively he threw up his left arm to ward off the blow. He felt a crushing pain as the stone struck him and glanced away. He caught the triumph in the young Indian's eyes as momentum carried them past each other.

He was already half out of the saddle and knew he was going down. He struck the ground rolling. Panic grabbed him at the thought of being helpless in the midst of the Indians. He jumped to his feet, bringing up in both hands a chunk of wood he had rolled across. He swung it back over his shoulder, ready to strike anything which came at him.

The Indian could take him easily now, if he turned and came back. But he did not. Through the dust and the shouting and the shooting and confusion, Gideon saw Jimbo racing toward him.

"Swing up behind me!" Jimbo shouted. Gideon grabbed his friend's arm. He swung up partway, though not enough to secure himself behind the saddle. It did not matter. Jimbo caught hold of him and spurred downriver out of the fray, giving Gideon a chance to pull himself into a better position. Gideon looked fearfully behind him, sure the Indians were upon them. But they were busy elsewhere. He and Jimbo were to themselves. Jimbo turned his horse and went back.

"Better jump down and get that gun," he said. Gideon did, acting from impulse more than deliberation. One lucid thought managed to come through. He hoped the Indians got that brown horse.

The brown had swum the river and was climbing out on the other side. The Indians, so far as Gideon could tell, were all still north of the river.

As suddenly as it had begun, the raid was over. The warriors were running their horses northward, yipping and yelling, driving a dozen or so head they had managed to cut from the bunch. They had missed the brown.

The lieutenant loped out to Gideon and Jimbo. His voice was raw with excitement. "You boys all right?"

Gideon couldn't bring out the words, but Jimbo had them. "Alive and kickin', sir."

The lieutenant gave Gideon his full attention. "I'm damned if I can remember your name, soldier."

Gideon licked dry lips and managed to tell him. "Ledbetter. Gideon Ledbetter. Sir."

"Ledbetter, I'd like to shake the hand of the man who got you to join the army. That was one of the coolest things I ever saw, the way you charged those Indians."

Words were slow to come. Gideon said, "It was the horse."

"I don't know that your judgment is as sound as it should be, but nobody can fault you for nerve. I'll tell the commanding officer about you, Ledbetter. He likes to know who his *soldiers* are."

Gideon was beginning to feel sick from the aftershock. "The horse ran away," he protested.

The lieutenant missed his meaning. He saw the US-branded horse on the other side of the river. "It's all right; we'll pick him up."

Feeling was coming back into Gideon's left arm. It ached as if it were broken. He gripped it with his right hand, giving in to the pain.

"They wound you, soldier?" Hollander pressed.

Gideon shook his head. "Just hit me with that club."

Hollander dismounted and felt of the arm, watching Gideon for reactions. "Counted coup on you. Indians take a lot of stock in that. You've made some brave mighty happy."

Gideon's sleeve was torn; blood began to stain the ragged edges. Incongruously he found himself worrying about having to pay for another shirt.

Hollander said, "Get that shirt off, soldier."

It hurt, but Gideon complied. The stone club's chiseled edge had bruised and gashed the flesh. Hollander said, "We'd better get those horses to the other side first, in case the redskins decide to make another try. Then we'll catch the pack mule that carries the medical supplies. I'll patch you enough to hold you till we get you to the post surgeon."

Many of the recruits gathered around, staring at Gideon with surprise and admiration. Jimbo declared, "The Indians are goin' yonderway, sir, and takin' some of our horses with them. Ain't we goin' after them?" The loss of horses shook him more than a fatality would have.

Hollander looked at the dust left by the Comanches. "You boys showed grit, but you're still green. They'd just circle back on us and take more horses—maybe all of them the next time. They might take a few of you, too. We'll leave well enough alone."

He turned again to Gideon. "The rest of them braced up when they saw what you did. I think they put up a better scrap than the Indians expected." A half grin tugged at the corners of his thin mustache. "Do you read the Bible much?"

Gideon didn't want to admit that he couldn't read. "I know some about it."

"There's a Gideon in the Scriptures, you know. A soldier. They called him a mighty man of valor. But I'll leave the Bible to the chaplain. *Charger!* That's what I'm going to call you. Charger, for the way you charged into those Indians."

Hollander turned away to see about getting the horses across the river. Gideon stood clasping his left arm. A trickle of blood was warm and sticky between his fingers.

"He wasn't even listenin' to me, Jimbo. I done my best to tell him the truth. That dumb horse just run away. I was scared flat to death."

Jimbo smiled. "Always tell white folks what they want to hear and you'll never get no whip marks on your back."

Four

THE COLORADO RIVER and the skirmish lay far behind them as the rough hills and the red clay gave way to grass-blanketed flats and prairie-dog towns sloping gently southward toward the Conchos. A movement to the left caught the eye of Frank Hollander. One of the black recruits shouted, "Indians!"

Hollander supposed the curved horns of an antelope might resemble Indian feathers to the uninitiated, still trembling in the aftermath of their first brush. "There is no recorded case of an antelope ever shooting a United States soldier," he said loudly enough that most could hear. "Jimbo, come forward with me."

The antelope—twelve or fifteen—broke into a run, paralleling the soldiers and the horses until they had moved well ahead. Then, in single file, they cut in front, white rumps flashing in the sun. Hollander pushed the sorrel to a lope. When he was within good range, he pulled his carbine from its scabbard, stepped quickly to the ground and flipped the reins at the wide-eyed Jimbo.

He dropped to his right knee, propped his left elbow on his left knee and aimed, leading the last antelope to compensate for its fleet stride. The carbine coughed black smoke. The antelope tumbled, rolled once and lay kicking.

In fright at the shot, the horse jerked the reins from Jimbo's hand. Jimbo spurred to catch up, grabbing the reins and wrapping them around his wrist. Hollander held his breath because a man could get dragged that way. But Jimbo was strong and determined. He brought the sorrel to a stop and led it back, talking gently and calming it down.

Hollander smiled. He could not remember that he had ever encountered a man who seemed to have such an easy way with horses. If he could keep the other officers from catching on too soon, he would get even for the shameless way they had collaborated to fleece him at poker and keep him near poverty. He patted the horse on the neck before mounting. He rode to where the antelope lay, its open eyes dulling.

"You know how to gut him, soldier?"

Jimbo said, "I've slaughtered a many a hog."

"Do it then, please. There'll be smiles in officers' mess tonight."

In Hollander's opinion, compared to venison or even buffalo, antelope left something to be desired. But it was fresh and would help break the monotony for his fellow bachelors. As the rest of the troopers came up, Hollander had one of the loose horses caught. It rolled its eyes in fear at the smell of blood. Jimbo had to rub its neck and talk to it of other things while the antelope was tied across its back. The rest of the pronghorns were long gone across the flat. Unlike deer, they preferred the open where they could see an approaching predator and use their one defense —speed. They could outrun a horse but not a bullet. Frank Hollander might privately concede that as an officer and a gentleman he had a minor shortcoming or two, but poor marksmanship was not one of them.

Gideon Ledbetter rode up close as Jimbo remounted. Hollander noted Jimbo's quick solicitude. He would use his influence to see that they were assigned to the same company—*his* company. Gideon held his bandaged arm tightly against his chest. Hollander asked, "Hurting bad, Charger?"

The recruit shook his head. "Ain't nothin' much, sir." The cloudy look in his eyes gave the lie to his words. Hollander suspected he was running a fever.

"The fort is only a little farther now. See where the big pecan trees line the river? Hold on tight."

Something in Gideon's stolid face reminded the lieutenant of a faithful dog, holding up a hurt foot but not whimpering. Hollander felt as if he should pat him on the head. This, in a way, had been his feeling about all the black soldiers he had liked. He had never allowed the rest to clutter his emotions.

The fort sprawled south of the river. Space seemed endless here, so the post had been spread liberally across a large block of land that the wise men of Washington had not seen fit to buy from the state of Texas. It had been so far from civilization that it seemed unlikely anyone would care to claim it. But some sharp Texas speculators had bought it after the army had put up several permanent structures. Now the government was paying a handsome yearly rent for the use of the ground.

On the north bank clustered a motley assortment of raw picket shacks and Mexican-style *jacales*. Saint Angela was a whisky village subsisting entirely from the fort. Hollander compared it to a wood tick which attached itself to a cow's ear and lived on blood. A new stone building of some pretensions had been started in his absence. The tick was swelling, he thought darkly, and he was bringing fresh blood to feed it.

Damn them, they wouldn't get any of *his*. Very little, anyway. He bought an occasional bottle of indifferent whisky there, but he never drank it on their unholy premises. He made it a point to contribute as little as possible to the mud-and-stick village. More Fort Concho soldiers—black and white—had been killed or maimed in Saint Angela than at Indian hands.

Jimbo was showing a sharp interest and perhaps warm anticipation. "I didn't expect to see no town way out here."

Hollander's eyes narrowed. "It's hardly a town. It's more like a boil on a soldier's butt."

He led the troopers around the outer edge of the village to the shallow ford. A Mexican prostitute, dark of skin, waved from a rude *jacal* of pecan limbs, brush and mud. Jimbo shouted at her, as did several others.

Hollander advised, "You'd better stick to army horses, Jimbo. These fillies have tricks you've never heard of."

A horror story the officers always recounted to new recruits was the experience of a white bugler in the fort's earliest days. He had been given a narcotic by one of Saint Angela's soft doves so she could separate him from his money. After weeks near death his body finally recovered, but his mind remained a shambles.

The river ran deep in most places. Unwary soldiers who tried to sneak across in the dark of the night had been known to miss the fords and drown in the cold, treacherous waters. The men were especially vulnerable after partaking too long of cheap snakehead whisky peddled for their pitifully few dollars.

Up from the south bank loomed the sturdy stone corrals which Colonel William R. Shafter had built to protect post horses from thieves, red and white. Someone there had seen the recruits and the remounts coming, for a blue-clad trooper swung one of the wooden gates open, then stepped aside so he would not booger the horses away from the entrance. Hollander swung his arm. "Let's put them in."

Without being told, Jimbo loped ahead and took a position at the left to haze the horses through the opening. Hollander looked in vain for someone to do the same on the right without having to be told. He set his jaw grimly. He thought, *For a bunch of Ethiopians, I suppose one out of twenty-odd isn't too bad.*

A black soldier rode out of the gate and took the right-hand position. He sat straight in the saddle, his back rigid as a flagpole. Sergeant Esau Nettles bore himself like the commander-in-chief of all the armies. There was not another like him in the Tenth Cavalry and perhaps not in the entire service. Hollander had quietly laughed at him in the beginning, taking his manner for pretentiousness. He had not laughed in a long time.

He had developed a disquieting feeling that had Esau Nettles been born white, and in favorable economic circumstances, he might well have *been* the commander-in-chief of all the armies.

Hollander watched until the bell mare trotted through the gate so he could be sure the rest would not spill and have to be chased down. Horses and men shared this lamentable trait at times. He rode up to Nettles, who sat on a big horse named Napoleon, as black and shiny as a crow's wing. Nettles gave a sharp, self-consciously proper salute. Hollander's slack response would have earned him a demerit in old days at the Point.

"Good to see you back, sir," Nettles said. The tone was genuine. Hollander took that as a compliment. Rather than say what he did not mean, Nettles would have remained silent.

"Good to see you're still here, Sergeant." He studied the black face, trying to decide if a touch of levity was in order. With Nettles he could never be sure. Nothing made the sergeant freeze up faster than the suspicion that a white officer was condescending to him. Hollander saw that Nettles' face bore the faint stirrings of a smile, an event worth noting in his diary, for that happened about as often as a good rain in this dry country. The lieutenant said, "I was afraid they might ship you off to another post while I was gone. I'd hate to break in a new top sergeant."

Nettles' smile was small and carefully rationed. "I was afraid they'd keep you back East, and I'd have to break in a new lieutenant. Sir."

Hollander relaxed. He had caught Nettles on a good day when none of the men in his charge had committed any serious breaches of good judgment or the articles of war. "Who's the C.O. now?"

"Still Colonel Thomas, same as when you left, sir."

Hollander grunted in satisfaction. Fort Concho was notorious for frequent changes in command, even by the unstable standards of frontier posts in general. A post commander who oversaw the planting of a garden seldom stayed to enjoy all the season's produce.

He watched the horses and the recruits enter the corral in a thick veil of gray dust. "Sergeant, I've brought you some fresh meat."

"You mean the men, sir, or the horses?"

"Both. I know you'll be kind to the horses."

"And the men. Chastisement is often a kindness, sir."

"If that be the case, then the army has been kind to us all."

The sergeant's smile left him. "I see you come back all by yourself, sir. I ain't countin' the recruits."

Hollander looked away. He had expected questions from his fellow officers. He had not been prepared for them to start with the sergeant. "I'm alone."

The sergeant nodded solemnly. "Yes, sir." It was as far as he would pry into Hollander's privacy.

The last of the horses trotted into the corral. Hollander waited for the dust to clear, then followed. Several black soldiers in canvas fatigue clothes had been cleaning corrals. They gathered to stare at the new recruits and to catcall admonitions that they would be sorry.

One fierce word from Sergeant Nettles scattered them like quail.

The recruits sat on their mounts along the corral fence, some staring worriedly after the departing soldiers, wondering if they were right.

Hollander said, "Sergeant, I turn these men over to you until they are assigned. All but one. We had a brush with Comanches. I'm taking the wounded man to the post hospital."

"I can take care of him, sir. I expect you got other things to do."

"This one is special, Sergeant. I want to be sure some hospital orderly doesn't slough him off."

Nettles said nothing, but Hollander read a critical thought in the half-closed eyes: *The lieutenant has picked him a pet.* There was, among some of the men, always an attempt to gain the favor of an officer so they might earn soft duty as orderlies and errand boys. Nettles had no more use for that kind than for the centipedes and scorpions which often infested the barracks' stone walls. Defensively Hollander said, "He showed conspicuous gallantry in battle."

Nettles had picked the slumped Gideon from the crowd. "He's quiet, sir. He don't look like the type."

"They seldom do." Hollander asked Nettles to see that his antelope was delivered to the bachelor officers' mess, then beckoned for Gideon to follow. The other men watched impassively. Nettles pointed in the general direction of one on the end, nearest the gate. "Daddamn you, soldier, can't you see the lieutenant is fixin' to pass? Open the gate for him!"

In their haste to comply, two troopers bumped each other. One went down. "Get up from there!" Nettles barked. "Least you can do is to *act* like soldiers instead of fools!"

Hollander suppressed a smile that might compromise the sergeant's unbending discipline. Nettles ordered the men to line up their horses. They were slow and sloppy about it. That situation would be corrected.

The lieutenant skirted eastward around the storage buildings and the guardhouse. Just off the southeast corner of the parade ground stood the largest building in Fort Concho, the almost-new hospital with generous wooden porches all the way around, shading and cooling the native-stone walls. The two-story middle section reminded him of a camel's hump. In its very center, rising to third-story level, was the glass-windowed belvedere, standing like a tall sentry over the post.

He tied his horse. Several black soldiers in gray canvas fatigues were raking and picking up litter. All snapped to attention and saluted, except one. He stood half a head taller than the others, a larger man than the army usually accepted for the cavalry. It loaded the horses down with so much heavy equipment that the weight of the rider had to be limited. Making a show of his delay, the big man gradually brought himself to a reasonably straight stance and gave a belated and sluggish salute that carried more of defiance than of respect.

Hollander smiled thinly, refusing the bait. "Well, Dempsey, I see they left the guardhouse door open again." Dempsey made no reply, staring at him with thinly concealed resentment.

The hell with it, Hollander thought, his smile gone. He saw Gideon dismount stiffly and make an effort at tying his horse. "Dempsey, can't you see the man needs help?"

Dempsey took one step forward and stopped. "He can do for hisself."

"Help him or I'll sic Nettles on you."

Hollander pushed the door open and automatically held it for Gideon before realizing that the soldiers outside were watching. It was not good form for an officer to be so solicitous of enlisted men, especially blacks. *The hell with that, too*, he thought.

Post surgeon Buchanan stood in the hallway, his white jacket rumpled but clean. His light-colored beard needed combing. By that, Hollander assumed the hospital was busy as usual. This country was hard on men who hadn't become acclimated to it. Few of the black troopers had been here long enough to have fallen into tune with its seasonal rhythms: its summer heat and its deceptive winter cold, its spring dust, its autumn asthma.

Buchanan stared in surprise. "Hollander! I hadn't heard that you'd gotten back."

"I just rode in."

Buchanan smiled. "Well, where's the bride?" He looked at Gideon. "I know *that's* not her!"

Hollander's jaw went tight. "There *is* no bride. What I've got here is a fierce Indian fighter, and he's taken a wound in the line of duty. I have to come to see that he gets the best of attention."

Buchanan appraised Hollander and saw he was not making fun. "Well, I suppose some married junior officers on this post will be glad you didn't bring a wife with you. You'd have bumped half the families on officers' row. That's bad for their morale."

"It would've been good for mine, though," Hollander said ruefully.

Until more permanent officers' quarters were completed, it was standard operating procedure for some or all of the bachelor officers to be billeted on the hospital's second floor. Hollander looked toward the stairway and cringed with dread at the thought of resuming residence up there amid the odor of disinfectants, listening to other officers complaining about the conduct of their foot-dragging troops, or recounting and grossly embellishing for the twentieth time old tales of past conquests, military and female.

He pointed his chin at Gideon. "I've still got a man standing here bleeding." That was an exaggeration. The bleeding had long since stopped.

Buchanan beckoned with his finger. "Follow me, soldier." Gideon glanced quietly at Hollander for confirmation, then complied. Hollander trailed him to the examination room. When he saw that Buchanan meant to cut off Gideon's sleeve, he protested. "The army will make him pay for that blouse, likely as not. Let's save it if you can." He carefully helped Buchanan slip the sleeve off Gideon's stiffened black arm. Gideon winced but made no sound.

The surgeon felt impassively around the wound, exerting no particular care to spare the soldier pain. "Arm's not broken." His brow wrinkled. "That's not from a bullet, nor from an arrow."

Hollander didn't give Gideon the opportunity to answer for himself. "One of those stone axes the Comanches use to scatter brains. This soldier charged in like he meant to wipe out the whole tribe." He told the story.

Buchanan grumped at Gideon, "It sounds to me as if they missed your brain by a long way. It's probably in your feet."

"It was my horse," Gideon said. Nobody paid any attention to him.

Hollander said, "Mark my words, Buchanan, this man will make corporal before his first year is out."

"If he lives that long." The surgeon began to wash the wound with something that smelled like bottled death and burned like unstoppered hell. Gideon clamped his strong white teeth to keep from crying aloud. The surgeon said, "This wound won't kill you, soldier, but it'll probably weep for a few days."

When Buchanan was through and his routine paper work given its customary lick and promise, Hollander accompanied Gideon out the door. He spotted Big Dempsey giving the army nothing but his presence. "Dempsey, come here."

The big man complied slowly enough to show his independence without culpable insubordination.

"Take this man back to the corrals and turn him over to Nettles."

Dempsey's narrowed eyes said that Gideon could just as well find his own way back, but his voice said, "Yes, sir."

Hollander turned to Gideon. "Charger, you do what Sergeant Nettles tells you, and you'll get along fine. Cross him and you'll think you've crawled into a den with three grizzly bears."

"Yes, sir," Gideon said. He walked stiffly along the porch, his teeth set in what Hollander took to be pain. At the end of it, he turned and said with a flaring of impatience, "Sir, it *was* the horse."

Hollander blinked in surprise and wondered whether Dempsey's manner was that contagious. He attributed it to fever, gone to Gideon's head. Anyway, sometimes these blacks seemed to speak a foreign language.

A headquarters building was in the fort's plan but had not yet been built. Hollander rode down to the adjutant's office, a small structure at the south edge of the parade ground. Tying his horse, he lifted off the saddlebags containing the Fort Sill dispatches and stepped through the door. He saluted the officer of the day and noted with some disappointment that Captain Richard Newton held that honor. Newton returned the salute without getting up from his desk.

"Hollander. I didn't think you'd ever come back."

"I just took a leave, not a separation."

With a faint touch of malice, Newton said, "I expected your new in-laws to use their political pull and get you a soft post back East."

That would have pleased Newton in two ways. It would have rid him of Hollander, and it would also have given him legitimate grounds to grouse about the army's lack of fairness . . . not that he had ever waited for legitimate grounds.

"As you can see, Captain, I am here. I brought some remounts and some recruits from Sill." He flopped the dusty saddlebags on the desk.

Newton made an annoyed show of waving the dust away. "I hope they're better than the last bunch. They were hardly worth the bringing."

"The men or the horses?"

Newton's eyes narrowed. "Either. There's not much difference between one and the other. How did we get ourselves trapped into a black regiment, Hollander?"

"It looked to us like an easy ticket to promotion. Not many officers wanted the assignment."

Newton snorted. "Easy ticket? Trying to teach the impossible to the incapable? It's rare when one of these darkies can even read and write. We sit up half the night doing paper work that would be delegated to enlisted men in a white outfit."

"A price we paid to avoid competition."

Newton frowned. He had never appreciated Hollander's disconcerting way of stripping matters down to bare essentials. Naked truth was like naked men: unattractive and sometimes ugly. Like them, it needed dressing up. But Frank Hollander knew exactly why he and most of the other officers were here. Nor did he entertain any lofty illusions about the motives behind the organization of the Ninth and Tenth Cavalry, or the two infantry regiments that shared their blackness. Negro units had served the Union during the war, and the new regiments were in part an effort to utilize this military experience. But of stronger immediate interest to a revenge-minded Reconstruction Congress had been the opportunity to humiliate the defeated South by occupying it with black troops, giving the slave authority over the master. That later events had turned these soldiers into Indian fighters was incidental, and more or less accidental.

Newton demanded, "And when are you going to let us plebians see the blue-blooded bride?"

Hollander had long sensed Newton's resentment over his correspondence with the daughter of a New England merchant who had access to influential offices in Washington. Newton's own wife was a plain and complaining woman who sent his hard-earned money home to her hapless father in some Illinois crossroads town. That gentleman could not influence the outcome of a dogfight, much less the outcome of national legislation, or the promotion of a deserving son-in-law to higher rank in a comfortable post worthy of his abilities and family connections.

Hollander admitted grudgingly, "There *is* no bride."

It might have been his imagination that a fleeting smile touched Newton's face. Newton stood up and looked out the front window at the half-completed officers' row. "At least we won't have to listen to all the junior officers' wives cry about being bumped to lesser quarters."

The door opened. Colonel Mahew Thomas stepped inside. Hollander saluted. Smiling, Thomas responded with an offhand salute that wouldn't be tolerated from a recruit. "Buchanan told me you just rode in, Frank. I hope you brought something with you to brighten the post?"

Hollander knew what he meant. "No, sir, unless you count some fresh horses and fresh recruits."

Thomas' smile faded. "I thought that was the purpose of your leave."

"I thought so too, sir."

Thomas nodded sympathetically and let the matter rest. He was a large man, wide of shoulders, beginning to soften and spread around the middle as his rank kept him tied more to garrison and allowed him less time in the saddle. He was one of that large, almost faceless and nameless pool of colonels scattered among the army's many western garrisons, a man of competence but not of the uncommon and dynamic abilities shared by such previous Fort Concho commanders as William Rufus Shafter or Ranald Mackenzie. Thomas had given up dreams of military glory and had resigned himself to quietly performing his duties with neither flash nor complaint until he was of age to draw his pension.

Newton moved aside so the commanding officer could thumb through the dispatches Hollander had brought.

Hollander told the colonel, "You'll find the horses eleven head short, sir. A raiding party hit us at the Colorado crossing."

Thomas blinked. Other than vague reports of horse theft in the hill country, this was the first excitement in several weeks. Hollander told it all, including the valorous counterattack by new black recruit Gideon Ledbetter. "I realize it is up to your discretion to apportion the recruits, sir, but I would consider it a personal favor if you would see fit to assign that man and his partner to my company. I believe that my Sergeant Nettles could turn them into top soldiers."

Thomas nodded. "Write their names down for me. This post needs all the *good* soldiers it can get."

Captain Newton mulled over the report. "Hollander, you are telling us that you let a dozen or so Indians get away with eleven horses? And you with thirty men at your command?"

Hollander stiffened. "Command is hardly the word for it. They were recruits. Most of them didn't even appear to know how to fire a rifle. If I had gone in pursuit I would more than likely have gotten men killed without recovering the horses. I thought I was fortunate not to lose more than eleven head."

Newton's mood was dark. "Fighting is what they're paid for. Better to train men in battle than in retreat."

Hollander felt no necessity to explain himself to Newton, who outranked him but nevertheless was only a company commander, as was Hollander himself. He turned to the commanding officer. "I had to make a decision in the field, sir. It was my judgment that the best course was to minimize my losses. But if you would like to put the matter before a board of inquiry, sir . . ."

The colonel shook his head. "No, Frank. I am satisfied with your report. If we court-martialed every failure against those damned Indians there would not be half a dozen field-grade officers left west of the Mississippi."

Newton's long military experience had taught him when to pursue a subject and when to drop it. He would not wish his own failures enumerated. "I was just inquiring, Hollander. No offense was meant."

"None was taken," Hollander said, but his voice was brittle.

Colonel Thomas set the matter to rest. "My wife has been looking forward to welcoming your bride, Frank. I do not want to be the one who disappoints her. I propose that we step over to my house and you tell her yourself, over a glass of brandy."

"I'm a bit dusty and trail-worn, sir."

"If that perturbed her, she would have turned me out thirty years ago."

Hollander had rather serve three days as officer of the guard than explain the unpleasant details to Elizabeth Thomas. But the matter was settled. Looking at officers' row, he felt the sting of his loss. He had expected to be moving into one of those houses with a warm and smiling wife at his side.

It was a short walk to the commanding officer's quarters, a modest stone structure with a wooden porch, looking about the same as the other buildings completed thus far on the south side of the quadrangle. The army saw little reason for variations except minor ones of size, to recognize differences in rank. Hollander scraped his boots carefully and stamped each foot to dislodge some of the dust. This was more a matter of form than of substance, for Texas dust had a stubborn way of clinging. Like the flies, it might rise momentarily, only to return to place as quickly as the disturbance was over. Putting rank aside, Thomas held the door open. The lieutenant removed his hat.

"Elizabeth," Thomas called, "I've brought a young lieutenant to pay his respects." It was customary for an arriving officer to pay a duty call upon the C.O.'s lady, though Hollander was hardly new here.

Elizabeth Thomas, a small, thin woman whose large, alert eyes saw everything, appeared in the kitchen doorway. Deep tracks had been etched in the corners by what those eyes had seen. Before she spoke, she removed her apron quickly, laying it across a plain high-backed rocking chair. She took quick, happy steps. "Frank Hollander! I had begun to wonder if you were ever coming back. Welcome to this house." She extended her small hand, the long fingers well suited to playing the piano, a pleasure she had long been denied at a succession of frontier posts. Hollander bowed slightly and kissed her hand in a manner that some were beginning to regard as old-fashioned. He noted the dark spots spreading on her skin, betokening the years. "The greatest pleasure of being back, Mrs. Thomas, is to see your smile."

It was the sort of thing a young officer was expected to say, but he meant it, more or less. He could not in good conscience have said the same thing to Richard Newton's wife, for he had seldom seen that woman smile.

Mrs. Thomas looked expectantly past the two men, her thought transparent. Hollander said, "I came alone, ma'am."

"Then she is to follow you later?"

He shook his head. "There was no wedding."

Mrs. Thomas released a long, disappointed sigh. She forced a quick, shallow smile. "There will be. Love always triumphs in the end."

"I am afraid that *was* the end, and it didn't." He sensed that his eyes betrayed the banked coals of anger he had been suppressing.

She said, "I'm sorry, Frank," and turned toward the small sitting room. "I have tea making on the stove. Or perhaps you men would prefer something stronger."

The colonel said, "Frank has had a long trip, and I lured him here on the pretext of giving him brandy."

"Then brandy it shall be. You men have yourselves a seat."

Hollander waited until the senior officer had seated himself, then eased into a well-used horsehide chair that some previous commander had not seen fit to take with him when he left. It was not army issue. The chair had existed on borrowed time for years. In the adjacent dining room was a small, somewhat battered walnut china cabinet, its doors originally fronted by etched glass. Except for one surviving section, the glass had been lost years ago in the moves from one military post to another. In the cabinet were remnants of a fine china service, gradually reduced by the hazards of frequent packing, hauling, unpacking and packing again as the colonel's restless career led him backward and forward across a hundred long and bumpy military roads. There was a saying among army wives: three moves was as bad as one fire.

Mrs. Thomas took a cork-stoppered bottle and two small glasses of etched crystal from another cabinet. "These are, I fear, almost the last survivors of what was once a proud and noble company. Mahew's parents gave us a set of crystal and china when we were married. Please don't ask me how long ago that was."

She poured Hollander's glass full of a nut-brown brandy, then filled her husband's. "If you men don't mind, I shall confine myself to tea. The spirit is willing, but the stomach is weak."

As she retreated into the kitchen, the colonel explained, "Something has upset her the last few days. I fault the water."

Hollander stared after her, reflecting on the daily hardships endured by army wives in such outposts, denied simple comforts other women took for granted in the smallest of towns in the East. If they were fortunate enough to have a house instead of a boarded-up tent, that house was likely to be hot in the summer and drafty in the winter. Here at Concho the stone walls and rough wooden floors regularly yielded up scorpions and centipedes, and occasionally a rattlesnake crawled in over an open threshold. Aside from whatever the military families provided for themselves, the furnishings were most often plain and thriftily utilitarian. Whatever possessions the woman might own were at the mercy of careless enlisted men and uncaring mules every time a move was made. Aside from game, the food tended toward the bland and monotonous, bordering on the inedible. The water was never to be trusted. The prudent boiled it before use.

Few western garrisons had ever suffered direct Indian attack, so garrison women ordinarily faced that danger only on the move. But they were always exposed to the frontier's less spectacular but even deadlier perils such as cholera, malaria, or those mysterious and incurable maladies of a dozen manifestations lumped together simply as "the fever."

Man, woman or child, these hazards respected no noncombatants.

Elizabeth Thomas returned carrying a saucer and a steaming cup. Hollander stood up quickly and waited until she seated herself before he sat down again. While out of sight, she had seized the opportunity to brush her long, graying hair, to button the sleeves she had rolled partway up while she worked in the kitchen. Here on this isolated post, she tried diligently to present a symbol of polite civilization as she remembered or imagined that civilization to be. She was an island of gentility in a huge, rough wilderness, a tiny candle in a dark night, a reminder to those who saw her that somewhere life was—or had been—different.

The effort was well intentioned, and Hollander acknowledged that it needed to be made; the alternative was total surrender. But often he felt it was futile. In the end, the wilderness would overwhelm these little islands and bury them without a trace.

He tried to picture Olivia Walburton where Elizabeth Thomas sat. The transfer did not fit. Probably everything had turned out for the best. But knowing didn't make it hurt any less.

Mrs. Thomas said, "I don't mean to pry, Frank, but are you certain there is no hope?"

"It's over. I'm not what she wants."

"I can't understand that. Any young woman would be lucky . . ."

"She didn't feel that way, nor did her mother and father. Especially her father. He tried to persuade me to leave the army and work in his mercantile business. He said he could use his influence to get me an immediate separation. He said a soldier could never support his daughter in the style to which she had every right to remain accustomed."

Mrs. Thomas argued, "You won't always be a lieutenant, Frank. Someday you'll be a captain, then a major, and eventually a colonel. . . ." She stopped, looking around the spartan room, seeming to realize how hollow her case sounded. Her husband was a colonel, and yet they lived on the edge of poverty.

Hollander continued, "Her father said any man content with a soldier's lot had little ambition. And a man who would associate himself with black soldiers obviously had no ambition at all. It amounted to an ultimatum: stay in the army and lose Olivia, or leave the army and she would condescend to accept me."

Mrs. Thomas automatically took a partisan position. So long had the fabric of her life been interwoven with the military that she thrilled like an old soldier to the piercing call of the trumpet or a sharp roll on the drum. So long had she endured the dust and the leaking rain, the smothering heat and the back-bending cold that their challenge had worn away. She ignored them when she could, and when she couldn't she confronted them head-on with a virtuous sense of duty met and served. Any insult to soldiers in general was an insult to her in particular, for she was army to the bone.

"You did the right thing, Frank. There are lots of other young women."

He felt a sense of privation, of denial. "Not out here."

After the breakup, he had stopped off in Washington to get gloriously drunk and had temporarily worked off his frustrations and pent-up hungers in one of the gaudy, red-tasseled institutions that specialized in such service to officers and other professional men of moderate means. He had not left until his means and his hunger were well spent. On the long trip back, the hunger had returned, but not the means.

He stared at the Tenth Cavalry coat of arms hanging on the colonel's parlor wall. Atop it was the shaggy form of a buffalo, symbolizing the black "buffalo soldiers," and beneath it a war-bonnet and pair of crossed tomahawks, symbolizing their mission. The troopers were proud of that emblem, and he supposed he should be, too. It had cost him enough.

A movement at the kitchen door drew his attention. He saw a slender, large-eyed girl wiping her hands on an apron. He stared in surprise. Because she stood in shadow, it was a moment before he realized she was not white. She was a mulatto, or perhaps a quadroon, her skin nearer olive than black. Her eyes rested briefly on the lieutenant, studying him with open curiosity though she spoke to the colonel's wife.

"You ready to put the roast in the oven, Miz Thomas?"

"Go ahead, Hannah."

"Yes, ma'am." The girl backed through the door, watching Hollander until she disappeared into the kitchen.

He said, "I don't remember seeing *her* before."

Mrs. Thomas replied, "She showed up on the post after you left. She lives with her granny over on laundry row. She works for me part of the time and helps the old woman wash and iron soldiers' clothes the rest of it."

"I would wager that she has the full attention of all the troops."

Mrs. Thomas shook her head. "Her granny watches her like an old brood hen. I've seen caning marks on Hannah."

"I would think the old woman might have to use her cane on some soldiers, too."

Mrs. Thomas frowned. "They would deserve it. If they can't control their baser natures, they can indulge them in that sin-trap across the river. They need not debase my kitchen help."

The girl came back to the door and asked Mrs. Thomas about the seasoning for the roast. The colonel's wife shrugged apologetically and retreated to the kitchen.

The colonel turned in his chair to be sure she was gone, then said, "I strongly suspect that at least a couple of my bachelor officers have taken a new interest in cleanliness since that girl has been on laundry row."

"She's black," Hollander pointed out.

"Not *very* black."

Five

GIDEON SENSED ANIMOSITY in the silent Big Dempsey as they walked toward the corrals from the hospital, leading his brown horse. He felt alone and ill at ease, for the post was new and large and full of strange people. He had never met people easily. On the plantation, he had never had to. His left arm, freshly bandaged, seemed dead except for a dull throbbing that just bordered on pain. He felt sluggish, wrung out, wishing he could crawl somewhere cool and dark and be forgotten for a day or two.

He tried to make conversation. "Is this Concho a good place?"

Dempsey growled, "When you're a nigger, there ain't no good place."

They reached the corral. Dempsey studied Gideon's stiff arm with suspicion and stood back, letting Gideon slide the bar and open the gate for himself. Leading the brown in, he could see that his fellow recruits were briskly currying and brushing their unsaddled horses while Sergeant Esau Nettles restlessly stalked among them, hands knotted into hard fists set threateningly on his hips. The crackle in his eyes was as loud as a shout. "You missin' a place there," he told a nervous black trooper. "You ain't done till I can't see one speck of dust, one trace of sweat. On the horse, I mean. I want to see lots of sweat on *you*."

He turned his challenging dark eyes to Gideon and Big Dempsey. "Dempsey, this ain't where I put you to work."

Dempsey did not cringe. "Your favorite lieutenant sent me to guide his pet pup back. Afraid he might get lost or somethin'." He turned and walked toward the hospital building.

Gideon felt the sergeant's eyes focus upon him. He had seen more friendliness in a white overseer the morning after a bad drunk. "Private Ledbetter, sir." He saluted the best he knew how.

Nettles was not impressed. "You don't salute sergeants—not even a top sergeant like me. You don't call me *sir*, neither. That's for the white officers."

"Yes, sir," Gideon murmured in confusion. He had never gotten it straight in his mind who was an officer and who wasn't. It seemed to him he caught hell from everybody who had one stripe or more on his sleeve.

Nettles gave him a hard stare that Gideon's eyes couldn't meet. "You got lost time to make up. Get the saddle off of that horse. Grab you a brush and a currycomb. Around this outfit the horses get groomed and fed before the soldiers do."

"Yes, sir." Flustered, Gideon unbuckled the girth. It was awkward, working with only his right hand. He tried to use his left, but it hurt.

Jimbo abandoned his own horse and stepped around to help him.

Nettles' hands went back to his hips. "Daddammit, trooper, what do you think you're doin'?"

"Helpin' him, is all. He's kind of one-handed."

"You got enough to do takin' care of your own job. If it *ain't* enough, I'll find you somethin' else. On this post every man totes the load for hisself."

Jimbo glanced apologetically at Gideon and hurriedly retreated.

Gideon slipped the light saddle off, picked up a brush and began trying to work the dust and sweat out of the brown horse's hair.

Nettles said, "The harder you brush, the better he'll shine."

Jimbo made one more effort to help. "Sergeant, old Gid got his arm hurt by them Indians."

Nettles withered him with another stare. "The only time you speak without permission is when I tell you to." He turned back to Gideon. "Maybe you really got that arm hurt, and maybe you're lookin' for the lieutenant to give you a soft time of it. But around here it ain't the officers you need to be scaredest of—it's *me*."

Gideon already was. "Yes, sir." He brushed harder, forcing his left arm into service.

Nettles declared, "I got eyes in the back of my head. I don't have no trouble seein' through a soldier that's tryin' to slack his duty."

"Yes, sir."

Nettles fell silent, but Gideon could feel the eyes on his back. He brushed. The pain rose. His left arm felt hot.

"Just a minute, trooper."

Gideon turned. Nettles parted the torn sleeve. A red stain was seeping through the fresh bandage. The work had made the wound bleed. Nettles' eyes were still fierce.

"Why didn't you tell me, soldier?"

Gideon looked at the ground. He couldn't meet that sharp scrutiny.

Nettles beckoned to Jimbo. "You, the one that talks all the time . . . Since you're so daddamned anxious for extra work, come here and finish groomin' up this horse."

Jimbo grinned and saluted. "Yes, sir."

Nettles gave him a glance that branded him a hopeless case. He jerked his head at Gideon and walked out of hearing of the other men. He leaned against the stone fence. "They told me what you done out there. I don't put no stock in daredevils. They're generally crazy or else tryin' to work some shenanigan to get theirselves soft duty."

Gideon hoped somebody—someday—might listen to him. "Sergeant, it wasn't none of them things. That brown horse just got afeered and run off with me, is all."

Nettles studied him in surprised silence.

Gideon added, "I tried to tell them. None of them didn't want to hear what I was sayin'. Lieutenant says I'm a hero. Doctor says I'm just crazy."

"And the truth is that you just can't handle your horse."

"I reckon that's about it."

Nettles grunted. "Well, we'll teach you how to do that. As for the rest, I don't see no need to disabuse the lieutenant of his notions by forcin' truth on him when he don't want to hear it. You got somethin' to live up to now. Maybe it'll make a better soldier of you."

"But there ain't no truth in it. I ain't no hero."

"In this army, you're what the officers say you are. Let them down and they'll stomp on you. Then I'll come along and finish what's left. That tell you what's expected of you, boy?"

Gideon shrugged, burdened by the heavy weight of expectations. "I don't know what I'm supposed to do."

"You just do what I tell you. You satisfy *me* and them officers won't be no hurdle atall."

The officer who recruited Gideon and Jimbo in Louisiana had conjured up pictures of them wearing splendid blue uniforms, cutting a dashing figure as they rode gallantly across the plains protecting the helpless settlers from the merciless savage. The settlers' gratitude would be boundless, and the soldiers' selfless efforts would help build beautiful cities in a waste and a wilderness.

After more than a month at Fort Concho, Gideon thought it probable that the recruiter had had some other place in mind. Gideon had not been more than a mile from the post since his arrival. The only settlers he had seen were a rude lot in that huddle of stone and mud and stick houses known as "Over the River." He had ventured across to Saint Angela one night with Jimbo; neither had money for more than one drink of whisky, but both were eager for a try at the ambrosia they had heard about all their lives. Neither had been allowed to taste it on the plantation. Gideon had expected it to have the kiss of angels about it because of the sacrificial lengths to which men would go. The drink had been painful and disillusioning. It had tasted more of the devil than of angels. When Gideon and Jimbo finished their only drink and did not buy another, the barman brusquely told them to leave the crowded place and make room for thirstier customers. So much, then, for the grateful settlers.

As for savages, since that day on the Colorado River he had seen none—unless he counted the man in the bar. Neither Gideon nor the other recruits had been sent to chase a single Indian. What they had done instead was to feed, curry and comb the horses; to drill afoot and on horseback until he sometimes forgot which was his left hand and which was his right; and most of all, to work as laborers on the construction of the post. They carried cut stones for the German masons whose language was incomprehensible but whose frequent displeasure was manifested in ways unmistakable. With picks and shovels and crowbars they hacked and punched ditches and foundation footings into a ground that seemed nothing but alternate layers of solid rock and hard-packed dirty-white material known locally as caliche.

If the recruiter had not lied, he had left a lot out.

Gideon and Jimbo had spent much of the morning helping dig a ditch destined to become a latrine. The glowering Big Dempsey was with them, as well as a little man named Finley whose incessant talking would worry ants out of a hole. The hard ground resisted every assault and gave up no more than a few chips at a time. Dempsey cursed as he swung his powerful shoulders behind the pick. Often the point struck sparks, and the handle shuddered with the impact.

Sergeant Esau Nettles stood above the men at the top edge, looking down upon the results of their labor and finding them meager. "You tryin' to break off too much at a time," he advised Dempsey. "Take a thinner bite and it won't fight back so hard."

The big man gave him a look not far from rebellion, but he said, "Yes, sir, Sergeant." He kept on striking the point of the pick in the same place.

Finley worked little but talked much, so that the others would have been glad to dispense with his help to be rid of the noise.

Gideon was using the shovel a little farther down the ditch, in a layer of caliche already loosened by the pick. He felt the sergeant's disapproving eyes light upon him. He was convinced that

Nettles watched him more than any other man in the company. When he spoke to Gideon individually, it was always with a curt order, a sharp criticism. Nettles had no respect for any recruit, and he seemed to have singled Gideon out for particular displeasure.

Gideon swung a shovelful of dirt and caliche toward the rim of the ditch, but in his nervousness he scraped the edge and spilled most of the load. Nettles scowled. "Ledbetter, when you was a slave and worked for nothin', you was overpaid."

Gideon gloried in but fiercely suppressed a wild notion of throwing the next load into the sergeant's black-whiskered face. Like others in the company, he had lain awake nights, his body wearied to the bone, and had dreamed of finding an appropriate revenge someday. No method properly fiendish had yet presented itself. But it would; he had faith. The Lord provided to those of patience.

Lieutenant Hollander walked out from the corrals. Nettles said, "Tech-*hut!*" The men dropped their tools and snapped to attention, despite cramped backs and aching arms and legs. Hollander returned Nettles' salute and look dispassionately at the ragged hole that could not yet properly be called a ditch. "You men carry on with what you were doing."

Dempsey swung the pick. He omitted the cursing, not out of respect but out of better judgment. Jimbo raised a crowbar and drove its point at the edge of a rock layer. Not a chip broke off.

Gideon forced his shovel into the caliche. Hollander said, "Good morning, Charger. Your arm still doing all right?"

Embarrassed, Gideon paused. Hollander's attentions had earned him a lot of hard looks from other men in the company. "It's healed, sir."

"That's fine. I want you in good shape the first time we go out after Indians. I want you to show these other men what a *soldier* can do."

Warmth came to Gideon's face. He stood there feeling foolish, still holding a shovelful of earth. The sergeant frowned at him.

Hollander jerked his chin. "Sergeant Nettles, I need to talk to you. Let's go up to the corrals."

"Yes, sir." Nettles looked at the men. "Keep on workin'. I've seen a prairie dog move more dirt than all of you."

As soon as Nettles was gone Big Dempsey cursed and pitched his pick aside. He sat down heavily, hanging his legs into the hole. He glared at Gideon. "Your name ain't Charger."

The sergeant had told them to keep working. Gideon pitched his half load of caliche over the side.

Dempsey insisted, "How come you let him call you a name like that?"

"He's a lieutenant. A lieutenant does whatever he takes a notion to."

"Makin' you his pet nigger is what he's doin'."

Gideon didn't know how to meet Dempsey's malice. "It ain't so," he declared, knowing it was. He had a strong feeling it was at the root of his difficulty with Nettles. A sense of guilt hung over Gideon, and a sense of helplessness. He hadn't asked for this.

Slave society had structured itself into layers, each insulated to a degree from the others. He remembered the envy and resentment of the field hands toward the "house niggers." He said, "Sergeant told us to keep workin'."

"The sergeant." Dempsey spat. "They ain't no meaner man on earth than a slave when he gets to be a master. One of these days I'll tell him . . ."

Jimbo rubbed a sleeve over his sweaty, dirty face. His smile was thin. "And right after you tell him, we'll hear the guard-house door slam shut."

If he was attempting to draw heat away from Gideon, it worked. Dempsey responded angrily, "I been locked up aplenty times. Ain't nothin' they can do worse than what's been done to me before." His voice coarsened with remembered hatred. "One time back in Mississippi they called me a bad nigger and tied me to a wagon wheel and whupped me because my back hurt too much to bend over and pick cotton. They rubbed salt in where the whip cut me and throwed me in a root cellar without no food or water. Told me to either heal up or die. Come winter, they chained me in a corn crib and near froze me to death. Yankees come, finally. They told us we was free to do anything we wanted to. I taken me a singletree and laid it up beside old massa's head. I didn't stay around to see if he lived or not." He looked at Gideon with eyes afire. "I take care of myself, and I don't let nobody make a pet dog out of me, neither."

Gideon flared. He took a step forward, hands tight on the shovel.

Jimbo moved between the two men, probably saving Gideon from a beating. Dempsey could have had him for breakfast. "Sit down, Gid. Rest yourself. You got to watch that arm."

Gideon let the shovel sag to the ground. He raised his right hand unconsciously and rubbed the place that was still sore to the touch.

Dempsey had never gotten to his feet. He had not acknowledged Gideon as any challenge. "I never did believe that arm was hurt as bad as you made out. Just an excuse to shine up to the lieutenant. But you better remember about them white folks, Ledbetter. They only talk nice as long as they can use you. When they don't need you, you ain't no more to them than a dog, and not as much as a good horse."

Finley took advantage of the pause to start an outrageous lie about the dire revenge he had taken upon *his* master one time. He floundered in the telling, working under the handicap of a poor imagination.

Jimbo jerked his head. "Old Nettles is comin' back."

Gideon picked up his shovel, the anger still smoldering. Dempsey grumbled and retrieved his pick. He concentrated his anger on the rock, making the steel ring and the sparks fly.

Nettles peered critically at the hole. "You-all ain't a bit deeper." He glared at Gideon. "Ledbetter, put some muscle into it."

Lieutenant Hollander might play favorites, but Nettles didn't. He gave hell to one and all. "You got to finish so you can drill this afternoon."

Dempsey groaned. Nettles faced him. "You say somethin'?"

Dempsey shook his head, not looking up. "Just workin', Sergeant." He swung the pick harder and faster, attacking the earth as if he were digging Nettles' grave.

To Gideon, drilling was harder than plantation work—possibly because he saw so little tangible result come of it. If he plowed and planted a field, he saw the seed go into the ground and the plants come up. If he harvested a crop, he saw feed go into the shock and cotton into the sack. But drilling was like digging a hole, then covering it up. Nothing ever looked or felt different for their having done it. It seemed futile, this marching up and down the practice grounds, learning how to move in straight lines, how to respond in unison to the shouted orders of corporal or sergeant to "Forward march! To the right flank, march!" Gideon reasoned that they would never be called upon to trample any Indians to death. The manual of arms seemed particularly pointless to him. They would never kill any Indians with an empty rifle. They hadn't even been allowed target practice with their war-relic Spencer carbines. Ammunition cost too much.

In Gideon's view, horseback drills were not much better. Their only superiority was that the officers and noncoms would stop when the horses became tired; they had no such consideration for the men.

Older hands had told Gideon the saber was never actually used in the field; even the officers left them behind when they went on patrol. Nevertheless, saber drill was part of the routine. The sabers were too dull to cut butter, and the men were afforded nothing to sharpen them with. Yet hour after hour, on the ground, they were drilled to draw, present, carry and return, to point, to cut, to parry. When that had been mastered, after a fashion, they were obliged to repeat on horseback.

Gideon had never approached Jimbo's horseback proficiencies. Where Jimbo's lifetime alliance with horses had been of whole heart, Gideon's had been of tolerance.

Sergeant Nettles had assigned Gideon the brown horse which had surrendered so quickly to the enemy at the Colorado River. The brown was fearful of the saber, turning his head uneasily to watch its movements, white showing at the rim of his eye. He danced and wrung his tail. When Gideon accidentally touched the point of the blade near the brown's flank, the horse squealed and went up like an exploding powder keg. Gideon was not with him on his return, but landed separately and noisily.

As the dust cleared, Gideon looked up at a scowling Nettles. "Ledbetter, you use a saber to cut the enemy. You don't job your own horse with it."

The men around him were laughing. Gideon sensed that they thought he needed a comeuppance. The heat of shame came to his face. Nettles saw to it that the laughing stopped quickly.

It took Jimbo to calm the brown horse enough for Gideon to remount. Gideon looked down angrily upon the horse's nervous ears. He said brittlely, "Judas, I see buzzards flyin' yonder, waitin' to make your acquaintance."

Jimbo smiled. "Judas ain't no name for a horse."

"It fits this one."

Not until the horses were groomed and fed did Sergeant Nettles divulge that the paymaster had arrived. By companies, the men lined up. After deductions, the little Gideon had left jingled nicely against Old Colonel's gold piece in his pocket.

Jimbo seemed in some danger of grinning himself to death. "Gid, it's time we done ourselves some funnin'." He pointed north. "I been studyin' on goin' over the river and havin' some more good whisky."

"*Good* whisky? If that's good whisky, I don't want to taste no bad."

"I think I could get partial to it if I could afford it more."

"Well, you can't. Anyway, them people ain't friendly."

"They'll be friendly when we bring money."

Gideon frowned. "Everybody on the post has got paid. You heard what the old soldiers been tellin' us. Somebody's apt to get killed."

Jimbo shrugged. Trouble had never bothered him; he simply refused to recognize it. "Nobody gets hurt that ain't lookin' for a fight. If you don't go with me I'll find somebody else. Big Dempsey, maybe."

Gideon considered Dempsey a doubtful choice of company for anyone as easily led as Jimbo. "I promised Old Colonel I'd look out for you."

"Old Colonel ain't here."

"I thought we'd take our clothes over on laundry row and get them washed by a sure-enough washerwoman 'stead of doin' them ourselves."

Jimbo laughed. "Washerwoman? I druther have the whisky."

After supper, the stone barracks emptied as if somebody had announced smallpox on the post. Gideon dolefully watched Jimbo leave with Dempsey and Finley and some others, hollering as if they had good sense. He was the only man left in the barracks except for an unsmiling Sergeant Waters, who had been in the Tenth almost since it was organized. Waters, subordinate to Nettles, kept to himself as much as a soldier could, considering the group life military men had to lead. The only friend he had was an old fiddle. Through it, sitting in a corner alone, he put into sound the feelings he never put into words. Some nights his music danced, some it soared. Tonight it seemed to cry.

Gideon had never been able to draw him into conversation. Nor did anyone else, often. Waters' eyes were like closed doors. As he played, he was somewhere else, far away.

When the music stopped Gideon asked, "You ain't goin' over the river to stomp and holler?"

Waters seemed a little startled at his presence. "I done got that out of my system."

"Whisky ain't all that's over there. They got women."

"Got that out of my system, too."

Gideon felt an invisible wall rising between them. "I'm fixin' to take my clothes to be washed. Where had I ought to go?"

Waters seemed impatient to be rid of him, as if Gideon were trespassing on old memories. "This company been usin' an old woman that moved in awhile back. Second shack from the east end of the row. Name's York."

That evidently was all he meant to say. Gideon thanked him, rolled his laundry into a shirt and tied the sleeves around it. As he started through the door Waters called, "If you see a young woman, you walk way around her. Old woman's liable to take an ax to you."

Every frontier post had a suds row of some description. Sometimes the laundresses were wives of enlisted men, trying to earn a few dollars to stretch their husbands' miserable pay. Sometimes they were single women and widows, trying to survive in an environment where survival at even the barest subsistence level was no mean accomplishment. And sometimes, Gideon had been told by old army hands, when laundering did not bring a woman all she needed—or all she wanted—certain ones augmented this income by catering to other needs common to men trapped in an all-male society.

The army had plans to build a solid structure for the laundresses at Concho, but so far they were still housed in a crude set of picket shacks, much like the Mexican *jacales* over the river—except that they were positioned in a military line. The smell of wood smoke was strong. A common denominator of all these houses was one or more blackened pots in back, where water was kept aboil to take out the sweat and the grime and even the lice so often an affliction of the soldier.

Second from the east end, Waters had said. Gideon heard the splashing of water, the strike of a bucket against a tub. He skirted the shack, looking for the old woman. He stopped suddenly, staring with strong interest at a very young woman dipping water from a steaming pot and pouring it into a nearby tub. She did not see him at first, for the steam was in her eyes. A lock of black hair had slipped from under the big red kerchief around her head, and that, too, was in her way. She was slender, lighter-skinned than the women on the plantation. The unacknowledged daughter, probably, of some slave owner in the old times before Mr. Lincoln. His pulse quickened. She was uncommonly handsome.

She walked back to the pot and dipped more water. She struggled, lifting it out.

Gideon set down his laundry. "I'll help you with that."

Startled, she dropped the bucket into the boiling water. She grabbed at the handle, trying to grasp it before the bucket sank. The edge of her long black skirt swept the fire. In her anxiety she did not notice the flame that caught it.

"Look out!" Gideon shouted.

She screamed and jumped back, letting the bucket sink. She seemed to freeze, her hands against her cheeks as the flame spread.

Gideon grabbed wet clothing from the tub and slapped at the

fire. In blind panic she started to run. He grabbed her arm and kept slapping until the flame was dead. He dropped to one knee and rubbed the wet cloth against the edge of the garment, pressing it to her legs until most of her skirt was soaked. The fire was dead.

She started to sob. Holding the ash-blackened wet clothing, he felt awkward and unsure now that it was all over. He didn't know where he had gotten the inspiration to beat out the flames with wet cloth. He could remember no conscious thought process. It had seemed to come to him from nowhere—as if another mind had controlled his own.

He wished he knew he *had* thought of it himself. He said, "Everything's over with. It burn you much?"

She didn't know. She bent and rubbed her hand up and down her legs, feeling. The sobbing stopped. "No, reckon not. I was almighty afeered, though."

"I was afeered *for* you."

"Good thing you was here. I might've burnt up."

"If I hadn't of boogered you, you wouldn't of caught fire in the first place. I didn't go to cause you harm."

"I reckon my mind was on somethin' else, and all of a sudden you was standin' right there."

"Goin' to have to patch that skirt," Gideon observed.

"Won't be the first time by a long ways." The tears had gone from her eyes, though their trail still glistened on her almond-colored cheeks. "How come you here in the first place?"

"I brought some laundry over. Lookin' for a woman named York."

"My name's York."

"She's supposed to be an *old* lady."

"My granny. She's in the house."

"How come she didn't hear you screamin'?"

"Old Granny don't hear nothin' anymore 'less you holler in her ear. Or 'less you talk straight at her. She can watch your lips and tell what you say. Git where she can't see you, and you can say what you want to."

Gideon didn't really want to talk about laundry or about a

deaf old granny. But staring at those big brown eyes, he would
have stood hitched for any subject.

She said, "I better go get Granny."

He felt no inclination to move. "I been here over a month, and
I ain't seen you before."

"Some of the time I help Miz Colonel Thomas with her house-
work and her cookin'. Rest of the time I help Granny wash
clothes."

"How come I ain't never seen you, then?"

She looked at the ground, hiding her eyes. "Old Granny don't
let me talk to no soldiers. Soldiers come and bring their washin',
she makes me go inside so they don't look at me."

"She afraid we goin' to eat you, or somethin'?"

"Somethin', maybe."

"Well, I'm here, and I ain't done nothin'—only put out a fire."

"I'm much obliged to you . . . whatever your name is."

"Name's Gideon."

"Gideon?" She repeated the name as if trying it for taste.
"Gideon's a funny kind of a name."

"Come out of the Bible. Preacher read me the story one time.
There was a Gideon in the Bible that was a soldier."

"Like you."

He shrugged. "There's an awful lot I don't know about sol-
dierin'."

"You think quick—the way you put that fire out. That ought
to count for somethin' with a soldier."

He wished he could feel honest about taking the credit. He
floundered, trying to keep the conversation going. "I didn't hear
your name."

"I'm Hannah."

Hannah. Hannah York. Had a nice sound to it, he thought.
"Hannah York, be all right with you if I was to come over here
sometime of an evenin' and maybe take you walkin'? It's nice,
down by the river."

Alarm came into her eyes. "Granny don't allow none of that.
She don't allow me to talk to no soldier."

"But I ain't meanin' no harm. If you think that I . . ." He
broke off, knowing what was in her mind, sensing that even to

deny it would lend strength to the notion. A girl this pretty, there had surely been a-plenty tried. He would probably try too, when the time was right.

The back door of the shack flew open. An old black woman rushed out, bearing down on him. She fastened him with eyes that reminded him of the hooks he had once used to grab cotton bales. "Soldier boy, what you doin' back here?"

So startled that speech left him, he backed off. He found his tongue and reached down for his bundle. "I fetched over my clothes, to get you to wash them for me."

"I don't allow no soldier trash around this girl of mine. You got any notions about her, you git them out of your head."

"I got no notions. I only just now met her. She caught afire, and . . ." He realized she couldn't hear him.

She shook a long, bony finger in his face. She was a small, wiry woman with an evil countenance that chilled him. She looked much like an aged conjure woman back home, freed by her master years ahead of the Great Emancipation. Folks whispered that she had witched him into it, and indeed she had a reputation for putting people under a spell and turning them into owls or frogs or whatever low creatures her half-crazy mind lit upon. In his later years, Gideon had decided all that talk was made up to keep people at a distance—but for safety, he had continued keeping his.

The old woman shrilled, "You got clothes to wash, you bring them to the front door and talk to *me*. This gal ain't for you, nor no others the likes of you."

Gideon shrank back. He had never been able to stand his ground against any angry woman, and especially an evil *old* woman. It was, perhaps, a holdover of boyhood fear about that wizened old conjurer. He turned and started away.

"Soldier boy!" the woman's voice lashed at him. "You brung them clothes for washin', didn't you?"

He realized he still had his dirty laundry under his arm. He watched her warily over his shoulder. "Yes'm."

"I can't wash them if you don't leave them."

He dropped them on the ground. He gave the girl one quick glance. She was hurrying into the shack, her head down. He suspected that the tongue-lashing he had received was nothing compared to what the girl would get.

His first intention was to put a comfortable distance between himself and that witchified old woman. The most open area, free of fences and houses, was down toward the river. He walked briskly at first, slowing as he took a better hold on the rush of emotions, the mix of dread and helpless anger. He began feeling foolish, letting himself be cowed by a little woman who couldn't have done any bodily injury to him. He could have carried her down here under one arm and dropped her in the river. That comforting thought was fleeting. He wouldn't have touched her —or let her touch him—for a saddlebag of pure gold coin.

He stood on the high bank and looked down through gathering darkness at the whispering flow of the North Concho. It soon set his mind drifting homeward. He found himself wishing he could be back there where life, though sometimes harsh, was at least predictable and ran by a rhythm that he understood. He sat down on a flat rock outcrop and stared down at the moving water. He realized it bore little resemblance to the Mississippi except in being wet. The water here was clear and fast-running in a channel narrow enough that he could sail a rock across it. Except after a rain, he had never seen it muddy. At this point it was running almost due east, but folks had told him it came from somewhere north, a day's ride and more, from country that still belonged to the Indian. For all he knew, Comanche horses had drunk from this very water, this very day. The notion prickled the hair on his neck, and he forced his mind to other things.

Gazing at the clusters of lamplight on the north bank, he pictured the various forms of vice that the devil must be witnessing there. He could hear the occasional whoop and holler of a soldier celebrating the fact that Uncle Sam had rendered him his due. He thought of Jimbo and Dempsey and the others burning their goozles raw on that malevolent breed of whisky with which Saint Angela merchants freed the soldiers of the excessive weight in their pockets. He heard a woman's laugh, high-pitched and false. Those women over there were earning the army pay much faster than the soldiers had, and easier.

He heard the laugh again, and it reached him in a different way this time, coming so soon after his experience with the girl Hannah. Suddenly he felt a strong temptation to go across the river. He was dissuaded only by the knowledge that any love he found there would be as false as the laugh he heard. Only the money was real. Starting back in the general direction of the barracks, he skirted laundry row, leaving several houses between himself and the waspish old woman. He looked that way, nevertheless, searching for lamplight in the window. He could see the faint glow, dimmed by plain cotton sacking. He stared a minute, knowing the futility of it.

He became aware of a dark shape coming toward him in the night. He recognized the purposeful stride and brought his hand up in salute. "Evenin', Lieutenant."

Frank Hollander halted, awkwardly returning the salute, for he carried a bundle under his arm. "That you, Charger?"

The name "Charger" was unpleasant, but Gideon accepted the fact that it had been fastened on him like a chain. "Yes, sir, Lieutenant."

A glowing cigar lighted the officer's face each time he puffed. "Already had your night over the river? It's early."

"Ain't been, sir. Ain't nothin' I want bad enough to pay their price."

Hollander nodded. "First time I saw you in action, I knew you had more sense than most of these . . . soldiers. Carry on, Charger."

Gideon watched him disappear into the darkness with the bundle under his arm. Somehow he had never considered that officers got their clothing dirty, too. They always seemed to be above that sort of thing. It jarred him a little, seeing the lieutenant carrying laundry just like some black recruit. It seemed in an odd way to bring him down to Gideon's level, a contradiction to the training of a lifetime.

Reaching the rear of the barracks, he heard the mournful sound of Sergeant Waters' fiddle. He walked in quietly and stopped. Waters was unaware of him. A half-empty bottle sat on the wooden floor beside the man's bunk. It was probably a violation of twelve different articles of war to bring whisky into the barracks, but it was a prohibition honored more often in the breach than in compliance. Gideon was in no mood to face the isolation of being in a room with a man who kept a high wall around himself. He backed away and retreated outside. He leaned against the building, looking toward laundry row and its faint spots of lamplight. In awhile, he saw the light blink out in the York house.

After a long time Waters' fiddle went quiet. Gideon concluded that the man had drunk himself to sleep. He could think of nothing better to do, so he entered the dark, quiet barracks and carefully picked his way down the aisle past the rifle stand and the cold iron heater, bumping his toes against the wooden chest at the foot of his bunk. He spoke a few words which had curative powers.

Lying in his bunk, he kept seeing the face of the girl. In his mind, he tried to bring a smile to it, but he could not. He saw only fear.

The door opened. He heard a man's footsteps, slow and careful. He could see a dark shape against the windows. The man struck a match, and the flame revealed the face of Sergeant Nettles. He appeared surprised. "Ledbetter?"

"Yes, sir, Sergeant."

"Didn't you like it over the river?"

"Never did go."

"Got paid, didn't you?"

"Not that much."

The sergeant went to his own small room. He was the only man in the barracks who had the privacy of a wall and a door.

Gideon drifted off to sleep thinking about the girl.

The awakening was sudden. Loud laughing, cursing, singing, a stamping of heavy boots on the wooden floor put a harsh end to sleep. Somebody lighted a lamp. Somebody else stumbled into the big round heater. Gideon blinked to bring the blue-clad men into focus. Jimbo hollered, "Hey, Gid, you asleep?"

Gideon sat up irritably, sorting him out of the blur. "I ain't now."

"You ought to've gone with us, Gid. You'd of had the time of your natural life."

Gideon was jolted fully awake by sight of Jimbo's face. Dried blood streaked it, and one eye was puffed. He looked beyond Jimbo at the others. "You-all look like you got in front of some runaway mules."

Swaying, Jimbo laughed. "Not mules. Mule*skinners*. We whupped up on them real good. I wisht you'd of been there to see it." He waved Dempsey over. The big-shouldered man gave Gideon cause to fear he might lose his balance. It would have been like having a mule fall into bed with him.

Jimbo said, "We was just drinkin' whisky and lovin' on some of them Mexican-talkin' gals. Havin' a big time. Well, some of them white teamsters come in—you know the ones that haul rock to build the buildin's with? They commenced to passin' remarks. Finally a big feller about two ax-handles broad, he come over and says to Dempsey, 'You're about the blackest nigger ever I seen.' I wisht you could of been there for the fight."

Gideon asked sharply, "How much you got left of your pay, Jimbo?"

Jimbo thrust his hands into his pockets. They came out empty. "Anyhow, I got somethin' to remember till next payday."

"Especially tomorrow. You better get to bed. They'll be blowin' that bugle directly."

"Bugle be damned," Jimbo shouted. "I still feel like dancin'." His heavy boots began pounding the floor. Some of the other men took it up.

Even louder than the stomping feet and the raucous singing came a commanding voice. "Tech-*hut!*"

Sergeant Nettles stood at the door of his room, his feet bare, his black body covered by gray underwear and blue trousers. His face looked like a winter storm. "This is a military barracks, and you are soldiers," he thundered. "Payday is over. Now git to bed!"

Clumsily, sheepishly, the men made their uncertain way to their bunks. As they hurriedly undressed, Nettles' eyes cut like a whip from one to another. "Every daddamned white man over the river will tell you they ain't no sense nor dignity in a black soldier, and you-all bust a gut to prove they're right!"

He cut his gaze to Dempsey. "I believe you just may *be* the blackest nigger I ever seen." He stopped at his door. "Last man in bed blows out the light. And he works tomorrow in the company sinks."

Six

INDIAN RAIDS WERE always to be expected. Nevertheless, each seemed to burst upon the West Texas settlements as a total surprise.

Sergeant Nettles had put the company on police detail. The name had promised an interesting task, but Gideon soon learned it meant raking manure from the corrals or picking up miscellaneous litter from the post grounds. Wearing their gray fatigues, he and Jimbo were cleaning the parade near the adjutant's office when a civilian loped past them, leaving Gideon blinking away the sting of dust. Without taking time to tie his horse, the man pushed through the office door.

Gideon and Jimbo stared at each other in silent curiosity. The horse trembled in exhaustion, its shining hide dripping sweat. Jimbo's resistance to temptation had always been marginal. He said, "We better go tie that horse for the man."

Gideon knew what he was thinking. "It's too tired to run off."

"You never can tell about a horse."

Jimbo walked purposefully. Gideon followed, looking back over his shoulder for sign of the sergeant. Nettles was contrarily single-minded about seeing that any job he assigned was properly finished. Standing with Jimbo near an open window, Gideon heard the name "Ben Ficklin," and "Comanche."

Ben Ficklin was a stage stand and a small village near the confluence of the South and Middle Conchos, a few miles south and west of the fort. It was named for a frontiersman and former Union officer who owned the San Antonio–El Paso mail line. The little settlement was made up mostly of stageline employees and farmers who raised feed for the company and the military. It was as staid and respectable as Saint Angela was wicked and wild. It offered little to hold the average soldier's interest.

The civilian hurried out of the adjutant's office.

Jimbo volunteered, "We tied your horse for you, sir."

The white man gave him no acknowledgment but trotted briskly toward the residence of the commanding officer. In a couple of minutes, he came back with Colonel Thomas, both men taking long strides. Jimbo had spilled several bits of paper out of his sack, and the wind had fortuitously carried them against the building, near the open window.

Gideon stiffened and saluted as the commanding officer approached. Thomas halted. "Trooper, do you know where to find Lieutenant Hollander?"

Gideon still held the salute, for the colonel had not returned it. "I seen him at the corrals."

"Go fetch him for me. Tell him it's urgent. If you see Sergeant Nettles, send him, too."

"Yes, sir." Gideon set out in a trot, looking back in envy at Jimbo, who bent by the window innocently picking up loose paper he had dropped there in the first place.

The lieutenant and the sergeant were at the corral, Hollander trying out a new bay horse and showing unrestrained pleasure. Nettles seemed gratified. "I been havin' Jimbo ride him some."

"Good man with a horse, that Jimbo."

"Wisht he was as good with everything else."

Out of breath, Gideon saluted Hollander and leaned against the fence, his chest heaving. "Colonel . . . ," he managed. "Colonel says he . . . wants the lieutenant . . . wants you too, Sergeant . . . Indians . . ."

Nettles grumbled, "Taken you long enough to say so."

Hollander swung quickly out of the saddle. Nettles caught the reins and tossed them to Gideon. Hollander said, "Don't unsaddle him, Charger. I may be needing him."

After pausing to tie the horse, Gideon was too short of breath to match the men's brisk pace. He managed a quick glance at suds row, hoping to see Hannah York. He saw only the old woman, shoving dry wood into the blaze beneath her steaming pot.

Jimbo strode excitedly to meet Gideon. "We're finally fixin' to do somethin' besides drill and tote rocks. They're takin' us out after Indians."

Gideon had sensed it, but the reality stunned him. This was the duty for which they were supposedly trained. Yet, in the long waiting, it had become something remote, not quite real. A cold fear settled on him, and then shame for the fear.

Jimbo said, "Comanche raidin' party. Taken some horses from the Bismarck farm, then swung over by Ben Ficklin town. Knocked some Mexican feller up beside the head and run off a bunch of stock that belonged to the stageline." He pointed north. The Indians had gone in that direction, toward the plains. "A dozen of them, maybe. So the man says."

Gideon's chill persisted. Stories indicated that a dozen Comanches could hammer down the gates of hell.

Hollander and Nettles hurried out, the sergeant half a pace behind as befitted the demands of rank and race. "No bugle, Sergeant. That would just bring the other companies out."

Nettles beckoned first to Jimbo. "You'll find part of the company policin' around the hospital. Tell them to assemble." He turned to Gideon. "You get the ones at the corrals. I don't want to see nobody walkin'. Last man to fall in will clean out the company sinks."

The lieutenant wasted no time in explanations after the company formed in front of the barracks. Enlisted men were not entitled to them. "I have orders to take twenty volunteers. I want a nucleus of seasoned men, but I want some recruits to get field experience, too. Charger, you and Jimbo are going." He went down the line, picking his other volunteers. He tapped Big

Dempsey, who stood half a head taller than anybody else and was hard to overlook. The quiet Sergeant Waters was chosen as a matter of course. In all, Hollander selected nine recruits and ten experienced men. Nettles would make the count come to twenty.

Hollander frowned. "We can't be burdened with extra horses. If any man's horse is disabled, that man has to drop out and fend for himself. I don't think any of you want to do that—not where those Indians may lead us. So take care of your horses first and last. Depend on God to take care of *you*."

Hollander left, taking quick strides toward the hospital to gather his necessaries. Nettles stood with fists on his hips, his dark eyes crackling with threat. "There's a lot of white people don't think we're soldiers. But you'll *be* soldiers while we're out there. Any man disgraces his uniform, any man don't live up to his duty, he's goin' to wish it was the Comanches had aholt of him instead of *me*."

Nettles let no man take any step except in a run while they changed into their field blues, gathered what little they were to take with them and saddled their horses. Hollander and Nettles took the lead. Colonel Thomas stood in front of his house, watching. Hollander saluted. Gideon saw no more emotion in the colonel's face than if the men were being sent off to morning drill. He realized that the colonel had watched hundreds of such processions ride out of Concho and other forts. But this was Gideon's first. He found it difficult to accept the colonel's dispassionate attitude. They were innocents, most of them, riding into a big, strange country to hunt for Indians with the understood purpose of killing them if they could. It was also understood, if not stated, that the Indians could kill *them*. They rated a better sendoff than this.

The colonel's door opened, and Hannah York stepped onto the porch, drying her hands on an apron as she watched the troopers ride by. Gideon's breath went short. This was the first time he had seen her since that night they had met. Her eyes locked on him. Her hand came up as if she were about to wave, but she caught herself and looked around anxiously to see if anybody had observed the move. She quickly clasped both hands in the apron to keep them from trouble. She made Gideon think of a tiny bird, trapped and fearful.

He kept looking back at her until he was twisted halfway around in the saddle.

They rode west at first, following the river until it bent northward. They left it, heading generally westward with a tilt to the north. Gideon turned once to see the fort receding into the distance. The only thing which particularly stood out was the tall cupola atop the hospital. The army had not gotten around to putting up a flagpole because there was no suitable nearby timber to fashion one. The great pecans which lined the river were unacceptable.

Gideon had not been aware that he had developed any attachment to the post; it had not seemed home in any real sense. But as he looked back, it represented security of sorts. Leaving it, he felt vulnerable, somehow alone. The cold dread he had felt when he first came into this country returned to him now. It settled in his stomach like a leaden weight. Perhaps the other men felt the same fear but managed to hide it. Or perhaps he was the only one who carried this burden, the only coward in the company.

At length the detail came upon the Middle Concho, which flowed from the west. Gideon had heard Hollander tell Nettles that a civilian was to follow the Indians' trail to wherever it crossed this river. There he would wait, putting the troops hours closer to the raiders.

Gideon regarded that as a mixed blessing.

He knew the recruits needed this outing to give them a feel for the campaign, a grasp of the wild country, but it seemed to him that this purpose could be met without their fighting Indians the first time out.

In due course a horseman spurred toward them. He rode a big sorrel with two stocking feet, a blaze in its face. Jimbo leaned forward in his saddle, giving the horse his full attention. If he felt any concern about Indians, he hadn't shown it. He looked as happy as if he had good judgment. "That there is a *horse*, Gid."

The civilian did not salute, though he came close with an upward motion of his hand. His stern military bearing gave Gideon a notion he had had some army experience, probably with the Confederacy. He was a blocky man, not in the least fat. His face was covered by a short brown beard that did not hide his eyes, or the misgivings in them as he surveyed the black soldiers. "Frank," he said, "I'm glad it's you instead of Captain Newton, or one of them other damnyankee dimwits."

Hollander accepted that as a compliment, after its fashion. "I happen also to be a Yankee, Pat Maloney."

"In your case I have not put the *damn* in front of it. Yet."

Gideon felt Maloney's eyes pass over him, but they did not single him out. Maloney appeared to see little merit in any of the men. "Army had some *soldiers* out here in the beginnin'. Yankee government may be mighty, but it can't turn black into white."

Gideon looked quickly at Nettles. The sergeant stared off to the north, his jaw set hard, the cheekbones stretching his black skin.

Hollander said, "I volunteered these men myself. They'll do."

The trail was plain enough that Gideon felt he could have followed it himself. But the realization that it had been made only a few hours ago set a chill to playing along his spine. For a time the troops followed it in an easy pace, northwesterly across rock-edged rolling hills, down long, wide valleys where the thick turf was like a grass carpet. Clusters of brown buffalo looked up from their grazing and scattered in an odd, rolling lope. Once Gideon's eyes caught a movement to the west, and his breath stopped. What at first appeared to be feathered Indians became pronghorn antelope racing in single file, cutting in front of the soldiers and passing on.

Hollander reached down to his carbine but changed his mind. Regretfully he said, "One of those would make us a good supper."

Maloney grunted. "May not *be* any supper."

Long miles passed beneath the horses' hoofs, leading the troops toward the middle section of the North Concho. The soft, rounded contours of the hills made them appear deceptively gentle, a promise proven empty by closer acquaintance. Rockier ground made tracks harder to see. Maloney slowed. At length he told Hollander, "I better move out in front. You-all stay behind me a ways. If I have to double back to hunt for lost tracks, I don't want you and them blackbirds coverin' them up."

Hollander came near smiling. "I'll take care of my blackbirds, Pat. You just worry about the tracks." He turned in the saddle and searched the ranks. "Charger, come up here. Jimbo, you, too."

Hollander seemed to feel he was doing the pair a favor. "I'm giving you boys a chance to prove your mettle. Mr. Maloney needs to devote his full attention to the tracks. You'll ride up there with him and watch out for Indians."

Gideon's stomach drew into a knot. Jimbo showed not the slightest concern. Gideon was certain that he did not comprehend the situation.

Maloney's eyes narrowed suspiciously. "You boys look to me like a pair of greenies."

Hollander said, "They're good boys. You can bet your life on that."

Maloney growled, "No, *you're* bettin' my life on it." He set the sorrel into an easy trot. Without hesitation Jimbo moved out beside him. Gideon did hesitate, then had to use his tiny spurs to catch up. When the three were a hundred yards ahead, Lieutenant Hollander started moving, keeping the pace set by Maloney.

Maloney jerked his thumb first to left, then to right. "You boys spread out twenty-thirty yards on either side of me. Keep a sharp watch. One of you goes to sleep, I'll shoot him and tell God he just died."

Maloney need not have been concerned. Gideon saw everything that moved, from jackrabbits flicking their long ears to a distant hawk making slow circles, watching for something its size to reveal itself on the prairie. As the long afternoon wore on toward dusk, Maloney said nothing. Whatever his occasional problems in seeing and following the tracks across hard ground, he shared none of his thoughts or feelings except in his troubled face. Awhile before dark, they came to the river. Tracks indicated that the Indians' horses had watered but had not crossed over. Maloney motioned for Gideon and Jimbo to stand their ground while he swam his horse over and rode a little way up and down to be certain. Presently he came back, evidently satisfied, but not saying so. Gideon felt a tug of resentment. He could tell them *something*. Their being just soldiers—or being black—did not mean they were uninterested.

Gideon asked, "What river is this?"

Maloney looked at him in surprise. "The North Concho. Everybody knows that." He compromised his silence, but not much. "Same river that runs by your fort. We'll be comin' to the head of it up north and some west of here. Past that, the next livin' water is the big spring."

Gideon knew nothing of the big spring. He had not seen a map and could not have read it if he had. A piece of pecan bark bobbed along with the flow of the current. He stared at it, imagining himself taking a small log and floating on it all the way back to the post. It was a foolish notion, and he did not toy with it long. He wasn't even sure he wanted to go back. For all his apprehension, it came to him that this was one of the few days since his arrival that he had not dug a ditch, toted rocks or drilled in the hot sun until his nose bled.

Maloney circled his hand over his head, signaling Hollander to come up. He showed the lieutenant how the tracks were going. "Dark's comin'. We won't be able to see them much longer. Chances are two to one they'll head for the big spring. If you want to gamble, we can go straight to it and not worry about tracks. Dark won't have to stop us."

Hollander frowned. "Two to one. But what about that third chance? It's showered up here lately; I've been seeing potholes with water in them. The Indians don't *have* to go to the spring."

"Indians never *have* to do anything. That's why the army hardly ever finds them."

"If we guess wrong, they'll be gone for sure."

"Might be just as well." He studied the troopers, his doubts visible. "Half of these men are raw recruits."

"We have the Indians outnumbered."

"Indians are never outnumbered. One of them is good for three or four of your Yankeefied blackbirds. Meanin' no disrespect, of course." His expression showed he meant all of it.

Hollander's eyes followed the tracks upriver. "We'll stay with

the trail as long as we can see it. Seems to me they've been getting fresher. The Indians will have to rest, too."

Maloney laughed harshly. "What army manual did you read
that out of, Frank?" He set out following the tracks and the
river. He did not waste a glance at either Gideon or Jimbo, but
expected them to know their duty and to do it. The two
troopers rode side by side; it seemed unlikely the Indians would
charge from across the river.

Jimbo gloried in his work and seemed not in the least tired or
worried. "I wisht the army could be like this all the time."

When dusk faded into full darkness, Maloney held up and
waited for Hollander. "There'll be a sliver of moon directly. I
could still find you the spring."

Hollander shook his head. "We'll rely on the tracks." He
turned to Esau Nettles. "Sergeant, have the men water their
horses, then set up a picket line. Cold supper, no fires. We don't
want the Indians to know we're here."

Maloney grunted. "You could climb up on that hill yonder
and build a fire big enough to roast a horse for all the difference
it would make. Them Indians know where we're at."

Hollander said, "The army has its way."

"I know. And I've never figured out how you Yankees ever
beat us."

Because they were deep into country better known to the Indians than to most white people, Hollander had a third of the detail on guard at any one time all night. Gideon thought it was
just as well; he lay sleepless in his blanket most of the time anyway. He heard every call of the night community and wondered
if they were really birds. Every time a horse stamped its foot on
the picket line, he expected a war whoop. He stood his guard
tour with hands sweaty-cold on his carbine, and he spent the rest
of the night lying on his back listening, wondering if anyone else
was getting much sleep. He didn't have to wonder about Jimbo.
Jimbo snored.

Gideon was not simply worried about what the Indians might
do. He wondered what *he* might do. Could he stand his ground
like a soldier or would he cut and run? He kept remembering
that skirmish on the Colorado. He remembered fear; he remem-

bered helplessness. He wondered what he might have done had the frightened brown horse not taken choice out of his hands. He was haunted by a feeling that he might have run.

There was no bugle to awaken the men. None was necessary. As soon as Hollander stirred, Sergeant Nettles was up and around, giving brusque orders, nudging sleeping men with the toe of his boot. Gideon had slept a little the last couple of hours, when it was almost too late. Now he had to struggle to get up. He found he was under Nettles' hard and demanding stare.

The sergeant turned his attention to another man singularly unwilling to depart from his blanket. "Leatherman, git up before I boot you up. You're the most triflin' piece of nothin' I ever had in this company."

Leatherman complained that it wasn't daylight yet. Nettles booted the reluctant trooper hard enough that today's ride was likely to be painful. Hollander allowed no fires. Gideon would have enjoyed coffee, but he settled for hardtack and river water.

Maloney looked to the rising sun and said impatiently to Hollander, "If you can get your boys to wipe the sleep-boogers out of their eyes, we'd best be movin'. Indian don't take much sleep on the trail. He'll catch up when he gets home to where the squaws do the work."

Hollander sought out Gideon and Jimbo with his eyes. "Boys, you know what's expected of you."

Gideon had just as soon someone else were allowed to share the honor, but Jimbo grinned. "Yes, sir." Gideon mounted the brown Judas and rode out with Maloney. His eyes were heavy, his stomach uneasy from missed sleep.

Maloney eyed him suspiciously. "You don't look good to me, boy."

Gideon doubted that any black soldier looked good to Maloney, but even in his infirm state he had the judgment not to say so. Old Colonel would have been proud of his tact.

The river narrowed and shallowed and finally disappeared, along with the taller grasses. The country had the look of always needing just one more rain.

Past the feeder springs which gave the North Concho birth,

the trail led along the rim of a rough hill. The steep and treacherous hillside was strewn with large rocks broken off by time and erosion from the ancient sedimentary layer which formed the ragged crest. Maloney gave the hillside a moment's suspicious study but continued to circle the rim.

Even Gideon's untrained eyes could see that some of the horse tracks led downward. He pointed them out to Maloney. The guide's furrowed brow showed that unsolicited advice was unwanted advice. "A few of their loose horses, was all. Main bunch went along the rim to find an easier way down. That's what we'll do."

Presently Gideon saw that most of the horses—and presumably the Indians—had indeed found a longer though gentler descent. The trail was steep, but mostly clear of bad rocks. Gideon let Maloney take the lead, then followed at what he thought was a safe distance. Halfway down, Gideon's brown horse lost footing and sent a shower of small stones rolling past Maloney.

"Boy," the tracker barked, "you got the whole wide world to ride in. Don't be ridin' on my horse's hind feet."

Jimbo chuckled. Gideon did not see the humor. He gave the white man more room and half-hoped an Indian was waiting down there. Maloney's luck held. He reached the bottom without incident. In the clear, he waited for Gideon and Jimbo to reach him.

The horse trail was plain at the foot of the hill. Maloney rode out a short distance and stopped, turning to watch the troopers make their slow descent single-file, the way he and Gideon and Jimbo had come. Hollander was first. Sergeant Nettles stayed behind to see all the others down. Though the breeze swept away the sound, Gideon could see by the sergeant's gestures that he was shouting orders to the men picking their way down.

Two troopers were holding back. Just as Nettles turned to get them started, they came on their own, straight down the hillside the way a few of the Indians' loose horses had done.

Jimbo pointed. "Ain't that Leatherman?"

Gideon had to squint. "Yeah, and Ripley. Takin' a shortcut."

Jimbo cursed under his breath. "Damn fools, liable to break a horse's leg that way."

At the top Nettles waved his arm and shouted words picked up and carried away by the wind. It was useless. Once the two men had started, there was no stopping or backing up. Their speed increased. Two-thirds of the way down, Leatherman's horse fell heavily on its right shoulder, rolling over, kicking wildly. Leatherman threw himself out of the saddle in time to keep the horse from rolling on top of him. He slid, ran and slid again, carried forward by the momentum. The soldier finally stumbled on a small boulder and finished the last few feet sliding on his belly and hands.

The other man's horse lost footing once but managed to catch itself. At the bottom, Leatherman pushed shakily to his feet and dusted himself.

Hollander shouted, "Your horse, man. See to your horse!"

When the horse struggled to its feet at the bottom of the hill, it was obvious it would do no more running for a while. It picked up one forefoot and hobbled about on the other three, trembling from pain and fright, the saddle turned on its side.

Leatherman's companion Ripley reached the bottom, still in the saddle. His horse limped, though less badly.

Jimbo reached Leatherman's horse ahead of anybody else and jumped down, grabbing the reins, talking to the frightened animal. He rubbed his hand along the horse's neck and down its shoulder. He felt carefully of the hurt leg. When he stood up, his eyes were ablaze.

In their years of growing up and working together, Gideon had heard Jimbo curse only a few times. It had always been over someone's abuse of a horse or mule. Jimbo gave Leatherman one of the roundest cursings Gideon had ever heard. Lieutenant Hollander rode up primed to the same task but bowed to a superior talent and kept his silence. When Jimbo ran out of steam, Leatherman stood with head down, well chastened. Jimbo turned to Ripley. He had used up the words, but his angry eyes made the message plain.

The lieutenant ordered Ripley down from his horse. He asked Jimbo, "What about Leatherman's mount? Is its leg broken?"

"Not broken, sir, but he's spreened it pretty bad."

"Take a look at Ripley's."

Jimbo felt that horse's leg. "He ain't fit to ride either."

Hollander fixed the two men with a punishing stare they couldn't meet. "You remember what I said before we left? See after your horse before yourself, or you'll walk. Well, now you'll walk. You're of no use to us afoot, either of you, and we can't afford to break down two more horses by having you ride double with someone else. You'll have to walk back to the post and lead your horses."

Leatherman took fright. "Just the two of us?"

"You brought it on yourselves."

Leatherman's fear was contagious. Ripley looked as if he had been kicked in the stomach. "They's liable to be Indians out there."

"You should have thought of that. Backtrack to the river, then follow it back to Fort Concho. And stay off of those horses. If I find out that either of you has ridden a step, I'll hang you up by the thumbs."

The two men were shattered. Leatherman pleaded, "Lieutenant . . ."

But Hollander was through with them. He sought out Maloney with his eyes. "We're losing time."

Maloney said dryly, "If I was you, Frank, I'd just shoot the both of them. It'd be a fine object lesson to the rest."

Hollander stared at him. "Were you ever an overseer of slaves?"

"Nope. I was always a poor man. Always had to do for myself."

"A pity. You have all the natural talents."

Maloney gave him a flat, dry grin. Gideon sensed that between the two men stood a contradiction in attitudes; on one hand, an old animosity going back to the war and to the vastly different social and cultural codes of their upbringing. Yet, on another level, he discerned a mutual respect, a recognition by each man that the other was capable.

The lieutenant might have been finished with Leatherman and Ripley, but Nettles was not. He gave them a blistering look that withered them like cornstalks before a flame. "When we get back . . ." He let them finish it in their imaginations, where fancy was more terrible than fact.

Maloney took his forward position, following the tracks. Gideon and Jimbo moved out to flank him. Gideon looked back once. He watched the two troopers leading their limping horses. In the distance they looked terribly alone, two tiny figures almost lost in a sun-bright expanse of hill and rock and short-grass prairie.

Maloney began running into trouble. He would lose the tracks on long stretches of hard and gravelly ground. When he found them again, where they moved off into softer ground that yielded better to the cutting hoofs, they would be fewer than before. Ultimately he came to a point where the main body of horses had disappeared. He found himself following what he was certain was just three horses and riders. Motioning for Hollander to come up, he pointed to the ground.

"They split up. Them Indians have fooled us."

Hollander's mouth hardened. "Not us, *you*. *You're* the one to whom the army pays an exorbitant fee for tracking service."

"Exorbitant, hell!" Maloney lost an hour trying to determine where the main bunch of stolen horses had left the hard ground. He finally settled for following the three horses. "Most times," he told Hollander, "they split up to confuse you, but they get back together farther on."

The tone of his voice was less hopeful than his words. Before he had gone far, the tracks swung west, then suddenly south again. Maloney's eyes were grim as he again signaled for Hollander. "They doubled back."

Hollander did not seem surprised. Nothing the Indians ever did surprised him much. "To what purpose?"

"Sometimes Indians like to circle around behind folks that's followin' them and hit them from the rear."

"Three Indians wouldn't hit this many soldiers."

"They might if we was straggled out. A scalp or two, a horse —they don't ask for much."

A thought chilled Gideon to the bone. "Leatherman and Ripley."

Maloney and Hollander stared at each other. Maloney nodded.

Hollander spoke a few words under his breath and turned his horse around. He set out in a long trot, not waiting for the other men. Maloney spurred up to take his place in front, though now it was only a matter of form. They would follow their own backtrail, not Indians.

In a little while they were back at the foot of the hill. Like the earlier descent, ascent could safely be made only in single file. Gideon looked around to see who would go up first, and while he waited, Jimbo started. Gideon set in behind him protectively. Maloney gave them a little time, then began. Scrambling to keep its footing, Jimbo's horse sent a cascade of small stones and gravel rolling back. Gideon slowed to allow him more of a lead. The horses plodded and labored; in a while, they were at the top. Glancing back, Gideon saw Maloney lagging. Jimbo kept going.

"Hold up, Jimbo," Gideon called uneasily. "Let's wait for the others."

"What for? They ain't no Indians here."

That was by no means Jimbo's first error, but it stood strong odds of being his last. Gideon heard the strike of hoofs. From behind a clump of thick green junipers seventy yards away, three Indians charged on horses streaked with paint. Gideon's heart went wild. He stared in stunned fascination at a spectacle of running horses, of bright colors, of feather-trimmed shields. One Indian began loosing arrows at an amazing speed. The other two carried rifles. When they had cleared half the distance, one started to whoop. The other two picked it up.

Gideon was too startled to find his voice. He tried to tell Jimbo to whip his horse around and run. Before he could get it said, Jimbo was doing just that.

Maloney reached the hilltop but sat at the edge, rifle in his hand. It was forty yards back to him and less distance to the rapidly closing Indians. Gideon jerked Judas around and jabbed spurs into him. This time the horse didn't carry him headlong into the shouting Comanches. One of the warriors fired his rifle. The shot went astray. An arrow buried into the breast of Jimbo's horse, halfway to the feathers. The animal fell. Carbine in his hand but never fired, Jimbo rolled.

Gideon's momentum carried him past Jimbo. For a moment he seemed benumbed, not knowing what to do. With his eye, he measured the distance to the Indians and the impossible distance to Maloney and Hollander, just coming up onto the rim. Maloney had begun firing, but he had not moved toward the stranded pair of soldiers.

Gideon was not conscious of any thoughts; he spurred back automatically to the downed Jimbo. Jimbo was on one knee, aiming, firing. Gideon kicked his foot out of the stirrup so Jimbo could swing up behind him. He tried to shout, but his throat seemed blocked. Jimbo stayed on one knee, levering a new cartridge into the chamber.

Gideon's breath was short, his face hot. They had to make their stand right here. No one was coming to help them; no one could. The first Indian was near enough that Gideon could see his painted face, the leather shield with jagged lightning streak and red animal tracks. Later, when he had time, he would reflect that he had seen a shield like it on the Colorado.

His bullet struck something; he saw a puff of dust. An eagle feather floated away, cut to ribbons. The slug had ricocheted from the heavy shield. Even so, the impact made the Indian loose his arrow too soon. His rush carried him past Gideon and Jimbo.

The other two were still coming. One jerked as a bullet struck him—Gideon didn't know whose. The warrior dropped his rifle and threw his arms around his horse's neck, trying to hold on. He did not lose his shield—it was looped to his arm. The third rider jerked the trigger as he passed Gideon. Gideon was sure he felt the heat of the blast, though the bullet missed. The Indian thrust the smoking muzzle forward and tried to touch Gideon, to count coup. In that, also, he was unsuccessful.

The wounded Indian rode a little farther, lost his hold and fell heavily to the ground. He pushed to his knees, badly stunned.

To Gideon's amazement the other two turned back. He thought they were going to charge at him and Jimbo again. Instead, they leaned from their running horses and grabbed up the fallen warrior between them. They were coming straight at Gideon, but he could only stare in wonder at what they had done. They swung around and galloped away, carrying the third man by the arms.

Several more soldiers were on the hilltop now, joining Hollander and Maloney in their firing. But they seemed to have no luck at such a rapidly moving target.

Gideon's heart pumped hot and fast. It suddenly occurred to him that his fear had vanished. He felt a wild, almost drunken exhilaration. He was enjoying this moment in a way he had never enjoyed anything before. He found himself shouting for the Indians to come back.

Instead they set the third man down, and one caught the runaway horse. When the wounded warrior was back on his mount, one of the others—the one with the lightning-streak shield—yelped defiance and waved something over his head. By the time the last of the soldiers reached the hilltop the Indians were gone, descending at another point three hundred yards away.

Unaccountably, Gideon was laughing. His heart felt swollen, and his whole body tingled. "We stood them off, Jimbo. Me and you, we stood them off!"

He saw the rifle the wounded Indian had dropped. On impulse, he spurred the brown horse to get there and retrieve the firearm before someone else. Jimbo shouted, "Gid, there's liable to be more of them!"

There weren't. Gideon returned with the rifle, shouting, his blood still racing. Jimbo stared at him as if convinced he had gone crazy. Gideon wondered too, for never had he felt a light-headedness quite like this.

Jimbo wasn't laughing. He knelt and ran his hand along the shoulder of his fallen horse, down to where the arrow shaft bobbed with the last gasping breaths of the animal's life.

Gideon found voice to warn, "Careful he don't take a spasm and kick you."

Jimbo's eyes were soft with pity. "He's past kickin'. He's past anything. He was a pretty good horse." To Jimbo they were all good. He had even had kind words for Gideon's Judas. Now that Gideon thought about it, he realized the brown hadn't threatened to run this time.

Jimbo laid his hand on the neck of Gideon's brown horse, just forward of the heavily laden McClellan saddle. "If you hadn't of come back for me, Gid, they'd of butchered me like a hog."

Gideon said nothing. His action had been instinctive, just as when the York girl's skirt caught afire. He didn't feel right in taking credit. He had a guilty suspicion that if he had had time to consider, he might have kept going. "You come after *me* that other time."

Jimbo was sobered by the loss of his horse and by what could easily have happened to himself. "I reckon we're both kind of dumb."

Gideon began laughing again. He could not control himself. It was a release from tension, and it was infectious. Jimbo laughed, too. The other soldiers, holding their carbines, had formed a semicircle. They stared in silent suspicion that the pair had lost their minds.

Lieutenant Hollander studied them with apprehension, then relief. "Charger . . . Jimbo . . . I take it that neither of you suffered a wound."

Gideon said proudly, "They never touched us."

Maloney leaned forward in his saddle. "Don't you boys let it go to your heads. Far as I could see, you didn't touch them either."

Gideon quit laughing. He had not given the tracker much thought during those anxious moments. Now it came back to him that Maloney had stayed at the rim of the hill. He cast aside the caution Old Colonel had warned him to keep. "You didn't come out and help us none," he accused.

Maloney could have taken violent offense. Instead he replied flatly, "You boys made a mistake ridin' out there by yourselves. I'd of made another if I'd gone after you. Anyway, I did more good where I was at. I shot the one that fell off of his horse."

Gideon reluctantly decided to give Maloney the benefit of the doubt, and as he thought back, he realized how much room for doubt there truly was.

Hollander smiled. "I knew it from the first, Charger. You have it in you to be a first-rate soldier."

Troopers who had been resentful of Gideon before began congratulating him for staying by Jimbo. It was a good feeling, while it lasted. But when the congratulations were through, Gideon and Jimbo still had to face Sergeant Nettles. With him, kind words were as rare as July snow. "If you-all had had the sense God gave a jackrabbit, you'd of stayed at the edge of the hill till the others got there. So now you've lost a horse. You can't break the other one down by ridin' him double. You got to take turns, one ridin' and one walkin'."

After the elation, it was as if Nettles had poured cold water on Gideon's bare back.

Hollander said, "Maloney, we'd best be moving. We've still got two men back there somewhere."

Maloney took a battered cigar from his shirt pocket, leaned way over and scratched a match on the shank of his Mexican spur. The cigar had been partially smoked earlier, then saved. "*Had*, Frank. Had." He jerked his chin at Gideon. "Let's see that rifle you picked up."

Gideon held it out. The lieutenant took it. "Spencer carbine," he said with surprise. "Army issue."

Maloney nodded grimly. "And still in army hands up to an hour or so ago, I'd wager. Did you see what that Indian waved at us, just before they skinned out?"

Hollander's face showed he was beginning to suspect. "At the distance . . ."

"Scalps, Frank. Two fresh woolly scalps."

Gideon's skin prickled and went cold. He saw horror strike Hollander, then turn quickly to anger. The lieutenant slapped his palm helplessly against the pommel of his black saddle. "Damn fools! I told them . . . Sergeant Nettles, a column of twos."

Finding the men was easy. Leatherman and Ripley had gone less than a mile from the edge of the hill. Leatherman seemed to be kneeling, his forehead touching the ground. Ripley lay on his back, his sightless eyes open; he had died staring into the sun. Each man had three arrows driven deeply into his body. The two horses were dead.

Maloney said, "When the Indians found the horses lame, they killed them. They made sure the army would never use them again."

Gideon did not want to look, but he could not pull his eyes

away. His stomach turned over. He feared he might disgrace himself by throwing up. Two other recruits did. Gideon had seen dead people before, but most had died of natural causes. The worst sight he had ever seen was a slave on Old Colonel's plantation, many years ago, who had sought a place to hide while he drank a bottle of bad whisky. He had made the mistake of getting himself trapped in a high box stall by a mean mule, which had kicked and stomped him into a sodden mass his own mother could not have identified. Old Colonel, though he liked a nip himself, forced his slaves to view the remains as an object lesson on the evils of drink.

Hollander made similar use of the two hapless soldiers. "Sergeant Nettles, I want all the men to come by in single file. I want every soldier to take a good look." His voice was brittle and strange. He raised it so everybody could hear. "I want all of you to remember what you see here. I want you to know what can happen when you abuse your horses, when you disobey orders, when you get off to yourselves. Out here, every man depends on every other. Any man who gets careless, who shirks his duty, is a danger to everybody around him. So look, Goddamn it, even if it makes you sick at your stomach. Look and remember!"

Gideon would remember. If he lived to be a hundred and six, he would never forget. He would always wish he could.

But he knew he would remember something else: that unaccountable soaring of spirit when he had faced his enemies and stood his ground as their equal. He would always respect this country and its dangers, but he would never be afraid of it again. He had stood up to its challenge, and he had prevailed.

He looked far ahead toward the thin line of trees that marked the beginnings of the North Concho River. Suddenly, nothing about it seemed strange any longer.

To the Comanche a name was not a permanent and sacred thing to be fastened upon an infant and worn unchanged throughout life. An old name could be abandoned, a new one adopted. Many a young warrior insisted upon it, shedding a nondescript name from his childhood and assuming a new one befitting his status as an adult skilled on the hunt and in war. Thus had Cub With a

Bad Foot become Bear That Turns to Fight as soon as he had returned from his first horse-gathering trip down into the settlements of the *tejanos*. That name was of his own selection. To
those young men of his own age group who knew him best, he
was known with a faint derision as Bear That Growls All the
Time. Inasmuch as the use of this name tended to make him
want to fight, and using the name of his own preference did not
suit the others, he was most often simply called Bear, a compromise that left everything understood and nothing settled. Conse-
quently, Bear was usually growling about something.

He had been particularly embittered about Gray Horse Running and his cousin Limping Boy. Sent off to scout, they had
come upon and taken a small horse herd without first returning
to the rest of the party to give everyone else a chance to share
honor. The other young men had been pleased enough simply to
get the extra horses, since the results of their own efforts to that
point had been meager. But Bear had made an issue of it and did
not drop the argument until the party's leader, Eagle Feather,
told him to quiet down or go off by himself.

Bear and Gray Horse were blood kin—distant cousins—but
Gray Horse reasoned that Bear's perpetual sourness must have
been visited upon him by unshared ancestors. He had to show
Bear some deference inasmuch as Bear had attained his personal
medicine two full years earlier and had gone on the war trail that
much sooner. And though Bear was known in council as one
who talked more than was necessary about his own exploits—no
small thing among warriors who waited impatiently to talk of
their own—at least he had those exploits to talk about. Gray
Horse begrudged him nothing except what he regarded as a jeal-
ous attempt to keep other young men from acquiring the same
degree of honor.

Gray Horse considered that his medicine had shown him the
way to the horses. Sent to scout west of the main party, which
came along with a dozen animals stolen laboriously by ones and
twos along the edge of the German hill-country settlements,
Gray Horse and Limping Boy had come upon a wolf, a big male,
a worthy specimen of his race. Gray Horse was certain the
amber eyes had gazed directly into his; then the wolf had

changed directions and trotted to the northwest. Most Comanches would have regarded this as a bad omen and changed
their own direction, but Gray Horse had the wolf medicine. He
took it as a sign that he was meant to follow. Presently the wolf
led them to a trail left by driven horses, a trail so fresh the droppings were warm. Shortly Gray Horse and Limping Boy hauled
up behind some twenty horses being driven by a lone man, a
Mexican, judging by his dark skin and broad straw hat. He was
singing a song that had an alien and almost painful sound to
Gray Horse's ears; his mind seemed to be on things other than
danger.

The Comanches had an ambivalent attitude toward Mexicans.
With joy in the sport, they rode hundreds of miles to plunder,
kidnap and kill in Old Mexico. Yet they maintained an open-
handed trading friendship with Mexican Comancheros to the
west, often bartering to them the livestock taken from kinsmen
to the south. It was a self-feeding process; the brisker the trading, the more intensive the raiding. This seemed to trouble the
Comanchero conscience very little, the Indian, none.

There was no ambivalence in the Comanche attitude toward
tejanos. They hated them all. When they found Mexicans living
among the *tejanos*, they killed them, too.

Limping Boy fitted an arrow to his bow, but Gray Horse
counseled that there was more honor in bringing down an enemy
hand-to-hand than in ambushing him. With his war club, Gray
Horse had taken his first coup against the buffalo soldier on the
Colorado River. With the same war club, he would count coup
again and throw the matter into the face of Bear, who liked to
kill, but always at a fair distance. Drumming his heels against the
ribs of his pony, Gray Horse took a firm grip on the club. He
gave a war whoop so his enemy would face him before the blow,
for that added to the honor. The startled Mexican had a rifle in a
scabbard beneath his leg. He reached down and pulled it out too
late. The stone club sent his straw hat sailing. The Mexican went
down heavily, falling upon the rifle and driving its muzzle
deeply into the ground. Limping Boy grabbed its stock and
pulled it out of the dirt, touching the stunned Mexican with the
barrel and sharing Gray Horse's coup.

The action boogered the horses into a hard run. Gray Horse
had it in mind to finish the Mexican and take his scalp, but this
might cost him the horses. He chose to retain the greater prize.
The rest of his life, the *vaquero* would have a story to tell and a
scar to prove it by.

Limping Boy was beside himself with pride in his cousin's feat,
and in his own good fortune at sharing it. They were a year
apart in age. As far back as Gray Horse could remember, Limping Boy had followed him like a pup, always a step behind in his
training but always grateful to learn. Gray Horse had been given
his first small bow and reed arrows by his maternal grandfather.
He had soon learned to kill birds. Gray Horse, in turn, passed
the bow and the lessons on to Limping Boy, whose own maternal
grandfather had been killed by Texas Rangers in a reprisal foray.
Limping Boy, then only five or six, had gained his name and a
stiffened leg in that same attack upon the family's buffalo-hunting camp in a bend of the Colorado River. If he had let it, the
handicap could have turned him into a saddlemaker or other useful craftsman like most of the Mexican boy captives. But he had
grown up following Gray Horse, determined to become a warrior in the best tradition. Slow and awkward afoot, he was as
good on horseback as any youth of similar age in the band. The
wound to his leg had done no damage to his heart.

At the least, Bear had demanded later, the captured herd
should be divided among the other warriors cheated of honor by
the selfishness of Gray Horse. Gray Horse spiked this argument
by declaring that it had been his intention from the first to add
these horses to the common herd. It would be up to Eagle Feather
to divide them as he saw fit when they returned to the main encampment far to the north. All Bear could do then was carp over
the fact that they had not taken time to lift the Mexican's scalp,
for the whole camp could have enjoyed an invigorating scalp
dance around it upon their return. Gray Horse replied quietly
that he thought they would enjoy the horses more.

Bear continued to badger Limping Boy as they brought up the
rear together, driving the horses. He reminded Limping Boy of
his seniority, of the fact that his father had often brought meat
to the tepee of Limping Boy's widowed mother. In exasperation,

Limping Boy gave him the rifle he had retrieved from the fallen Mexican, together with the scabbard and ammunition taken from the Mexican's horse. However, Limping Boy failed to tell him the barrel was full of dirt. When Bear fired at a rabbit the barrel split, blackening and burning Bear's face.

Bear blamed Limping Boy, of course, and declared that if it had not been for the strong power of his protective medicine he might have lost his eyes. Bear's guardian spirit was supposed to impart wisdom, but Gray Horse judged that the spirit did not talk to Bear very much.

Perhaps indulging a warped sense of humor, Eagle Feather dispatched Gray Horse, Limping Boy and Bear as a rear guard, dropping way behind to watch for sign of pursuit and do whatever was necessary to slow it. Ahead lay the open plains. Once they had the horses over the caprock, raiding parties historically had been able to assume a high degree of safety. Rarely did the white or buffalo soldiers pursue them far onto that great ocean of grass. The *tejanos* were more inclined to try, particularly the Rangers, though even they rarely carried the pursuit to conclusion and confrontation. Usually it was sufficient to decoy them back and forth until they ran out of water and were forced to turn back. Water—or lack of it—was the most critical factor on the Llano Estacado.

Bear took it upon himself to be the leader of the rear guard, giving orders that Gray Horse accepted only because they made sense and not because he recognized Bear's self-ordained authority. There was, among Comanche warriors, no absolute compulsion to follow anyone's orders. A man was always free to refuse and withdraw. There were no generals in the white man's tradition, or even in the war-chief traditions of many other plains tribes. There were only advisers, followed so long as the others regarded their advice as sound.

From a stand of junipers, the three watched the cavalry patrol make its way carefully down the steep and rocky hill where the raiding party had come with the captured horses earlier. They watched, puzzled, as two troopers took a shortcut and let their horses fall. They watched later as these same two troopers led their horses back up the hill while the rest of the detail went on.

The three warriors held the nostrils of their horses while the main body of soldiers passed, following the trail. Gray Horse noted that a *tejano* seemed to lead them, two black soldiers flanking him as his guard.

Bear gave vent to an ancient Comanche hatred. "I would like to have that *tejano*'s scalp to hang in my lodge."

"It is yours," Gray Horse said, letting malice creep into his voice. "All you have to do is kill all those soldiers first."

"They are buffalo soldiers—not even white," Bear observed. "The only white faces I see are the *tejano* and one other. He is a chief, more than likely."

Gray Horse had heard it said that the black soldiers were slaves of some kind, perhaps like the Mexican youths or the occasional young Utes or Apaches the People captured and allowed to live as menials. But he had also heard it said they could be bitter fighters. He remembered that the one he had struck with his club on the Colorado had been coming to meet him, not running away.

It was not the Comanche custom to attack a greatly superior force, but Gray Horse let Bear believe he contemplated it. "If you think so little of the black soldiers, you take all of them, and Limping Boy and I will take the two with the white faces."

Bear said, "We will take the two buffalo soldiers who turned back. That will be honor enough for one day."

They waited until the main body of soldiers were far away before venturing out of the junipers. Bear used the time to paint his face for war, streaking black paint along one side and yellow on the other. Gray Horse and Limping Boy followed his example. Gray Horse painted the lightning on his face and the lightning and wolf tracks on his body that he carried on his shield.

Bear took the lead in climbing the hill. Far ahead they saw the two lonely soldiers, still walking and leading their horses. The whole thing was so pathetically easy that Gray Horse took little pride in it afterward, though Bear would always make it seem a great encounter in the telling. They came up behind the soldiers undetected until one of the limping horses looked back, pointing its ears. By then the warriors were too near for their arrows to miss. One of the black soldiers raised his rifle in self-defense, and

Gray Horse put an arrow into him. The other soldier dropped his rifle, fell on his knees and began to sob. Gray Horse judged that he was pleading for his life, though the words had no more meaning to him than the barking of a camp dog. Bear shot this one through the heart, his arrow turning slightly upward as it struck the breastbone. Each warrior put an arrow into each soldier, so they shared equally in the kill, but Bear claimed both scalps inasmuch as he was in charge. The killing was cold and mechanical, done without passion or pity, for the Comanche was taught from childhood to despise his enemies, to know that all but the People themselves were something less than true human beings. White people—and these blacks were only white people with a different look—were fair game wherever found, like the antelope or the buffalo.

Gray Horse watched dispassionately as Bear worried with the short, kinky black hair, trying to peel enough for a proper display. He cursed the soldiers for cheating him and marked them with his knife to show his displeasure.

Curious, Limping Boy tore open the shirt of the soldier who lay on his back, eyes glazing. He rubbed his hand against the skin and looked at his fingers. "I have heard they are white people painted black. But the paint does not come off."

Gray Horse said, "Their blood is red."

Disdainfully Bear said, "They are *teibos,* just like all the others. They have lived in the sun more. The black skin does not make them different inside." He touched his chest, where the heart was.

Bear took the shiniest rifle and reluctantly gave the other to Limping Boy. He glanced at Gray Horse to be sure his cousin realized he was purposely left out. He gathered the ammunition belts and canteens, which would be useful. He finally chose to give Gray Horse a pistol taken from one of the soldiers, not feeling it necessary to point out that it was a lesser item than a rifle. He puzzled over the heavy steel picket pins hanging in a ring on each saddle. They were too short to use as a club and much too large for an awl. Gray Horse suspected their true purpose and suggested that he and Limping Boy might find some use for them.

Because both horses limped badly, they would be more liability than asset. Bear was about to try his new rifle when Gray Horse suggested the shot might be heard by the other soldiers. They used arrows instead, afterward digging them out with their knives for use another time. Good arrows were not to be wasted. Those in the soldiers' bodies were left alone. An arrow which had killed a man was never used again.

The incident had taken a lot of time. Gray Horse worried aloud that the main body of soldiers might overtake or at least harry Eagle Feather and the others. Bear finally agreed, though he took time to multilate the soldiers a bit more, to cause them embarrassment and impotence in the afterlife, if the scalping did not rob them of it entirely.

With the caution drilled into them from boyhood, the three dismounted and looked over the edge of the hill without skylining themselves for anyone below to see. It was a fortunate precaution; the soldiers were returning, giving up the trail of the stolen horses. They were climbing this hill in single file. Gray Horse and Bear looked at each other, and for once they found nothing to argue about.

Bear said, "Perhaps the *tejano* will come first."

Whoever came first, they would get him, Gray Horse replied. If they were lucky, they might get two or three before so many soldiers reached the top that they had to leave. If the spirits were pleased, they might even take two or three more horses with them.

Gray Horse hunched at the rim, watching to see the order in which the men were making the climb. He pulled back from the edge before straightening and running for his mount. "Two of the buffalo soldiers are ahead of the *tejano*. If we wait until all three are on top, we can kill them and be gone before the others can do anything."

Bear growled, "The *tejano* is mine."

Gray Horse saw that Bear intended to use his newly acquired rifle. He worried, "Do you really know enough about it yet?"

Bear snorted. "If it will work for a soldier, it will work for me."

Gray Horse saw that Limping Boy intended to use his, too.

He was almost glad he had not been given a rifle. He knew the bow, the arrow.

He expected that the first soldiers to reach the top would stay at the edge until they were reinforced. That would have been the prudent thing. It would also have bunched them better for attack. To his surprise, the first black soldier kept riding, the second following and calling.

The tension was too much for Bear. Before the *tejano* had properly reached the top, Bear whooped and charged from behind the stunted cedar. Almost at once the *tejano* and both soldiers were firing. Gray Horse loosed an arrow that found a soldier's horse and brought it down. The other soldier instantly went to the downed one's rescue, as a Comanche would. The one on the ground fell to one knee, bringing his rifle into use. Gray Horse seemed to be looking straight down a gun barrel at the desperate wide eyes and black face behind it. He swung his bullhide shield around, its feathers and buffalo tail flaring. A bullet struck with the force of a heavy war club, almost ripping the shield from his arm, tearing off one or more of the feathers. But the convex shape, hard as flint, sent the slug whining away.

From the rim, the *tejano* was firing with calm and deliberation. The ferocity of the resistance startled Gray Horse. He saw Bear slump forward and drop his rifle. Limping Boy got off one shot, which struck nothing, then jammed the unfamiliar weapon. He tried in vain to touch the soldier.

There was no more time for arrows. Bear slipped from his horse and hit the ground. Gray Horse and Limping Boy turned back, their eyes meeting in agreement. Bear was rising to his knees, stunned. From boyhood, Gray Horse and Limping Boy had trained for this emergency. To leave a fellow warrior wounded or dead on the battleground, at the mercy of enemies, was cowardice of the worst kind, as unforgivable as the murder of another Comanche. Leaning down, passing on opposite sides, they caught Bear under his arms and lifted him up between them. The rescue run carried them toward the soldiers, and bullets passed them like angry hornets, but neither man questioned the need. They turned, Gray Horse taking the outside of the pivot. At a fair distance they pulled up and eased Bear to the ground. Limping Boy loped on to catch Bear's loose horse.

The soldiers remained where they were, perhaps waiting for all the others to reach the top before they moved. They continued to fire, but their marksmanship was not good. Gray Horse did not care. The wolf medicine had proven itself when his shield had turned the black soldier's bullet aside. He was immune to bullets, just as the wolf itself was. To kill him they would have to find something more potent than their rifles.

Gray Horse saw that Bear's wound was high in his shoulder, far from the heart. He would always have the scar to brag about. Because this was Bear, Gray Horse knew he would.

Limping Boy brought Bear's horse, and they helped Bear onto him. Gray Horse's blood ran hot, fired by a wild exultation bequeathed him by uncounted generations of warrior ancestors. He was reluctant to turn away from the fight. He jerked loose the two scalps Bear had tied to his rawhide bridle, and he waved them over his head with a loud shout of defiance. The bullets that passed him were as gnats, not even a decent nuisance. He shouted once more, alluding to the soldiers' ancestry, and the *tejano*'s. Then he led Bear and Limping Boy down the rough hillside, leaving the soldiers far behind.

Eagle Feather was known as a generous man as well as a good warrior. This helped make young men eager to follow him, for they could expect a fair share of whatever plunder was taken if they had acquitted themselves acceptably on the raid. Long before the party reached the main camp, Eagle Feather made the division. He saw that each man received one particularly good horse and two others of perhaps less evident value but sound of foot and wind. He kept only two for himself, both good ones, announcing it as his intention to present the best of the pair to his father-in-law as a gift. This, indirectly, would be recognized as an honor to his wife Antelope, as well as to her father. Gray Horse decided there was much he might yet learn from Eagle Feather.

Gray Horse had been given a stout-bodied sorrel with three stocking feet, a big patch of white on its belly and a spot on the left side of its neck. It came very near being a paint, he thought, glad it had come no nearer. Eagle Feather probably would have given it to his father-in-law.

Bear was given a black with a white star on its face. His expression of vague disappointment made it clear he thought Gray Horse had been favored, but he did not speak his feelings aloud. It was Eagle Feather's prerogative to make the division as he saw fit. Bear silently nursed his notion of persecution along with his wound.

There was a proper procedure for entering camp after a raid, one fashion for an unsuccessful one—particularly one that had cost a warrior his life—but a joyous and boastful fashion for a successful raid such as this one. The party camped the last night a short way out of the main village so it could make its triumphal entry in the morning. Limping Boy, youngest of the warriors and a novice on this trip, was given the honor of going in first to announce the victory. The rest of the men used handfuls of dry grass to brush their horses and make them shine. They preened themselves, using porcupine-quill combs to dress their hair, tying in all their feathers. Bear had a long braid of which he was proud. He had plaited in extra hair which he had gotten from some girl to make it even longer. Bear again streaked black paint on one side of his face, yellow on the other. He painted circles around his wound to make it easier for everyone to notice. Gray Horse used red and black paint, putting on the wolf tracks that had turned bullets away.

A singing, shouting, laughing group from the village came triumphantly up the hill, led by an elderly woman whose sons had been honored warriors and had all died bleeding. She carried a scalp pole. It would have been good form for Bear to have tied the two buffalo-soldier scalps to it and do her honor, but he chose to carry them himself so all in the village would know who had taken them, and would see as well that he had brought home a wound. Eagle Feather led the warriors. It was custom that he choose those who had done the most and let them follow immediately behind him. Bear pressed forward, for he had the scalps, but Eagle Feather chose Gray Horse to come second. Bear and Limping Boy rode third and fourth. A merry throng formed two ragged, cheering, singing lines for the horsemen to pass between. Bear, who lived alone, was first to turn in, placing his scalp pole in front of his lodge to be sure no one missed seeing it and knowing what he had done. Bear was as yet a bachelor. When he had need of a woman he borrowed from one of his brothers, who expected him to honor the custom someday when he had a young and pretty wife of his own.

All along the way, Gray Horse's heart stirred to the cheers. But he felt a growing disappointment as he vainly searched for a particular pair of happy black eyes. Nowhere in the crowd did he see Green Willow. Of all people, beyond his immediate family, he was most eager for her to see his position in the procession before it broke up. He wanted her to see the sorrel horse. It ran through his mind that he might present it to her father as a gift, a token that he was putting a claim on Green Willow.

Limping Boy turned off at the lodge of his widowed mother. His father had had no brother to take her to wife after her widowhood, and she was not so well favored with beauty that other men had chosen to do so out of charity. It had been left to her sons and to the generous hearts of the camp to support her.

Gray Horse pulled up presently before the lodge of his uncle-father, peace chief of the camp. He received a joyous greeting from his mother and his aunts and from Black Robe. His sisters smiled, proud tears in their eyes, but they stood back from him. He was a man, and sisters did not touch a grown brother lest fleshly temptations lead to incest, one of the greatest abominations the People knew. Though it was rarely done, a man had a right to kill a sister who tempted him.

Gray Horse's mother quickly brought food, which he dutifully ate, though he felt no hunger. Black Robe was eager to know the details of the trip. Every so often the elder, who no longer rode the war trail, would interrupt with an exclamation of approval. An actual father could not have been prouder than this uncle who had taken Gray Horse as his own.

"Eagle Feather is a good leader," he acknowledged, "but without my son, he would not have brought back half so many horses."

Gray Horse did not argue the matter. False modesty was not a weakness of the People. If a man did not acknowledge his own accomplishments, who else would? If his deeds were not known, how would he acquire honor?

Black Robe predicted, "My son will be known after this as a great warrior. You could lead a raid yourself now. Many young men would follow you." The statement was not an idle boast; it was a challenge. Gray Horse's heart swelled at this tribute.

Black Robe ran his fingers over Gray Horse's shield and the dent left by the soldier's bullet. "Your mother will sew you a cover to protect its medicine. You should leave it outside the camp so that no accident can steal its power."

Many things could spoil good medicine. Grease was one enemy. The touch, or even the presence, of a woman in her menstrual period was almost certain to destroy power. A warrior could never be too careful.

Black Robe admired the sorrel again. In a moment of pride and overflowing gratitude, Gray Horse gave it to him. He realized too late that this left him no gift worthy of Green Willow's father. He would find that venerable soul another on the raid he planned to lead.

At dark, the people of the camp gathered for a scalp dance, a celebration which might or might not end before daylight. Gray Horse could remember some which continued for days, though he hardly felt that this raid and its results were of a magnitude to justify that much observance. Bear's two dark scalps were raised high on a pole. A fire was lighted, and the dancing and feasting and story-singing commenced. One by one the young men who had followed Eagle Feather were called upon to tell their stories. As his turn came, Gray Horse took pleasure from the approval he could see in the crowded circle of eager faces, the firelight and the shadows leaping back and forth among them as the fire flared and dulled and flared again. And there, in that circle, he saw at last the face he had sought. Green Willow was listening attentively. He dared not stare at her as he talked, for that might be noticed and commented upon. It was not seemly for a young warrior to make bold with a maiden under the eyes of the village. Comanche society gave the aggressor's role entirely to the girl, though even she was expected to remain discreet.

Occasionally, after Gray Horse had moved into his own tepee, alone, one girl or another would come to him in the darkness of night, crawling through the low opening where the skins had been rolled up from the ground for ventilation. She would slide into the robes and initiate the lovemaking which custom had made her prerogative rather than his. These girls had taught him much which he was happy to learn. It was expected that he maintain the pretense of not recognizing them so that there need be no shame in the daylight. He had known them all, of course. To his disappointment, none had been Green Willow.

Gray Horse almost stumbled in the telling of his story because his mind was on the girl. It came to him that he might ask some older person—perhaps Limping Boy's mother—to intercede for him and make his feelings known. The woman, a distant aunt, was always trying to do something for Gray Horse in gratitude for the help and friendship he had given her handicapped son. Perhaps he would do it tomorrow, if this dance ever ended.

It did end, earlier than he expected, for two soldier scalps were not major trophies, especially since they were taken with so little resistance. Bear seemed disappointed that the affair broke up before dawn. He had wanted the rising sun to add its warmth to his glory. He sat alone, smoking Mexican trade tobacco in his bone pipe after the crowd went home.

Gray Horse was tired. The trip had been long and the rest periods short, and he had done much dancing through the night. He had his bed made on the west side of the tepee, facing the flap so the rising sun would touch his eyes when he awakened. His mind raced like a runaway horse, touching on one memory and another and another as he relived the evening and its praises. After a time, he dropped off to sleep.

He awakened suddenly to the touch of a small, warm hand that gently stroked his face. His eyes opened quickly to darkness, though he could see the form of the girl who leaned over him. Her breath was warm on his cheek. He lay quietly, letting her start. She was unpracticed and unsure. His patience and reserve did not endure. The wanting surged in him. He grabbed her in his arms and turned over with her. A soft, eager laugh told him what he had suspected.

This was—finally—Green Willow.

She would have to leave before dawn so that she would not be seen making her way back to her own family's tepee. But there was as yet no sign of light through the open flap. They lay in each other's arms, whispering.

He made no pretense of not knowing who she was. "If someone else comes and ties horses at your lodge, turn them loose and drive them away. You will be *my* wife, and no one else's."

"That is for my father to decide."

"My father says if I lead a raid, many young men will want to go. I will bring back many horses and give my share to your father."

"Am I worth so many?"

"All I can find. And more."

"My father is getting old. He wants a son-in-law who will bring meat to the lodge and keep him rich in horses. He will not wait much longer."

"I will begin looking for warriors today."

"Then I will see that he waits, at least awhile. Do not be too long, Gray Horse."

She snuggled beneath him again. He knew he would not want to be away from her a day more than would be necessary for him to find and bring back the best horses this camp had ever seen.

Seven

MORE AND MORE, Gideon enjoyed scouting expeditions far from the fort. Despite its relative comforts and the dependability of its plain but ample food, garrison life tended toward numbing monotony day after day. Over and over he went through the same tiresome drills. He was subjected to the endless drudgery of digging holes and ditches for the gradually expanding post, of hauling rocks and shoveling sand, of raking stables and hoeing the post garden, of cleaning sinks and working the company mess. On post, he felt more mule than man.

Scout detail was different. True, the riding was long and bone-wearying. Meals were sometimes cold, often postponed and occasionally missed altogether. Water from a canteen frequently substituted for coffee from a cup, and times even the canteen went empty. But never did he suffer from monotony. Every hill he climbed spread a fresh and different scene before him. It was not a planned and ordered land, with houses and fields and well-defined roads, but a new and unspoiled country with a random scattering of creeks and rivers, of mountains and prairies violated by only a few twin-rut military roads sometimes hard to distinguish from the buffalo trails that led the way to water, when there was any.

Sometimes Gideon had the feeling that he had set foot there the day after God had finished it, for man had made little mark upon it. The Indian neither built nor tore down, and the white man, for the most part, had not yet claimed it.

Somehow, after that second skirmish with the Indians, his fear for this big, open land had left him. But the awe remained. The country would change one day, probably soon, and Gideon realized he would play a part in bringing that change. But he could always remember that he had seen it the way it was.

A week after their return from the unsuccessful chase after the Indian horse thieves, Lieutenant Hollander took him and part of the company on a long scout west, first along the pecan-lined Middle Concho and the rough hills which flanked it, on beyond to the gentler land where pecan trees did not grow because there was not permanent water for their roots to rest in. They passed the last wet-weather springs and moved onto the semi-desert flatlands which sloped gradually westward toward the Pecos River, harsh and inhospitable. Grass was sparse, and trees did not grow at all, except for a scattering of the indomitable mesquite. Gideon had heard that this thorny plant sent its taproots halfway to China and had long since sucked all the water out of hell. Great open flats were covered by low shrubs like the lotebush and the greasewood, and on harder ground, up the sides of arid, stony hills, grew a wicked-looking cactus plant whose curled leaves grew in a circular pattern with the sharpness and toughness of short, bent swords. The scout Maloney called them *lechuguilla*. Gideon saw few buffalo beyond the head of the Middle Concho, and he reasoned that those few he saw were lost. This land seemed better suited to the stiff-bristled, belligerent little wild hog known as the javelina, whose sharp tusks could take off half of a man's hand if he were foolish enough to offer it. A trooper named Davis shot one but tried to claim possession before it had finished its dying. He lost all of one finger and part of another. None of the soldiers would eat the pig because it had fed on human flesh.

Maloney found it delicious.

They followed an old immigrant, stage and military road through a line of low, hostile, flat-topped mountains and into a

tight pass which Hollander called Castle Gap. From the mouth
of the pass the road led down across a wide, gently sloping and
arid flat toward the narrow gash that was the Pecos River. The
horses were thirsty, for the only water since the head of the
Middle Concho had been at a wet-weather hole known as China
Pond. Gideon had wondered why it bore that name. Maybe it
came from the deep-growing mesquite roots.

Sergeant Nettles cautioned the men not to stop and drink from
the potholes west of the gap and not to let their horses drink
from them. They contained enough alkali to kill man or beast.
Maloney told a horror tale about some cattlemen named Goodnight and Loving who had brought a trail herd this way soon
after the war, starving for water from the time they left the
head of the Concho. Many cattle stampeded to these inviting
holes, drank of the bad water and fell dead.

The Pecos was certainly no Mississippi, nor was it like any of
the three Conchos. For all Gideon had heard, he was surprised at
how narrow it appeared. He could have hurled a rock across it
with a sore arm. But the water was swift, and he sensed that it
was deceptively deep.

Maloney seemed unable to distinguish most black soldiers from
one another, but he had become used to Gideon and Jimbo. He
chose them to ride with him for some distance upriver, then
down, looking for any sign that horsemen had crossed the Pecos
in the recent past. He found none. He seemed satisfied that no
Indians had been here in a while.

Gideon had discovered that most white men wouldn't automatically take a whip to him if he asked a sensible question.
"How do you know?" he asked cautiously, not wishing to
provoke Maloney into irreverence.

Maloney was having a patient day. He swung his arm in an
arc, pointing vaguely at the river. "See how steep the banks are
here? Both sides. You can't hardly get into or out of it anywhere
for a day's ride in either direction. Bunch of them Goodnight
and Loving cattle jumped in off of the high bank, piled up and
drowned. Horsehead yonder is the only decent crossing for a
long ways, north or south. If Indians didn't cross there, they
didn't cross anywhere."

They camped the night, and Gideon found just how unfriendly the river really was. Its salty water went through him
like a heavy dose of medicine. He was constantly having to drop
out the next day until the malady ran its course. He was not
alone; nearly every other man had the same difficulty to some
degree. Maloney seemed mildly amused over the black men's discomfort and embarrassment. He was unaffected.

"You boys ain't drunk enough of that Saint Angela whisky,"
he said. "It'll make you immune to anything short of strych-
nine."

They followed the river southeastward to its next crossing far
below, where an old military and mail road led from San Antonio toward El Paso del Norte in the distant west. High up
from that crossing stood the skeletal remains of an old an-
tebellum fort known as Lancaster. They camped a night there,
where a full moon accentuated all the spectral aspects of the
dead military post. Some of the men did not sleep well. Gideon
had no problem, except that which remained from his first encounter with Pecos River water. If live Indians had not killed
him, he expected no harm from long-vanished soldiers.

From Lancaster they looped northeastward in the general direction of Fort Concho. At one point Maloney was lost for a
while, and in his casting about he led the detail to a spring and
fair-sized waterhole not on Hollander's map. It took Gideon
awhile to fully appreciate the lieutenant's pleasure and excitement.
For himself, he was gratified at the chance to fill his empty canteen. There was ample sign that the spring had been used by Indians for at least a temporary campsite, and not long ago.

Hollander was meticulous in penciling the location onto his
map, along with the few landmarks that would help point the
way to it. "One less sanctuary," he said.

Gideon did not want to expose his ignorance by asking
Hollander, and he would not ask the grimly silent Nettles. But
he had come to feel a limited ease with the civilian Maloney.
When he and Jimbo were out front with the scout, he asked
what a sanctuary was. Maloney told him, and he explained that
the more of the secret watering holes and campgrounds the sol-

diers could find, the harder it would be for future Indian raiders
to disappear.

Up to then, Gideon had assumed this expedition to be a failure, for they had not seen an Indian or even the fresh tracks of
one. Maloney explained that every scouting trip had value if it
yielded up fresh information about this huge and almost trackless
country. Officers' maps were almost as important as the soldiers'
rifles.

"But don't you ever tell them stiff-collared Yankees I said so,"
Maloney cautioned. "I like to keep them on the *de*fense."

A second expedition took them up the North Concho, to and
beyond the point where they had turned back on their search for
stolen horses. They visited the big spring Maloney had described.
From the spring they rode northwestward for a day. A chill
played on Gideon's spine as he realized they had moved onto
that mysterious land known as "the plains." Men talked of it in
the same mystic tones they applied to heaven and hell. The horizon line appeared absolutely level, without a tree, a hill, anything
to break the flatness of it. Up there, somewhere beyond the
shimmering heat waves, lay some dark and hidden stronghold
known only to Comanche and Kiowa. Few white men had done
more than guess at what it was like, for nature guarded it even
more fiercely than the Indian. Time and again, white soldiers and
civilians had trailed raiding parties this far and farther, only to
lose all sign of them and have to turn back when their water ran
out and they could find no more. Time and again, men had come
off the edge of these plains half-crazed with thirst, leading their
horses or leaving them behind.

Somewhere there must be water, or the Indians themselves
could not survive. But it was hidden, and nature and the Indians
seemed to have conspired to keep it so. Now and again a military
scouting party would find a seep or spring not mapped before,
but the secrets were yielded up slowly and grudgingly, at heavy
cost to men and horses.

Hollander made a wide circle, hoping to cut some sign that
might lead to a previously undiscovered playa, one of the shallow depressions which would become a temporary lake after a
rain; his trip was in vain. By the time the detail trudged back to

the big spring, the men were afoot, sparing their horses, trying to conserve in them what little strength was left. Thirst had swollen Gideon's tongue and blurred his vision. He could see nothing except directly in front of him, and even that was not plain. It would have been a good time for an Indian party to drop down and hit the troopers, for they would have been hard put to defend themselves.

Sergeant Nettles delayed slaking his own thirst until he had overseen the men, preventing them from taking too much water at first, cajoling and reasoning and booting them into drinking only a little at a time lest they make themselves sick, or worse. Gideon's reason all but left him at the first touch of water on his wooden tongue, and only the rough hands of Esau Nettles dragging him back from the edge stopped him from frantically filling his belly all at one time.

The sight of the half-starved black troopers floundering, fighting Nettles to get back to the water, brought Maloney to frown in disgust. Painfully thirsty himself, he was too well seasoned to succumb to panic. The men were nowhere as near starvation as they imagined, and he knew it.

He said thickly to Hollander, "To think, Frank, me and you went to war and fought each other over the likes of *them*."

"They'll toughen. Next time they'll stand more. They'll be better soldiers for this experience."

"They'll still be a flock of blackbirds."

Hollander decided to camp a day at the spring. Big Dempsey complained darkly, where the lieutenant couldn't hear him, that the decision had been made for the sake of the horses, not of the men.

Sergeant Nettles had suffered like the rest, but it was hard to tell from watching him. He seemed to be everywhere. He seemed to know what every man was doing, every minute. He made each do his part of the cooking, the cleanup. He made certain every man stood a share of the watch without dropping off to sleep. Because of the spring's popularity among the Indians, Nettles ordered a double guard.

Gideon was about an hour into his tour of duty when Nettles came around in the darkness, making certain every man was alert, not giving in to the fatigue and the temptation to sleep. He gritted, "If I was an Indian, Ledbetter, I'd of slipped up on you and killed you."

"No, you wouldn't," Gideon countered. "I heard you a way over yonder, and I've had this gun on you ever since."

Gideon didn't know why, but the sergeant seemed satisfied. Nettles asked, "Did you hear what Maloney said about us this mornin'?"

Gideon had.

Nettles said, "You'd like to make a liar out of him, wouldn't you?"

Gideon hadn't thought on it much, but he sensed that the sergeant had deep feelings. He said conservatively, "I don't reckon I'd mind."

He realized that was not the answer Nettles was looking for, because the sergeant stalked away into the darkness. Gideon grimaced, wondering what he should have said.

He had expected that they would ride from the spring directly down to the head of the North Concho, then follow the river home. He learned once more that it was idle to try to outguess white officers. Hollander conferred with Maloney, and they made a wide, looping swing more or less southward, across yet another stretch of dry country Gideon had not seen before. Not until they struck the Middle Concho did he find what he considered familiar ground. They encountered a scattering of buffalo and some antelope out on one of the wide valleys, but not once did they see any clear-cut sign of Indians.

About midafternoon of the fourth day from the spring, they came in sight of the fort. They rode in just south of the twin mountains that lay several miles west of Concho and Saint Angela. Jimbo declared that this well-matched, well-rounded pair of promontories reminded him of Big Ella. He laughed, but Gideon considered the remark disrespectful.

The two of them, riding with Maloney, jumped a buffalo cow out of a grassy swale. Lieutenant Hollander gave chase, putting two bullets through her lungs before she went to her knees and rolled over, kicking.

"Bleed her for me, Charger," he said.

Gideon's brown horse was none too keen about getting close. Gideon didn't know whether it was the smell of blood or simply the buffalo herself that gave the animal such a severe case of the keep-aways. He had to dismount and hand the reins to Jimbo, then walk the last forty or fifty feet to the downed cow. She still kicked convulsively and tried to lift her head.

Maloney warned, "Give her more time, boy. She flings that head just right, them sharp horns'll rip you from gut to goozle."

Gideon waited, his hand trembling a little. This was the closest he had ever been to a buffalo. He had not realized how large they were, even a young cow like this one. When he slashed, gushing blood splashed hot on his hand. To his dismay, it took her awhile to die. He didn't watch. He was relieved when Hollander detailed someone else to do the gutting. He figured she would go to the officers' mess. What the officers shot usually did, along with whatever the enlisted men shot in the officers' presence. But Hollander said, "Half of her goes to the company mess."

Jimbo raised a cheer, which several others took up. Even Big Dempsey looked surprised, though he did not cheer, or even smile.

Hollander said, "According to my calculations, the paymaster should have come and gone. If so, that means we're due to be paid when we get in."

That brought another cheer.

The lieutenant added, "Now, I'd hate to know that any men of my company did anything so foolish as to go across the river tonight and get drunk. So whatever you do, don't tell me about it."

Sergeant Nettles frowned. "Surely the lieutenant don't mean to encourage these men to drunkenness and sloth?"

Hollander winked at Maloney. "As I told them, that's the last thing I want to hear about."

Gideon had never lost time worrying about the fact that he could not read or write. Few black people he had known could. Those few had usually made him uneasy. Intentionally or not, they seemed always a little superior, the way house help had always looked down on the field hands. He had tolerated his subordinate position to white people because he had been born into the custom. Acceptance had been drilled into him from as early as he could remember by both whites and blacks, with words and looks, with a cane, a few times with a whip. He did not like it, and occasionally he had flared up against it at considerable pain to himself. But usually he had stood it as he stood bad weather and mud, bad water and bad food. It was life. A man came to terms with it.

But he did not appreciate other black people making him feel inferior to *them*. He had always resented and resisted.

The situation came to a head at the pay table. The men just in from the scout lined up for their pay, signing a receipt as the adjutant counted out greenbacks and coin. Like the other soldiers, Gideon scratched an X.

Sergeant Nettles stood beside the table to keep order. He had only to be there, his frown, his brittle and wicked eyes silently putting every man in his proper place. He had not spoken a word to the other men, but he spoke to Gideon. His voice cut like his eyes. "Ledbetter, is that the best you can do?"

Gideon stammered in confusion. He had stood quietly in line. He had not made any commotion or crowded anybody. Big Dempsey had done both, but Nettles had said nothing. He had only given the trooper a cold stare that would wither a cactus in full bloom, and Dempsey had gone on his best behavior. Gideon's resentment began to stir. Why was it that no matter who aroused his displeasure, Nettles always seemed to light on Gideon alone?

Nettles jerked his head in summons and walked to one side, out of earshot. He turned, his eyes cutting like black steel. "You enjoy bein' backward, Ledbetter? You want to be just another ignorant nigger the rest of your life?"

Anger leaped into Gideon's face. He had to clench his teeth to keep from answering Nettles in kind. To him, *ignorant* meant stupid. He knew he was not stupid.

Nettles demanded, "Ain't you ashamed to sign your name with an X?"

Gideon hadn't thought about it one way or the other. "Everybody does."

"*I* don't. White soldiers don't, most of them. Ain't you as good as a white soldier?"

Gideon hadn't thought much about that either. "White folks don't think so."

"I ain't askin' white folks. I'm askin' *you*. You tellin' me you ain't as good as a white soldier?"

Gideon's face was hot. *How come he always picks on me?* "I ain't sayin' that."

"Then you're sayin' you *are* as good as a white soldier."

Gideon looked around quickly to see if any officers could hear. They wouldn't like the tone of this. "I am."

"You ain't if you can't read and write your own name."

Gideon looked at the other men waiting in line. They couldn't do it either. Why didn't Nettles jump on *them?* "Nobody ever taught me how."

"If a man wants to learn bad enough, he can teach hisself."

The longer Gideon considered that, the less sense it made. "How can a man teach hisself somethin' he don't know in the first place?"

"A man with gumption can do anything he sets his mind to. You want to learn, Ledbetter?" It was less question than challenge.

The way it was put to him, Gideon's pride would not let him back away. In anger his voice rose almost to a shout. "Yes!" Almost immediately, he sensed that Nettles had baited him into a trap.

A half grin fleeted across the sergeant's leathered face, then was gone as quickly. "Remember, you volunteered. I believe you're acquainted with Chaplain Badger?"

Every Sunday that Gideon had been on the post and had not been standing duty he had attended Badger's services. Faith had been drummed into him from as far back as he could remember, by his mother, by Big Ella, even by Old Colonel. Slave owners by and large had always encouraged religious teaching among their chattels, especially those parts that dwelt upon obedience.

Nettles said, "Chaplain Badger gives classes of a night. I been goin'. If you got any pride in yourself, you'll go, too."

Gideon frowned, looking back at the pay line. "Tonight?"

"Tomorrow night. Brother Badger is a servant of the Lord, but tonight's the devil's night to preach." He stared morosely at the pay table.

Already paid, Jimbo waited uneasily for Gideon. He pointed his chin toward Nettles. "You been up to somethin' I don't know about?"

Gideon shook his head. "He wants me to go to Chaplain Badger's night-learnin'. Wants to learn me to read and write."

"What for? You ain't got nobody to write to."

"I don't want to do it by myself. I wisht you'd go with me, Jimbo."

Jimbo jingled his newly acquired wealth in his pocket. "To-night?"

"Tomorrow. Ain't goin' to be much learned tonight."

Jimbo smiled. His eyes sparkled with mischief. "Tell you what: you go with me to the learnin' across the river tonight, and I'll go with you to the Bible learnin' tomorrow."

From where he stood, Gideon could see part of the sprawling line of buildings that made up the principal business district along Concho Avenue, parallel to the river. From this side the view was of back doors and fluttering clotheslines, of outhouses, of trash heaps that strung themselves halfway down the river-bank. Saint Angela had not yet felt the stirrings of civic pride that insisted on hiding the unsightly. That would come later with the "better sort" of people. As yet, the town existed principally upon the spillage of the fort, and what did illiterate black soldiers know of civic pride, or of pride in *any* form? Folks said Saint Angela was good enough for who it was for.

"All right," Gideon conceded, "but I ain't takin' more than three-four dollars with me. When that's gone I'm comin' back."

"Three-four dollars will be like water spilt on a hot stove."

"Then I'll get to bed early."

Not since last payday had he mustered the nerve to go back to Old Woman York's on laundry row. From the stables and corrals he had occasionally caught a distant glimpse of Hannah

York bending over the washtubs or struggling stoop-shouldered with buckets of water on their way to the blackened pot or from it. Invariably her granny would be nearby, like some shriveled old witch stirring her caldron. Occasionally Gideon saw the girl at or near the colonel's house, but there, too, she was out of bounds. A common soldier did not tread in the vicinity of the officers' houses unless on business that would stand close inquiry. The married officers had a constant dread of black violation against their womenfolk, a conviction that the animal drive was strong among Negro troops, that none could be trusted where white women were concerned.

Carrying his dirty clothing rolled and tied by shirtsleeves, Gideon at last had a legitimate excuse and the money to back his claim. He suspected the old woman would compromise her suspicions in the interest of coin, if the white people across the river could compromise their racial feelings in the same cause.

The girl saw him before her granny did. She paused a moment from scrubbing clothes against a washboard. Her even white teeth were shining in a broad smile, and the sight lighted a glow to warm him like a bright lantern in a dark night. The officers could keep their pale, washed-out, blue-eyed wives. This girl was —hands down—the prettiest feature Fort Concho could offer.

When the old woman stopped rubbing clothes and looked up from a steaming tub, Hannah York quickly turned her face away so her granny could not see her. Gideon's long shadow fell across the old woman's tub. She brought herself slowly around, squinting painfully into the sinking sun. He guessed the years had not been kind to her wicked little eyes.

"Who you be?" she demanded sharply.

"Name's Ledbetter," he said. "You done clothes for me once."

She jerked her head irritably. "Git yourself over thisaway to where I can see your face without the sun in my eyes. I can't hear a thing you say."

He realized she "heard" him mostly by watching his lips. He moved partway around the tub and repeated what he had said. His position let him appear to look at her while he looked over her shoulder at the girl.

Hannah had not resumed her scrubbing. "How you been, Gideon?"

He was momentarily surprised that she remembered his name. It had been a long while. "Just fine. How you been?"

She shook her head. "Don't answer me back whilst she's lookin' at you. She can't hear it thunder, but she can tell what you say long's she can see your mouth."

The old woman said, in response to the question she took to have been directed toward her, "I got the miseries some, but they ain't fixin' to put me under the ground yet." Her eyes were suspicious; she knew perfectly well that Gideon didn't give a damn how she felt.

Hannah said, "I was about decided you wasn't comin' no more. I figured Granny put a spell on you."

Gideon contrived to turn around as if looking for the proper place to put his bundle down. The old woman could not see his lips. "I been wantin' to come see you. They been keepin' me busy."

"I know. I seen you go out one day with a bunch after the Indians. I heard later a couple of men got theirselves killed. I was scared to death it was you, till I seen you over to the horse pens. I wisht you'd of told me you was all right."

"I didn't have no idee you was worried."

"Well, I was."

Gideon's face warmed.

The old woman poked at his arm. He drew instinctively away from her touch. She said sharply, "I told you to look at me."

"I forgot. Where you want me to put these clothes at?"

She pointed her thin, crooked finger at a crude wooden bench put together of warping pecan lumber, pegs and rawhide strips. "Yonder."

He took advantage of the chance to turn away from her again. "I'd like to come see you sometime. Without your old granny around."

"I wisht you could. But I told you, she don't allow none of that."

"She goes to sleep of a night, don't she? If she's all that deef, I could come up and whistle. She wouldn't hear you slip out of the house."

"If she was to find out, she'd take a whip to me."

"She ain't goin' to find out—not if we're careful. I'll come tonight."

Hannah was a minute in answering. "Granny's got company comin'."

"Company don't stay all night, does it?"

"Not tonight, Gideon. Please."

He had gotten farther with her than he had expected, yet he felt a keen disappointment at being put off even for a night. He turned, prepared to press his case, and looked straight into the malevolent face of the old woman.

She shook her finger at him. "You tryin' to talk to my gal. Don't you lie to me; I can smell a lyin' soldier as far as I can see him. I don't allow no nigger trash messin' around with my gal, you hear me? Now you git yourself away from here, and you stay away when you ain't got no business." She started mumbling, more to herself than to him. "I'm goin' to git me a dog, a real mean dog."

Gideon maneuvered into the setting sun. "You be listenin', Hannah. I'll come whistlin' for you."

He left there humming to himself. If that old woman had it in her head that she was going to keep him away from Hannah, she was way off in her thinking.

Among the many things the army had not gotten around to building at Fort Concho was any proper sort of bathhouse for the troops. At dark, Gideon and Jimbo and several others headed for a spot just downriver from the town and splashed around in the Concho to wash off the dirt and the sweat and whatever else had accumulated on the scouting trip. A few people in town had complained about this practice and the contamination of the river. The commanding officer had always promised to take the matter under advisement, suggesting the townspeople might help by petitioning their Congressman for an appropriation to build a bathhouse. The complaints about contamination from the soldiers had been generally laughed at by the men of the fort, white as well as black. Most of the people in town got their drinking water hauled to them in barrels by a Mexican who had two mules and a two-wheeled cart. Many a time he had been observed with his cart out in the river. He would be filling barrels while his mules stretched themselves and emptied their kidneys into the current.

That, some of the soldiers had suggested, was probably what gave Saint Angela whisky its peculiar kick. It was also why soldiers didn't drink water while they were in town. One reason, anyway.

Jimbo had always been proud of his uniform. Even at its dustiest and most abused, and even when a harsh summer sun made it unbearably hot, it was brighter and smarter than the tattered rags he had worn most of his life around Old Colonel's stable. Mirrors were few at the fort, but Gideon noticed that Jimbo seldom missed an opportunity to pass by one and smile at the image that smiled back at him. Those few times Jimbo had a chance to take himself a night in town, he went shining. Every button was buttoned, every wrinkle flattened the best he could make it.

Jimbo critically pointed out to Gideon, "You got a little spot of grease on your britches, down at the knee."

Gideon had little of Jimbo's deep attachment to the uniform. "They ain't goin' to be put out over no spot of grease. They just goin' to want to know what's in the pockets."

"What is?"

"Three dollars, like I said. When it's spent, I'm comin' back."

He resented spending even that much. He had rather leave it rolled up with most of the rest in a pair of socks at the bottom of his footlocker. Someday, when that sock was good and full, he was going to buy something for his own. A piece of land, or a store, or maybe a shop of some kind. He wouldn't always be a soldier.

Jimbo dusted his uniform once more. Big Dempsey said sourly, "Don't matter what you look like, Jimbo. Long's you got money, you're a customer. When you're broke, you're just a nigger again."

Because the rest of the garrison had been paid while Hollander's company had been out on scout, and their wages were spent, the town was not crowded. That meant most of Saint

Angela's attentions were focused on a relatively few soldiers, hardly an unmixed blessing. It meant the vendors of whisky and other wares could devote more time and surface-smiling assistance to each individual in helping relieve him of his earnings rather than run everybody through en masse like cattle at the slaughter. On the other hand it gave Gideon less chance to melt into an anonymous crowd and enjoy the jollified atmosphere without investing much in it.

Small as it was, that town frightened him more than the half-explored Indian lands that stretched almost to infinity beyond it. He had tasted that land now. For all its strangeness, its continuous threat of disaster, it produced a stimulation he had never known before. Out there he seemed set free from the constraints of his blackness. The land made equal demands upon all men and neither gave credit nor demanded extra for their color.

In Saint Angela he was aware every minute of being black, tolerated only for the money in his pockets. Even when mouths smiled, the eyes showed hate.

He drank beer. It was milder than the liquefied fire the other men favored. It went down slower and cheaper. The religious side of him suspected it was just as wicked.

He followed along with Jimbo and Dempsey and the rest as they roamed up one side of Concho Avenue and down the other, looking into each place that offered refreshment and entertainment. Some of the men who had been on post longest offered advice about the places which watered their whisky or were careless in counting change. They had advice about the ones where the women were likely to give the men a little something extra to take home—something they hadn't counted on and didn't want. Gideon had always found Jimbo rash about matters of this kind, and he marked it to his credit that Jimbo seemed willing to listen to good advice. Sometimes.

As the evening wore on the newly paid men were liberally scattered up and down the street. Gideon found himself sitting in an adobe-walled gin dispensary with Jimbo, Dempsey and three others, listening to a one-legged old black fiddler make tunes of indifferent quality but commendable energy. Dempsey seemed to know a lot about the pegleg. It always surprised

Gideon how much Dempsey knew about everybody, and most of it bad. Dempsey said this old man didn't even have a shack to live in. He slept in a crude picket lean-to behind the saloon. He scratched out a living by such menial chores as toting slops down to the riverbank and spilling them over the edge. At night he fiddled for whatever small coin the customers might see fit to give him.

Gideon observed, "He'd of been better off to've stayed a slave. Least he had a roof, and some proper vittles."

Dempsey turned on him furiously. "He's free."

"Free to starve to death, looks to me like, or die of the ague from sleepin' in the rain."

Dempsey looked eight feet tall as he leaned across the table, his eyes crackling. "For a growed man, Gideon Ledbetter, sometimes you don't understand a damn thing!"

Gideon settled back in his chair, smarting a little. Excepting, perhaps, Esau Nettles, Big Dempsey was the most difficult man he had ever tried to get along with. Gideon looked away from Dempsey and concentrated on the proprietor as he slowly sipped his beer. He tried to decide what breed the man belonged to. He had the voice and manner of the Southern white trash from back on the delta, but there was a darkness to his face that seemed neither Negro nor Mexican. Gideon supposed the man enjoyed the privileges accorded to a white in this part of the country, yet he seemed not altogether white. By the general slovenly look of him he probably could never make much of a soldier, and it was evident he was no kind of a Christian. Yet, by his manner of addressing and looking at them, he left no doubt that he considered himself superior to the black soldiers whose spending he depended upon.

Gideon shrugged. That was the way things were, and if anybody was to lose sleep over it tonight, he would let Big Dempsey be the one.

There had been one girl in the place when the soldiers first came in. The proprietor whispered in her ear, and she left. In a while she was back with enough other girls to go around, one to each man. Gideon could easily see that this meant twice as many drinks sold in the same amount of time, and the girls weren't paying for any of them.

The "girls" of the town were mostly Mexican, a few Negro. Gideon had been told that most white women who had formerly plied the street had drifted out of Saint Angela when the garrison's makeup shifted to predominantly black. The few who remained kept their respectability by doing business only with the white men such as the stonemasons, the teamsters, the hunters, the post's officers. Most of these women looked as if they could give a man more problems in three minutes than he could cure in three years. Gideon had known little of such things on the plantation, but a military barracks taught lessons on some subjects that Chaplain Badger's classes never touched upon.

One of the newly arrived girls was black. Gideon was tempted momentarily, but Big Dempsey grabbed her. In a minute, a little Mexican girl, somewhat plump, seated herself unceremoniously on Gideon's lap. Feeling foolish, he bought her a drink. She didn't order cheap beer like his; she took whisky. Her English was broken, so he didn't understand all she said, but her busy, roving hands spoke a universal language.

Dempsey soon left with his girl. Jimbo was dancing with a tall, lithe Mexican woman to the scratchy tune of the pegleg's fiddle. Gideon was so caught up in what his plump girl's hands were doing that he didn't notice when Jimbo and his companion slipped out the door.

Gideon's blood raced, his face warm. He felt himself trapped in a situation he had not intended, though it was becoming frighteningly pleasurable. If he didn't bring it to an end quickly he was going to be embarrassed right here in public. He was torn between sitting passively and running like a thief.

He was not a complete novice. He had been attracted to girls on the plantation, and from time to time they had followed their instincts. But they had always found some remote place; it had never been a public performance.

The urge to flee finally won out, not a minute too soon. He bought the girl another drink and told her to wait for him. He slipped out the back door as if going to the toilet, but when he hit the night air he kept walking until he was across the river and on the post. Looking back, he struggled between relief and frustration. He hadn't had enough money left in his pocket to have paid the girl's price.

He could hear the old Negro's fiddle, or perhaps some other, and he was tempted to go to the barracks for more money. The girl was probably still waiting for him. The coolness of the night and the passage of time subdued the urge. He adhered to his resolution to stay south of the river, though the choice was not without pain and regret. He felt a little ashamed.

The idea of returning to the barracks left him cold. Sergeant Waters would be sitting there drinking himself into solitary oblivion, wrestling with his own private demons to the tune of his resin-streaked fiddle. Gideon's thoughts turned to Hannah York, and conscience began to plague him. He was sure she would think ill of him if she knew how near he had come to sin and shame. Gradually the frustration gave way to a sense of relief that he had not betrayed her. In a little while, he found himself standing by her shack, looking at the darkened windows. He remembered her admonition not to come tonight, but he could see no harm in it now. Obviously the old woman's company had left. Granny York was probably asleep.

Temptation found little resistance. He whistled softly by one of the windows. The old woman could not hear it. He waited a little, then whistled again and stepped closer, listening intently. The house was still quiet. He tried a third time and spoke her name. "Hannah. Hannah?"

Disappointed, he finally gave up. If he called any louder, he would wake up half of the post. He walked away from the shack, moving back down toward the river to sit awhile on the bank and listen to the voices whispering in the water. He walked slowly, aimlessly across the top of the high, rough bank, looking down at the river ashine in the moonlight. It was no longer mysterious to him, for he had seen its headwaters and the land across which it meandered on its way to this place. From here on, flowing eastward, it moved into relatively safe and civilized country, cutting through the pitted prairie-dog towns of the Lipan Flat, on past the old Indian painted rocks and finally to a great junction point Gideon had not yet seen, where it joined its waters with those of the Colorado. People lived out there. Not soldiers, but *real* people who had houses and fields and cattle, people made secure by the presence of this fort and the soldiers here. Perhaps someday, when he had saved enough, he might buy a farm there and break out his own field and build his own house. It wouldn't be anything grand, like Old Colonel's, but it would be better than the shack Gideon and Jimbo had shared so long. It would be better than the shack where Hannah lived with the granny woman. If he managed to please the Lord, perhaps Hannah would share that house with him.

He heard splashing. He thought at first it was the river beating against some rocks. Stopping out of curiosity, he could see someone standing waist deep, bathing. Moonlight shone on a woman's breasts.

Embarrassed, he knew he should leave quietly. But the same urges which had kept him in the saloon quickly overrode his resolve. He knelt so he would not be conspicuous. At the distance he did not know if she was black, brown or white. It made no difference. She was slender and female and a beautiful sight to behold. He watched while she rubbed soap over her body, then dipped under to rinse it off. She lingered, which suited him well, for he was in no hurry to go back to the barracks. The longer he watched her, the more his mind turned back to the girl in the saloon and to wondering if he had done the smart thing in leaving.

After a time, she came up out of the water. Gideon saw a towel at the edge and a dress spread on a large rock a little farther up the bank. As she dried herself, she moved toward the dress. The moonlight touched her face, and Gideon knew her.

Without intending to, he spoke aloud. "Hannah!"

She gave a small cry and covered herself quickly with the dress. "Who is that?" she demanded in a frightened voice.

"It's Gideon. I didn't go to scare you."

She was a moment in saying anything. Once the fright had passed, she said, "Gideon, you oughtn't to be here."

"I didn't know you was down there."

"You turn your back till I put my dress on."

It was a needless gesture. He had seen about all there was. He said, "I'm comin' down."

"You oughtn't to."

He found no real resolve in her tone. He picked his way down the bank and stood before her in the moonlight, a few feet from the water. Buttoning the dress, she asked suspiciously, "You follow me from the house, Gideon?"

"No. I didn't know you was here."

"Then how come you on the river?"

"Just walkin', thinkin'. I taken a bath myself along here a few hours ago. It's a good place for it."

She seemed to want to believe him. She said, "I come down here sometimes late of a night, when there's nobody around. Bath feels awful good sometimes. Seems to wash away more than just the dirt."

They stood in uneasy silence, and again her suspicions came to the surface. "You was watchin' me from up there."

"I didn't know it was you."

"You always go around lookin' at naked women?"

He had seldom had the opportunity, but he knew better than to say that. "I was brought up Christian."

"Lots of people is brought up Christian, but it don't take much to turn their head."

"If I'd known it was you, I wouldn't of looked."

"But if it was somebody else, you would."

She had trapped him, and his face warmed. She touched his hand. "It's all right, Gideon. You're a man. Men can't help bein' turned thataway. It's in their nature."

"How would you know? You're too young."

"Granny. That's why she don't let me have nothin' to do with no soldiers. She says they all got the animal in them."

"You think I got an animal in me?"

She shrugged. "You're a man. You *did* watch me from up yonder." Her suspicion was still not satisfied. "You sure you didn't follow me?"

"I didn't. I went by your house. I whistled for you and called you, real quiet. I figured you was asleep and didn't hear me."

"You better not do that no more, Gideon. You'll get me in trouble."

"Old woman can't hear. She don't ever have to know."

"It ain't just her. It's others."

"What others?"

"Well, like Miz Colonel. She ever gets a notion I'm messin' around with a soldier, she won't let me work in her house no more. She might even tell Mr. Colonel to kick me and my granny off of this post."

"Ain't nothin' wrong with a man and a woman seein' each other."

"They is around here."

She still had his left hand. He touched his right hand gently to her cheek. "Hannah, I don't understand this. Old Colonel back at the plantation, he was religious, too, but he didn't raise no fuss over a man and a woman seein' one another. He always said they's things in nature that people can't stop and oughtn't to try. I want to see you, Hannah. I want to see you all the time." He didn't understand his feelings, for he had never had any just like this before. He wanted to cry but didn't know the reason for it.

She laid her head against his chest. "I want to see you, too. But it ain't that easy here. We got to be careful."

He could feel the warmth of her body through the thin cotton dress. He drew her firmly against him. She did not resist. He moved his right hand from her cheek down to her chin, raised it and kissed her lips. They were warm and soft and sweet to the taste. A sudden intoxication raced to Gideon's head. He half-crushed her while he kissed her hungrily again. She seemed momentarily surprised, but then she responded. Her hands pressed against his back, and her legs pushed against his.

There was no asking, no telling. It seemed as natural as breathing for him to sweep her into his arms and carry her to a grassy place beneath the steep bank and lie down with her. He crushed her again and felt the heat in her face like that in his own. Her whole body trembled.

"Gideon," she whispered, one arm around his neck, the other pressing insistently against his back.

He raised up on one elbow to look down at her. "What?"

"Nothin'. Just . . . Gideon."

They lay locked together a long time. Finally, both naked, they splashed into the river and washed one another, laughing and giggling like schoolchildren. They dried and dressed and started back to the post, arms around each other's waists. They walked slowly, wanting to make it last.

From across the river came the sound of a fiddle and an old tune from years ago. He reached back into memory, and the words came. He sang them softly.

> The years creep slowly by, Lorena,
>   The snow is on the grass again.
> The sun so down the sky, Lorena,
>   The frost is where the flowers have been.

Not far from the old granny woman's shack they pulled into the black shadow of a corral and clung awhile. Reluctantly he let her go. She held to his hand until their arms were stretched. She squeezed his fingers. "I want to see you again, Gideon."

"I'll be walkin' by the river real often from now on."

He watched until she was gone from sight, and a little longer. Body tired, but heart singing like that distant fiddle, he walked to the barracks. He stumbled over a boot someone had left in the aisle.

Jimbo raised up in his bunk. "That you, Gid?"

Gideon blinked in surprise to find Jimbo and the others in bed ahead of him. "What you-all doin' back so early?"

"It ain't early. It's up into the mornin'. Where'd you run off to, Gid? You missed a lot of fun."

Gideon smiled, though Jimbo couldn't see it in the darkness. "I didn't miss nothin'."

Eight

In FRONTIER ARMY posts, the chaplain had an extra duty beyond that normally levied by God and the military. He was expected to minister to men's minds as well as their souls, especially in black units where illiteracy ran near a hundred per cent among the enlisted men because of their previous condition of servitude. It was the chaplain's duty to teach reading and writing to men who had never encountered these skills or had brushed against them too lightly to have been scratched. This was not pure altruism on the army's part. Though much was said and written about the government's desire to elevate the Negro's position in society, the practical purpose of this coaching was to produce men capable of handling at least some of the endless clerical work and writing of reports in duplicate, triplicate and quadruplicate that sometimes made the suffering of a long scouting expedition far preferable to garrison duty for field-grade officers.

On Sundays, Norman Badger's wind-whipped chapel tent near the hospital served as a church for all the garrison, black and white, and for the minority of Saint Angela's civilian population who were inclined toward religion. On weekdays it was a schoolhouse for children of the white officers. It was the position of the army—and of most army wives—that living in an outpost of civilization made study of that civilization particularly imperative.

On as many weeknights as garrison routine made possible, the chapel tent became what some on the post euphemistically called the Concho Academy, teaching black troopers how to read and write their names and, if they stayed hitched long enough, how to handle more advanced material.

Gideon found a certain fascination in schooling. It had long been a source of wonder to him that one man could make what appeared to be hen-scratching, and another man could glance at it and know what he said. The concept had seemed somehow akin to the dark magic that a few black people still attempted to practice as a heritage from forgotten ancestors across the big waters. But when the chaplain printed Gideon's name on a slate and told him that was the way it had always looked and would always look, and pointed it out to him on a page in his thick black Bible, Gideon had enthusiastically committed himself to learning.

The chaplain slapped his hand on the black cover of the Book. "You keep studying, Gideon. Apply to learning the same vigor that your biblical namesake applied to war, and you'll someday be able to read this good book yourself from one cover to the other."

Gideon allowed that it was a mighty big book, and he was getting a late start.

The chaplain smiled. "There are children on this post who can sit down with this book and read page after page."

Gideon reflected on two or three who surely *needed* to. Captain Newton, for example, had a couple of boys who were an unholy terror to other children, to the post dogs, and to most of the black troopers, who feared to take any reprisal. Gideon had it in mind that once he was able he might volunteer to read them a little Scripture. Especially if he ever caught them again working cockleburs into his brown horse's tail.

It was several weeks before Gideon was sent off the post on another detail. This gave him ample time to attend classes at night, which was to his liking, though Jimbo had given up after a week. It also gave Gideon a chance, after class, to slip away in the darkness to old Granny York's house. Now and again he would find the shriveled little woman sitting out in front, her corncob pipe glowing in the dark like one eye of the devil. Nights like that were a sharp disappointment. Though he went around by a side window and whistled softly, Hannah never came out. Other nights he would whistle and hear a soft answer from inside, telling him to wait a little. Presently, when the old woman was snoring, Hannah would come out and hurry away into the night with Gideon.

He had had feelings from time to time before about one girl or another, but never had one fired his soul like Hannah. Always before, the fire had flared briefly, then burned itself out. With Hannah the flame seemed to build higher. The wanting was never satisfied. It was always there.

Days, he drilled and curried horses. He quarried stone from Ben Ficklin crossing or mixed mortar or dug ditches and pits. These were physical things that called only upon his body, leaving his mind free to be with Hannah, to walk with her by the river, to swim with her, to lie with her in the darkness. He planned their future together and tried to figure, though he was vague at ciphering, how long he would have to save to buy them a farm. Hannah had told him that was her dream, to have a little farm where they could live alone and never worry about pleasing anyone, white or black, except each other.

The air was sharp with the breath of coming winter the night he found her waiting outside without his having to whistle. She had a towel in her hand. When he touched her, she seemed to draw away.

"Let's go to the river," she said tightly. "I need a bath real bad."

"It's cold to be swimmin'. You'll take yourself a chill."

"That's better'n feelin' dirty like I do."

"You been workin' too hard."

"I don't know no way I can stop it."

He found a touch of bitterness in her voice that he had not heard before. He put his arm around her and felt her flinch again, drawing herself in. Angrily he decided she had quarreled with that old granny. The witch had caned her, more than likely. It had happened before, leaving Hannah bruised and hurting.

He said sharply, "Someday I'll take a stick to that old woman."

"Wouldn't do no good. I'd still belong to her."

"Nobody belongs to nobody anymore."

"I belong to *her*."

"If you got to belong to somebody, belong to *me*. We could get married."

Hannah missed a stride. Gideon stopped, turning back to face her. For a moment, she stared at him in hope, but the bitterness held on. "You just don't understand. I still got to do what she tells me to."

Gideon chewed his lip as they walked to the river. He thought about taking off his clothes and going in with her, but the raw wind changed his mind. He stood on the bank and held the towel and watched her walk hesitantly into that cold water. She used the soap and washed quickly and hurried back to the bank, shivering as he wrapped the towel around her. He held her against his body to give her warmth.

She also gave him warmth, and his hands began to move. She caught them with cold fingers. "Just hold me, Gideon. That's all I want."

She shivered against him, and he sensed that it was not all because of the wind.

"Have patience, Hannah. From now on I ain't spendin' a dollar. We'll have us that farm before long. You'll see."

"Takes a bunch of money to get a farm."

"We'll have it."

"Takes more than money. Takes a lot of knowin', too."

"I already know about farmin'. I done it all my life. And lately I been learnin' other things. Looky here." He knelt and traced six block letters in the sand. "You know what that is?"

"Just scratchin', is all I can see."

"Them letters say *Gideon*."

She was dubious. "How do you know?"

"Chaplain Badger told me. He's a Bible man."

"Maybe he's just puttin' a bunch of foolishness in your head. White men, they tell you anything to get what they want."

"Chaplain's a good man. He wouldn't lie. Lyin's a sin, and he's hard set against sin."

"They all against sin except when *they* want to do it. Then they just call it somethin' else."

He frowned. He had never seen her so resentful. "What's got into you, Hannah?"

"You're just so trustin'. White man tells you somethin', you take it for the truth. They ain't none of them you can believe."

"There's a-plenty good white folks, Hannah. You just got to know them, is all. There's men like Colonel Thomas. And Lieutenant Hollander—he's good to the men."

She said tightly, "His clothes ain't no cleaner than the rest of them." She doubled her fist. "Wait till somethin' don't suit him—then you'll see what the other side of his face looks like. This is their world. We're just here to do what suits them, and nothin' else."

She pulled out of his arms, unwrapped the towel and put on the freshly washed clothes she had brought. "We better get back. It's cold out here."

It was, Gideon thought, in more ways than one. He walked with his arm around her waist, but she did not cling to him. Even as they moved side by side, she seemed to be putting distance between them. He sensed that the underlying cause was not of his doing, and he felt a momentary resentment for being the victim of it.

His silent message seemed to reach her. As they paused in the shadow of the corral, where they usually took their goodnights, she turned into his arms. "I didn't go to take everything out on you, Gideon. You ain't done nothin'. You just wait a couple nights before you come back to see me. Everything'll be all right by then."

"Couple nights can be an awful long time."

"A little waitin' makes things better when they *do* come. Everything'll be back like it's supposed to be for us." She kissed him and hurried into the moonlight.

He watched until she was out of sight and listened to be sure the old woman didn't awaken and raise a ruckus, though he didn't know what he could do about it if she did. He started toward the barracks, head down, his mind awhirl with confusion. He had never imagined things could turn so contrariwise with a woman.

A voice from behind startled him so that he jumped. "Wait up."

Gideon turned quickly. Sergeant Nettles walked slowly toward him from the corrals, taking his time as if to make clear that he was in charge.

Gideon blurted defensively, "I ain't done nothin'."

"That's all in the way you look at it." Nettles jerked his head, beckoning. He walked to a fence and squatted with his back braced against it. He motioned for Gideon to sit down beside him. Gideon complied hesitantly. He had never gotten closer to Nettles than duty demanded and had kept as much distance as circumstances allowed.

Nettles let Gideon stew awhile in apprehension. When he finally spoke, his voice was quiet. "Been awhile since the bugler blowed taps."

"I heard it."

"Taps means you supposed to be in bed, restin' for another long day."

"I was to the chaplain's, learnin'." It was a thin excuse, and futile, for Nettles had been in the same class. Where Gideon was still learning his letters and reading a few small, easy words, Nettles was already working out of a blueback speller.

The sergeant said, "That was over with a long time ago."

"I just taken me a little air before bedtime, is all."

"Air's kind of fresh down on the river."

Gideon's face warmed as he realized the sergeant had followed him. Apprehension clutched him. It would be in Nettles' power to send him away from Hannah, or even to send Hannah away from this place. He found himself fearing this man, and hating him because of the fear. "Sergeant, is it against the rules for me to see a girl? Most everybody does it sometimes."

"The others, they get theirs across the river."

"She's a good girl. I don't want you gittin' no wrong notions."

"I expect she's good, all right."

"She ain't like them over yonder. Reason we got to sneak around is the old woman. We have to wait till she goes to sleep of a night before Hannah can come out to see me."

"How much money that gal got off of you?"

"No money. It ain't thataway atall. I'm savin' up my money so's we can get married."

The sergeant looked surprised. "Married?" He fell silent, twisting one rough hand over the other. "Back home, didn't you ever think you was in love and find out you wasn't?"

"It wasn't like this."

"There's more to marryin' than just layin' a girl down in a cotton patch, or on a riverbank. Things turn out different than you figure. Women ain't always what you thought they was, when the blood cools down." His hard gaze was fixed on Gideon. "Bet you lived in one place all your life."

"Since I was a little boy."

"Bet you never seen the outside world . . . towns, and like that?"

"I seen our town, lots of times."

"But it wasn't no Saint Angela. Bet you didn't know there was places where they sell women the way they sell whisky."

"Hannah ain't one of them. I'm goin' to marry her."

Nettles swept his hand in a small arc, pointing in the general direction of the barracks. "They ain't but few married soldiers here, exceptin' the officers. You ever ask yourself how come? They just ain't no proper home for a soldier's family. They ain't enough pay without the wife takes in washin' and God knows what else. Most of the washerwomen here is soldiers' wives, tryin' to keep theirselves and a bunch of runny-nosed kids from starvin' to death. They's some that'll sell theirselves for the price of flour and salt pork, and their husbands pretend like they don't know it. Is that what you want?"

"I ain't always goin' to be a soldier. I'm goin' to have a farm for me and Hannah."

"You put your mark on the enlistment paper. You got to stay four years. Run off and they'll ride you down like a strayed mule. You want that?"

"Four years ain't forever."

"It can feel like forever." The sergeant twisted his hands some more. "Ledbetter, you got the makin's of a good soldier in you—maybe the best soldier in this company. You'll make corporal someday, maybe even sergeant. I don't want to see you throw all that away."

Gideon blinked in surprise. "Everything I ever done, you jumped on me. You've rode me like a mule, harder than anybody in the outfit."

"A good soldier has got to take punishment without it cavin' him in. I've tried to see how much you could take. You got it in you to be as good a soldier as there is in this army, black or white."

"I got it in me to be a good farmer, too."

"That all the ambition you got, to be a farmer? There's farmers everywhere, but there ain't that many good soldiers. Not good *black* soldiers."

"Black . . . white . . . what difference does it make?"

"Plenty. You think we're free just because Mr. Lincoln said so? Go ahead, save up your money and try to buy yourself a farm amongst the white folks. You'll find out how free a black man really is. Like as not, they won't let you buy it in the first place. Even if you buy it, they'll squeeze you out or burn you out. If that don't work, it ain't no big thing to kill a nigger; it's not much more than shootin' a stray dog. You ain't free if they don't want you. And they sure as hell don't want you.

"They didn't want us in the army, neither. You got no idee how much hell was raised when they started to put the Ninth and Tenth Cavalry together, or the two black infantry regiments. A lot of them fine Yankee officers that talked about how they freed us from bein' slaves, they talked out of the other side of their face when somebody wanted to make us soldiers and put us amongst them. They're still fightin' us. They want us to fail, Ledbetter. That's why I don't let no man shirk his duty or do less than I know is in him. This company ain't goin' to fail; I ain't lettin' it. And I ain't lettin' no good soldiers get away. Includin' you."

Nine

GRAY HORSE AWAKENED suddenly from an uneasy dream about the buffalo. He had seen a broad valley covered by bare white bones, and a gaunt reddish buffalo calf staggering in the midst of them, bawling weakly.

Blinking, he saw a show of color through the open end of the small hunting tent which Green Willow had set up for the two of them last night. His pony stirred on its tether, but the camp was not yet awake. Gray Horse leaned on his elbow and looked down into the peaceful face of his wife, her head resting on a pillow of hair-stuffed rabbit skins.

His thoughts were drawn back to the dream, and he wondered if that was all it had been. Sometimes it was difficult to know a true vision from a simple dream. This one had lacked the clarity and strength of a vision, he thought. Moreover, it was a preposterous dream, for in it all the buffalo were dead except the calf— all the buffalo in the world, it had seemed. He was sure no force except the spirits themselves could ever destroy all the buffalo. The People never killed more than they needed, nor did the lesser tribes which shared their hunting range by consent or stealth. Sometimes the white *tejanos* sent small hunting parties onto the fringe of the range to take haunches, humps and

tongues, but the few they killed—though begrudged and prevented when possible—had never been half as many as were
taken by the hungry wolves which always trailed the drifting
herds.

Gray Horse had heard stories, drifting down from their northern allies the Cheyenne, of heavy slaughter far beyond the many
rivers by white men who took only hides and left the meat to
rot. It seemed hardly reasonable. Even the *tejanos*—the wick-
edest and most destructive of all men—had never been so waste-
ful as that. Surely there were not enough white men in the world
to equal the buffalo.

He decided the dream had come about because he had gone to
sleep worrying over the elusiveness of the buffalo. He was with
Eagle Feather and a group of hunters and their assorted working
womenfolk looking for fresh meat to serve the main camp. They
were two days west of the encampment and had not yet seen
enough buffalo to keep half the women busy skinning and cutting up meat. They had watched for the ravens to tell them
where the buffalo were. Those thoughtless birds had given them
no sign. The horned toad was well known for pointing the way
to buffalo, but so far no hunter had seen one of them, either.
Eagle Feather had talked confidently. Still, last night's hunting
dance had lacked exuberance.

The village was not in immediate danger of going hungry; it
still had dried meat from the last concerted hunt, and individual
parties continued to bring in fresh game other than buffalo. But
time had become short to put up the final dried meat and pemmican for the lean months of winter. Though the Comanches of
modern times had rarely known extended hunger, old stories
from their forefathers held up the specter of starvation in the
long-ago time when the People had lived farther north and had
not acquired the horse to help them ride down the buffalo.

Green Willow's father, Counts Many Coups, talked frequently
of it to impress his son-in-law about the necessity of diligence.
He reminded Gray Horse often that it was his duty as son-in-
law to see that his wife's parents were never wanting. It was no
more than his right to demand this, for Many Coups had been
one of the best hunters and warriors in the band before arthritis

and failing eyesight had forced him to join the elders around the council fire, talking of olden times. Gray Horse could remember his leading home many a triumphant war party, many a group of successful meat hunters. He respected him for all that but wished age had not made him quite so garrulous about the superiority of past generations.

It took little time to strike camp, for the hunters and their women had not brought tepees. For shelter they used a couple of buffalo skins thrown across a short pole supported by forked sticks. What this lacked in comfort, it made up in quick mobility. The men were soon riding in the lead. The women came along behind with the pack animals which would carry the meat and hides.

Bear That Turns to Fight pointed southward. "The buffalo are that way. I dreamed about them last night."

Eagle Feather laughed. "A dream does not mean a thing is true. I dreamed four beautiful women came to my bed. But when I woke up, there was only my wife, and she was asleep."

Gray Horse said nothing, but he thought that one woman like Eagle Feather's Antelope should be enough for any man. It was common knowledge that she loved her husband with a passion bordering on ferocity. She had even defied her father to take Eagle Feather before he had gained his reputation. Her father had chosen for her another; an older man whose honors were secure, who already had two wives to spread the workload and make life easier. Antelope had run off with Eagle Feather on the war trail to escape this unwanted marriage and had taken the scalp of a *tejano* foolish enough to lower his rifle because he saw that she was a woman. A wife with that kind of fire was highly prized even though she had borne Eagle Feather no children. Some of the older women speculated that she had tried too hard to be a man and had lost womanly attributes such as the ability to conceive. But Gray Horse had seen and heard enough pass between the couple to know she had not lost them all.

Bear kept insisting that his buffalo dream had meaning. After a time, he persuaded Eagle Feather that it might be worthwhile to turn south. Gray Horse said nothing about his own dream because it had been a bad one, and a dream told in less than four days was likely to come true. He had little faith in Bear's notion, however, and was on the verge of saying so when he saw the wolf.

It trotted onto a small knoll no more than fifty yards away. It turned to look at the horsemen, and it seemed to Gray Horse that its eyes met his. He glanced around to determine the other hunters' reactions and was surprised to find that none had even seen it.

"Look at the wolf," he said to Limping Boy. Limping Boy's gaze followed Gray Horse's pointing, but he saw nothing.

A chill ran through Gray Horse. Perhaps the wolf was invisible to all except him. Perhaps the wolf meant his message for Gray Horse alone. He watched, trembling, as the wolf looked westward, glanced back once at him, then set out in a trot toward whatever he had looked upon.

"The wolf," he said aloud. "I believe the wolf is trying to talk to us."

The other men looked, but the wolf had disappeared. Bear scoffed that Gray Horse had probably seen a jackrabbit and did not know the difference.

Gray Horse said tightly, "The rest of you follow Bear and his dream. I will follow the wolf."

"To a nest of jackrabbits," Bear grinned.

But Eagle Feather was a believer. He recognized that some spirits might speak to one man but not to another. He had his own, which he never discussed lest their power diminish, and he respected those of others. "You follow your wolf," he told Gray Horse. "Part of us will go with Bear and the rest will go that way." He pointed in a direction midway between the one chosen by Bear and the one which Gray Horse's wolf had taken. "If anyone finds the buffalo, he will build a fire and signal to the others."

Gray Horse glanced at Limping Boy, who automatically pulled over to his side. Wherever Gray Horse went, there Limping Boy would go also. It did not matter that he had not seen the wolf; if his cousin had seen it, that was enough.

Eagle Feather sent the youngest man back to tell the women to stay. If they saw a signal smoke, they were to go to it. If they did not, the hunters would all return to this place. The men split into three groups, Gray Horse's the smallest. Only Terrapin and Says Little chose to join him and Limping Boy. Most chose to follow Eagle Feather, who had neither dream nor wolf to guide him, but relied on instincts that experience had shown to be good.

Riding across the rolling prairie, Gray Horse went out of his way to climb each high point for a long look that sometimes showed him what lay miles ahead. He hoped each time to see the wolf, but he was disappointed. The wolf had delivered its message, then dropped out of sight. It might even have been a spirit wolf that simply vanished like a mirror image when the mirror is turned away. But it had pointed the direction, and that had been enough. One did not demand from a benevolent spirit but felt grateful for whatever it saw fit to give.

When Gray Horse felt hungry, he munched dried buffalo meat and drank from a deer paunch of water carried on his rawhide-covered saddle. Several times Says Little indicated his name was not well given, for he suggested they turn south and find the others. They had not seen so much as one outcast bull driven from a herd by a stronger one. Gray Horse kept on doggedly, holding his growing insecurities within himself. More than not finding buffalo, he dreaded having to listen to Bear's derision if he returned empty-handed. Granting that Bear had proven himself a warrior and hunter, there were times when a man wanted to take a club to him and mark him from shoulder to thigh. It was not simply for himself that Gray Horse dreaded criticism; he did not want Green Willow to hear it and wonder if her father's misgivings might have been properly placed. Old Many Coups set high standards. He was certain that the People's hunting and fighting ability had peaked with his own generation and had declined in recent years.

Once Gray Horse told Limping Boy defensively, "I *did* see the wolf. It looked at me and pointed the way."

"I know," Limping Boy said confidently. "They know, too." He glanced at the two riders who trailed behind them. "But they protect themselves so they can say later that they doubted you."

Once Terrapin and Says Little stopped and let the other two

move well ahead of them. When Gray Horse looked back, he could see their hands moving briskly in the sign talk that accompanied an argument. The next time he looked they were coming ahead in a long trot, catching up, still giving him the benefit of an increasing doubt.

It was Limping Boy who lifted the growing weight from Gray Horse's shoulders. He loped off to the right and ascended a knoll. As soon as he reached the top he signaled excitedly. Giving the other two men a quick over-the-shoulder glance, which told them to follow, Gray Horse set his hunting pony into a run. Before he reached Limping Boy he saw part of the sight that had aroused his cousin's enthusiasm. In a broad valley stretching beneath them, down to a brush-lined creek and far beyond, hundreds of buffalo grazed with the plains wind to their rumps, moving them gradually southward.

Limping Boy's face glowed like a warm fire on a cold night. In triumph he turned half around to face the doubting warriors as they rode up belatedly to the crest of the knoll. "When a wolf speaks to my cousin, everyone else should hush their talk and listen."

The two men gazed a moment in surprise and pleasure. Terrapin glanced southward. "I see no signal smoke anywhere. No one else has found buffalo."

Limping Boy declared, "No one else saw the wolf."

It was with difficulty that Gray Horse restrained himself from shouting. He did not want to appear to disparage any other hunter. That sort of thing he would leave to Bear.

Says Little said, "I'll build a fire so the others can see where we are."

Limping Boy objected. "No. Gray Horse led us to the buffalo. It is for him to build the fire."

Using flint and steel acquired from the Mexican Comancheros, Gray Horse kindled a small blaze and built it up with wood brought to him by the other three. A heavy gray smoke laid out almost flat and spread across the prairie under the drive of the north wind. It never occurred to him that it might be seen by Rangers or soldiers. Though they occasionally penetrated this great buffalo range, they were always transient, always strangers in an inhospitable land that rejected them quickly. This was Comanche land, and it always would be.

Gray Horse accepted compliments with grace as the other hunters gathered in reply to the signal smoke, though he smiled wickedly at Bear. Bear said he remembered seeing many larger herds of buffalo.

There were a hundred times more of them in sight than this little band of hunters could kill or the women could skin and dress. It was randomly decided that the effort should be directed against one specific bunch grazing a pocket hidden from the others by the knoll to which Limping Boy had ascended. This would avoid alarming and scattering the rest. Some of those might be needed later. As was customary among the buffalo, the bulls were at the outside of the loosely scattered herd, the cows and calves at the center. The hunters approached them from the south, downwind, the men all watching Eagle Feather for a signal. The women waited on the knoll, where they could watch the kill and come down to start their work as soon as the men were done.

Eagle Feather motioned for the men to spread in a semicircle, approaching the herd with their horses in a walk. The buffalo had weak eyesight, made poorer by a thick and curly growth of hair over its eyes. A big bull saw the riders, however, and belligerently shook its head, flinging a strand of mucus from its black nose. Eagle Feather gave a shout and charged forward. The riders at either end of the semicircle pushed their horses into a lope and rounded the herd.

Startled, the animals began to run, but the hunters forced them into a circle that made them easy game. The cows and calves were mostly in the center of the dusty maelstrom, the bulls on the outside. His blood racing, Gray Horse kneed his running pony in close to a lumbering young bull. His hunting arrows were so notched that when he fitted one to the string the head was vertical and could, if necessary, pass between the ribs of the animal. His war arrows, on the other hand, were notched to keep the arrowhead flat in its flight, to pass between the ribs of a standing man. He aimed between the hip bone and the last rib, where the arrow could pierce the vitals with the least resistance. His first arrow drove almost to the feather. Gray Horse pressed with his left knee to turn his pony quickly aside. The wounded buffalo whirled in rage and attempted to gore the pony but sank to its knees and was unable to rise. Gray Horse gave a whoop of joy at his first kill and reached back for another arrow from his quiver. When the killing was over he would be able to return and identify every animal he had brought down, either from memory, which would hold in most cases, or from his individual markings on the arrows.

His blood ran hot, his heart pounding, as the circle continued and the slaughter went on. Next to war, the hunt for buffalo was the most exciting and rewarding aspect of life. It was a mortal necessity for both body and spirit. The hide sheltered and warmed the body, while the flesh and the blood fed it. The chase fircd the spirit, giving each man a chance to test his courage and expand his soul by looking death in the face and not pulling away.

Though most of the hunters relied on bow and arrow, Eagle Feather demonstrated his daring by using a lance. That compelled him to draw in closer than the bowman. With his hunting horse almost rubbing its shoulder against the running buffalo's haunch, Eagle Feather would raise the lance high above his head and plunge it downward at an angle with all the power in his strong shoulders. The buffalo's own natural tendency to turn against its antagonist gave Eagle Feather extra leverage that drove the lance even deeper. He would then pull out the weapon and leave the animal to die while he rode on to kill another.

He had done it many times, and it was another reason he had the respect and admiration of his band. But this day his luck ran its course. As Eagle Feather made his sixth kill, his horse bumped against the buffalo and stumbled. The enraged bull turned back upon its tormenter, its sharp black horn tearing the horse's chest open. Screaming, the horse went over the buffalo's hump with both forelegs, its lifeblood gushing across that black, shaggy head. Eagle Feather clung to him, stunned by the heavy impact. The horse went down, its rider partially under him. Eagle Feather's leg snapped with the sound of a dry mesquite limb broken for a campfire. Horse and buffalo and man lay in one bloody, threshing heap.

Gray Horse was the first man there, for he had been trailing behind Eagle Feather, watching his style, hoping for his courage. The dying buffalo kept slinging its massive head, a mortal danger to anything it struck. The horse lay kicking in its death throes, its hoofs also perilous. Gray Horse grabbed Eagle Feather under the arms and tried to drag him. Eagle Feather cried out in agony from the broken leg, pinned beneath his dying mount. Limping Boy and Terrapin were there in seconds, moving quickly, warily. They worked the gasping warrior free and dragged him to safety while the bull struggled and bawled in the fury of its dying. A few hunters continued to try to hold the surround, but too many had pulled away to see about Eagle Feather. The rest of the buffalo broke free and stampeded over a rise, clattering off into a shallow ravine to be hunted another day.

Eagle Feather clenched his teeth and struggled to be the fearless warrior who knew not pain. His body felt cold, his forehead wet, his eyes glazing from shock. Gray Horse looked him over quickly and found no bleeding wounds of account, but the awkward slant of his left leg showed it was broken—probably shattered—below the knee.

If he lived, his hunting and fighting days were probably over. Gray Horse felt a welling of sympathy, as much for that as for the pain he knew the hunt leader suffered. It would be a mercy for Eagle Feather's guardian spirits to let him die now and spare him the agony of helplessness and dependence.

The women had seen the incident from their vantage point and had recognized that the hunt was over. It was customary for them to race to see which would be first to touch a buffalo. Eagle Feather's wife was far out in front, drumming her heels against the ribs of the bay mare she rode like a man, but her interest was not in the buffalo. She did not allow the mare to slow until she was almost there, then slid her to a stop and jumped off, her small moccasined feet hitting the ground running. Antelope fell to her knees by her man's side, seeing at hardly more than a glance the extent of the injuries that showed. No one could know if he was torn internally.

She allowed herself only a moment of tears, then began giving orders like a chief. Green Willow cast Gray Horse one quick look to assure herself that he was not hurt. That worry behind her, she fell in to helping Antelope prepare a travois to carry the injured man away from this unlucky place, back to the main encampment where he would have all his family around him and would receive the benefits of a shaman's healing magic.

No one had to tell Antelope, before she rode away with her half-conscious man, that all of Eagle Feather's meat and more would be delivered to his lodge. That was a matter of honor understood without being spoken. Should he live, other men would take it as an obligation to see that hunger never came to one who had so often proven himself and who in his better days had been known for his generosity to the less fortunate. Should he die, they would see that his widow had food until such time as some man saw fit to take her to wife and put her under his individual protection.

The somber mood was temporary, for the excitement of the hunt still ran high. Eagle Feather's travois was not out of sight before the women began their task of skinning. The jubilant spirit returned, and laughter drifted over the bloody field where the buffalo lay. Gray Horse and other men helped lift some of the dead bulls up onto their bellies so the women would have an easier time, but the more mundane work they left to their chattering wives and daughters.

There was an air of celebration as the first buffalo were cut open with the flint knives and those of steel traded or stolen. Gray Horse dipped his hands into the steaming innards and cut off a slice of hot, quivering liver, which he ate raw, slicing another piece for Green Willow. They stared joyously at each other while they relished this delicacy of the hunt.

Presently he rode back up onto the knoll where Limping Boy had first seen the buffalo. He took down the pad he had used for a hunting saddle and spread it on the ground. From here he could see across a broad plain more buffalo than the People would ever need. The relatively few they had killed today made no showing against the major herd.

Lighting his pipe, he blew smoke toward the sun and the earth and the four winds, giving thanks to the wolf spirit which had guided him. His soul was warm with the knowledge that his medicine was strong, that it was useful not only for him but for all of his band. That gave his life a special value which many men could never claim. He felt a twinge of sympathy as his mind went back to Eagle Feather. That accident would not be forgotten, but no one would dwell upon it in conversation or thought on this hunt. It was a price someone was expected to pay occasionally for the bounty the spirits had spread before the People in this great land. Gray Horse himself might have to pay it someday.

But not this day. This day he had been in his glory, his medicine tested, his ability as a hunter demonstrated. He had no real idea how large the world was, how far it might be to its corners. But he doubted that anywhere in it was there a man so happy, so content with the life the spirits had given him as a Comanche warrior whose woman was loving and whose medicine was strong.

He looked back down to the killing ground and watched Green Willow as she diligently went about skinning the buffalo his arrows had slain. The sight of her put fire in his blood. There would be much dancing and singing in camp tonight. He and Green Willow would celebrate, too, at the dance and afterward, in the privacy of their hunting tent.

There was not a man alive with whom he would trade places this day.

But the day was over, eventually, and the rejoicing of the night. Sometime up in the early hours before dawn he awakened, trembling, chilled. The dream had come back to him. He had seen the red calf again in the midst of the buffalo bones.

Ten

THOUGH GARRISON days were monotonous and the building work exhausting, nights made them bearable for Gideon. Hannah eased his mind as he swung pick or shovel, as he sleepwalked through rifle and saber and horseback drill. Routine left little mark on his consciousness, for the phantom Hannah lifted all burdens and softened all indignities.

But inevitably a day came when the army had business for him elsewhere. Lieutenant Hollander chose Gideon and Jimbo with Big Dempsey and garrulous, irritating little Finley as a guard detail to go north to abandoned old Fort Chadbourne. There they were to meet and relieve a similar detail accompanying the paymaster down from Forts Sill, Richardson and Griffin. While the company stood at attention, Hollander put Sergeant Nettles in charge. "Take pack mule and rations, Sergeant, because you may have to wait a day or two at Chadbourne." He spent a moment studying each of the four men, standing two steps forward of the company line. "We've had no Indian sign for some time, but don't let that lead you to complacency."

Jimbo whispered to Gideon, wondering where Complacency was, speculating that it must be somewhere past Chadbourne.

The lieutenant added, "Remember that if you don't bring the

paymaster in here safe and sound, the men on this post don't get paid. *You* don't get paid. In such a case, I had rather face the Indians than my friends."

The rest of the company was sent off to mundane duties, and Gideon stared after them, wishing he could stay, too. Being away from Hannah for three or four days took all the luster out of an assignment he would have welcomed awhile back. Jimbo discussed politics and weather with the recalcitrant mule while Gideon and Dempsey packed it. Gideon tried to see the York shack through the dust but could not.

Only after Nettles gave the order to mount could Gideon get a look at laundry row. Hannah stepped to the wash pot and poked wood into the flames beneath it. He waved, and she caught the motion. She seemed to realize he was leaving the post. Face sad, she waved back.

Lieutenant Hollander noticed the movement and half-turned, staring first at the girl, then back to Gideon. He looked surprised.

When the detail crossed the river and moved up the opposite bank into the east edge of Saint Angela, Gideon looked behind him once more. In the distance, he saw Hannah hurrying with more wood while the old granny woman gestured briskly at her. Catching hell again.

He paid little attention to the village. It was of only fleeting interest that a few more stone buildings were going up to replace the transient adobes and brush *jacales*. Saint Angela still resembled nothing so much as the scab on an old sore.

The horses settled into a steady trot on the twin-rutted Chadbourne road, angling northward and a little east to skirt the red clay and rock peaks, ancient relics of a great caprock. This was the road over which he and Jimbo had first come to the fort months ago, and for a while older memories masked those of Hannah York. He recalled the spot, more or less, where Lieutenant Hollander had shot the antelope, and he remembered the shock and pain which had dulled that experience for him. He anticipated without pleasure their arrival at the Colorado River crossing where he had had his first encounter with hostile Indians. Hannah glided gracefully through his mind, but other images intruded harshly, getting in the way. His sharp eyes caught every movement of jackrabbit or chaparral hawk, every waving of frost-bared mesquite limbs in the sudden gusts of cool wind from the south and west.

They unexpectedly encountered a small herd of buffalo, which snorted and ran away in their clumsy, rocking gait. They were drifting southward into this region as the weather turned colder. Veterans of past winters at Concho had told him they would number thousand upon thousand by Christmas.

Dempsey pointed at the buffalo. "Fresh meat for supper, Sergeant."

Nettles grunted. "We couldn't take but a little with us. Waste is as wicked as sloth."

"It *all* goes to waste if we don't take none."

"Nature don't waste. She got a use for everything."

Crossing this prairie, Gideon realized that though the buffalo were the most visible of the wild animals, they were not really dominant. In terms of total mass and weight, the lowly prairie dog was far and away the most important. Their "towns" of holes and little mounds stretched as far as Gideon could see.

He stayed watchful. It was said that the Indians were seldom bothersome once cold weather began. They seemed to hole up in their winter camps and subsist on supplies of buffalo meat they had dried and preserved during the long hunts of the fall. But Gideon kept an eye on the scattered buffalo and was mindful of the strong affinity that existed between buffalo and Indian. It seemed logical that wherever the buffalo went, there also might be the Comanche.

He and Jimbo rode side by side. Behind them the little trooper Finley kept up a one-sided conversation with a reluctant Big Dempsey. Finley had tale after tale to tell of the days before Mr. Lincoln and the tricks he had played on his old master to keep out of heavy work, the ruses he had used to steal food and whisky out of the master's big house on the hill and blame it on passing white trash and Confederate soldiers. They were the kind of stories the bitter Dempsey would have enjoyed if he could have believed there was any truth in them. But Dempsey hunched his shoulders and ignored Finley as best he could. The little man would lie to St. Peter himself in the unlikely event that he ever reached the Pearly Gates.

Nettles rode in front, by himself. Even with a company of men, he seemed alone. His eyes were on the trail ahead or on the countryside. His black Napoleon set a steady, mile-eating pace humane to the horses. Nettles expected the men to keep up without his looking back.

The noon stop was unceremonious. Nettles simply pulled off of the trail in the middle of a short-grass flat where they could see for some distance in any direction. "We'll eat," he said. He gave no time for fixing coffee. The men ate bread and cold hash left from breakfast mess and washed it down with water from their canteens. Finished, he pushed to his feet silently, got into his saddle and set out. The others hastened after him. Finley had to finish eating in the saddle because he had been chattering on while the others had wolfed down a cold and tasteless meal. Finley's horse shied as a jackrabbit darted out of the dry grass, and the little soldier dropped what was left of his lunch. That brought on the only smile Gideon had seen from Big Dempsey in a week.

Gideon vaguely recalled landmarks in the red clay land. He remembered cone-shaped Mount Margaret, which somebody said was named for the wife of a Fourth Cavalry officer who had served at Concho during the Mackenzie time. It was only a hill, but it served for a mountain where nature had neglected to provide a real one.

A chill ran down Gideon's back as a line of frost-nipped trees, all shades of brown and gold, marked the river ahead. He imagined he felt pain in his arm again. Nettles did not have to tell the men to be on the lookout. Gideon laid his carbine across his lap.

He saw no Indians, but he spotted something else which had not been there before: the walls of a rough cedar-picket cabin, not yet completed. It stood back from the south bank, out of the main floodplain. At a blur of movement he brought up the rifle. Halfway between the cabin and the trail a small girl was walking, trailed by a barking mongrel. She wore a plain gray cotton dress that lacked only a couple of inches reaching her bare, dirty toes. From the half-finished cabin came a woman's frightened shout. A man stepped into the open with a rifle in his hands. A woman ran down toward the trail and the little girl.

Nettles raised his hand for a halt. He gave the rifleman time to recognize them as soldiers, then started his horse in a slow walk off the trail and toward the cabin. The little girl watched the on-coming soldiers with curiosity. The woman grabbed her up and she dropped a rag doll. She knelt so the girl could retrieve her toy from the red dust. The woman could see that the riders were soldiers, not Indians, but nevertheless she hurried to the shack. She reached the protective shadow of her husband and his rifle before she turned. Gideon saw fear in her face. Black soldiers were not trusted.

The sight of the woman brought Hannah to Gideon's mind. He made a quick and unfavorable comparison. This woman's face was sunburned despite her slat bonnet. Long blondish hair strung down beneath the bonnet, tangled and windblown. Her hands were rough and red from hard labor. Gideon supposed white men might find her handsome, but he had never been able to comprehend white men's judgment.

The dog took a protective stance between the soldiers and the white people and kept barking. From a line of timber beyond the shack and beside the river, a second white man galloped up bareback on a workhorse. Breathing hard, he slid from the ani-mal's back and joined the other man. He also carried a rifle.

The man who had been at the cabin spoke first. "Hush up, Tige." The dog glanced back at him but kept barking. "Tige. Over here!" The dog retreated to the woman and little girl. The man lowered his rifle to arm's length, leaving it clear that he could raise it in a second. "Howdy, troopers." His untrusting eyes were upon Nettles because of the stripes on the blue sleeve.

Nettles nodded. "A good afternoon to you, sir . . . ma'am." He touched the brim of his dusty hat, showing a little of the deference of old slave days. He was not dealing with subordi-nates.

The woman decided the soldiers were not to be feared. She eased the child to the ground. Staring, the girl said, "You're nigger soldiers."

The mother moved quickly to quiet her. Esau Nettles broke

into a chuckle Gideon had not heard before. "Leave her be, ma'am, please. A child don't know better than to speak the truth." He leaned forward in his saddle and smiled at the girl. "You're almighty pretty, little Missy. You got a name?"

The smile was contagious. "I'm Susie. I'm five."

Gideon had pulled up abreast of Nettles and watched him with surprise. He saw the broad smile die. Then, slowly and painfully, Nettles brought it back. It was not so free and warm as before.

"Your doll got a name, too?"

The rag doll was homemade of cotton fabric scraps. The face was of faded yellow cloth, the eyes, nose and mouth stitched in coarse black thread. It spoke more of mother's love than of art. "She's Susanna. She's five, too." Susie paid no attention to the other four blue-clad horsemen. Her eyes were glued to the sergeant. "Do you have a little girl?"

Nettles was slow in answering. "Used to have. Her name was Susie, too."

"Where's she at now?"

"Gone with the angels, I expect. Been a long time, missy."

Nettles turned his attention to the settlers. "We didn't know anybody was living here. All I seen here the last time was a covey of blue quail."

The larger man said, "We just come out from Erath County, me and my wife and my brother here. We laid by a crop of corn on another man's farm and come out here to take up land for our own. We couldn't see nobody had a claim on this parcel, and it's handy to the road and the river."

Nettles frowned. "Indians think they got a claim on it."

"They don't use it. They don't farm it. All they do is pass through here once in a while, kill a buffalo and move on. Land belongs to people that'll stay on it."

Nettles' eyes returned to the little girl. "Be a shame if somethin' was to happen to *her*."

"We ain't goin' to let it. Our family has fought Indians since my old granddaddy Cooper come to Texas from Tennessee. Besides, looks to me like the Indians have gone to the reservation."

"No, sir," Nettles said. "Not all of them."

Gideon judged that the settler was old enough to know he should not set himself down in the middle of Comanche country. Seemed to him these folks could have found a safe place among the farmers and cattle raisers clustered where the Concho and the Colorado rivers ran together, a day's ride east. He saw a canvas-covered wagon beside the unfinished walls of the cabin. The family was probably living in that wagon—sleeping in it, anyway—until they could get a roof raised. He hoped the men were fast workers. The first real winter storm was likely to break any time now. From what people had told him of Texas blue northers, he wouldn't care to meet one under a thin canvas tarp stretched over wagon hoops. But he judged these people were tougher-raised than the white folks on the delta. These two sun-darkened, wind-whipped men who held their rifles unthreateningly but ready seemed capable of charging the devil's stronghold with a sharp stick and a bucket of water.

Nettles gazed speculatively at the land beyond the cabin. "You figure this is proper soil for raisin' corn?"

"We're farmers. I could raise corn on the rocky side of that mountain yonder if I was of a mind to. Come summer we'll have feed to sell to you soldier boys as you go up and down the road."

Nettles slowly returned to his smile. "You'll have to talk to our officers about that, sir. Now we'll bid you folks a good day and be a-travelin' on."

The girl waved. Nettles turned in the saddle and waved back. Gideon caught a glimpse of a softness, a sadness he had never seen in the sergeant's eyes. The two men and the woman said nothing, seeming relieved to see the black soldiers move on. The horses took the shallow ford, cold water lapping at their bellies. Gideon raised his feet to keep his boots dry and hoped Judas wouldn't slip on the slick rock base. The brown horse was still inclined toward error.

The little girl kept waving as the men climbed the low bank on the north side.

Big Dempsey grumbled. "You see them faces? They'd of shot us for a little of nothin'." He looked back. "Serve them right if the Comanches come and take their hair."

Nettles whirled his horse, a savage anger in his face. "Dad-damn you, Dempsey! Don't you ever say such as that again!"

Dempsey drew back like a child unexpectedly struck. He out-weighed Nettles by thirty pounds, but he would never think of using that advantage.

Nettles said sternly, "Don't let me ever hear any man say such as that. Any man!" He cut his angry eyes from one trooper to another.

Dempsey was a long time in saying anything, and then only when Nettles was far enough out in front that he couldn't hear. "Least they could of done was to invite us to eat."

Gideon said, "Didn't look to me like they had much. I believe they're worse off than we are."

Dempsey shook his head. "The hungriest day they ever have, they'll still be white."

Much later, when Nettles had had time to calm down, Gideon asked the question that had bothered him about these settlers. Nettles said, "These people ain't like your plantation farmers. For a hundred years they been comin' West a generation at a time with a plow handle in one hand and a rifle in the other, and a Bible in their pocket. Kill one and two more comes up behind him. They ain't no stoppin' them."

Arriving at the abandoned fort before dusk, the troopers turned their horses into a corral that had been maintained in good condition. They fed a bait of corn and proceeded to cook supper for themselves. The fort's stone buildings, though empty and silent, remained in a reasonable state of repair because the army periodically used them as an outpost.

Finley was a close-eyed little man who had serious short-comings as company but whose cooking was of a higher than standard order. This made his presence at least tolerable. Jimbo's carbine had brought down a couple of cottontail rabbits, small and scrawny, not to be despised when the alternative was hardtack and salt pork. Finley converted them into a fair-to-middling stew.

Jimbo expressed satisfaction that the paymaster and his escort had not arrived. "Our horses need the rest."

Dempsey had no interest in the horses. "Every day we spend

out here is one day we ain't diggin' no holes or totin' no rocks to
give some white officer a place to lay his head down."

Nettles had listened without complaint to Finley's irritating
lies, and he had challenged Dempsey's light treason but once.
Now he seemed compelled to challenge him again. "You ain't
done bad, Dempsey. You never had a better roof over your head
than you got at Concho. You ain't never et so regular or had
clothes half as good."

Dempsey moved away, grumping. "Man can't even speak his
mind."

Nettles said grittily, "Man's got to have a mind before he can
speak it."

In the dusk, Gideon and Jimbo and Dempsey walked around
the empty buildings, leaving Finley to talk to himself while he
grudgingly washed the supper utensils. They felt grandly wicked
exploring the officers' houses and the post headquarters, something Gideon was sure no black soldier ever did except under
strictest observation when the post was active. Now there were
no sentries, no locks. It was akin to the feeling he had the time
he and Jimbo had slept upstairs in Old Colonel's mansion.

Because there were no white officers to flout, Jimbo invented
his own. He stood in the empty office which they assumed to be
the commander's, and he dressed that gentleman down in the
most inflammatory terms, reviving all his past sins of commission
and omission, speculating upon his ancestry, upon his future at
the hands of old Lucifer.

"You," he declared, pointing at the spot where a splintered
floor indicated years of chair scraping, "are a fat old goat, and
you ain't got the good sense God give a mule. You got a mean
soul and a evil eye."

Big Dempsey entered into the spirit of the occasion. He used
words Gideon was not sure he had even heard before. Where
Jimbo had talked for fun, Dempsey became carried away by
emotion. His voice was loud and angry, his fist-shaking violent.
Gideon had an uncomfortable feeling that Dempsey really saw a
man there. He glanced at Jimbo and saw the beginnings of alarm
in his friend's eyes. Jimbo backed away, putting room between
himself and Dempsey as the big man gave vent to pent-up

hatreds, rages suppressed for God knew how long. Gideon sensed that Dempsey was dangerously near the edge of a deep and dark pit.

He became aware of another presence in the room. Sergeant Nettles stood in the doorway, listening passively while Dempsey wore himself down. At last Dempsey also became aware of the sergeant. Sullenly he faced around, his eyes challenging. The sergeant's disapproval was silent but clear. Dempsey's shoulders slumped. He was unable to meet Nettles' quiet stare.

Nettles said, "I hope you got it all spilt out."

Dempsey did not reply.

"You ever have the poor sense to say such as that to a real officer, they'll put a twitch on your tongue and draw it out by the roots."

Jimbo tried nervously to grin the whole thing away. "We was just funnin', is all."

Gideon grimaced. It had been fun at the start, but it had changed tenor when Dempsey joined in.

Nettles said, "Funnin' like that can cause you misery. It can give you notions and make you forget what you are."

Dempsey demanded, "And just what are we, Sergeant?"

"We're soldiers. But that uniform ain't changed our color. And talk ain't goin' to change people's minds. Only *doin'* will fix that."

Because Finley had done the cooking, Nettles gave him the first tour of guard so he would not have to break into his sleep. Dempsey grumbled, but only after the sergeant was gone. Gideon saw no discrimination; he had rather take a middle-of-the-night guard than cook. They built a fire in one of the barracks fireplaces to ease the night's chill. Nettles sat to himself on an old spider-webbed bench, whittling thin mesquite branches to uniform lengths. They were still green and pliable though autumn had begun drawing the sap to the roots. Using leather string, he began lacing the thin limbs together.

Gideon watched with curiosity, but not enough to ask questions. When he was warm he rolled in his one wool blanket on the hard floor. He stared at the dancing firelight reflected from the ceiling, his thoughts running back down the Concho road to

Hannah York. He was making love to her in a dream when Jimbo shook him awake. The fire had burned down. A chill had invaded the room. Gideon put wood on the fire, then took his blanket to wrap around himself on guard in the early morning hours.

The dark loneliness of the place added a chill of its own. Every time a horse moved, the wintry night magnified the sound. It had been easy enough, in the daylight, to dismiss thoughts of Indians. Darkness, however, produced them in every black shadow.

The remembered warmth of Hannah's body helped a little. Gideon's mind ran to the settler family at the Colorado River. He had seen little in the way of tangible property—a horse, a wagon, an ox team, a moldboard plow. Surely it did not take a terrible amount of money to buy these things. The land was free, so far, and plentiful. By the time the state government or somebody came to lay claim, a good farmer should have enough money saved to buy it free and clear. Give him a toenail hold and he would make it the rest of the way.

Maybe he had already saved enough to buy the few things he and Hannah really needed. He could make do with an old cheap wagon. Worst come to worst, he could build a serviceable plow of hard oak. If he couldn't buy a yoke of oxen, he could train his own. It seemed to become easier as he sat thinking about it. His enthusiasm blossomed. He would go to Hannah as soon as he got back to Concho. He would tell her there was no need for them to wait any longer.

But reality returned like a lash laid across his back. He wasn't free. He didn't belong to himself now any more than he had belonged to himself in olden times. Old Colonel had owned him then. The army owned him now.

There was a way. The thought had come to him sometimes in slave days, though he had never acted upon it. He could just up and run off. This was a big country. A man could go a long way and lose himself.

Or could he? A white man might, but black faces stood out. He wasn't sure what the army did when it caught a runaway soldier, for there had been only a couple during his time at Concho.

The low desertion rate was a point of pride in the Tenth. But Gideon remembered well what slave owners did to runaways in the olden days. They made it a point that other slaves be required to watch, so they would remember. Gideon remembered, and that memory made him shudder even now, years afterward.

The next day passed pleasantly enough, though Nettles considered idle hands a dangerous thing and made the men police up the deserted fort, to do what they could to retard nature's relentless reclamation. Small mesquite trees, sprouted from dried horse manure, were growing in tromped-out corrals where they had little competition from grass and transient weeds. Sunflowers had made their season and stood now in skeletal gray stalks, their shattered heads turned black. Dried tumbleweeds lodged against the buildings and piled in the corners of the corrals. Nettles worked side by side with the men. The fires they kindled in disposing of trash threw off a pleasant warmth that warded away some of the wind's cold.

Gideon had mixed feelings about the smoke. He did not know whether it might be a deterrent or a magnet for drifting Indians.

Late in the afternoon, Jimbo loped in from the flat where he had watched over the grazing horses. He pointed at the Griffin trail. "Folks comin' yonder, Sergeant."

Carrying his carbine, Gideon climbed a fence. He saw a wagon accompanied by four horsemen. "It's the paymaster."

Nettles nodded. "Jimbo, you trot back out yonder and bring up the horses. We don't want to be leavin' them for some fast-fingered Comanche. You other men, fall in. We goin' to look like soldiers when the man gets here with the money."

The thought of money brought a broad smile to little Finley. Gideon decided it hadn't occurred to him he would have to wait until they got back to Concho to be paid. Even if they had the money here, there wasn't a drop of anything to spend it on. But he said nothing, for he saw no gain in depriving even Finley of small pleasures.

Nettles saluted smartly as the Daugherty wagon pulled to a halt. The weary, graying major on the seat returned the salute with the typical halfhearted gesture Gideon had decided was standard procedure for officers, though they would burn the britches off of an enlisted man for such laziness.

The major asked, "All secure, Sergeant?"

"All secure, sir. Welcome to Fort Chadbourne."

The major cast a dark glance at the abandoned buildings and grunted. To the ranking noncommissioned officer on horseback, a black sergeant like Nettles, he said, "That chest goes inside, and I want a guard mounted on it immediately."

As he climbed stiffly down, Nettles stepped up to give him a hand. The major shrugged him off. "I can manage, Sergeant."

Dempsey muttered, "Don't want no black hand touchin' him."

The words seemed not to reach the officer, or he ignored them. But they reached Nettles. He gave Dempsey a withering glance.

The major walked a small circle, stamping circulation back into cramped legs, rubbing hips pained by a long day in the seat. He asked Nettles, "Have you seen anything amiss around here?"

"No, sir, ain't been nothin' moved but prairie dogs and rabbits."

The major stared at the trail over which he had come. "We believe we glimpsed a party of mounted men an hour or so ago. Just a moment, and no more."

"Indians, sir?"

"Logic would tell us so, would it not? I tried to look at them through my telescope, but they were gone. There is, of course, always the chance that it was simply a band of wild horses." It was clear he did not believe that.

Nettles showed some apprehension. "If you want to keep movin', sir, we can be mounted and ready in ten minutes. Five."

The major demurred. "It is almost dark. We could not go far on these tired horses. There is no place on the road half so well suited to meet the challenge as this old fort."

Nettles frowned. "We come up on some folks down to the Colorado crossin'. They ought to be warned."

The major seemed a little surprised. "Moving or settling?"

"Settlin', sir. Buildin' them a cabin."

"If they are staying, then they have to assume danger all the time and be vigilant. The army cannot watch over every outly-

ing cabin of every ex-Confederate foolish enough to expose himself to the hazard of Indians."

"They's a family, sir. They got a little girl, about this high."
Nettles made a sign with his hand.

The major shrugged. "There are always children, Sergeant.
Why these people persist in putting their lives and the lives of
their families at constant peril, I cannot begin to understand. Nor
can we begin to protect them all." Still obviously not believing
it, he said, "Probably it *was* just wild horses." Clearly, he was
through with that subject. He turned a baleful gaze toward the
old buildings. "Not even a sutler's here for comfort." His eyes
were a bit watery, giving the major the look of one who enjoyed
convivial company and, above all, a glass or two of kindness to
pass the evening. But he was not at ease with the black soldiers
assigned to him at random as an escort from Griffin to Chadbourne. Nor was he likely to become better acquainted with
Nettles and his detail.

He turned to his Griffin sergeant. "See to the horses. Then see
to it that the men get their supper. I shall make quarters for myself with the chest, in that building there." He nodded toward
the one that had been post headquarters.

The sergeant saluted and went about his business. Nettles was
still distressed about the Colorado River settlers, but he said, "I'll
have my men carry in some wood and fix a fire for you, sir.
Night chill will be comin' on pretty fast."

The major seemed surprised by the solicitude. "I'd appreciate
it."

Nettles nodded to Gideon and Jimbo to carry the major's personal belongings, his bedding and his folding canvas cot. When
they had a nice blaze started in the open fireplace, the major extended his hands toward the warmth.

"This is comfortable," he said, relaxing some of his formality.
He warmed his front side, then turned and thawed the rear. At
length he said, "The sergeant seemed unusually concerned about
those settlers."

Gideon nodded. "He was right taken by their little girl, sir."

"Southerners, I suppose. The same ones who used to hold you
people in bondage."

"Them's poor folks, sir. I doubt as they ever had a slave."

Guard was heavy that night, half the men on duty at a time, each man getting only half a night's sleep, if that. The Griffin detail took the first watch, the Concho detail the second, past midnight. All the animals were placed in one pen and the gates lashed shut. Before dark the men had dragged large stones in front of the gates as a further obstacle.

Gideon was nervous during the first part of the guard, magnifying every sound, real and imagined. He had gotten past his old fears of Indians seen, but Indians unseen were more than he wanted to reckon with. The night was quiet, for most birds had flown south to Mexico, looking for summer. In a while, when he decided it was unlikely anything stirred beyond the fort, he let his thoughts stray to Hannah.

He became conscious of a growing restlessness among the horses. They stirred in the pen, circling the fence. Some made a skittish, rolling noise in their noses. It came to Gideon that the nightbirds were calling more. Owls hooted and answered from different locations at the perimeter of the fort. Listening, he came to a reluctant but compelling certainty that they were not owls—at least, not all of them.

In his loudest whisper, he demanded, "Jimbo, you hear all that?"

From across the corral Jimbo answered, "It's comin' from your side."

"Yours, too. They're all around us. Dempsey, where you at?"

Dempsey's voice came from some distance. He had never whispered in his life. "I'm here, and I'm fixin' to go tell Nettles."

Nettles said from somewhere in the darkness, "Stay at your post."

Gideon waited for orders. When none came he asked, "What we goin' to do, Sergeant?"

"Nothin', till *they* do somethin'. Hold tight, where you're at."

Hannah slipped away in the urgency of the moment. Gideon listened intently and watched for anything to move. He thought a time or two that he saw something, but he was afraid to fire. It could have been a trooper.

The owls stopped hooting, and the darkness went quiet. The

horses settled again, but Gideon did not. To him the night was a
week long. He was still wide-eyed when dawn's first promise
showed in the east. From noises within the post he knew the
Griffin troopers were up and moving. Smoke began to rise from
a couple of chimneys. As the night's gloom lifted he spotted
Jimbo at his station, and Dempsey and Finley at theirs. He saw
no sign that anything had changed in the night. The gates were
still tied. The big stones were in place. All the horses and the
pack mule remained where they belonged. He felt relieved and
at the same time foolish.

That major, and his talk of horsemen!

Sergeant Nettles walked a wide circle outside the corral, studying the ground. Watching him and catching up the major's
horses, Gideon and Jimbo laughed at their silly nervousness.

Returning, Nettles pointed with his chin. "They's moccasin
tracks out yonder. If we hadn't of kept guard, we'd be afoot.
Let's get movin'."

The night's chill came back to Gideon.

The major got coffee from Finley's pot, washing down hardtack and something out of a tin. He told the Griffin sergeant he
was countermanding the original orders, which were that the
Griffin soldiers return directly from Chadbourne. "When we get
to Concho, I'll write a letter for your officer, holding you
blameless. I believe under the circumstances it would be prudent
for me to retain your services." He turned to Nettles. "Sergeant,
I am placing you in charge of all the men."

The two sergeants were equal in rank. The major offered no
explanation for his choice. Whatever the Griffin sergeant's
thoughts might have been, they were not articulated. Those
three stripes had been hard to come by.

In fifteen minutes the detail was on the Concho road. Nettles
and his four men led on their fresher horses, the Griffin sergeant
and his detail a rear guard behind the major's wagon. Nettles set
a brisk pace. Gideon doubted the horses could stand up to it
long, but unless the major ordered otherwise, they would hold it
until they reached the Colorado. Nettles would have it no other
way.

The sergeant was well in the lead when he spurred down the

north bank and splashed into the river. Gideon heeled his brown but was unable to keep the sergeant from widening the gap between them. As he struck the water, he saw that Nettles was already halfway to the cabin. Gideon took the absence of smoke as a positive sign. He saw a movement and brought up his carbine. As the brown horse negotiated the gentle south bank, trailing water, Gideon saw Nettles jump from his horse and run afoot to the little girl. She had ventured only a few steps from the house at first. Recognizing him, she ran to meet him. The sergeant picked her up and carried her to the people waiting at the cabin.

By the time Gideon reached there, the two men and the woman were well into recounting the morning's adventure to Nettles. Cooper was saying, "It was Tige settin' up a racket that first stirred me and Jack."

Jack put in, "We never really seen no Indians, but we could feel them. If it hadn't been for the dog, they might of come in and taken our horses."

Nettles set the girl down. He was trembling. "You could of lost a sight more than that."

The major and the Griffin detail belatedly made the ford and pulled up as near the cabin as the wagon would conveniently go. The major looked angrily at Nettles, but if he had anything to say, he was saving it for later, where civilian ears wouldn't be listening to army business. "Good day, lady, gentlemen," he said in his most pleasant voice, touching fingers to the brim of his trail-dusty black hat. "Am I correct in surmising that we are not your first visitors today?"

The woman said, "You're the first one that's welcome. Git down off of your wagon, Captain, and we'll offer you what hospitality there is."

Gideon turned away to grin. The woman didn't know about army rank, and he suspected the major was chagrined at the arbitrary demotion.

The officer covered any resentment he might harbor against these daring settlers, always a nuisance to the military. "The offer is gracious, but no thank you, lady. We have business elsewhere." He introduced himself, noted the settlers' names and made the expected light fuss over the prettiness of the girl. The obligatory niceties done, he said, "We are pleased, of course, that the morning's visitation was of no greater consequence. In view of the fact that a recurrence is possible, I would offer you people an escort into Fort Concho."

The settler Cooper looked at his wife and his brother and seemed to find them in accord. "We're tryin' to finish this cabin before bad weather sets in. You soldier boys go ahead and take care of them that needs it."

The major shrugged, his duty done. "Good day to you, then, and good luck." He turned, looking for Nettles. "Sergeant?"

But Nettles had gone to the pack mule. He returned with the results of his handiwork during the waiting time at Chadbourne. From thin mesquite limbs and leather string he had fashioned a small, crude cradle. "Missy, I believe this'll fit your doll."

Innocent to the fact that he was black, she threw her arms around his neck. Gideon expected protest from the parents, but they smiled.

The mother said, "That was kind of you, soldier."

"Name's Esau, ma'am. Esau Nettles."

"You're a Christian, Esau Nettles. You take care of yourself."

The major was keeping his impatience under admirable restraint. Nettles turned to him. "You ready, sir?"

"Almost, Sergeant. Who is your best horseman?"

Nettles looked at Jimbo. "This man."

"It occurs to me that inasmuch as we now know those red heathens are moving in a southerly direction, it behooves me to send a galloper ahead to apprise the post. The colonel may wish to send out patrols."

"Yes, sir. Jimbo's your man, sir."

While the major licked a pencil point and scrawled out a message, uneasiness built in Gideon. Jimbo had never been dispatched alone with a responsibility before. Although Old Colonel used to trust him with his horses, he never sent him anywhere by himself. Jimbo had a way of jumping first and looking later.

Nettles studied Jimbo's horse critically. He seemed to wrestle with a dilemma before he said, "You better take my Napoleon.

He's got the constitution, and he can outrun anything them Indians is liable to have."

With his unabashed, wide-open grin, Jimbo resembled nothing so much as a happy pup. Not in the months they had been at Concho had he or Gideon seen anyone but Nettles ride black Napoleon.

Nettles frowned like a building thundercloud. "You're the only man I'd trust him to, and I ain't airtight certain about *you*."

Jimbo's grin never flagged. "Me and him, we goin' to get on fine." He patted the horse on the neck and talked to him in that quiet, confident voice he reserved for animals. In his pleasure over getting to ride the fine horse, he didn't seem to give a thought to the danger. Counting consequences had never been one of Jimbo's attributes. They always came upon him as a surprise.

Gideon volunteered, "Sergeant, don't you reckon I ought to go and help protect him?"

Nettles didn't even look around. "That fast horse is his protection. I ain't goin' to tie no drag on him."

The major finished his note. He personally stuck it into Jimbo's coat and buttoned the pocket. "Take this to the officer of the day and tell him I said it is for the colonel. If you encounter Indians, do not fight them. Outrun them. And do not dally along the way."

Jimbo saluted, his grin bright as sunshine. "Yes, sir." He swung up, sitting the sergeant's horse with the pride of a newly crowned prince. At this moment, a thousand Indians would not have frightened him.

Nettles grunted. "Jimbo, you let some Comanche steal that horse, or kill him, and I'll hound your reckless soul right into the fires of hell."

Jimbo laughed. "Any Indian gits this horse, that's where I'll be. In hell." He waved at Gideon and left in a lope.

A chill ran through Gideon as he watched the black horse raise a thin trail of dust on the wagon road. He felt somehow cut adrift. He had never been apart from Jimbo, not for so much as a day.

Gideon said quietly, "I sure do hate to see him go off by himself."

Nettles nodded. "So do I. But Jimbo'll take care of him."

The sergeant mounted Jimbo's horse, gave the little girl a wave and set out on the road, taking the point for the major and his wagon. Gideon watched Jimbo so long as he was in sight, and he watched the dust settle after Jimbo was gone. He listened for the distant sound of gunfire, but all he could hear was the plodding of hoofs and the rattling of trace chains.

Eleven

GIDEON HAD NOT realized how popular a white officer could be among black soldiers. Cheering arose from the post grounds as the paymaster's wagon pulled up on the south bank of the Concho, its wheels trailing water. The officer of the guard marched out a fresh detail to conduct the major onto the post in military style, allowing him to drop off the tired and dusty troopers who had accompanied him. Nettles pointed them to the corrals.

The fort had been handsome from out on the prairie, but most welcome sight of all was Jimbo brushing Napoleon's black coat. He had it shining like onyx.

Swinging quickly out of the saddle, Gideon half-crushed Jimbo's hand. He had much he wanted to say, but nothing intelligent would come out. "I see you made it. Run into any Indians?"

"Never seen a feather." Jimbo seemed disappointed. "I wanted to find out how fast Napoleon could run."

Sergeant Nettles took a slow walk around his black horse, lovingly rubbing him, critically inspecting him for the least sign of abuse. Jimbo stood with the brush against his hip. He was smiling and confident. Nettles' eyes showed he was pleased, but he would not say so. It was not military. It was not Nettles. "What did the colonel do when you taken him the dispatch?"

"He called in some officers right quick and got out a couple of patrols. Other companies, though—not ours." Jimbo's eyes brightened at the memory. "Officer of the day taken me right over to the colonel's house soon's he seen what it was all about. Colonel asked me a bunch of questions. Missus, she called in that washerwoman's gal, Hannah, to fetch me a dipper of cool water. After the water, Old Missus herself give me brandy. Out of her own hand, she done. I stood right there in the parlor like I was a white officer come, and not just a nigger."

Nettles' eyes snapped. "You are *not* just a nigger. You are a *soldier*, and don't you forget it!" The sergeant straightened and called, "Tech-*hut!*" He brought up his hand in a salute.

Lieutenant Hollander entered the stables. "At ease, men. Go on about your business." His eyes sought out Nettles and showed considerable pleasure at finding him. "Good to have you back, Sergeant. Things go to hell around here when you're off the post." The lieutenant did not wait for a reply. "Hello, Charger. I'm afraid you may have trouble living with Jimbo for a while. He's been over at the colonel's house picking in high cotton."

Gideon had never learned to be at ease with the lieutenant. He sensed that the officer expected some lighthearted banter, but he had none in him. He replied only, "Yes, sir." He still wished Hollander would cut out that "Charger" business.

Hollander said, "You men get your horses curried and fed as quickly as you can. We'll have company formation for the paymaster."

When the lieutenant was gone, Gideon turned back to Jimbo. "You seen Hannah. How'd she look?"

Jimbo's smile left him. "What you want to fool with that yeller gal for? Ain't nothin' but trouble, the colonel's missus ever finds out. Or that old granny woman either; she'll lay a curse on you."

Riding onto the post, Gideon had looked for Hannah working behind the shack where the wash pot was. His heart had sagged when she was nowhere in sight. As soon as he finished grooming and feeding the brown horse, and before the bugle's assembly call, he hurried to the west end of the corrals to look again.

She was at the smoking pot, stirring some boiling clothes. Glancing over his shoulder and not seeing Nettles, Gideon joyfully climbed the fence. He sprinted toward Hannah, keeping a watch on the shack in case the old woman should come out. Hannah's face instantly lighted up, but the smile was gone before he reached her. She watched the shack warily.

"Gideon, you crazy? Old Granny liable to come out here any time, and she goin' come out mad."

Gideon's voice was near desperation. "I just had to see you for a minute, Hannah." It took all the resistance he could muster not to make those last two long steps and grab her into his arms.

Her large dark eyes were distressed. "I know, Gideon. But you got to get goin' now."

"I'll be back tonight, Hannah. You be listenin' for me."

She shook her head urgently. "No, you stay away from here tonight. Old Granny, she got company comin' over."

"Company'll leave. I don't care how late it is, I'll wait."

Her eyes became fearful. "No, Gideon. Please, you stay away. Come another night. Please?" She turned her head toward the shack, pleading. "I think I hear her comin'. Git now, git quick, and don't you come back around here tonight."

Gideon was disposed to argue, but her frightened manner stopped him. Anger arose suddenly, helplessly. Damned old woman . . . "I'll see you, Hannah." He started backing off. "Don't you fret. I'm fixin' to take you away from her."

He made long strides toward the corrals, looking over his shoulder. When he reached the corral the old woman still had not appeared. He felt foolish about the haste of his retreat, and the foolishness turned to resentment.

He would make up for it. He would be here tonight. He would see Hannah if he had to wait till the roosters crowed over the river.

No matter how broke and desperate they had been for most or all of the month, soldiers on payday felt rich as New Orleans slave traders. A profligate spirit ran rampant on the post. Gideon

had seen men stand in the pay line and bet the meager wages not
yet in their hands on whether a restless doodlebug searching the
parade would cross a certain point or turn back. The late-afternoon air was too chilly for doodlebugs, but he saw Finley and
another trooper bet five dollars on whether one of the numerous
camp dogs nosing about for refuse would visit a certain tree or
not. The dog betrayed Finley. Gideon grimaced, knowing it
took the voluble little trooper more than ten days to earn that
five dollars.

Though one of the post officers counted out each soldier's
pay, deducting any fees shown on the company record as being
owed, the paymaster stood by, watching the operation. When
the reckoning was done and the last man had collected his due,
the major's gaze drifted to the Griffin soldiers. They had
watched with a certain forlorn air like unwanted strays. He
beckoned them with his finger.

They approached him and saluted, reluctant because they expected another duty assignment. The major drew a wrinkled bill
from his pocket. "Sergeant, I feel as if I have cheated you and
your men. You were obliged to forgo a rightfully earned celebration at Fort Griffin. I believe Saint Angela's fleshpots are the
equal of any at Griffin-Under-the-Hill. If you soldiers cannot get
comfortably drunk on five dollars, it is simply because you do
not make the effort. I trust you will make the effort."

The sergeant's grin was widest, but not by much. "You can
trust us, sir." He accepted the bill with a bow from the waist, a
relic of another time.

Gideon had no idea how much money a major made—maybe
as much as twenty or thirty dollars a month—but he knew five
dollars was no small gift. Even Dempsey would have to admit
that for an officer of such high rank—almost a general—the
major was a pretty good sort.

The Griffin troopers were billeted for the night in the barracks with Gideon and Jimbo and the others of Hollander's company. Gideon found them an agreeable bunch. There wasn't one
he wouldn't have traded little Finley for.

Because Jimbo kept insisting, and Dempsey and the Griffin
troopers kept backing him up, Gideon agreed to go across the

river with them for a while. He had to kill some time, anyway. They found Saint Angela in festive spirits. The paymaster's arrival was always grounds for celebration all around. Of whatever money arrived in the paymaster's wagon, most would be liberally distributed among the townspeople across the river by the time the first rooster crowed the following morning.

As always, Gideon made it a point to take only a couple of dollars. The rest was wrapped in a sock in the box at the foot of his bunk. His contingent started at the east end of Concho Avenue and worked its way westward, looking for the place where the music was the prettiest, girls the friendliest and the whisky tolerably drinkable. The combination was not easy to find.

Though Gideon found agreeable the warming and calming sensation which whisky gave him after it had settled into his system, he had not yet gotten to care much for the taste of it, or for the fire it lighted in his mouth and throat before it went down. He sipped it slowly and made it last. He watched Jimbo cut loose and dance alone on the packed earth floor of an adobe dive. He wondered if anybody anywhere had ever really had as much fun as Jimbo appeared to be having. He had a feeling that the hilarity was forced. It was as if the soldiers felt obliged to offset in one wild and uproarious night all the drudgery, all the indignities of thirty long days, and they realized that they never actually could. They tried to make up the difference in noise and show, convincing themselves they were having the grand time they felt was their due. Settling for less would be admitting that the system was cheating them.

Gideon knew that Sergeant Nettles did not indulge himself in this self-deception. That was but one of the differences between Nettles and the Griffin sergeant, who hollered as loud as any private on the street.

Gideon did not need this false compensation either. He had Hannah. As the evening wore on, impatience prickled his skin. He found it difficult to sit here passing the time, pretending to be having fun.

The situation was made more difficult by little Finley, who ran out of money early and tried to beg or borrow from his companions. Gideon bought a drink for him, which nearly exhausted what was left of his original two dollars. Finley was soon whimpering again, making a general nuisance of himself. Finally giving up, he left the saloon without explanation or a by-your-leave, his red-veined eyes resentful.

Gideon decided he too had had enough. Jimbo caught his sleeve. "Where you goin'? The night's young."

"It's gettin' old to me."

Jimbo made an excuse to the black girl who sat on his lap, and he followed Gideon to the door. Gideon kept walking, so Jimbo trailed him out into the dirt street, catching him by the arm and turning him around. "Gid, you fixin' to go to that laundry gal?"

It wasn't anybody's business. "If I take that notion."

The show of hilarity was gone. Jimbo was dead serious. "Ain't nothin' but trouble for you over there."

"What trouble? That little old woman? The day I take it in my head to marry Hannah, that old woman ain't goin' to amount to one good spit in the Concho River."

"There's more to it than you got any idee."

"Like what?"

"I can't tell you, Gid. I just wisht you'd stay away."

"You don't understand."

Jimbo shrugged, giving up. "Don't reckon I do." He stood hunch-shouldered as Gideon walked down the street toward the crossing.

Gideon's pulse quickened, his eyes searching eagerly for the laundress shack in the moonlight. Behind him followed the laughter, the mingled and discordant pianos and fiddles being played in half a dozen ginmills, the shouting of men and women trying to make the most of a short night. To his left he heard the shuffling of horses in the corrals, poking around for remnants of feed, a horse squealing as a more dominant animal drove him off with a quick snapping of teeth. Gideon hoped the victim was not his brown. Though he had reservations, he had come to some tolerance for the mount. Having often been put upon himself, he could muster sympathy for a horse in the same fix.

Coming up to the rear of the shack, he saw a couple of coals still glowing weakly beneath the pot. He thought idly that an ill wind could pick up sparks and move them into something combustible, like hay. Somebody ought to caution the washwomen about such as that. But it was not his job.

He saw no light in the shack and took that for a favorable sign; the old woman's company must be gone. He walked around to the front, whistling softly, knowing old Granny couldn't hear. He called, not too loudly, "Hannah! It's me, Gideon."

Too late he saw the tiny form sitting in a straight chair, leaned back against the outside wall by the front door. He saw the soft glow of her pipe an instant before the granny woman looked around. She jumped up from the chair with surprising agility. She came at him with the speed of a wild animal.

"Who you be?" she demanded shrilly. "What you doin' messin' around here?"

Surprised, Gideon took two steps backward. She was on him like a wildcat, her spindly little fingers closing over the lapels of his coat, reminding him more of claws than of hands. Her breath in his face was evil of tobacco and bad teeth. "I know you, nigger! I've told you before, ain't no common soldier goin' to sniff around my Hannah."

The front door opened. A man stood there in long underwear unbuttoned all the way down. "What goes on out here?" he demanded. It was a white man's voice, with the commanding tone of an officer.

The old woman had a surprising strength. In his confusion, Gideon let her whirl him around and push him toward the open door. He stumbled through it, into the officer who stood there. He threw up his hands defensively, striking the officer a weak, unintentional blow. The man's fist came around in a furious arc and sent Gideon crashing to the hard earth floor. His hat rolled away.

Hannah screamed, standing on her knees on the bed. 'Even in the reflected glow of moonlight, he knew she was naked.

Captain Newton grabbed Gideon's coat, attempting to pull him back to his feet. Gideon tried to draw away and stumbled.

"You black son of a bitch!" the officer exploded. From trousers hanging on the back of a chair, he pulled loose his belt and began to swing it at Gideon, using it like a whip. Gideon put his arms over his face. The belt hissed, most of the blows striking his coat, a few stinging fiercely across the back of his head and neck.

A momentary panic came over him—panic born of those few but awful remembered times when Old Colonel had taken a cane to him in moments of anger or retribution. He cried out.

The captain was shouting, "Damned lying, sneaking niggers! All alike, every one of you!" He stopped using the belt on Gideon and turned, acting for a moment as if he were about to use it on the old woman. She shrieked in fear. He yelled, "You told me she was clean. You told me no nigger had ever put a hand on her. You lying old wench, what do you call *that?*" He pointed his finger like a dagger at Gideon.

The old woman pleaded, "Lord God, massa, I didn't know. I has watched her, I has beat her, I ain't never let her git near no soldier. I don't know how this'n come to be here."

"Well, he *is* here, and it's a safe bet he's been here before. Him and God knows how many others. There is no telling what kind of disease . . ."

Newton swung his arm and slapped Hannah so hard that she fell against the iron bedstead. That brought Gideon up from the floor in a rush of anger. Newton reached to the chair again, and suddenly a pistol was in his hand.

"Come on, you black bastard," he said coldly. "There's nothing I'd rather do this minute than kill you. I ought to kill all three of you!"

Hannah broke down, crying. The old woman fell to her knees and begged. Gideon broke his rush, but he stood with his fists clenched, a wild and angry roaring in his head. The full magnitude of the situation had not yet reached him, but in the fury of the moment he was almost willing to risk the blast of that pistol.

Only the officer's cold voice stopped him. "Come on, Sambo. Come on and give me an excuse to kill you!"

Only then did a chill work down Gideon's back and force him to stop. He was closer to death than he had ever been in his life. This man truly wanted to kill him. Gideon's stomach tied itself into a knot, and cold sweat broke over his face.

From outside a voice demanded, "What's going on in there?" It was another white man's voice.

Newton shouted, "You keep out of here. Keep out, I say!"

Lieutenant Hollander pushed through the door. "Is that you, Newton? What kind of mess have you gotten yourself into here?"

"Stay out of this, Hollander. It's none of your affair."

It was too late now. Hollander was already in. He struck a match and held it high, taking in the whole scene before the flame licked down close to his fingers: Hannah naked on the bed, her head buried in her arms against the bedstead; the old woman on her knees, frightened to the point of collapse; Captain Newton in his underwear, pistol in his hand; Gideon Ledbetter standing with his hands half up, bleeding where the belt had cut him across his right ear.

To Gideon's amazement, Hollander smiled.

Newton said defensively, "This man struck me, Hollander. I have every right to shoot him."

Hollander was a moment in answering. He lighted a lamp and adjusted the wick. "I suppose you have, if that's the case. But do you want to stand in front of a court-martial and explain what you were doing here? Thing like this can be messy."

Newton lowered the pistol slowly. "All right," he conceded, "but I am going to see this man court-martialed. A soldier can be shot for striking an officer. Sent to the penitentiary, at least."

"You would be within your rights. But the same questions would be asked whether it is your court-martial or his. I wonder if you'd want your wife and children to listen. I wouldn't."

Newton's shoulders slumped.

Hannah pulled a blanket from the bed and covered herself belatedly. She remained on her knees on the mattress, sobbing.

Newton put on his clothes. His anger had drained largely and was replaced by shame. Faces peered curiously through the open door, one of them Jimbo's. The captain kept his back turned as he buttoned his coat. "Frank, could you get those people the hell away from here? This is bad enough without having every black heathen on the post staring. God knows what lies they'll tell."

Hollander said dryly, "God knows." He stepped to the door. "You people move along now. Nothing has happened here, and anyway it's all over."

Newton caught a glimpse of himself in a cracked old mirror and turned quickly away. His head was bowed. "Have I your promise as a gentleman that no word of this will get out?"

"I won't say anything. But I have no control over those people outside."

Anger flashed again in the captain's face as his gaze swept from Gideon to Hannah to the old woman. "You know the biggest mistake we made, Frank? It was in taking off their chains."

Hollander stared at the girl. She hid her face in the blanket. "Not *all* the chains." He pointed his chin toward the open door. "Wait for me out there, Newton. We'll go somewhere and talk."

The captain turned up the collar of the coat and pulled his hat low over his face. Without saying more, he stepped out into the darkness.

From the open doorway came voices on the crisp night air.

"Who is it?"

"One of them white officers."

"I believe it's Captain Newton."

Gideon had stared through a haze. He felt stunned, frozen, as if he had been kicked in the belly by a mule. He blinked now, but the haze was still there. He turned toward a wall, not wanting to look at anybody, not wanting anybody to look at him. He leaned his head against the rough plaster and cried quietly, his shoulders heaving, but no sound coming from him.

Jimbo entered the room and stood beside the lieutenant. They looked at each other in embarrassed futility.

A savage pain boiled up from the depths of Gideon's soul. He beat a fist against the wall until some of the poor plaster shook loose and fell at his feet. He turned on Hannah and cried out, "Why, Hannah? How come you to do it?"

She had no answer except to weep.

Jimbo said, "It was the old woman made her do it."

The granny woman couldn't hear, but she sensed that Jimbo was talking about her. She cringed fearfully into a corner.

Gideon turned to the wizened old witch so she could see his lips. "Why? She's your granddaughter. She's your own blood kin."

The woman hissed, "She ain't no blood kin to me. Old massa

given her to me to raise up after her mama was sold off. She's mine to do with what I want to."

Jimbo said, "Gid, I been wantin' to tell you, but I couldn't. This yeller gal been a white man's gal ever since she and that old granny come here. Old woman been sellin' her to them white officers right along. Everybody knowed it, just about, except you. You think all them other soldiers would of kept away like they done if they didn't know she was white man's stuff?"

For the first time in his life, Gideon wanted to kill Jimbo. In a searing rage he grabbed him by the collar and pushed him back against the wall. Jimbo did not resist except to lift his arms protectively over his face. "It's God's truth, Gid. I swear it."

Lieutenant Hollander laid a heavy hand upon Gideon's shoulder. "He's your friend, Charger. He's trying to help you. So am I. What he tells you is true—all of it."

Gideon wanted to close his ears with his hands, but his arms felt paralyzed.

Hollander said, "Jimbo was trying to keep you out of trouble, Charger. He followed you here. I happened to be coming along when the commotion started, and he ran to me for help. If it had not been for Jimbo, you might be lying on the floor now, dead."

Gideon tried not to listen, but the relentless words drove like nails into his brain. He let go of Jimbo and took half a step backward. He felt terribly cold, and he began to shiver. He looked at Hannah, though her face was turned away and mostly covered by the blanket. Again he demanded, "Why, Hannah?"

Her voice was so weak he could barely hear. "Because she told me to."

"You didn't have to do *that*."

"She's my granny. I belong to her."

"You don't belong to nobody. Nobody belongs to nobody. We got freedom."

"You don't know nothin' about freedom. She raised me up. I belong to her."

Gideon put his hands on her thin shoulders and shook her violently. "No, Hannah! You could of told her *no!*"

Hannah began to cry again. She tore herself from Gideon's grasp and fell face down on the bed, half uncovered. Gideon stared at her through the burning of his tears. Shamed for hurting her, he pulled up the blanket to cover her again. His soul still rejected what his mind told him was true.

He declared stubbornly, "I don't believe it. That captain's a hard man. He come here and forced her."

Hollander shook his head. "You're a soldier, Charger, and a man. You have to face up to facts no matter how much they hurt. Just about every bachelor officer on the post has been over here. Some married ones, too." He added with regret, "I've been here myself. Five dollars has been the standard fee."

The lieutenant tried to hold his eyes to Gideon's, but could not. Gideon covered his face with his hands and cried as he had not cried since his mother was buried.

Hollander said somberly, "I've done all I can do here, Jimbo. Too much, perhaps. See after him and get him to the barracks."

Jimbo nodded. "I'll see to him, sir."

The lieutenant paused at the door. "Can you hear me, old woman?"

She was reading his lips, the fear still in her eyes.

"Word'll get out quickly. I would advise you to be gone before it reaches the colonel's ears. Civilian teamsters are leaving in the morning with a supply train to Fort McKavett. They'll take you, for pay." He glanced at the girl. "I hope you'll pay them with cash."

He was gone, into the night chill.

Jimbo picked up Gideon's fallen hat. "Your ear's bleedin', Gid. Come on, let's go home and fix it."

"I love her, Jimbo. I don't want to leave her."

Jimbo took Gideon's arm. "Come on. This ain't no good place."

Gideon quit resisting. He paused at the door and looked at the girl. "Hannah, I'm comin' back."

Outside, in the cold air, he felt numb. He stumbled along, letting Jimbo pick the way across the post grounds toward the barracks.

A man rushed by them in the darkness, taking a shortcut from the barracks toward the river and Saint Angela.

Jimbo said, "That's Finley. Reckon he didn't get enough yet."

Gideon didn't care about Finley. He cared about nothing except Hannah. He leaned his shoulder against the wall of the dark barracks and surrendered to a hot rush of tears, his body shaking. Jimbo turned away, letting the moment run its course. Gideon beat his fist against the rock wall until the tears were drained out of him.

At last Jimbo put his hand on Gideon's shoulder. "You goin' to take the grippe standin' out here."

He led Gideon inside.

Frank Hollander sat at a small square table in an earthen-floored picket hovel and stared at Captain Newton's somber, drawn face in the dim light of a single lantern. Hand shaking, Newton poured the last whisky from the bottle into a streaked glass and glanced toward the sallow man who stood idly watching them from behind the plain bar of pecan timber. They were his only customers. Hollander motioned for the man to bring another bottle, and he laid some coins on the table. He could see dislike in the barkeep's eyes, though the man did not hesitate to accept his money.

Newton downed half the glass, a little of the whisky running on his chin. He rubbed a sleeve over it. "Be glad you never married, Frank. You have no idea the lengths a demanding woman can push you to."

Hollander toyed with his drink. In an hour, he had not put away quite a full glass. He had sat in this dingy saloon giving Newton support while the captain drank himself gloriously drunk. He was not even sure why he was here. He had never liked Newton; he had avoided his company when he could. But now, knowing the disaster that hung over the man like a dark thunderhead, he felt pity and an obligation to stand by him.

Newton said defensively, "It was her that caused me to join a black regiment in the first place. I was a second lieutenant and not getting anywhere. She kept nagging about me being a failure. I knew promotion came easier in black units because not many officers wanted the appointment." He made an angry sound deep in his throat. "I ought to've known that a man can't stoop to a level beneath himself and keep his self-respect. You can't fool around a tar bucket without getting some black on you." Newton downed the rest of his glass. "You know what they say everywhere else in this damned army? They say if an officer isn't fit for promotion the only way he can move up is to join a nigger regiment."

"That's not true."

"If enough people believe it, it had just as well be true. Stay with these damn people long enough and we'll turn black ourselves. Look at Colonel Grierson. They've tied his name to these black soldiers. They're calling them Grierson's Brunettes. It doesn't matter anymore that he led one of the boldest Union raids of the war. They've already forgotten about that. He's just a commander of nigger soldiers now, and that's all they'll ever let him be. That's all any of us can ever be, Frank. They've tarred us with the black brush."

"We can transfer out, any time we want to."

"You think so? Just try it. God knows I've tried. That wife of mine—she was glad enough to have a captain's pay, but now she nags at me to transfer to a white outfit. She's scared to death that some night when I'm out on patrol one of those black devils will break into the house and climb in bed with her." He grimaced. "If one ever did, it would be the disappointment of his life."

He began an inventory of her domestic shortcomings which left Hollander embarrassed, though he could understand why Newton had sought compensation along laundry row. At length Newton stopped and stared narrow-eyed at him. "You've never liked me, have you, Frank?"

Hollander simply looked back at him. He saw no point in denying the undeniable.

Newton said, "You should never condemn a man until you've tried his shoes on."

"I've never condemned you, and I don't now. But I can't agree with you, either. We haven't been banished from respectability just because we're officers in a black regiment."

Newton poured another drink. "You—bartender—come over here."

The man took his own time about it, making it clear that he was not subject to military discipline.

Newton demanded, "You don't think much of us, do you?"

The barman seemed to regard that as a challenge. He took a step backward, closing his hand over the back of a chair which he could use as a weapon. "I ain't let it bother me one way or the other."

"But it's true. You don't have much regard for us."

The bartender could not be accused of cowardice. He looked Newton squarely in the eyes. "If you was worth a damn, they wouldn't bury you in a nigger outfit."

Newton waved him away. "If that is the best opinion of a whisky peddler in a cesspool like Saint Angela, you can imagine how little they think of us in the rest of the army. An officer can be no better than his command. What is *our* command, Frank?"

Hollander felt his face warming. In his opinion, Newton had ample cause to feel humble. But Lieutenant Frank Hollander had no intention of conceding inferiority. "I'll match my black soldiers against anybody's white ones. There's not a sergeant in Mackenzie's Fourth better than my Esau Nettles."

"Can he write a report?" Newton knew the answer. "Damn lucky if he can read his own name. They can put a uniform on them. They can put them on the roster and even give them rank. But they can't make soldiers of them."

"I'll make soldiers of mine."

"Never in a hundred years."

Sometime far up in the night, the rest of the men came into Gideon's barracks—most of them, anyway. They were staggering, singing, laughing. Gideon tried to shut them out of his consciousness, but some of their talk soaked in. He was dimly aware that little Finley was not with them. He had not rejoined them after he had left the saloon. Someone suggested darkly that he might have drowned trying to cross the river in the wrong place, but someone else said he was so full of wind that he could not sink. They all had a laugh over that and worried no more about Finley. Gideon was relieved when the last man flopped heavily into a bunk and the lamp was out again.

Daybreak found him still staring at the ceiling. He had not slept. He had relived the terrible confrontation in the wash-woman's shack a hundred times. He had waited and listened the last two hours for the bugle, but it somehow caught him by surprise, making his heart jump. He sat up woodenly and swung his feet to the floor, shivering at the morning chill. His stomach burned like acid from his sleeplessness. His head throbbed. This day was going to be hell.

Nettles had been right. The weight of last night still lay as heavy on his shoulders as when he had gone to bed. He hardly touched breakfast, eating a little tasteless bread and sipping black coffee which only made his stomach churn. After a while he found himself in the stables, shoveling hay and manure and not even remembering how he had gotten there. He had been only dimly aware that little Finley had missed the morning formation and had been declared absent without leave.

To hell with Finley.

Jimbo had not spoken four words this morning, but he had contrived to stay near Gideon's side from the time they had made up their bunks. Gideon was both annoyed and thankful. Love could be bought, but friendship could not.

Raking spilled hay from the corral, Gideon could see the washwomen's shacks. Though he tried not to look, he could not help himself. He saw a big freight wagon pull up beside the York place and a white man step down, tying the reins to the right front wheel while the fresh mule team stood patiently with ears working backward and forward toward the source of each new sound. Hannah York came out, carrying a small trunk. The old woman followed, a bundle of clothing in her arms. She shouted angry instructions.

He had known they would probably choose to leave, but somehow the stark reality had not fully reached him until he saw Hannah and the trunk and the wagon. "Jimbo," he said in a stricken voice, "they're goin'."

Jimbo nodded. "And damn sure time, too. Them white officers goin' to want to skin them alive."

"I can't let her go."

"The hell you can't. Count yourself ahead that you was gettin' somethin' free when all them officers was payin' for it."

Gideon climbed over the fence. Jimbo grabbed at the gray

work uniform but caught nothing in his hand except the cold morning air. "Gid, you come back here. You'll wind up in the guardhouse with Finley, when they ever find him."

But Gideon struck a brisk trot, only dimly aware that Sergeant Nettles had come to the corral fence and was shouting after him along with Jimbo. His legs were so unsteady that he fell once and went to his knees. "Hannah!" he shouted. "Hannah!"

She saw him and stopped halfway between the shack and the wagon. Then she turned quickly and hurried into the shack. When he reached the door, she came out, carrying a wooden box that rattled with pots and pans.

"Hannah!" he pleaded. "You ain't goin'!"

She allowed herself only a quick look into his eyes, then dropped her chin. "We got to, else they'll bring us trouble."

Gideon pointed at the old woman. "Her trouble, not yours. She's the one that caused it all."

Hannah's big eyes filled with tears. "It was me she was sellin'. They'll come after me."

"Not if you ain't with her no more. You stay here with me, Hannah."

The old woman shouted, "Come on, gal. Man says we got to go."

Hannah turned to obey. Gideon caught her shoulder. "Turn around, Hannah. Listen to me." She turned, but she didn't look him in the eyes. He pleaded, "Marry me, Hannah, and she's got nothin' more to say over you."

"She's my granny."

"She's no blood kin. She said so herself. Anything you ever owed her, you've more than paid for. She don't own you; nobody owns you. Marry me and we'll live some way." She avoided his eyes. In desperation he gripped her shoulders and shook her. "Hannah, I love you!"

The old woman had climbed up onto the wagon seat, where a white man with black beard watched the scene with a faint amusement. She shouted, "You heard me, gal. I told you to come on up here!"

Hannah pulled herself from Gideon's strong grip and ran toward the wagon, crying. "I cain't, Gideon. I got to go with her like she says. I always done what she says."

She climbed up the wagon wheel and started to sit on the outside. The white driver gave the old woman a firm push and seated Hannah in the middle, his leg against hers. He said to Gideon, "You better move, nigger. This wagon is comin' through." He popped the whip past Gideon's face. Gideon stepped back. The wheels groaned against the axle, needing more grease than they had been given, and the wagon lurched past him. Hannah's head was down. She did not look at Gideon, but the old woman gave him a final glimpse of pure hatred. Had she really been a witch, he would have died then and there.

Gideon stood watching as the wagon pulled away, moving around the corrals to pick up the McKavett road. He wanted to run after it, but his legs seemed rooted to the ground. All he could do was stare—and weep inside.

Jimbo came up to him and stood in silence, offering friendship but not pushing it.

In a thin voice near the breaking point, Gideon said, "I told her I'd marry her. She'd of been free of that old woman. But it was like she was afraid to be free."

Jimbo nodded. "Some people don't know how *not* to be a slave." He put his arm around Gideon's shoulder, and the two walked back to the corrals.

It was upwards of noon when someone found little Finley dead drunk in the arms of a chunky belle in one of Saint Angela's picket hovels. He still had a few dollars in his pocket when he was brought back across the river under guard. It was a mystery to everybody where he had gotten the money. A mystery to everybody except Jimbo.

Grimly he turned to Gideon, who was paying no attention to the little man's troubles; he was grieving over his own. "Gid, you been keepin' money in your footlocker, ain't you?"

He had to ask a second time before the question penetrated and Gideon nodded.

Jimbo said, "You better see if it's still there."

Gideon rummaged through the box. The sock that had held his savings was limp and empty.

Jimbo cursed the little man for seven kinds of thief and black-guard.

Gideon just sat numb, shaking his head. "It don't matter. Everything I was savin' it for is gone."

Twelve

THE COMANCHE RAIDS came almost as a relief to the fort's dull early-winter routine.

Gideon could see excitement building in the brown-bearded face of the stocky civilian Maloney, for the Indians' trail appeared fresher with each passing mile. "Boys," he exclaimed, "keep your eyes open, for we're fixin' to come amongst them."

Gideon and Jimbo were riding alongside him to afford protection as the scout worked fifty yards in advance of Lieutenant Hollander's company, strung in a column of twos. In this case, Gideon had been thinking, the army could have saved whatever daily stipend it was paying Maloney. The greenest recruit in the company could have followed this trail on the run. The Indians had accumulated a considerable remuda of stolen horses. Gideon didn't know how to estimate them, but Maloney said there were possibly as many as fifty. He could not guess how many carried Indians, and that was a woeful intelligence gap.

Earlier, far to the south, the Indians had moved much of the time on rocky ground, splashing along the creeks and rivers to obscure their tracks. Now, with the Concho River behind them and the Colorado ahead, the turf was relatively soft. The horses' sharp hoofs bent and broke the hard-cured grass as the Indians picked their way between the prairie-dog towns and the rock-crowned red hills. They had abandoned cunning and had chosen speed, making an effort to reach the rugged caprock and climb with these horses onto that great plateau, that sea of wind-bent, autumn-cured grass which was their natural domain. There they would expect to disappear as if they had ridden up into that bright dome of brass and blue sky, as if they had been swallowed by the vagrant puffs of white cloud that sent shadows gliding silently across the vast expanse of grass.

Maloney was pushing at a long trot, all the speed he felt was prudent for the company horses consistent with the possibility that the chase might yet be a long one. Gideon kept finding himself pushing a little harder, getting out in front of Maloney so that the scout had to call to him to slow down. Maloney declared, "I never seen one of you blackbirds so damned anxious to get hisself killed."

Of late, Gideon had found himself angering quickly and at almost anything. He flared, "I thought we was supposed to *catch* them Indians."

"We will, and pretty soon, I expect. But it's apt to be a runnin' fight when we do. Last thing a man wants in a runnin' fight is a give-out horse. That brown of yours ain't the best plug on the post even when he's fresh."

Gideon felt resentment on behalf of the horse, though he knew Maloney's appraisal was true. Man and mount had come to a certain accommodation, if not full understanding. "He'll last as long as the rest of them."

"Only if the man sittin' on his back has more sense than the horse." Maloney's eyes narrowed. "You always been reckless, or is this a disease you've just caught lately?"

Recklessness had always been more an attribute of Jimbo than of Gideon, yet he realized he had been acting with a certain rashness. He had skirted dangerously near to insubordination several times, particularly with Lieutenant Hollander, avoiding the man's eyes, obeying every order with an exaggerated military stiffness, showing his resentment without quite resorting to any overt act that might land him on report or even in the guardhouse.

Maloney had no rank. Gideon owed him nothing beyond that undefined black-to-white deference which custom demanded and which was ingrained by Gideon's upbringing. Gideon said bitterly, "I hear there's people in Saint Angela that say the army is always careful not to let Indian tracks get too fresh."

"Saint Angela!" Maloney spat. "Since when you pay any attention to what *them* people say? I don't even drink their water, much less listen to their talk." He heard a horse coming up behind him and turned his head. "What's that sergeant think he's doin', crowdin' us again?"

Esau Nettles was coming up close behind them, well ahead of Hollander and the rest of the company. He had been doing it regularly.

Irritably Maloney turned in the saddle. "You want to take my place up here, Nettles?"

The sergeant made no apology. "Seems to me like, sir, that we can tell from the tracks whichaway they're goin'. They's hittin' for where the Concho-Griffin road crosses over the Colorado."

"I figured that out a long time ago. But if we push these horses too hard, we'll be fightin' a bear with a willow switch."

"They's people on that river. White people."

Maloney spurred into an easy lope, looking over his shoulder as if expecting Hollander to call him down. But Hollander picked up the speed. The reaction followed jerkily down the line of troopers like freight cars at the end of a train, responding to a surge of speed by the engine.

Gideon stared back at the lieutenant, resentment welling up like something rotten in his stomach. He had been unable to look at Hollander without conjuring up an ugly image of him lying with Hannah in that miserable laundress shack. The anger had simmered in him like stew over a slow fire.

Maloney shouted, "Boy, you better look in front of you, not behind. Up ahead is where the Indians are at."

Gideon tried to focus on the pursuit. The brown had swung into a leg-stretching run, his hoofs swishing as they reached through the dry grass. Quail flushed with a frantic flutter of wings that sent an involuntary tremor through Gideon and made him raise the carbine he carried across his lap. He topped a rise in the rolling ground and glimpsed a movement far ahead. A horseman.

Pointing, he shouted, "Yonder!"

Jimbo raised his carbine to his shoulder, then lowered it, for the rider was far beyond range, especially for a rifleman on a running horse. More than likely, the Indian was a rear guard.

Maloney turned to signal the lieutenant, but Hollander had seen. He spurred hard, leaving part of the company well behind him, rapidly overtaking the three men in front. Sergeant Nettles, on black Napoleon, moved up abreast of Gideon.

"Come on, Ledbetter!" he barked. "Don't let that horse go to sleep!"

The brown seemed to be putting out all the speed he had. The Indian, fully half a mile ahead of them, was keeping the distance constant, or perhaps gaining a little. Somewhere up yonder, Gideon realized, the main body of Indians depended upon this scout to bring them word of pursuit before it came too close.

Somebody fired a shot. Hollander shouted, "Hold your fire! He'll tell them soon enough!"

The pressure of the other horses closing the gap behind him did more to push the brown to exertion than Gideon's spurs had done. The electric excitement seemed to reach the animal, and Gideon could feel the response through his legs. From behind him the racing hoofbeats in the grass became like a low rumble of thunder. He found his heartbeat drumming like that of the horse beneath him.

From far ahead came the flat, distant echo of gunfire. The sergeant half-turned in the saddle, waving his Spencer. "Come on! Spur up!" It was the lieutenant's prerogative—not his—but Hollander leaned forward in the saddle as if in obedience to the sergeant's order.

Gideon heard a few more shots, then nothing except the rush of the horses through the grass. A grayish cloud began to rise. Smoke.

He saw fear in the face of Esau Nettles.

They broke over the last rise and into view of the Colorado crossing. The settlers' cabin was ablaze. Gideon saw a flurry of activity . . . men, horses, all in a swirl. Well beyond the river a faint dust cloud betrayed the stolen remuda, whipped into a hard run. Behind it, the warriors were on horseback or quickly getting mounted, spreading into a defensive line to protect the retreating herders. Gideon saw a puff of black smoke and a moment later heard the report. The range was still long. All the old hands said the Indians had not yet gained enough experience with firearms to be accurate. Just the same, Gideon ducked at the next black puff.

One sickening glance showed him that the two white men were dead. Their bodies lay twisted where they had been flung aside after the scalping. They bristled with feathered shafts. Beside the blazing cabin Gideon came upon the woman—naked—a single arrow in her back. Her eyes and mouth were frozen open in horror. Gideon's last meal almost came up.

A cry of rage from Esau Nettles brought him out of the numbness. The sergeant rushed after two Indians. One, who wore a buffalo-horn headdress, held something in front of him on his horse—something that fluttered like hawk wings. A dress. The Indian had the little girl!

Esau Nettles was fully thirty yards in the lead when big Napoleon hit the river in pursuit. The sluggish red current hardly seemed to slow him. The black horse was moving up the north bank before Gideon's brown struck the water. Gideon spurred across to try to help Nettles. He saw the second Indian fit an arrow to his bow and let it fly. The sergeant almost lost his saddle, grabbing at the neck of the black horse. The Indian reached quickly back to his quiver and brought another arrow over his shoulder.

Gideon did not have time for careful aim, even if the fast stride of the brown horse would have allowed it. He pointed in the bowman's general direction and fired. He knew even as the black smoke belched that he had missed. But Esau Nettles, lying over his horse's neck, squalled in fury and fired his pistol at close range. The Indian dropped the bow and twisted half around, hard hit.

The other warrior seemed to pause a moment, undecided, then threw the girl to the ground and raced to his wounded companion. He flung an arm around the man's shoulder to help steady him so he could stay astride. The two were gone as fast as their horses could run.

Gideon could not tell whether Nettles fell from Napoleon or dismounted so quickly that he could not keep his footing. The sergeant pushed to his knees and shouted at the girl. "Missy, come to me, quick!"

The child scrambled to the downed soldier. Clinging to him, she cried hysterically. The sergeant folded his arms about her. "Go on and cry, child. Just cry it all out."

Napoleon came partway back to the sergeant and stopped, nervous ears flicking.

Gideon reined up, showering the two with loose sand. The shaft of an arrow protruded from Nettles' bleeding hip. Impatiently Nettles waved him on. "Git on after them! Kill them, daddammit! Kill them all!"

Gideon wanted to stay and help, but he dared not defy the command in those furious eyes. With one foot already out of the stirrup, he heeled the brown into a run again. Much of the troop had moved ahead of him, but the brown quickly pulled forward into the ragged line. Big Dempsey and little Finley were both trailing.

The lieutenant reined over close and shouted, "Are they all right?"

Gideon did not look at him. "Sergeant taken an arrow in his hip."

"Damn!" the lieutenant exclaimed. That was all he had time for. The lead troopers had come within range of the rear-guard Comanches. The Indians had formed a protective shield behind the wounded rider and the one who had dropped the girl. A desultory firing began, one-sided because most of the Indians had only bows. Their arrows fell short. Gradually the Indians dispersed, fragmenting the pursuing troop into half a dozen groups angling off in different directions ranging from west to due north. Nevertheless, the unrelenting pressure forced the Indians to abandon the horse herd. They escaped with only the animals they rode.

Gideon had become separated from the lieutenant. He and Jimbo and the scout Maloney spurred hard to get around the tiring remuda. Gideon could feel the labor in the brown's slowing stride, and he knew Maloney had been wise about saving the horses. It was obvious that they would not catch the Indians— not now. But they had retaken the stolen stock. Gideon had been on the frontier long enough to learn that restoration of property went a long way in the absence of revenge.

The loose horses were not carrying a burden. It was all the three men could do for a time to trail along behind them and off to the side, keeping the gap from widening. The runaways slowed. Those in the rear dropped to a trot, then to a walk. The leaders soon realized there was no pressure from behind. Before long, the horses were stretched out for half a mile, all walking. Jimbo made a wide swinging motion with his arm. "We can handle them now, Gid. Let's be gettin' around them."

By the time the riders circled the horses and turned the leaders back toward the river, sweat was dripping from Gideon's mount. Maloney made note of it with a satisfied nod. "See what I told you, boy?"

Gideon saw no point in acknowledgment, for he had not argued in the first place. But Maloney assumed apology where none was offered, and he was feeling expansive. "I don't know as we killed any, boys, but we hit them where they holler the loudest. It kills an Indian's soul to give up a horse he's stole fair and square."

Gideon thought Maloney's pleasure was out of place. "They's dead folks back yonder. Gettin' these horses don't help *them* any."

Maloney shook his head. "But you tried, boys. I got to give you credit. You done better than I thought was in you. It wasn't in the stars for them poor people—that's all."

Gideon was surprised. "You believe in such as that, things bein' told by the stars?" It had long been drummed into him that superstition was the special province of black people. Big Ella had always called it the field hands' folly. She didn't believe in any of it—except black cats.

Maloney shrugged. "I believe everything that's goin' to happen to a man is already wrote up yonder, and there ain't nothin' he can do to get away from it." He noticed that Jimbo carried his rifle in his lap, the muzzle pointed Maloney's way. In sudden agitation he shouted, "Hey, boy, you point that thing some other place. You want to kill a man before his natural time?"

From afar off Gideon heard the bugle sounding recall, or an approximation of it. The company bugler was no credit to the post band. Stray troopers began to make their way back, abandoning the chase.

Hollander observed the recovered horses from some distance. He dispatched several troopers including Dempsey and Finley to help bring them in while he returned to the crossing and its carnage. Gideon stared sourly at Finley. He was inclined to give Dempsey the benefit of the doubt, but he strongly suspected that Finley had purposely held back during the charge, protecting the rear. Finley had always complained that the army gave him slow horses, but Gideon suspected that had the chase been reversed, Finley would have been at the head of the company rather than behind.

Finley took pains to stay on the far side of the horse herd, away from Gideon, for the matter of the stolen money remained unsettled. Finley had spent most of his time recently in the guardhouse or on hard labor detail, paying the army for his unauthorized absence. Payment for Gideon's lost savings had not been extracted, and Finley's careful avoidance indicated he expected that extraction to be made in blood. Gideon had no such intention; the money had been the smallest part of his loss. But it might be constructive for Finley's soul to let the little thief continue to fear the worst—and repent.

The chase had gone so rapidly that Gideon had only the vaguest conception of the ground covered. It seemed to him that it took an hour to return to the river. Lieutenant Hollander rode out to meet the herd, leaning forward in his saddle and making chopping motions with his right hand as he rough-counted the animals. Satisfied, he rode up to Maloney and Gideon, who were close together.

"Think you got them all, Maloney?"

The scout nodded his satisfaction. "All but what they was ridin'. If we knocked down any Indians, though, I didn't see it."

"Catching Indians is like trying to grab fish out of the river with your hands. But we *will* catch them—don't you doubt that." He shifted his gaze to Gideon. "Are you all right, Charger?"

"Charger" again. Gideon tried to stifle the flare of resentment. "All right. *Sir*." He looked away from the lieutenant, trying to locate Sergeant Nettles through the smoke of the ruined cabin.

He saw two men digging a hole up on top, back away from the riverbank. Three blanket-covered forms lay nearby. Gideon shuddered. He spotted Nettles then, sitting on the ground beside the settlers' wagon, his back braced against the wheel. The little girl huddled with him, her head against his shoulder.

Hollander followed Gideon's gaze. "Go on down there if you want to, Charger."

Gideon murmured a quiet "Thank you," and he rode ahead, aware that Hollander watched him all the way. He wondered what the lieutenant was thinking but impatiently pushed the question aside. It didn't matter.

Nettles looked up as Gideon swung from the sweating brown. Gideon volunteered, "We taken the horses back from them."

Nettles' eyes were only half open, but Gideon could see the pain. "You kill any of them heathens?"

"Not as I could see."

Nettles shrugged. "Wouldn't help Missy much anyhow. Or her folks. They's up on the hill yonder." His big hand tightened on the girl's shoulder.

Gideon felt unaccountable anger against the dead family. "They knowed the danger. That little girl could be layin' up there with them. What made them come out here all by theirselves?"

Nettles turned his head to look softly at the girl. Her dusty face was stained by dried tears. She snuggled quietly against him, worn out from crying. "They was poor folks, lookin' for somethin' of their own. White folks, but they wasn't free. They come here lookin' for freedom. Me and you, Ledbetter, we ought to understand that."

Gideon nodded, but he didn't really understand. Putting themselves at the mercy of every roving band of Indians seemed a long way from his notion of freedom. He knelt to look closer at Nettles' wound. "I see somebody pulled the arrow out."

"Done it myself. Everybody else was busy."

"You can't ride thataway."

"Could if I had to. But the lieutenant says they'll hitch horses to these folks' wagon and haul me and Missy back to Concho." He frowned. "Lieutenant figures on goin' ahead after them Indians."

"They already got away."

"They can be followed. They can be chastised to show them they can't do such as they done here and get away with it. I expect you'll be with the bunch that goes. Prove to the lieutenant what you can do."

Gideon grimaced. "Ain't important to me what the lieutenant thinks."

Anger leaped into Nettles' eyes. "It *is* important. You're a soldier. Show you're a good one." He softened a little. "The lieutenant's a better man than you know, Ledbetter. He's got his weaknesses, but that just goes to show he's a man like the rest of us. Time'll come, you'll know he done you a favor."

"Damn hard to see how."

"You're mighty close to bein' insubordinate, Ledbetter. If you don't want to clean out sinks with Finley, you mind what you say."

"Yes, sir," Gideon said, knowing he was not supposed to "sir" a sergeant. "You goin' to be all right?"

"I've had holes jobbed in me before." Nettles looked again at the girl. A tear rolled down his dark, dusty cheek. "I'll heal sooner than little Missy."

Lieutenant Hollander rode up and sat in the saddle, his expression somber. "I'm sorry, Esau. I sure hate to lose you right now."

Gideon blinked. He had never heard the lieutenant call the sergeant by his given name before. He took it at first for disrespect, but a look at the sorrow in the white man's eyes told him it was spoken in friendship that went beyond military considerations.

Nettles said, "Sorry to fail you, sir."

"You've *never* failed me, Esau. You tell Surgeon Buchanan I said he'd better have you back in the saddle in two weeks, or I'll pen a bunch of braying burros by his bedroom window. And you keep an eye out for that little girl till she's safely with her own people."

"You know I'll do that, sir."

It was the lieutenant who initiated the salute, unusually sharp and snappy. Nettles responded the best he could, under the circumstances.

Hollander turned. "Come on, Charger, we have work to do."

Badly as he hated to, Hollander was forced to divide his detail. He sent three men with the horse herd and one man to drive the wagon, hauling Nettles and the little girl back to Concho. He wrote a dispatch for Nettles to pass on to the colonel, telling of his intention to follow the Indian trail and render whatever additional chastisement might be possible. The lieutenant sat on the riverbank and watched the wagon start, Napoleon tied on behind. The recovered horses followed so their dust would not complicate Nettles' discomfort. When the procession was safely on its way he rode back to his company, five men short. He faced Maloney.

"What's the verdict, Pat?"

Maloney said, "You got some tired horses here, and some tired niggers."

"I would guess that somewhere out yonder are some tired Indians, too. You didn't answer my question."

"They flushed like quail and scattered seven different ways. They've probably got a place agreed on where they'll gather up later on. From here it could be lots of places . . . the big spring, the Double Mountains . . ."

"If we follow one trail and don't crowd them, we ought to find the place where they come back together."

"*If* we can follow it."

"We'll follow it. I am banking your reputation on that."

Maloney came near smiling. "I don't see where I got much to lose. The army don't rank us ex-Confederate soldiers much higher than it does these buffalo soldiers."

"Maybe we can prove the army wrong on both counts. Let's get started." He glanced at the silent Sergeant Waters, giving the order with his eyes for him to take up where Nettles had left off. Gideon saw uneasiness in the sergeant's face, but Waters put the

men into a column of twos. Hollander glanced at Gideon.
"Charger, you and Jimbo . . ."

Gideon saluted and followed the civilian Maloney, who pulled
up his collar against the chill of the north wind and moved in a
northwesterly direction, arbitrarily choosing a set of tracks to
follow.

Gray Horse had known they should not return to the settlers'
cabin on the Colorado River. The coyote had told him so. But
the insistence and greed of Bear That Turns to Fight had prod-
ded him into going against his medicine.

Looking behind him now, he could see that the whole raiding
trip had been a mistake in judgment. By now they should all
have been in the big winter encampment with the main band instead of here on the open prairie, running for their lives like
scattered rabbits. Bear's agitation had brought them to this, but
the decision had been Gray Horse's own. The blame would have
to be his.

Most of the band had already moved into winter camp where
tall canyon walls turned away the bitter north wind. But Gray
Horse, by custom, was traveling with his wife's family and some
other friends and relatives, setting up temporary hunting camps
and trying to get more meat to carry through the winter. Most
of the meat processed earlier had gone on with the main band,
and there had been some concern that it might not be enough.
The buffalo had seemed fewer this fall, the hunting more
difficult.

Green Willow's father, old Many Coups, had been chief of the
hunting camp. The crippled Eagle Feather had insisted upon
going along to hunt despite the slow mending of his broken leg.
His counsel had been good, but his riding ability was badly im-
paired. He was forced to spend most of his time in camp, where
his wife Antelope cared for him. It was just as well, for the
hunters found little game anyway.

The notion of a raid had sprung up one night around the
council fire as the men grumbled over their meager success. If
they could not find buffalo, they might at least ride south and
find horses in the settlements. The *tejanos* would have relaxed

their vigilance by now, for the autumn Comanche Moon, which they dreaded, had passed, and they would feel a false security since the cold winds had begun to blow. Supplied with horses, the hunters would not straggle into the encampment ashamed.

Gray Horse had been chosen leader despite his misgivings. Green Willow's stomach was beginning to swell. He would have preferred to stay close by her into the spring, when his son would be born. He gave no thought to the possibility that the firstborn might be a girl.

He could not in good conscience remain behind when Finds the Good Water was going. His wife was much further along than Green Willow.

Bear volunteered to lead in Gray Horse's stead, but only a couple of the men supported him. Since Eagle Feather was obviously unable, Gray Horse was the majority's choice. His medicine had been proven. His reluctance tempered by the new spirit he saw in the young men, he promised Green Willow a quick return and led the warriors south for one more accounting with the *tejanos* before the snow began to fly.

Their appetite was whetted early by the sight of buffalo soldiers on horseback accompanying two men in a wagon, but Gray Horse did not consider the few horses adequate to risk stirring up military pursuit so soon. They tested the defenses of the military party at the abandoned old soldier fort that night and found the stone corrals too well guarded. Daylight had brought them to the new settlers' cabin on the Colorado.

"They are spreading everywhere, like the flies," Bear had said bitterly. He wanted to lay waste to the place and take its prizes then and there. That would throw fear into the other land thieves and send them scurrying back where they came from. But Gray Horse reminded him that the men had come for horses, and horses were to be found in large numbers farther south.

"Time enough to kill these *tejanos* when we come back this way," he said, putting a temporary end to Bear's quarreling.

They did well in the days that followed. Near Fort McKavett, and farther south and east, they gathered up close to forty horses whose owners valued life more than property. The only disappointment was that none of the white men offered much fight, and no warrior was privileged to take a scalp or count coup.

In keeping with his promise to Bear, Gray Horse had pointed the returning warriors and the stolen remuda toward the Colorado crossing. Just north of the Concho River, and east of Fort Concho, they came upon Coyote, cousin to the wolf. He cut diagonally across their trail. A hundred yards away he stopped, looking back at them, circled twice and looked straight at Gray Horse. Then he changed direction.

The message was clear to Gray Horse if to no one else. The wolf spirit had sent Coyote to warn him that this party must change direction, too. Coyote meant for them to swing eastward, away from the big fort. The wolf spirit knew everything; it must have known that the soldiers were coming.

But Bear went into a fury. Coyote had always been a wily trickster, a mischievous spirit with no particular benevolence toward man. Coyote was never to be believed. Reminding Gray Horse of his promise, he threatened to go to the crossing alone if he had to. His insistence was so strong that he swung other men to his side. Even Limping Boy, though he did not speak against Gray Horse, did not speak in his behalf. His gaze on the departing coyote, Gray Horse reluctantly gave in. They would go to the crossing and teach those *tejanos* whose land this was.

The coyote disappeared as if the great cannibal owl had risen from the ground and gobbled him down.

They left the loose horses behind a little way to prevent the noise or the dust from alerting the farmers. Moving along in the cover of the scrub timber that grew down almost to the river's waterline, they came within fifty yards of the cabin unseen. Gray Horse thought the dog must be away hunting, or he would have raised a racket by now. The warriors took time to apply their paint, Gray Horse carefully making the lightning streak and the wolf tracks across his body to turn away bullets. He adjusted the buffalo headdress Green Willow had made for him from the first bull he had killed in the big hunt. When the men were ready, he led them through the last timber and paused to survey the ground.

He saw two men. One was on the roof of the cabin, applying

shingles. The other worked some paces away, strengthening the temporary corral where they secured their workhorses at night. Those two animals stood hitched to a wagon in which many cut timbers were stacked. Bear wondered aloud where the yellow-haired woman might be. As if in answer, she stepped out of the cabin door, wiping her hands on a white apron. The wind caught her hair and lifted it.

Two Beavers remarked to Bear how pretty that long hair would be on his scalp pole. Bear said, "I do not want her scalp. I want her alive. She can be a wife for me until I get a real one." He was still a bachelor, still borrowing his brothers' wives.

Gray Horse expected the attack to be easy. The ground the warriors had to cover was short, and the farmers would be taken by surprise. They probably would not even have time to reach their weapons.

He was wrong. He gave the shout, and the warriors rushed out of the timber a-horseback, shrilling the war cries that so often froze their enemies in fear. Almost in the same instant the man on the roof jumped down, grabbing up a rifle Gray Horse had not seen. The man in the corral dropped behind the stacked timbers and fired his first shot before the raiders were halfway across the open space. The woman shrieked and ran into the cabin, slamming its heavy door.

Gray Horse knew that these were not the weak-kneed white men he had seen at other times, running in terror at the sight of a feather. Though doomed from the first by superior numbers and the force of the charge, these two *tejanos* were of a breed that would fight until life had been hammered from them. The ferocity of such men seemed always a surprise to Comanche warriors who encountered them. It was as if these whites were part Indian themselves, for they yielded no ground and gave no quarter. Win or lose, they fought with a savage determination that did not quit short of victory or death.

Gray Horse struck with his war club and took first coup on one farmer. Bear got the other. The warriors rode them down, beating them to the ground and driving arrow after arrow into their bodies, yet the men struggled and fought until their last breaths had passed.

Such men should have been Comanches, Gray Horse thought.

The dog came rushing from across the river. It took three arrows to bring it down.

The woman stood her ground no less than the men. She opened a small rifle-port in the wall of the cabin and thrust out the barrel of a big muzzle-loading gun. The first shot hit no warriors, but the heavy cloud of black smoke choked the men who slammed their shoulders against the door, trying to break it in. Bear shouted for the men to put more force into it. Gray Horse jumped to the rifle-port, hoping to grab the barrel if she poked it out again. Bear brought up a heavy cedar post which the white men had cut for the corral. With it he and some of the others battered at the door. When the rifle barrel appeared, Gray Horse gripped it just behind the front sight. Despite the heat that seared his hands, he shoved it back violently against the woman's shoulder. It exploded, the fire burning the side of his face, the deafening roar hammering in his ears.

The door splintered. Whooping in victory, Bear rushed into the cabin. He came back dragging the struggling, screaming woman. She beat at his face with her hands. Bear was laughing. Soon he had all the volunteer assistance he needed to subdue her.

"You," he said, "are going to be my wife. I am going to teach you the first duty of a wife." He began tearing her dress while other warriors laughed and reached to help.

Gray Horse watched a moment, his own blood aroused by the woman's struggles. The men would expect Bear to share her. Gray Horse saw nothing wrong in that; this had been a long trip. The men had been away from their own women, just as he had been away from Green Willow. The People had agreed long ago that the first thing to do with a new slave woman was to shame and humiliate her, to show her she was nothing and that she must subject herself entirely to the will of her owner. The process had a ritualistic aspect; in dishonoring the woman, the warriors in effect dishonored her people. This was the way war had always been fought by the plains folk, whether against enemy tribes or against the Mexicans and the *tejanos*.

Limping Boy picked up an ax that had been driven deeply into a chopping log. It would be useful to take along. Against the cabin he chopped up a wooden barrel, retrieving its iron bands to file into arrow points. That was Limping Boy—always practical.

Gray Horse entered the cabin to see what might be worth taking. He picked up the smoking rifle first, then began pulling blankets from a crudely built bed. He heard a whimper from beneath it and swiftly drew his knife. He threw off a cornshuck mattress and found a small girl hiding beneath the bed. She screamed as he dragged her out.

He carried her through the door. Terrapin laughed, "Gray Horse has found himself a wife, too."

Gray Horse held up the crying girl for the others to see. He would take Green Willow a daughter to help care for their son.

He heard several of the men shout in dismay and draw back suddenly from the woman. She stood almost naked, her clothing in shreds. Her eyes widened as she saw Gray Horse carrying her little girl. She screamed and ran at him, her arms outflung.

Terrapin shouted, "Look out, Gray Horse! Do not let her touch you!"

In a blur of movement he saw Bear fit an arrow to his bowstring and draw it back. Startled, Gray Horse stood in confusion, holding tightly to the squirming, crying girl. The arrow drove into the woman's back just as she reached Gray Horse, the feathered shaft vibrating from impact. With a shuddering cry she grasped at the girl. Gray Horse turned away, and the woman caught hold of the medicine bag around his neck. Her other hand touched his arm. She clung for a moment, fighting for life, then slid to the ground. The leather string drew tight around Gray Horse's neck and broke. She lay face down at his feet, the medicine bag clutched in her dying hand.

Horrified, Terrapin walked way around her to reach Gray Horse. He said hoarsely, "She was bleeding. She has contaminated your medicine."

Gray Horse felt as if he had fallen shoulder-deep into icy water. His jaw fell, the enormity of the situation overwhelming him. He knew now why the men had stepped so quickly away from the woman. They had discovered she was in her menstrual period. To touch such a woman, or be touched by her, was a taboo that went back into antiquity. The spirits had given down the rule when the People were first granted dominion over the world.

Not only had Gray Horse been touched by her, but his buffalo-scrotum medicine bag was in her hand—the bag he had worn constantly since he had gained his wolf power. He looked down on her and trembled, his feet frozen to the ground.

Limping Boy brought a stick from a pile of firewood. With it he pried her fingers open without having to touch her himself. He flipped the bag away from her. He stared down at it a moment, building the nerve to pick it up, for there was no knowing what had happened to its magic. That magic might even be turned against any man who touched it. Steeling himself, he finally grasped it and extended it toward Gray Horse. Gray Horse only stared.

Hopefully, not wanting to keep holding it, Limping Boy said, "Perhaps no harm was done. She had it only a moment."

Still holding the sobbing girl, Gray Horse reached out woodenly and retrieved the bag from his cousin's nervous hand. He touched it against his body, hoping somehow he might feel its power and know nothing had changed. It felt dead to him, and cold. A shudder ran through him as he backed away from the woman.

A dead snake had been known to inflict a fatal bite to the man who had killed it. This woman, dead, might be taking a terrible vengeance.

In a flash of anger he drew back the knife and was about to slay the girl in revenge for what her mother had done to him. But her terrified eyes stared straight at him and stayed his hand.

A thought came to him, saving her life. Because the girl's mother had seemingly blighted his medicine, perhaps a strong shaman could use the girl in some way to lift the blight and restore lost power. He had no idea if such a thing was possible, but it was worth trying. In the meantime, Green Willow could use the girl's help around camp. Later he might trade her for a horse or two.

No one scalped the woman. All were afraid to touch her

again. But they cleaned out whatever was useful from the cabin, and Bear set it afire.

From afar, the sound of a shot penetrated the dark clouds of Gray Horse's mind. He saw a rear guard riding hard toward them from the south. Behind him rose a cloud of dust. Gray Horse could not see what made it, but he knew.

The soldiers!

He shouted for some of the men to get started with the stolen horses, to run them as fast as they would go. The rest would hang back, protecting the rear.

Robbed of the woman, Bear had not had enough of killing. He offered to dispatch the girl if Gray Horse lacked the power. Gray Horse turned his fury on his cousin. "It was *you* who had to come here. It was you who had to have the woman. Look, then . . ." He pointed toward the oncoming soldiers. "See what you have brought us to."

He swung onto his paint-streaked war pony, pulling the girl up after him. He shouted orders lost on the cold wind, for the warriors were racing after the horses. Gray Horse was the last to leave, waiting for the guard to come up. Limping Boy was gone, lost somewhere in the dust. Only Two Beavers hung back; the guard was his cousin.

As the guard passed him, shouting unnecessarily that the soldiers were just behind him, Gray Horse beat his fringed moccasins against the pony's ribs and put him into a run. The reddish cold water splashed into his face and half soaked the shrieking girl as they crossed the river. Hauling up on the far bank, he looked behind. One buffalo soldier was out in advance of the others, spurring a big black horse and coming as if a demon were in him. Two Beavers' mount stumbled and struggled to keep from going down, allowing that black soldier to catch up. The warrior loosed an arrow that struck the soldier in the hip and almost unhorsed him. A second soldier came up from the riverbank and fired a rifle, missing. Then the first one, despite the arrow that bobbed with every motion of the black horse, brought up his pistol and fired. Two Beavers fell across his horse's neck and almost lost his saddle.

Gray Horse hesitated only a moment. When a choice was to be made between keeping a captive and rescuing a wounded friend, honor gave a man no option. He flung the girl away and reined his horse sharply leftward. He put his arm around Two Beavers and urged both horses to speed.

Only once did he look back toward the river crossing, toward the dark smoke of the burning cabin. Though he quickly saw that he would be able to outdistance the soldiers and get Two Beavers away, he felt no elation. He was numbed by a conviction that he had destroyed more than those *tejano* settlers back there. Unwittingly he might have destroyed himself as well, for without power a man was nothing.

He should have followed the coyote.

Thirteen

IT WAS OFFICIAL army policy, duly documented in the handbook which went to every soldier whether he could read or not, that troops on the march ate and drank sparingly for reasons of health and comfort. This practice also eased the problems of supply and transport.

Hollander's company was not burdened by a great deal in the way of supplies. He had been sent into the field on short notice, and mobility was essential. It was understood that the men would remain on short rations until they returned to the post. Now Hollander had cut them even shorter, for he could not know how long this expedition might last. They rode until dusk the first day, trailing at a respectful distance behind Pat Maloney while he struggled not to lose the trail he had arbitrarily chosen out of the several available at the start. They made a cold camp and took their supper of hardtack and canteen water.

The trail had not followed a straight line. Jimbo had asked innocently once if the Indians might be lost, but Maloney had given him an exasperated look. "They're just tryin' to fix it so that *we* are," the scout said.

Wherever a rocky outcrop was to be found, wherever the ground was bare and hard and resisted tracks, the Indians made it

a point to travel. Once it had taken Maloney an hour to advance
two hundred yards. But he persisted, for he had a Scotch-Irish
stubbornness not in the least diluted by his several-generation status in this country. At last he found where the tracks led straight
again, for a time.

So long as they traveled, Gideon could concentrate on watching the trail and being wary of entrapment. But in camp his eyes
drifted resentfully to the lieutenant though he tried to fix his
mind on other things. He stretched out on his blanket and turned
away from the others. He heard the heavy tread of leather boots
and looked up to see Dempsey standing over him. Dempsey
squatted on his heels and spoke in a voice low enough that the
lieutenant would not hear.

"I seen you ridin' to the front today, Gid. You kill any?"

Gideon shook his head. "Did you?"

"Didn't try to. Them Indians didn't do nothin' to us."

"Didn't you see them dead people there by the river?"

"I seen them. They wasn't a one of them black."

"Just the same, they was murdered."

"Them people was stealin' the land, the way the Indians see it.
White folks ain't ever goin' to let *you* have no land, Gid, but if
they did, and somebody come along and stole it, wouldn't you
feel like killin'?"

Gideon didn't answer, but Dempsey did it for him. "Sure you
would, if you're a man. Them Indians are men. Me and you, we
ought to be fightin' *with* them instead of agin them. White man
taken away our freedom, and now he's takin' away the Indian's
land. What's worse, they got us helpin' them do it. And when
they've got it, you think they're goin' to let *us* have any of it?
Hell, no, Gideon Ledbetter. They'll use us as long as they need
us, and then they'll do to us what they're doin' to the Indian."

Gideon held his silence, for he knew Dempsey would not listen anyway.

Dempsey went on, "I hear there's black folks livin' with the
Indians, even fightin' on their side. We could go and join them.
We ain't got no friends here."

"We ain't got no friends amongst the Indians, either. You seen

for yourself what they done to Leatherman and Ripley last summer."

"I'll bet you them two tried to fight instead of make treaty."
Dempsey looked behind him, his eyes narrowed, then leaned
closer. "We could kill Hollander and Maloney, and then the
whole bunch of us go join up with them Comanches."

Gideon wondered for a moment if Dempsey had smuggled
some whisky along. But he realized that if Dempsey was drunk,
it was on hatred. "You're crazy. Ain't a man in this outfit go
with you on that."

"Not even you, Gid? After what Hollander and them others
done to you and your yeller gal?"

"Not even me."

Dempsey seethed. "Gid, you're like a baby kitten that ain't got
its eyes open yet. Time you finally see, it'll be too late." He
pushed to his feet and tromped away.

Gideon turned over in his blanket, trying vainly to sleep.
Dempsey had brought him fully awake. He lay there, the hardtack and water lying cold and heavy in his stomach. His
thoughts ran uncontrolled. In the darkness, his mind's eye saw
Hannah York as he had seen her that warm summer night, bathing in the river, but he could not hold onto that pleasant image
long. It was pushed away by the imagined sight of her on that
iron bed with Hollander and the other white officers. He struggled to put the picture out of his mind, and in its place came the
fresh and chilling sight of that white woman lying dead with her
eyes open. He had to fight to keep the hardtack and water from
coming up.

Fatigue overtook him, and he drifted off into a troubled sleep,
where Hannah came again unbidden, as she had done every night
since she had left Concho with that miserable old woman. In his
dream he found himself fighting with Captain Newton, the thing
he had really wanted to do instead of turning his head away and
taking the officer's whipping. He had the captain by the throat
when a hand gripped his shoulder and shook him hard. Startled
out of sleep, he sat upright.

Jimbo said, "Guard."

Gideon shivered at the sudden cold. He felt as tired as when he had stretched out on the ground. He pushed stiffly to leaden feet, for he had not removed his boots. He wrapped the blanket around him to ward off the bite of the north wind, picked up his rifle and followed Jimbo to the picket line. The horses stood quietly, taking their needed rest.

Jimbo said, "Wisht I was a horse. They never stand guard duty."

Gideon looked in the direction where Hollander had rolled out his blanket. "Just as well wish you was a lieutenant. They don't either."

But in a while he saw a vague shape moving toward him in the stingy light of the waning moon. Hollander spoke in barely more than a whisper. "Who's on guard?"

Gideon didn't answer. Jimbo said, "Me and Gideon."

Hollander stopped a pace from Gideon. "Well, Charger, I hope you're awake and alert."

Gideon listened for condescension in the voice. "Ain't slept much. Sir."

Hollander grunted. "Neither have I. Maybe I can sleep better now, knowing who is on guard." He waited as if he expected Gideon to thank him for the compliment. It was a long wait. At length the lieutenant said, "Charger, a wall has come up between you and me. We need to talk it out."

Gideon remembered Nettles' warning about insubordination. He measured his words carefully. "Seems to me like it's all been said."

"Perhaps not." Hollander groped. "Charger, I never had any wish to hurt you. If I'd known you felt so strongly about that woman . . ."

Gideon caustically put words in his mouth. "You wouldn't of told me."

"No, I wouldn't." The lieutenant paused, trying to get it all lined up properly. "I had a hunch you were seeing her, but I didn't know it was serious with you. I assumed you were like the rest of us—just taking a little pleasant diversion."

"She wasn't no diversion to me. I was set in my mind to marry her."

"I had no idea." Hollander let it go at that, but Gideon thought he could fill out the part that went unspoken. Because he was black, he couldn't love a woman as deeply as a white man could. Because he was black, his feelings were shallow, passing easily and without importance.

Gideon said grittily, "Maybe we'd just best not talk about it no more. There ain't no turnin' back what's been done."

"I suppose. But I've never had a soldier on my conscience before, black or white. I'm sorry, Charger."

"Name's Gideon. Gideon Ledbetter."

"You'll always be Charger to me."

"I expect that's where part of the trouble is at, Lieutenant. Charger is somebody you just made up in your mind—a make-believe nigger you been tryin' to turn me into. But I ain't no Charger. I'm Gideon Ledbetter, and that's who I'll be when I go to my grave."

Hollander walked back toward his blanket. Gideon supposed the lieutenant didn't understand what he had tried to tell him. There was a lot the lieutenant didn't understand.

Jimbo came up when the officer was out of hearing. "Gid, you as crazy as Dempsey. You goin' to get yourself throwed in the guardhouse."

"How come you listenin'?"

"It was loud enough. You could of lied to that lieutenant a little bit, told him you'd done forgot about that yeller gal. Ain't no sin in a *good* lie. He'd of gone off happy and maybe give you soft duty when we get back to Concho."

"I been playin' that game all my life, never tellin' the white man nothin' he don't want to hear. I don't feel like it no more. Maybe the army has changed me."

"One thing it ain't changed—you're still black. If I was you, I wouldn't be forgettin' that so easy."

They were up at daylight and rode several hours, mostly in a walk, for the trail was difficult. Maloney compromised his religion several times in the process of picking up a new thread after the old one was lost. Eventually, while Maloney toiled with a tough problem, moving afoot in a zigzag pattern back and forth across the Indians' line of travel, Hollander let the men build small fires that wouldn't yield much smoke. They boiled coffee and repeated the previous night's slim supper, calling it breakfast. Gideon held Maloney's horse while the scout hunted for sign. Jimbo rode back to the nearest fire and fetched coffee. Maloney took none until he turned up tracks and was fairly sure about their direction. Then he gratefully accepted the hot coffee.

He told Hollander, "Good thing I talked you out of headin' straight for the big spring. Don't look to me like they're goin' there."

"I never suggested doing that in the first place," Hollander said defensively, then seemed to realize Maloney was baiting him harmlessly. Not often did the Texan have the army at his mercy. In this situation he was indispensable, and he knew it.

The obscure trail led eventually to a small spring—or, more correctly, a seep—near the foot of an oblong hill. Gideon could plainly see moccasin tracks and the hoofprints of two horses in the mud. The water had a suggestion of gyp, but it was not too bad to drink. Maloney, Gideon and Jimbo filled their canteens before starting out to follow the trail further. The rest of the troops, coming up behind, did likewise. It was a cardinal rule never to leave a watering place without refilling all canteens.

Hollander fought the wind to spread his map on the ground as Maloney started away. The lieutenant would try to pinpoint this location and pencil in the spring if the map did not already show it. Another cardinal rule was that any time a watering place was discovered, it was added to existing military maps. That information might mean life instead of death to some future party.

Numerous times they could have shot an antelope for fresh meat, and once they flushed several buffalo out of a deep draw where the grass had cured up thick and brown, and where mixed brush afforded protection from the raw north wind. But Hollander forbade any shooting. Until the search was either successful or abandoned, the only shots fired would be at Indians, he said.

Maloney came to another problem, a rocky ridge over which a herd of buffalo could have trampled without leaving sign other than their droppings. The scout wasted only a little time on the ridge itself, moving down to the flat ground which stretched north and west of it, confident that he knew the direction and could pick up the trail. His confidence was ill-founded. He cut back and forth across the flat without turning up a trace. A long, cold shadow spread eastward from the flat-topped hill across whose foot the Indians had ridden. The winter sun was camping for the night. Hollander reluctantly ordered his troops to do the same.

Maloney's words carried assurance, but his tone of voice did not. Obviously doubting, Hollander agreed with him that he would do better with a fresh start in the morning. Trailing was usually easier in the early hours and the late afternoon, when the upper rim of each track caused the faint depression to fill with shadow.

Gideon read anxiety in the two white men's faces, but he knew that most of the troopers would be just as happy if it turned out the Indians had ridden straight up that hill and off into the clouds. Whatever eagerness they might have felt at the beginning of this search had been worn away by the monotonous plodding mile after mile and the nagging hunger that could not be satisfied by short, cold rations. Gideon's own feelings were mixed. The initial drive fired by the sight of those murdered settlers and by the running skirmish had about run its course. They had come a long way since. He could only guess how much farther they might still be expected to go. Slim rations and gyppy water had left his stomach in none too good a shape.

But he could not forget the fury in Esau Nettles' face. If they turned back now, Nettles would take it as a failure on the part of the troops, and as such a personal failure. It would hurt even more if word drifted to him that the good folks over in Saint Angela were chuckling about the burr-headed soldiers concluding another successful Indian hunt up onto the plains . . . "successful" meaning they found none and were not shot at.

Because he had slept so little the night before, Gideon was tired enough to disregard his queasy stomach and drop off to sleep. Even Hannah York made but a fleeting visit to his fading consciousness. By morning he was rested and feeling better about the expedition, especially when Hollander permitted them to dig shallow firepits and boil coffee while Maloney resumed his search.

An hour dragged by, and more. Without being ordered, Gideon and Jimbo assumed their usual positions not far from Maloney, guarding him, though attack seemed unlikely. Discouragement deepened in the scout's face. The feeling was mirrored in the droop of Hollander's shoulders as the lieutenant waited afoot with the rest of his men.

The cold north wind set something to fluttering in the short grass. Curiosity pestered Gideon until he eased Judas over to give the matter a look. From the saddle he saw it was a feather, but not an ordinary one. It was an unnatural crimson. Swinging to the ground, he picked it up and rolled it between his fingers. It was dyed, the end wrapped in thin leather string, partially unraveled.

He shouted at the scout, forgetting to "mister" him. "Maloney. Maloney. Over here!" The scout stared at him grudgingly, reluctant to waste his time. The futile search had left him ready to snap at anything or anybody.

"If you've found tracks, Ledbetter, they're probably your own. You've left them all over."

Gideon silently extended the feather toward him.

Maloney's interest quickened. "Where'd you find that?"

Gideon pointed to the ground.

Maloney grunted. "Come out of a buck's hair, or maybe off of a shield. Wind could of blown it from anyplace."

But he dismounted and bent from the waist, walking in a tight circle, studying the ground. He dropped to one knee and shouted, "By God!" He looked straight down, then raised his eyes. Soon he found another fragment of track, enough to set the direction. He hailed the lieutenant jubilantly. Gideon saw Hollander's shoulders straighten as the two men talked.

Maloney said, "God must of give that boy sharp eyes to atone for paintin' him black."

Already cold, the trail drew colder as the day wore on; Maloney could not move at the pace of the Indians who had made it. The tracks led the party on a meandering course between and around the rough, stony hills in a direction that varied from due north to generally northwest. At the foot of a red clay hill topped by a ragged rimrock, Maloney came to a mound of rocks freshly stacked, dirt still clinging to many.

Gideon shivered. The brown horse shied away, smelling death.

Maloney grunted. "Looks like somebody done better shootin' than we thought. Some Comanche got this far and turned into a good Indian."

Gideon guessed this might be the one who had wounded Esau Nettles and had in turn been shot by the sergeant. He voiced the thought.

Maloney nodded. He saw simple justice in that proposition. "You boys be sure to tell the old sergeant. He'll be right tickled."

Jimbo said, "I always heard that the Indians put their dead folks up on a platform, closer to heaven."

Maloney shook his head. "Not the Comanches. They try to bury theirs. Puts them closer to hell."

Gideon pointed out some wisps of horsehair on the ground.

Maloney said, "His partner buried this one with all his weapons and stuff. Probably cut off a bunch of his horse's tail and put it in there with him so he could ride to the happy hunting ground and not have to walk."

Jimbo laughed at the thought. Maloney narrowed his eyes. "Boy, don't you ever laugh at somebody else's religion—even an Indian's. Might be somethin' to it. When the Lord gets tired of our errant ways and calls us home, we're liable to need all the help we can get."

Though the rocky nature of the country still was not conducive to plain tracks, it appeared that the surviving Indian had quit giving so much attention to obscuring his trail. Perhaps he thought pursuit would have ceased by now, or perhaps he was so shaken by the death of his companion that he had become careless. For whatever reason, Maloney began making better time.

To the northwest a line of flat-topped mountains began taking shape, their distance painting them a dark blue. Ahead, still a long ride away, a pair of equally blue mountains began to rise out of the rolling prairie, well to the east of that other line

which marked the caprock of the great staked plains. Gideon
sensed that these might be the Double Mountains.

Maloney picked his way carefully—often losing the trail, then
finding it again. Late in the afternoon, the tracks cut sharply
westward. Maloney puzzled over that unexpected development
until he reined up and shouted joyfully. He motioned to Hollander. Without being bidden, Gideon and Jimbo moved in too.
Maloney paid them no attention. He directed the lieutenant's attention to the ground.

"Like I told you, Frank, when they split up, they generally
come back together farther on. Here's where two of them rode
in from yonder, and ours cut across to join up with them. What
do you think of old Reb Maloney now?"

Hollander was pleased, but he suppressed the showing of it.
"You had nothing to do with their coming back together."

"But I told you they would."

"I knew they would, too. I didn't come out here just last
week. I've learned a few things about Indians."

From his jubilation, Maloney moved quickly toward exasperation. "They'll be easier trailed now. Three Indians leave more
sign than one."

"Then get to it and stop crowing. Earn that money the army
is paying for your services."

Maloney grumbled, "Damn you, Frank, you're like all them
other damnyankees. Never give a man credit."

"It would only go to your head. You want me to set Ledbetter
and Jimbo in your place and let you go back to Ben Ficklin?"

"You'd probably show them more appreciation. But I've come
this far."

Gideon sensed that Maloney's show of indignation was not all
pretense. Between these two white men existed both a friendship
and a restrained animosity brought about by their differences in
station, geography and politics. Even if they lived to become old
together, some of that strain would always rise between them.

At twilight the soldiers were still riding. Maloney sat straight
and proud in his saddle. A couple of times, shortly before dark,
the scout reined up and signaled for quiet. He stepped down and
stood away from his horse, listening. Gideon heard only the

leathery creak of his saddle as his brown horse breathed heavily. Maloney tilted his head back and seemed to be sniffing the air. The second time, he motioned for Gideon and Jimbo to come up beside him.

"You boys have got good eyes. How's your smellers? Take a deep one off of that north wind and tell me if you catch anything."

Gideon tried. He smelled nothing except perhaps the sharp presence of ice in the air. He took another deep breath through his nose, this one slower. It might have been his imagination. "Wood smoke?"

Malonely smiled thinly. "You sure?"

"No, sir, I ain't sure. Just got a tetch of it, and then it was gone."

Maloney looked at Jimbo. Jimbo shrugged. "Maybe it was."

Maloney's smile widened. "It was." He glanced back at Hollander, sitting far behind them. "You boys game to make a little ride with me?"

Gideon was instantly suspicious. "A ride to where?"

Maloney pointed his bewhiskered chin north, where the tracks headed. "Yonderway. That smart-aleck Yankee's been wantin' Indians. I got a strong notion we can give him some."

Gideon asked dubiously, "What we three goin' to do—surround them?"

Maloney laughed quietly. "We'll just make sure if they're there. If they ain't, we don't have to say nothin' he can snicker at. If they are, *we* can snicker for a change."

"Ain't they liable to be some risk?"

"There was risk the day you taken leave of your mammy's womb. There'll be a risk of hellfire after you're dead."

As Gideon considered the proposition, Maloney said, "Think of the glory in it, boys, if we find them Indians."

Gideon found himself borrowing from Dempsey's philosophy. "They ain't goin' to let you and us have no glory, Mr. Maloney. We're too dark complected, and you're a Texican."

Maloney held his smile, but no humor was left in it. "They're goin' to have to watch you boys. You've gone to *thinkin'*."

They made another dry, cold camp, eating bacon cooked dur-

ing their noon stop when the small fires wouldn't show. They
drank water and for coffee had the memory of noon. Gideon
heard Maloney tell Hollander he wanted to reconnoiter and take
Gideon and Jimbo with him.

Hollander's eyebrows arched. "You expect to find a camp?"

"I'd just like to find out if there's anything ahead of us."

Hollander was suspicious but gave his consent. "If you find
any hostiles, return and report. Do not engage them."

Maloney's smile bordered on being dangerous. "We'll save
them for you."

They rode into darkness, making an arc from the direction the
tracks had been taking so they would not obscure the trail. They
had left all unnecessary equipment that might bump, rattle or
impede them if speed were called for. Gideon looked behind him
and found the camp instantly swallowed up in darkness. He
wondered how they would ever find it again. Maturity had
taught him to question white men's judgment, but experience
had taught him to keep the questions to himself. He laid the carbine in his lap and stayed silent.

Every so often, Maloney dismounted and handed the reins to
Jimbo or Gideon. He would walk off a few steps to listen and
test the air. Finally he said, "There's a little creek yonder ahead
of us. The camp is a short ways up it. You got them guns
cocked?"

Gideon took long, deep breaths to compensate for the rising
tension. Jimbo showed no more anxiety than if he were fixing to
mount a new and untamed horse. If anything, he seemed eager.

"I never seen an Indian camp before," he whispered.

Maloney cautioned, "You don't want to see *this* one too
close."

They walked the horses, picking their way carefully not to
slip or slide on the broken ground that led down to the creek.
When Gideon smelled wood smoke he acknowledged that the
scout knew what he was talking about. He heard the distant
barking of a dog. They came up on the east side of a small hill,
and suddenly he was looking at several points of firelight.
Maloney raised his hand for a halt. They stared, trying to make
out the main features of the camp in the poor light of a thin

moon. Gideon's heart beat quickly to the realization that he was gazing into a hostile Comanche camp, that he could be dead in a minute.

He dimly saw the conical shapes of tepees set in a half-moon fashion, facing eastward. The buffalo skins were partly translucent, scraped down so much that the light of the fires inside made a faint glow even where the flaps were closed against the cold night air. From one he heard a baby's cry, and the voices of women calling to each other. Gradually, as he concentrated upon the camp, he began to see wooden frameworks set up for the drying of meat, for the stretching of animal hides. The sound of a horse's pawing caught his attention, and he noticed that horses were staked near several tepees.

Gideon's brown horse swung its head around, ears pointed forward. It raised its head to nicker. Gideon froze.

Jimbo reached out quickly and closed his fingers over the brown's nose, pinching off the sound.

Gideon held his breath as long as he could, then expelled it in relief, his heart thumping. "Damn horse is goin' to kill me yet."

"Just friendly," Jimbo replied.

Maloney pondered, "I wonder where their horse herd is at?"

Jimbo pointed off into the darkness, vaguely northwestward. "It's up yonder."

Maloney blinked. "How do you know? You can't see nothin'."

"I just know—that's all. I got a feelin' about horses."

Maloney was silent a moment, deciding whether to believe. He shook his head. "Sometimes you boys are so much like Indians that you scare a man half to death."

Gideon did not understand Maloney's gift for direction, but he came to respect it more and more when the scout took them straight back to the place where the troop had halted. From dead ahead, a voice barked in the night, "Halt! Who goes there?"

Maloney grumbled, "Who the hell do you *think* goes there? Go tell the lieutenant I want to see him."

The lieutenant's voice was forbearing. "Never mind, sentry. I heard him. So did any Indian within two miles."

Maloney dismounted. Gideon sensed the triumph that bubbled in him. "They're a little further than that, Frank, but not much."

Hollander was impressed. "You found them?"

"It's what the army pays me for, ain't it? Hell, yes, I found them, me and these boys here. I think we're due a little more credit than we been gettin'."

Hollander said dryly, "I'll see that you get a special letter of commendation, written by the corporal of the guard. If I can find one that can write. What did you find?"

"Ten-twelve lodges, best I could see. We didn't ride through there and take inventory. Temporary camp, I'd call it. They probably figure to move on north to wherever the main winter camp is as soon's all their boys get in from the sashay through the settlements."

"Ten lodges doesn't sound like many Indians."

"You damnyankees are all alike—greedy from the husk to the center of the cob."

The lieutenant hunted around for a bare spot on the ground. "Show me the lay of the camp."

The two white men knelt, and Maloney drew a rough sketch showing the creek and the relationship of the tepees to it. The moonlight was poor, but Hollander seemed to see the map well enough. Maloney told him the lodges appeared to be semicircled along the foot of a hill, following the long bend of the creek.

Hollander asked, "Where is their horse herd?"

Maloney followed Jimbo's intuition. He jabbed the point of a stick into the ground. "Right about there, up the creek."

Hollander studied the map and wasted no time making his decision. "We'll hit them at first light."

Fourteen

THE LONGER Gray Horse rode, the more obvious it became that Two Beavers was not going to live. He was able to stop the bleeding for only a while, then it would break out fresh again. The buffalo soldier's bullet had bored deep and lodged where Gray Horse could not get at it. The wound needed the attention of a medicine man whose powers were strong, not a warrior whose powers had been weakened if not stolen away. He used what he could find to stanch the wound—dry grass, that great healer, the buffalo chip—always applying a split pear pad afterward. But life was ebbing away. He could see the gray color of death spreading around Two Beavers' dulled eyes.

Gray Horse looked often at the backtrail. He had heard the bugle and had seen the soldiers turn back. Nevertheless, he had a feeling of being followed. Wherever possible he took evasive measures, riding upon tight ground, on the rocks, up or down the small and gyppy streams he encountered before he found a firm surface to climb out on the other side. But the uneasy sensation stayed with him. Somewhere back there, an enemy came after him. Were he not saddled with Two Beavers, he would circle back, coming up behind whoever trailed him. It was a measure the Comanche often employed, one which had brought death to many an unwary white man and occasionally even an Apache or Ute who should have known better.

Except for missing Green Willow, he dreaded having to return to camp with bad news. At the least, the war party had lost all the horses it had taken. All the effort of the trip was wasted. At worst, they might be compelled to paint their faces black and ride into camp with the sad tidings of death, touching off grief and much wailing. Two Beavers' wife had already been widowed once. She had been married to his older brother, killed by vengeance-seeking *tejanos;* part of his body had been chopped up, cooked and devoured in a blood ritual by the Tonkawas, those man-eating allies of the soldiers and the Texans. She still bore the scars from her first grief-stricken self-mutilations. What she would look like after this time, he shuddered to imagine.

After a long while, he lost the feeling of being trailed. The longer he rode, the more he was convinced that the soldiers, as always, had lost heart and had turned back. Recovering the horses was much more than they usually accomplished; they should be satisfied with that.

The time came when even tying Two Beavers to his saddle was not enough. Gray Horse regretfully eased him to the ground, spreading his blanket and laying him upon it. He knew he could do nothing more except be at his old friend's side when the soul departed, and to bury the body so that no enemy would defile it or wild animal devour it. He sat and smoked and sadly talked to whatever spirits might listen. He told them of Two Beavers' strong qualities—his courage, his stealth on the raid, his daring but vain attempt to rescue his brother's body from the *tejanos* and the Tonkawas, and the wound he had taken in that effort. No man had ever questioned his word or his valor, and that should be enough to take a good warrior west of the setting sun to the great valley where hunting was good and thunder never made the ground tremble.

Gray Horse did not know just when Two Beavers died. He touched his hand and found life gone. He reverently placed the warrior on his horse and carried him to the side of a clay hill, where he wrapped weapons and shield and body together in a blanket and covered them with rocks. In another time and under other conditions, he might have killed Two Beavers' horse and left it for him to ride on the long trip west. But in recent generations it had become acceptable to cut off some of the animal's tail and leave it with the body. A live warrior was likely to need this horse.

The burial over, he smoked again and called upon his spirits, wondering if they would answer or if they had turned their backs upon him. He heard and felt nothing. It occurred to him that in the long miles since the battle he had not seen a single wolf crossing that big open prairie. Feeling cold, he broke off the smoke and put this sad place behind him.

The disaster at the river had not been expected, but war parties always planned for such contingencies. It was customary to split up and confound the enemy, meeting later at some rendezvous point agreed upon in advance. Gray Horse no longer felt the need for evasive tactics and reined his horse directly toward a spring south of the hunting camp. He rode Two Beavers' bay horse part of the time to relieve his own of the burden.

Eventually he saw two riders to the west, topping a hill and stopping to look around before moving down onto a broad clay-colored flat. He watched them cautiously until convinced, then quartered in their direction. They pulled up and waited. Limping Boy and Terrapin looked whipped and apprehensive, as if they expected him to chastise them for failure. But the failure was not theirs, it was his own. He had been the leader.

Limping Boy gravely eyed the animal which Gray Horse was leading. "That is Two Beavers'."

Gray Horse acknowledged the fact. "He put an arrow in the soldier who killed him." At least that was some compensation.

Bear and a couple of the others were encamped at the spring, waiting. No one made much talk; all looked like dogs whipped out of camp. Bear avoided Gray Horse's eyes, which was just as well, and contrived to stay out of his cousin's way. Gray Horse had difficulty choking down the resentment. One word from Bear would have been enough to start a fight. He made up his mind that if Bear said anything which could be taken as criticism, they would have an accounting that Bear would remember as long as he lived.

The last of the men came eventually, and there was no longer any excuse to delay the homecoming. The thought of it made Gray Horse cold. He cut hair from the tail of his horse and smeared black paint on his face. The others followed his example. They rode off singly and by twos to straggle into the camp. Limping Boy held back, electing to wait for Gray Horse, who would be the last to go. Gray Horse sat by his tiny fire, drawing little warmth, delaying as long as he could the disgrace of returning in defeat. When he knew the others had had time to reach camp and spread the news, he arose, kicked sand over the fire to prevent its escape into the dry grass, and mounted his horse. He did not look at Limping Boy, or speak.

Riding into the cluster of tepees set along the small creek, he could hear the wailing of Two Beavers' widow in her lodge. He saw a handful of black hair lying in front of it, and a splotch of blood where she had laid her hand upon a piece of firewood and chopped at her fingers. It was his duty to go in and speak to her. He stepped to the ground and handed his reins to the silent Limping Boy. He tied Two Beavers' horse by the tepee, steeled himself, then opened the flap and stepped in.

He was not quite prepared for the bloody scene. The widow sat before the fire, naked to the waist. She had cut her hair short and had slashed herself across the breasts and arms and legs. Blood still trickled from the stubs of two fingers. She stopped her wailing for a moment, recognized Gray Horse and went on keening, louder than before. One of her sisters, a wife to Terrapin, stood by her side, chanting. Gray Horse waited dutifully for them to reach a stopping point. He avoided using Two Beavers' name. He said simply, "Your husband died a good death. He put an arrow in the soldier who shot him." He expected little response and saw none. "His horse is tied outside. I will give you another, from my own." He turned and left her to her grief.

He led his horse down to his lodge and tied it outside. The smell of wood smoke was strong and good. Green Willow had a fire going. He stepped through the flap and stopped. She stood at the far side, her stomach larger than when he had left. He strode

quickly to her, circling to the left of the fire, and took her in
his arms.

After they had clung to each other awhile, she asked him if he
was hungry. She had stew cooking in an iron pot he had brought
her from another raid. He looked in it. "Rabbit?" he asked. He
had wanted buffalo meat; it had been a long and hungry trip.

She said apologetically, "There is not much meat left in camp.
Even Eagle Feather has been out hunting on his bad leg. It is
time we left for the winter encampment."

Gray Horse gritted his teeth. He would not go into that big
camp hungry—another indignity added to the one just suffered.

"I will take some of the men out tomorrow," he said. "There
must be buffalo left somewhere. We will carry fresh meat into
the big camp; we will not go in begging."

They moved in a column of twos through the darkness,
Gideon and Jimbo as outriders a short distance from one flank,
two other troopers performing the same function on the opposite side. No sign of daylight showed in the east when they
broke camp, and little more sign when they struck the creek
some distance from the Indians. Hollander waited there for the
sun to rise.

Gideon watched him narrowly but silently, wondering why
he couldn't have let the men sleep longer rather than have them
sitting here on their horses, nervous and unstrung. He remembered times on the plantation when Old Colonel had booted
every slave out of bed long before daylight, then had them waiting in the fields an hour or two for the morning sun to dry the
dew so they could pick cotton.

It seemed an hour before the first color betrayed approaching
daybreak, and another hour before enough light had spread that
the men could see a hundred yards. At length Hollander and
Maloney glanced at each other and shook their heads at the same
time. Hollander motioned for the men to gather around him. He
spoke just loudly enough for all to hear.

"Surprise is the main thing. They have some horses tied in
camp, so it won't help much to run off the horse herd first. We

have to hit them so fast and hard that none of the warriors in camp ever have a chance to get mounted. They'll swarm out of the tepees like so many hornets, I think. It is not my intention to leave one of them alive."

Gideon said, "They's women and children there."

"We are not here to kill those, but we are not here to *be* killed, either. When in doubt, shoot!" He studied Gideon a moment, then looked at some of the others. "It is not army policy to brutalize these people, but it *is* army policy to see that every transgression is punished. If you feel any weakening of your resolve, remember the woman you saw murdered on the Colorado."

Maloney said, "Them reservation Quakers will raise hell."

Hollander responded grimly, "They are there. We are here. When *they* are here, they may do as they see fit." He sought out Finley, who hung back toward the rear. "Finley, come up here." The little trooper obeyed reluctantly. Hollander eyed him fiercely. "I saw you hanging back in that other engagement. In this one, I want to see you in front of me at all times."

Trembling, Finley nodded. The moment he had a chance he would drop back and hope the lieutenant had forgotten him under the pressure of more important business.

Hollander touched spurs lightly to his horse and led out, the men following him along the creek. As the edge of the sun's red ball pushed over a low hill to the east, he drew rein within sight of the first tepee on the creek. No alarm had been sounded. The lieutenant shivered, first sun pushing the cold down upon him. But he flattened the coat collar he had turned up earlier against the sharp wind. He drew his pistol, looked around him to be certain everybody was ready, then said, "Bugler . . ."

Most of the men had pistols in their hands, but Gideon was one of those who preferred his carbine. He had never come to trust a pistol. It seemed like a live thing in his hand, with a will of its own.

At the first notes, the lieutenant spurred into a run and fired his pistol toward the upper part of the tepee. It struck just below the point where the lodge poles were joined and tied and where the smoke vent indicated a morning fire already going. A woman screamed. A man stepped through the opening, to be hit in the face by the morning sun and two slugs from troopers' carbines.

The camp was a din of shrieking women, screaming children and barking dogs, of ragged gunfire and shouting men, of horses' hoofs beating a tattoo across the hard-packed ground.

Horses tied by the tepees broke their hair or rawhide ropes and stampeded through the camp along with the soldiers. Ahead, Gideon saw a warrior jump upon a horse and start to charge into the fight, only to be cut down before he could fit an arrow into his bowstring.

In less than a minute the vanguard had reached the far end of the small camp. Gideon's carbine smoked from shots he had fired at Indian men who had leaped from the hide tepees to face the invaders. He did not believe he had hit one. He whirled Judas around and looked back for the lieutenant. Through the gray swirl of gunsmoke and dust, he saw him. Hollander's eyes and mouth were wide as he spurred into another run. Maloney gave a piercing yell that had chilled many a Yankee soldier and plunged after the lieutenant. Gideon rode neck and neck with a laughing, shouting Jimbo who seemed drunker on excitement than he had ever been on whisky.

They dodged among crying women and children, who ran desperately for the creek and splashed headlong into its frigid waters. The first charge had cost the Indians heavily. Several dead and dying lay in Gideon's path. He saw a crippled warrior on a makeshift crutch, trying desperately to cover the flight of his young woman by loosing arrows as quickly as he could draw them from the quiver and fit them to the bow. The crutch made him awkward. Hollander and Maloney fired almost together. The warrior fell back, dead before he hit the ground. Maloney's horse shied aside, and it bumped against Hollander's. Both stumbled and almost went down. Gideon heard the Indian woman scream as she rushed back and fell to her knees beside her man.

Farther down, an elderly warrior appeared from somewhere, wearing a ceremonial feathered headdress, his face streaked with paint he had taken time to apply. He loosed two arrows before bullets cut him down.

By the end of the second run the camp's defense was finished.

The trailing soldiers, including Finley, encountered no resistance.
A number of women and children had made their way to the
creek or across it. Gideon's observation had been hampered by
speed and stress of the action, but he doubted that a single adult
male had survived. The last to fall had been a young man—actually, a boy—who came riding hard from the northwest, where
the horse herd was. He looked more Mexican than Comanche.
He had probably been stolen in Mexico and brought up as a servant.

At the upper end of camp, where the first rush had begun and
the second had ended, Hollander pulled up, breathing heavily,
and tried to survey the devastation. His gaze fell on Sergeant
Waters. He made a sweeping motion with his arm and shouted at
the sergeant to take the handiest six men, cross the creek and
bring back those women and children. A few had fled up the hill
to the rear of the camp. He sent three more men to encircle
these and haze them down.

"Now," he said to the men gathered around him on pawing,
hard-breathing horses, "we'll take this camp one lodge at a time
and make sure we've cleaned it out." He spied the unfortunate
little Finley, who had hung back despite orders. With a malevolent smile, the lieutenant said, "Finley, you make sure nobody is
still in that first tepee."

Finley seemed tongue-tied and frozen. Hollander said threateningly, "Finley . . . ," and brought up his pistol. Cowed to the
point that tears began to run down his dusty cheeks, the little
man hunched his shoulders, hesitated at the flap, then stepped inside, pistol in his shaking hand. Nothing happened. He came out
near collapse.

Big Dempsey watched the lieutenant in resentment. Hollander
was about to order Finley into the next tepee, but Dempsey
preempted him by taking that one himself, with the same nega-
tive results. He disliked Finley, but he hated Hollander. A
snarling dog challenged Dempsey as he stepped out, and he
dispatched it with a shot. All up and down the camp, and well to
either side, other dogs were in a frenzy of barking. Gideon
judged that most would starve now, for they were too dependent to live in the wild. They were not wolves.

The women and children, too, would starve if they were left here. He watched them herded back across the creek and down the hill, weeping in fright and grief. A chill that shook him came less from the bite of early-morning frost than from the desolation he saw in these people.

Somehow he had never considered Indians in terms of women and children. He had thought only of warriors, free and wild as the winds that searched these rolling plains and the broken hills of the caprock country. Certainly he had known there must be women and children somewhere, but these had been only phantom wraiths, not quite flesh and blood. Now he looked at the terror in their eyes, and they were very real, very vulnerable.

One by one the tepees were searched. Gideon stared in wonder at the first he entered, for it seemed larger inside than outside, the bedding and horseback accouterments and cooking vessels arranged with considerable order, a fire crackling in the round firehole at the center. A dozen strange odors assailed his nostrils.

A trooper named Jolley walked to the open flap of the next tepee and stumbled back with an arrow in his shoulder. Two troopers rushed past him, firing through the opening. One stepped inside swiftly, and a final shot sounded. Black smoke preceded him out the open flap. He told a concerned Hollander, "They was a fightin' woman inside, sir."

Gideon watched two friends pull the arrow from the wounded trooper and try to stop the blood. His attention was diverted by a woman's wailing. The one who had run to the crippled warrior felled in the second rush was keening a song tuneless and alien to Gideon's ear. He shivered. He sensed it was religious—probably a death or grief song. From somewhere she produced a knife, and he instinctively brought up his carbine. But she used the knife only against herself, first hacking off handfuls of her black hair, then slashing her brightly beaded deerskin dress. It fell away from her shoulders, baring her arms and her body to the waist.

He watched in cold disbelief as she gashed her left arm from wrist to shoulder, then switched hands and did the same to the right arm without a break in the wailing song. She made a slash just below her throat, sending blood streaming down her breasts.

Gideon watched, transfixed, unable to move. The woman's eyes burned with a determination he had never seen.

Lieutenant Hollander pulled his horse around in consternation. "My God! Why didn't you stop her? She'll bleed to death."

Gideon had no answer. He had seen grief among his own people at death, at enforced separation under slavery, but he had never seen the equal of this. He kept shivering.

The woman's eyes went to Hollander. She gave a shout that crackled with hatred as she recognized her husband's killer. From beside the warrior's body, she grabbed up his fallen bow and an arrow. She fitted the notch of the arrow against the string and drew the bow with a strength Gideon could not have believed those slashed and bleeding arms still possessed.

Hollander defensively aimed his pistol at her. The hammer fell on a spent cartridge.

Crying out in protest at what he had to do, Gideon squeezed the carbine trigger at close range. The impact drove her backward. The arrow wobbled harmlessly past Hollander, and the bow fell from her hand. Through the smoke she stared at Gideon with burning black eyes that seared his soul. She sank slowly to earth, her cry choked to a whimper. She stared at Gideon through glazed eyes after the last flicker of life had gone.

He lowered the smoking carbine, tears scalding his eyes.

A woman! God help him, the first person he had ever knowingly killed had been a woman.

A hand rested on his shoulder. He did not turn to look, but he knew it was Hollander's. "Thank you, Gideon. She'd have killed me."

For one wildly resentful moment, Gideon wished she had. "A woman!" he cried. "How come it had to be a woman?"

Hollander said evenly, "Not an ordinary woman, an *Indian* woman. They're not like ours, or yours."

Yours. Gideon stared at the dark face and for a moment saw Hannah York. She, too, was dead to him. At that moment he hated Hollander as he had hated few men in his life.

Several troopers gathered around him. Through the blurring of tears, he made out the towering form of Big Dempsey. He heard Hollander say, "Jimbo, you'd better take your friend aside and talk to him. The rest of you, we have work to do. We're going to destroy this camp."

Jimbo did no talking. He didn't have to; he simply had to be there. Gideon brought himself to look again at the woman's face. The chill still gripped him, and the feeling of sickness.

The women and children were herded into one group. Maloney had counted the Indian dead. "Six grown men and one big Mexican boy is all I can find," he reported to Hollander. "I don't think any got away. Maybe all that raidin' party hadn't got back yet. I find three women shot dead and another one fixin' to die. One youngun dead—run over by a horse, I expect."

Hollander said, "It worries me, there not being more men. Is there a possibility we hit the wrong camp?"

Maloney shook his head. "Tracks led straight here."

Jimbo put in, "This is the right camp. Looky yonder at that little girl. See what she's got in her hand?"

A small girl, possibly four years old, grimly clutched a doll. It was a faded cotton doll with yellow face, with eyes, nose and mouth of black thread. Gideon remembered that he had seen it in the hands of the little girl, Susie.

Jimbo reasoned, "One of them dead Indians was this young-un's daddy."

Maloney sat on his horse and studied the captives. They totaled twelve women, mostly young, and five children. "What you goin' to do with them, Frank? If we burn up everything, they'll starve to death."

"Would you have me shoot them?"

"It'd be a mercy, I expect. But the army don't pay me enough to shoot women and younguns. Even Comanche."

Hollander counted them for the third or fourth time, frowning. "We'll have to take them with us."

Maloney glanced southward, dubious. "It's a long ways to Concho."

"These are hardy people. It seems to me that having them as

prisoners at the post might give us leverage to help force their kinsmen onto the reservation."

"Indians can always get theirselves more women and kids. They're birthin' new ones all the time. Looky at them women. Half of them are in a family way. See the one with all the beads? I'll bet you a pretty that she drops hers before we get to Concho."

Gideon's eyes were drawn to another young woman, obviously pregnant but not so far along as the one under discussion. Big brown eyes were the outstanding feature in a dark, roundish face. Because of those eyes and their resemblance to Hannah's, he felt a particular concern for her.

Hollander asked, "Pat, how good are you at sign language?"

Maloney shook his head. "I never let myself get close enough to learn."

"Try it anyway. See if you can make them understand they're going with us. Make them understand they're to take along blankets and clothes and food enough for the trip."

Maloney beckoned a couple of fearful women into a tepee and handed them blankets. "You take," he declared firmly, in the only language he knew. "We go much far." It took awhile for the women to get the idea and to understand that the soldiers did not intend to abuse or kill them. They talked excitedly among themselves, gesturing, arguing some, then went to their individual lodges under guard, retrieving items they considered necessary.

Hollander dispatched Gideon and Jimbo and three others to gather the scattered horse herd. Gideon was relieved for even a brief escape from the bloody camp.

Big Dempsey was among the detail. As they rounded up the horses and started back with them, he pulled close to Gideon. "Bet you feel proud of yourself, Gid. How's it set with you to kill a woman?"

Heat rose in Gideon's face, but he said nothing.

"She'd of killed that damn lieutenant if you'd stayed out of it."

"They'd send us another one to take his place—maybe worse."

"With him gone, we wouldn't have to go back to Concho. We could just take our horses and ride off."

"Where to? East is Fort Griffin and Richardson. North and west ain't nothin' but Comanches."

"We'd go join up with the Indians."

"You're crazy."

"At least I ain't got no dead woman on my conscience."

Gideon hunched in the saddle.

Hollander had decided to put the prisoners on horseback in the interest of speed. Walking them to Concho would add days to the trip. Gideon wondered about the danger to the pregnant women.

Maloney replied to his question. "Hell, havin' a youngun ain't no more to them than havin' a calf is to a cow. You couldn't kill one with a *bois d'arc* club."

Hollander stared worriedly at the woman nearest her time. "I'd leave that one, but I'm afraid they never would find her."

Maloney shrugged. "Look at the bright side, Frank. You may count off more Indians at Concho than you started with."

Hollander managed to convey to the women an order to prepare the horses they would ride. From the tepees they dragged out crude saddles of wood framing and rawhide. He and Maloney puzzled aloud over the little food there seemed to be in camp, just some roots and berries, a little dried meat that looked like dog but was probably possum or badger or some such thing. Maloney said a Comanche would starve before he would eat dog. The scout reasoned, "Camp damn near run out of anything to eat while the menfolks were makin' their wild sashay. That's probably how come we didn't find many men here; they're out huntin' fresh meat."

Hollander accepted that theory as plausible. "If that be so, let's leave them nothing but ashes."

Gideon brought himself to look again at the woman he had killed. "Sir, we ain't goin' to leave these dead folks for the wolves, are we?"

Hollander took a long, sweeping look through the camp. "Drag them to that cutbank yonder. We'll cave it over them."

They took all the horses except a couple that were lame and three that were very poor. At Hollander's order, these were shot. Jimbo looked away, drawing himself into a knot. He had taken the deaths of the Indians in stride, but he would not watch horses killed.

An hour later the procession pulled away from the burning camp. Maloney's tracking services were not required, but he pointed the way south anyhow, Gideon and Jimbo automatically taking their places as his flankers. Hollander insisted on a brisk pace at the beginning to put as much distance as possible between them and any straggling Indians who might follow. He also reasoned that the sooner they could get the women and children away from the country they knew, the less eager they might be to escape.

Gideon noticed that Sergeant Waters moved woodenly, his eyes drawn again and again to the weeping captives. He seemed to hate this as much as Gideon did.

The pall of dark smoke hung low over the site of the camp, behind them. Maloney said this was a sign of bad weather coming. The north wind was raw and cold, and Gideon pulled his coat collar up around his neck. He faced south and looked back no more, for his heart was sick. He had left something of his soul in that terrible place.

They pushed the horses hard all day and took little time for rest. Hollander figured the more exhausted the women and children became, the less the likelihood that any would slip away that night. Near dark he came across an arroyo with sides too steep for climbing. He put the prisoners into it and had the gravely silent Waters station guards on either side of them.

Gideon's sentry duty was to be after midnight, on the picket line. He dropped off to sleep dreading it, for he was paired with Finley. When Jimbo awakened Gideon after his own time on watch, Gideon arose grudgingly, knowing that the voluble little trooper would make the next two hours hard on his ears. He was surprised to find Big Dempsey waiting for him where the horses stood tied to the line.

He said, "I thought Finley was supposed to be here."

"I traded off with him. I wanted to talk with you, Gid."

Gideon stiffened. "About that Indian woman? I don't care to talk no more."

"Time for talkin' is past, Gid. Time now to be *doin'*."

"Too late for that too. She's buried."

"We can't undo that, but we can make up for it. Our rightful place is up yonder with them that knows who the real enemy is." He pointed his chin northward. "I'm fixin' to go join up with them Indians. I got a notion you feel like I do. Come and go with me."

Gideon could not see Dempsey's face plainly, but the voice was intense. He could imagine the eyes. "Them Indians ain't our friends."

"We'll *make* them our friends, me and you. We'll help them run the white folks clear back to their cotton plantations. Then we'll be free, Gid, really free. Won't be nothin' out here but the Indians and the buffalo and us. Won't be nobody callin' us nigger, not ever again."

"We ain't no wild men," Gideon argued. But on reflection he decided Dempsey always had been, in his own way.

He could feel Dempsey's eyes burning at him. Dempsey said, "You ain't goin' with me." It was a statement, not a question.

Gideon shook his head.

Dempsey said, "Then you'll holler for the lieutenant, minute I start. You'll have to, else they'll throw you in the guardhouse."

Gideon didn't see Dempsey's fist coming. He fell on his back, his head exploding. He was dimly conscious of Dempsey towering over him. Dempsey said, "I'd druther not treat you thisaway, Gid, but at least they can't blame you."

Dempsey struck him above the ear with something harder than his fist. Lights leaped in Gideon's head, and he lapsed into unconsciousness.

He could not know how long he lay there before he mustered strength to push up onto his hands and knees. He heard himself weakly calling, "Jimbo! Jimbo!"

In a minute several men had gathered around him. Jimbo was helping him to his feet. Gideon swayed and almost took Jimbo back down with him.

Lieutenant Hollander demanded, "What happened, Ledbetter?"

Gideon managed to say that Dempsey had struck him. Sergeant Waters made a quick survey and brought Hollander the
bad news. "He's gone, sir. If I count right, they's four horses
missin'."

Maloney had counted too. He had a little more bad news. "He
taken your good bay, Frank."

Gideon didn't know Hollander had whisky with him, but he
did. He forced a little down Gideon and demanded to know
what, if anything, Dempsey had said. Gideon told him as briefly
as he could.

Maloney reasoned, "He taken the extra three horses as a gift,
more than likely. Figures to buy them Indians' friendship."

Hollander asked, "Think he can do it?"

Maloney shrugged. "Comanches are partial to horses."

The six hunters had been out two days without finding
buffalo, though they had managed to kill several antelope by
tying a streamer of cloth to a bush and waiting hidden until the
animals' insatiable curiosity drew them within range. There was
little chance of running the antelope down, for the horses were
gaunt and tired from traveling on the long raid with little time
to graze and rest. The frostbitten grass lacked strength. The
Comanche tried to be easy on his horses during the wintertime.

The hunt had been a necessity, or Gray Horse would not have
left Green Willow again so soon. During the two long cold days
he could not keep his gaze from turning back toward the camp
they had left behind. A strange uneasiness had set upon him even
before they left, and it had grown during the time they were
out. The buffalo dream had come to him again, but this time the
starving calf had not made the sound of the buffalo. It had cried
like a human baby. His baby, perhaps.

A bitter north wind was at his back as he pointed the hunting
party down the long slope that led to the creek where the camp
had been made. Often a thin cloud of gray smoke hovered above
such a camp in winter, when every lodge had a fire for heat. He

saw no smoke but thought little of it, for he reasoned that the wind was strong enough to carry it away.

The first sight of charred ruins made him haul his horse up so abruptly that the rawhide reins cut its mouth. He stared in stunned silence a moment before setting the pony into a run. By instinct more than reason, he brought an arrow from his quiver and held it near the bowstring. He could hear the dismayed shouts of the other men as they loped in behind him.

Gray Horse reined to a stop in what had been the center of camp. Where the tepees had stood, he saw only ashes and charred remains of buffalo hides and lodge poles. Debris littered the ground. Several dead horses had begun to swell. Limping Boy jumped down and shoved his hand into a pile of ashes. "Barely warm," he said.

It took Gray Horse a minute to believe what he saw, to realize the camp was totally destroyed. He saw no sign of life except a few bewildered dogs. Perhaps some of the People had escaped into the timber. He began calling. "Green Willow! Green Willow!"

Other men called for their women, their children, their elders.

They quieted then, listening. The only sound was the north wind crying in the trees along the creek, and the barking and howling of dogs.

"Who could have done this?" Gray Horse demanded, trembling.

Bear found the answer. He picked up several brass cartridge cases and held them in his palm for all to see. "Soldiers. These are from the soldier guns."

"But where are our people? They would not have killed them all. Not all the women . . . the children . . ."

Tears welled into his eyes as his mind raced wildly, picturing the slaughter. He slid to the ground and ran to the place where his own tepee had stood. He grabbed up a half-burned lodge pole and began to throw aside charred remnants of buffalo skins and blankets and parfleches, fearing that beneath them he would find Green Willow. She was not there. He turned and cried with all the voice he had left, "Green Willow!"

It was Terrapin who found the freshly caved cutbank. Feverishly, using whatever implements they could find, Gray Horse clawing with his bare hands, the men dug through the soft earth. Gray Horse found a woman's moccasined feet—the kind Green Willow wore. Crying without shame, he called for help and dug faster, more desperately, until he had uncovered the woman and brushed the dirt from her face.

"Antelope!" Limping Boy said.

Gray Horse stepped back, his shoulders heaving from exhaustion. For a moment he felt relief that it had not been Green Willow. But other men kept digging. They found what was left of Eagle Feather, and one of Terrapin's badly trampled children. When they found old Many Coups, Gray Horse gave up. He dropped on the ground and wept.

Hope left him. There was no use digging any further. The soldiers had killed everybody in camp.

He saw the same despair in the men around him. Some sat as he did. Others stomped about, cursing the perfidy of all white men. Bear, who had lost no one close to him, rode out alone and began to search for sign. He returned after a while and sat challenging the others with a hard stare.

"Do you want to stay here and cry, or do you want to take revenge?"

Gray Horse looked up at him through a blur.

Bear turned and pointed. "I find many horse tracks leading south. They have started back to the soldier village."

Gray Horse struggled for voice. "How old are the tracks?"

"What does it matter? They will get fresher if we ride fast."

Gray Horse pushed to his feet, looking around him. He did not need to ask. The other men were ready. "First we must cover these people," he said. "And we must kill all the dogs, or they will dig up the bodies when they get hungry enough."

That did not take long. As they finished, a distant sound ran a chill along Gray Horse's neck. Somewhere in the hills, a wolf howled. He listened but did not hear it again. Without saying anything, he led the grim procession along the trail that Bear had found.

Hunger gnawed at him, but he did not take time to stop and

cook meat over a fire. He chewed pemmican unused on the raid and kept his position in the lead, following the horse tracks. The relentless cold wind and a light rain had partially obscured them farther south but had left enough trace for him to see. His mind seethed, bitterness and grief and anger all mixed together. It was filled with memories of Green Willow, with ruined images of the son they were to have had, of the grand times Gray Horse had a right to expect, teaching him the ways of the hunter and warrior, the old ways of a man untrammeled on a land broad and free.

Preoccupied with his thoughts, he did not see the four horses until Limping Boy touched him and pointed ahead. A man rode one and led the other three. Gray Horse's mouth dropped open. He could not imagine what warrior might be out here alone. As the rider neared, he proved not to be a Comanche at all.

Bear gritted, "It is one of the soldiers. A buffalo soldier." He seemed not to believe what he saw.

Gray Horse blinked and cleared his eyes. True enough, this was a black soldier—a tall man broad of shoulder. Gray Horse turned and looked at the other men, finding them as incredulous as he was.

Terrapin, grieving over his young son whose body he had seen and the rest of his family he had not seen, said angrily, "He must be a fool. He sees us, but he still comes on." He fitted an arrow to his bowstring.

Gray Horse said, "Wait. It could be a trick."

It was a common ruse of warriors to bait their prey into chasing them into an ambush. He had no intention of chasing this soldier into a wall of blazing rifles. But on closer study of the terrain, he saw no place for an ambush to be set. He could see a long way beyond the trooper.

Clearly nervous but determined, the big black soldier rode up and stopped so close that Gray Horse could almost have touched the horse's nose. The man raised his right hand, palm out. "I am a friend," he said. "My name is Dempsey."

Gray Horse glanced at Limping Boy and Terrapin. The man's words meant nothing to him. They were no more than the growling of a camp dog.

Dempsey said, "I have come to join up with my friends the Comanches. We'll fight the white people together. Looky here, I've brought horses. They're a gift for my friends." He tried to smile, to show his assurance, but the smile froze in uncertainty. His eyes cut from one warrior to another, looking vainly for a sign of acceptance. He waved his hand toward the horses again.

Gray Horse said, "I think he wants to give them to us."

Bear laughed without humor. "He *will* give them to us. All four of them."

Dempsey's eyes betrayed the beginnings of alarm. "I come to you all on my own. I've left the soldiers. I hate the white man same as you do. I want to be your friend."

Terrapin drew his bow. Dempsey caught the movement and looked toward him, seeing to his horror what the warrior intended to do.

"No," he protested in a shout that was half scream. "I'm your friend."

The arrow drove through his chest to the feather and pushed out his heavy blue coat in the back. Choking off a cry, Dempsey extended both hands as if trying to push back the other arrows suddenly aimed at him. It was a futile gesture. Three more struck him before he finished the cry that had started in his throat. His big horse shied aside and kicked at his body as he fell heavily to the ground. He was not quite dead when Terrapin stepped down and began cutting his scalp, which was his right.

Limping Boy mused, "I wonder what he was trying to tell us."

Gray Horse looked down in bitterness at the open-eyed buffalo soldier, quivering in the moment before death came over him. "It does not matter. No white man says anything I want to hear."

"He is a black man," Limping Boy pointed out.

"They are the same."

Terrapin raised the scalp over his head and gave a whoop that startled the soldier's horses and set them into a run. Some of the men had to lope after them and bring them back.

Bear had taken possession of the bay horse the soldier had ridden. It was the largest and deepest in the chest. Terrapin argued that he should be entitled to the animal inasmuch as his had been the first arrow, but Bear held fast to the reins. Terrapin grumbled and settled for one of the others.

Gray Horse said impatiently, "We did not come here to fight like children over a few horses. We came for vengeance."

Bear said, "We have had vengeance. We have killed a soldier."

"*One* soldier. They killed many more of us."

Bear argued, "The rest of the soldiers are far ahead of us. It is cold, and we have nothing much left to eat. I say one soldier is revenge enough. It is time to go back."

That was easy enough for Bear to say; he had lost no close family. But to Gray Horse's dismay he found other men tending to agree. Most had been on a vengeance raid at one time or another; usually one enemy scalp was sufficient to end such a foray and send the participants home to dance and celebrate.

This time was different, he argued. These men, most of them, no longer had a home to go to. They had lost their families. But he could see he was losing. They were tired; they had been on a long raid, then a hunt, and now this vengeance quest. Even Terrapin, who had seen his little son's body, seemed drained now that the black soldier had paid the price.

Terrapin said, "It is a long way to the winter camp, Gray Horse. You have parents there. Most of us have people there, and friends. We have the winter to heal our wounds. When spring comes, we will ride out again and hit the *teibos* from every side."

The anger still boiled in Gray Horse. One soldier was not enough, he cried. But he saw that he was fighting uphill. The others began pulling away from him, all except Limping Boy and Terrapin. Terrapin gripped Gray Horse's arm. "Patience, brother. We have time enough to take more revenge. Let's go back before our ponies die, and *we* die."

Gray Horse declared, "I am not through with them. You may all go back, but I am going to follow and kill some more."

Terrapin glanced questioningly at Limping Boy. Limping Boy said, "Wherever my cousin goes, I will go."

Terrapin accepted that. "May your medicine be good," he

said, and threw his leg up over his pony's back. The others had taken everything worth taking from the soldier's body. The wolves would soon finish the rest, for the winter looked lean.

Terrapin's words rang hollow in Gray Horse's ear. *May your medicine be good.* If his medicine had been good, all these bad things would not have happened.

He said harshly to his cousin, "It would be better for you if you catch up to them while you can. I bring bad luck to everyone around me."

"You have never been bad luck to me, brother."

Gray Horse did not always know how to show gratitude. He did not always try. "Let's go, then. They are still a long way ahead of us."

They did not stop that night until it was too dark to see tracks. They found a hollow where he was confident that their small fire would not show, and they made a rude camp. He huddled near the flame and fed it all night, sleeping little, crying softly to himself as his mind kept going back to Green Willow and their child. Limping Boy slept, and Gray Horse realized how exhausted his cousin really was. He should have made him go back with the others whether he wanted to or not.

The wind let up a bit the next day, the chill easier but still there. It took more effort to keep the animals going at a strong pace, but Gray Horse could tell that the tracks were getting fresher. Because their direction had changed little all day, it was obvious that the soldiers were going back to the fort as directly as they could. Gray Horse took a chance and kept riding after dark, closing the distance.

The wolf could have warned him, but it did not.

Dead ahead of the two Comanches, an army mount heard them and nickered on its picket line. Before Gray Horse could move to stop it, his own pony nickered in answer.

Gray Horse saw a shadowy movement. Almost near enough for him to have touched with a lance, a sentry shouted, "Halt! Halt!"

He and Limping Boy had ridden right into the dark camp, unaware. Startled, Gray Horse started to jerk his pony around. The soldier's carbine blazed. Gray Horse felt as if he had been struck by a buffalo bull. He fell back on the pony's rump, the breath knocked out of him, a searing agony in his chest. He would have fallen to the ground if Limping Boy had not caught him.

Gasping for air, he heard the soldier camp coming awake. More shots were fired into the darkness.

He did not know how he found the strength to grip the pony with his knees as Limping Boy whipped it around and plunged away into the darkness, one arm around Gray Horse.

The soldier camp was thoroughly aroused, but the troopers did not venture into the darkness. For all they knew, half the Comanche nation might be out there. They fired wildly, missing the warriors.

The last thing Gray Horse heard before he lapsed into unconsciousness was a wolf howling somewhere in the night. It had not chosen to warn him before. It howled now, perhaps in laughter.

Fifteen

THE INDIAN women kept looking back over their shoulders toward the flat blue mountains, expecting rescue. Lieutenant Hollander shared that expectation and pushed the horses steadily. Big Dempsey's theft had forced some of the men to trot along afoot, by relays, which limited the pace. Hollander could have made the captives ride double, but he knew they needed no extra encouragement to slow the column.

Gideon looked back often, half hoping Dempsey would change his mind and catch up to them. The passage of time gradually killed that hope.

The second-night attempt on the picket line finished all questions for Lieutenant Hollander. At first light, he broke camp and put the company on the move. They did not stop to sleep again until they reached the stone-house camp on the North Concho. By noon of the following day they rode into Fort Concho from the west. The Indian women pulled closely together and hunched down in fear as their eyes swept the strange place where the pony soldiers lived. One wailed a death song.

News of the Comanche captives raced ahead of the column. The unoccupied people of the post lined up to stare. Some who had been gainfully occupied cheerfully left their duties to join the idle and curious. The commanding officer emerged onto the veranda of his stone house, his wife a step behind him. Their reactions to the prisoners were considerably different. The colonel immediately began talking in terms of the troublesome provisions that must be made to impound the women and children safely without imposing undue privations upon them. His wife, who had taken time only to throw a black woolen shawl over her thin shoulders against the chill, walked quickly around the weary, bedraggled and badly frightened group, then made a second, slower circle, expressing her sympathy for the unfortunate children and singling out for special attention a woman whose pregnancy was clearly nearing its term. She declared severely, "Frank Hollander, I shall be most surprised if you have not killed that woman's unborn child, and perhaps the woman herself. What do you mean, forcing her to ride this way?"

Hollander knew the colonel's lady well enough to have no fear of her. She would sear him around the edges, then invite him to tea. In a mildly defensive way, he said, "Ma'am, I could hardly have expected her to walk."

"You could have left her!"

"She'd have starved, ma'am. But the wolves wouldn't."

She shuddered but gave no ground. "Well, you could certainly have found a better way than this."

Hollander shrugged, for he had enumerated all the options he had seen.

The procession had stalled hopelessly. Gideon idly let his gaze run along the curious crowd until he saw the little girl Susie, rescued by Nettles on the Colorado. She was with some of the officers' children. She wore a dress of new calico, probably made for her by one of the women on the post. Gideon smiled, thinking that must please the sergeant.

Some of the officers' wives moved in closer, along with the colonel's lady. One reached up toward a baby an Indian woman clutched tightly and protectively in its cradleboard. The Indian turned as far around as she could, plainly fearing that the white woman meant to take her child from her.

The white woman gestured and spoke reassuringly until she made it clear that she wanted only to look at the well-wrapped baby. Reluctantly, but probably fearing they would take it by force anyway, the Comanche woman partially unfolded the blanket and exposed the dark-red, eye-squinting face of an infant perhaps three months old. The white woman reached for it again, slower and more carefully this time. The Indian woman handed it to her with misgivings.

Several of the post women clustered, making admiring noises about the dark-skinned baby.

Gideon considered curiosity about other women's babies to be a weakness of all women, whatever their color. He had seen aplenty of it on the plantation.

Lieutenant Hollander cautioned the women, "I'd be careful. There may be more in that blanket than just a baby."

The women paid no more attention to him than to the horses. They passed the baby and cradleboard from one set of arms to another, holding it low so their own children could see. One of the women made a closer inspection than the others and proclaimed it to be a boy. She encountered more than simply the proof of gender, however, and hastily returned the baby to the rightful arms.

Hollander observed the women with guarded amusement. He remarked to Maloney, "I'm afraid some of the good ladies will begin scratching themselves after a while. They'll learn not to ignore good advice, even from a lieutenant."

Maloney grinned. "No they won't. They'll forget you ever warned them, and they'll blame you for not sayin' anything." He turned his horse around. "Well, now that I've guided you soldier boys home, I have my own wife and family to go see about. I leave you with your ladies, light and dark." He winked at Gideon and Jimbo. "You're good boys. You watch out for yourselves."

Jimbo smiled, watching the civilian ride away. "That Maloney's not a bad feller, Gid."

Gideon frowned. "He rates us about the same as mules, and maybe not as high as horses."

Jimbo snorted. "It was high time Big Dempsey left us. You're gettin' to sound more like him every day."

Once before, captive Indian women and children had been

held at Fort Concho pending a prisoner trade and good-behavior agreement with their people. Tents were set up in a large stone corral normally used for horses and mules. The C.O. directed that the Indians be conducted to the corral and that provisions be made for them as quickly as possible. An extra guard would have to be mounted. Though it was the army's assigned mission to protect the civilian population, the military as a whole had little faith or trust in most of that population, especially the kind who lived in Saint Angela. The commander had more concern over some of the drunken local populace breaking in than over the Indian women breaking out.

The detail proceeded to the corral, where the women were directed through awkward sign language to dismount. Gideon watched the young one whose large eyes had caught his attention. She was hesitant about getting down. He raised his arms and helped her. She pulled away from him quickly, fearfully. He stared after her as she hurried to join the other women. For a moment, her face had been the face of the woman he had shot. He shivered.

Gideon would not have had the nerve to visit Esau Nettles in the hospital had the sergeant not specifically sent for him. He had always dreaded being sent to the place on cleanup detail. He hated its pervasive smell of sickness and strange chemicals. But he took a grip on himself, marching across the broad porch and through the door.

There he found the colonel's wife preaching at the medical officer in much the same tone she had used against Hollander. "Dr. Buchanan, that Indian woman has been forced through an ordeal at our hands. It is no less than our Christian duty to bring her to this hospital and see that she is given the best of care during her confinement."

The round-faced officer was straining at his outer limits to maintain a professional detachment. "Ma'am, she is not like one of our women. Those people live like the wild animals they hunt. Their women climb down from their horses, have their babies, remount and ride away. She doesn't need our special care. They take care of their own."

"Do you want me to send the colonel over here to talk to you?"

The surgeon quickly shook his head. "There will be no need of that, ma'am. I'll go down to the corral and see to her myself, if she will let me. If I determine that she has need of my services, I shall bring her here and give her a room all to herself."

The colonel's lady was not satisfied, but she accepted that compromise. "I shall be here tomorrow morning to see what you have done."

"It is always a pleasure to have you visit, ma'am," he lied.

Gideon found the sergeant stretched on a steel bed in a large whitewashed ward among a miscellaneous assortment of the halt, the lame and the lazy, all frightened of Esau Nettles. Gideon suspected that everyone in the hospital was afraid of him except the officers. Even those had to undergo the stern though silent judgment of intense black eyes that seemed to see through the surface to the hidden sin.

Somewhat to his surprise, Gideon learned that one of Lieutenant Hollander's first acts after attending to immediate necessities had been to visit Nettles, to inquire after his health and give him a report on the mission. The sergeant already knew of Dempsey's desertion. Nettles made several pointed comments to Gideon regarding Dempsey's ancestry and general character, not to mention his woeful lack of judgment. "He let hate twist him all out of shape."

"He was a proud man," Gideon said by way of defense.

Nettles shook his head. "No, you read him wrong. He was ashamed of bein' black. He hated it; he'd of given anything in the world if he could of changed his color to white. That was his biggest mistake. He never could see how you can take on the other man's game and beat him by makin' yourself better than he is. He could of been the best soldier on this post and done his people proud if he'd of set his mind to it."

Narrowing his eyes, Nettles abruptly changed the subject. "You been grievin' yourself over killin' an Indian woman."

Gideon could not deny those probing eyes. "I ain't slept good."

"War don't leave nobody out, and that's what we got here—a

war. That white woman over on the Colorado—I doubt them Indians ever give her a minute's thought after they killed her. Been black women killed, too. One time over close to Sill, right after the Tenth was put there, some folks come movin' across the country. They had a couple of nigger women for help. Indians killed them same's they done the white people. I don't reckon they seen no difference.

"Sides've been chose, and we ain't even been asked. We just got to take the hand that's dealt to us and trade for better cards whenever we can." He jabbed his finger against Gideon's breastbone. "You got the makin's, Ledbetter. Some people on this post ain't never goin' to be better than they are this minute. There's men that didn't know what to do with freedom when they got it, and they'll never do nothin' except waste it. But you can do ever what you set your mind to. Don't look back on what's past except for strength." He paused, searching Gideon's face hopefully. "You understand what I'm tellin' you?"

"I think I do."

"Keep studyin' on it. It'll come clearer as you go along." Nettles settled back on his pillow. "I don't suppose you've seen that little Missy gal?"

"I seen her. She was amongst the officers' children."

Nettles smiled thinly. "Colonel's wife, she been bringin' her every day to see me. Gal kind of looks on me like folks, till they find out if she's still got folks of her own."

The old sergeant looked up at the ceiling, his dark eyes softening. "It hit me the day we first seen her on the river with that doll in her hand. She's about the same size as my little gal was, last time I seen *her*. They sold her down the river from me, her and her mama both. Last I seen of her, she was driftin' away on that flatboat, holdin' onto an old rag doll."

Gideon turned away. The chemicals in the place made his eyes burn. "You never did find her, after freedom?"

"I tried, but you know how them slave traders shuffled folks back and forth. More'n likely she's joined the angels. Worse could of happened to her. She could be livin' the way that washer gal was. Wouldn't be her fault, because that's how luck goes for some people. But I'd as soon never know."

Gideon pointed out, "You told *me* never to look back."

"Only for strength. I take strength from rememberin' that baby girl and her mama. I tell myself that somewhere they're watchin' what I do. I've always meant to do them proud."

Nature spared the surgeon the choice between confrontation with the colonel's lady and bringing the Comanche woman into the hospital. That night, her first in the compound, the wife of Finds the Good Water was delivered of a healthy baby boy without the knowledge or aid of the U. S. Army.

The younger woman's baby did not come until near spring. She vowed she would not give it a name until she was reunited with her husband and the baby with its father. To the women of the compound, it was known simply as the son of Gray Horse Running.

Lieutenant Frank Hollander's gallantry in pursuit and the successful raid on the Indian camp was recognized by a personal citation sent down from regimental commander Grierson. The enlisted men of his company were accorded the pick-and-shovel detail, preparing the foundation for a new house on officers' row.

And Pat Maloney's compensation claim for civilian scouting services was disallowed because it was filed improperly.

Sixteen

THAT WAS THE winter the northern buffalo hunters broke the Medicine Lodge treaty and moved down onto the Texas plains. They had decimated the once-uncountable herd along the Arkansas River and began looking south to the forbidden lands beyond the Cimarron. General Phil Sheridan, wanting to rid the plains of that great drifting commissary which kept the horseback Indians independent, winked at the old treaty and said if he were a buffalo hunter, he would go where the buffalo were. Before the spring grass began to rise, hide men fanned across much of the previously unexplored Texas Panhandle, their Sharps Big Fifties booming, their great wagons groaning under the weight of cured flint hides. From concealment on the knolls and ridges of the Canadian River breaks, Comanches and Kiowas watched in growing anger and listened to the dark warnings of visiting Cheyenne meat hunters forced far south of their own ancestral hunting grounds. The Indians struck at isolated hide camps and killed a few invaders here and there, but it seemed that when one died, five more jumped up to take his place. Wherever the white men went, they left behind them desolation and the stench of rotting flesh while children whimpered hungrily in the lodges.

Limping Boy and Gray Horse spent much of that winter

alone. Gray Horse was so badly wounded and his mind so dark
that for a time his cousin almost despaired of keeping him alive.
He made camp first against a red bluff overhang on the Double
Mountain Fork, using what healing powers he had learned, wishing futilely for a medicine man. Gray Horse seemed to wait only
for death.

Limping Boy remembered the Medicine Mounds, which lay
several days to the north, beyond sight. Twice that he could recall, in times when strange sicknesses had been laid upon them,
the band had moved to camp in the shade of the four great
mounds where the healing spirits dwelled. Perhaps those spirits
might choose to help Gray Horse. If they did not, it would be a
holy place to bury him. He lifted Gray Horse up onto his pony,
tying him so he would not fall, and faced into the sharp north
wind.

A day before he reached them, he could see the four strange
hills rising from the uneven plain like nipples on the belly of a
sleeping wolf. In another place they might not have been particularly noticeable, but standing in isolation they were like surviving sentinel warriors, remnants of something far larger in the
long ages before the People came, when the spirits had been in
sole possession. It seemed reasonable the spirits would have
gathered to these lofty monuments to watch over the bountiful
land they had generously decided to share with their chosen people.

He crossed Pease River, whose waters pinched the drinker like
wild persimmon, and headed across the red breaks to the four
round peaks, which seemed to rise up from a sitting position to
await him as he neared. The southernmost pair were not so large
as the other two. The largest was farthest northwest, but he
remembered that the second from that end had a bubbling spring
on its southwestern foot. The water was gyppy enough to bring
tears to a strong man's eyes, but the medicine men had always
claimed it was curative. Nothing in life was granted without
some payment. Limping Boy took the horses up onto a bench
which lay along the mound's southern face. From there he could
see half a day's ride in three directions, so the soldiers could not
surprise him. He had hoped he might find others of the People

encamped here, but he was disappointed. He and Gray Horse were alone, except for the silent spirits who watched them. He chose a campsite amid the sheltering junipers, where strong waters broke out of the hill and murmured down toward the red gash of an eroded old buffalo trail, leaving crystals of gypsum to sparkle in the winter sun.

They need not hunger. He could see grazing buffalo by the thousands, scattered toward the long line of blue, flat-topped hills which lay far southward, toward the Double Mountains.

When camp was made, Limping Boy climbed to the top of the hill over soft and crumbling gypsum rock of varied but muted colors. The hillside was littered with slabs and shards of what once had been a protective caprock. At the top he shivered, struck hard by a high, chilly wind. From the summit he saw thousands more buffalo, scattered in small herds, grazing as far as he could see northward toward the blue cluster of the Wichita Mountains many days' ride beyond Red River. He sat down where a gnarled juniper helped deflect the wind. With some difficulty, he lighted his pipe, blowing a puff to the sun, one to earth, one to each of the four directions. He did not know to which spirit he should address his problem, so he talked to any and all who would listen.

It seemed to him after a while that the wind became calmer and warmer. He sensed the invisible presence he had come here to seek and was surprised that he felt neither frightened nor awed. It was as if he sat in the lodge of an old and revered friend who bade him welcome. He talked at length about the misfortune which had brought him here and asked the spirits, if it was their will, to bring Gray Horse back from the darkness.

Bone tired from the long ride, Gray Horse slept that day and all night. Next morning he awoke with his first hunger since he had been wounded. Limping Boy smiled and went out to kill a barren and fat young buffalo cow. But recovery was slow, and at times Limping Boy feared that Gray Horse did not really want to live. He talked little, and he never mentioned Green Willow's name, for it was not the People's way to speak the name of one so recently dead. Mostly he mourned in silence.

One morning Limping Boy tried to cheer him by pointing out

the great panorama to the south. "I have never seen so many buffalo in one place," he declared.

Gray Horse nodded grimly. "It is a sight I would have wanted my son to see." He turned away, facing toward the mound.

It seemed for a time that only by talking of revenge could Limping Boy kindle the flame of life in his cousin's eyes. Anger would sometimes bring the heart to a strong beat, for a while. And finally Gray Horse began to show an interest in small things around him, like the wind that spoke in his ear, and the winter birds which talked to him of faraway places he had not seen in a long time. Too, there was the grass. Gray Horse had always taken grass for granted; it was either there or it was not. But lying in the simple camp with nothing to do but observe, he began to remark on how many and how varied the grasses were. There were short ones, tall ones, curly kinds that seemed almost to twist themselves into knots. One which drew his particular attention had a stem thin and arrow-straight. The matured seeds clung to one side of it like scalps to a warrior's lance. Limping Boy took that as a favorable sign. His cousin was thinking in terms of war.

One day as he stood on top of the hill, looking for sign of anything human, Limping Boy heard the distant echo of guns. His first emotion was fear. Perhaps the soldiers were coming. He watched for a long time but saw nothing. Gray Horse, lying in the camp below, evidently had not heard. Limping Boy chose not to tell him until he investigated. He rode in the direction from which the sound had come, keeping to the protection of the juniper and the dry washes.

Two hours later he lay on a small rise, his pony tied in an arroyo, and gazed for the first time upon the bearded hunters making a *stand*, blazing away at a bewildered little group of buffalo they had trapped in a deep swale. They did not stop even at the young calves, for the kips would fetch a price of sorts on the eastern market. Limping Boy watched the slaughter in silent amazement, for he could see only two hunters. They killed more buffalo than twenty Comanche warriors would normally take with bow and arrow. When a few of the shaggy brown beasts escaped over a hillside, breaking up the bloody stand, Limping

Boy watched the hunters pick up their ponderous rifles and the tripods that supported them, wave their wagons in for the skinning, and go out a-horseback to search for more buffalo.

The skinners moved quickly and methodically. They would make a split along the belly and skin out the legs, then use a horse team to yank the hide off in one quick burst. They did in minutes what the women of the tribe might not finish in an hour.

These men, though dark from sun and wind, were not like the Mexicans he had seen, and their four-wheeled wagons were not like the great groaning two-wheeled carts the Comancheros used. These looked like the bearded *tejanos*. He had no way of knowing they were of yet another breed, the questing, ambitious, hungry Yankee, seeking not to settle the land but to take its bounty and move on to a more hospitable clime.

He waited until they were gone, then stole down and carved a chunk of hump from a likely cow. He could not understand why the white men had shown little interest in all this meat, for he had seen them take only a few tongues, a hump and a couple of quarters. The rest they left for the wolves, a shameful waste. He took the meat back to his well-concealed camp and cooked it over an open fire while he told the silent, brooding Gray Horse of the odd things he had seen. He could only surmise that these men worked for the soldiers, and that they needed the hides to build tepees for a great soldier camp somewhere to the east. But he still could not understand why they did not take the meat; surely soldiers ate like other men.

Next morning, after greeting the cold sun, Limping Boy moved Gray Horse southwestward, for it was no longer safe here. He told the buffalo he passed that they should move too, but they paid no heed except to drift away from him in their awkward gait, slinging their massive heads. If he had the buffalo medicine, perhaps they would listen to him.

Limping Boy made a new camp where he no longer heard the hunters' guns, and he watched Gray Horse slowly gain strength. One day, out looking for meat, Limping Boy unexpectedly came face to face with a small party of Kiowas on the same mission. He raised his hand in peace and waited uneasily while they returned it and moved up closer to look him over. From stories the old men told, he knew that Comanche and Kiowa had once been enemies, as Comanche and Apache still were. Allies now for a long time, often hunting and raiding together, they were still different in as many ways as they were alike. Though it was unspeakable for a Comanche to kill another Comanche, it was not unknown for disagreement between Comanche and Kiowa to lead to killing. For all Limping Boy knew, some old grievance might have gone unsettled, and these Kiowa warriors might see fit to kill a lone Comanche out here where no one but the spirits would ever know.

To his relief, he found that they bore him no enmity. Through sign language—their speech was totally alien to him—they told him they regarded themselves as his friends and wondered where the rest of his people were. Limping Boy told them of Gray Horse and of the great hurt he had suffered at the hands of the soldiers. The Kiowas generously took the two Comanches to their own camp hidden in the deep breaks at the bend of a little creek. There a Kiowa medicine man made incantations over Gray Horse. Limping Boy feared that the alien Kiowa spirits might undo the work of the Medicine Mounds, but evidently they were at peace with the Comanche guardian powers. With food and rest and the frequent ministrations of the tireless shaman, Gray Horse continued to regain his strength. A fire kindled in his eyes—an angry fire, different from the light of joy which had been there before. Gray Horse did not speak of the lost woman, or the unborn child, but Limping Boy knew they were much on his mind. When Gray Horse began practicing with a bow and arrows given him by an obliging Kiowa brother, Limping Boy knew that he intended a terrible revenge.

The two Comanches spent the remainder of the winter in the company of these strange but hospitable Kiowas. Before the new grass began to green, Gray Horse was riding with them to the buffalo. When news came that a party of white hunters had camped a few miles down the creek, his eyes glowed with a hatred Limping Boy had never seen. He rode in the lead, for the Kiowas agreed he was entitled to a chance at first coup in view of his great loss.

They struck the camp like a bolt of lightning, stampeding the stock, killing three skinners almost before the men had time to bring their rifles into use. A hunter, wounded in one leg, still stood after the raiders swept by. Gray Horse reined around and went back for him. He signaled that the white man was his. The hunter held one of those great and heavy rifles, those octagonal-barreled Big Fifties that so efficiently slew buffalo with a single shot to the lungs. The rifle had jammed or was empty, for the hunter made no effort to bring it to his shoulder as Gray Horse rode up to him in a walk, the Kiowas trailing silently behind. Gray Horse slid to the ground, knife in his hand, and walked those last few steps to where the white man stood. The hunter's eyes were full of fear, but he made no effort to defend himself. He seemed paralyzed. Gray Horse stood within arm's length of him a long moment, hypnotizing him with the ungiving hatred in his eyes. The Comanche buried his knife to the hilt in the man's stomach.

Dropping the useless rifle, the hunter slumped to his knees and groaned. Gray Horse stepped to one side as the man pitched onto his face. Without waiting for him to finish dying, Gray Horse put a foot on his neck, made a quick slash around the top of the head and jerked the scalp free. Turning, he raised it over his head and shouted in exultation. The Kiowas cheered him, then one by one came and touched the white man, taking coup for themselves.

Limping Boy did not count coup. He went off to smoke, to thank the spirits for bringing Gray Horse back from death.

Though these Kiowas were isolated, they were not without contacts with others of their kind. From visits by other Indians to their camp, and by lengthy conferences with hunting bands encountered on the buffalo range, fragments of news kept drifting in. White buffalo hunters had penetrated deeply into the treaty lands. On the reservation in what the white people called Indian Territory, there was great unrest among those who listened to the entreaties of the Quaker peacemakers and tried the white man's road. The government rations were not enough. Many people were reduced to eating their own horses and mules, and those they did not eat were in constant danger of being stolen by white renegade thieves who preyed upon them from both north and south. The Quakers and the Fort Sill soldier chiefs were long on promises but short on delivery.

As warm spring turned toward hot, dry summer, Gray Horse and Limping Boy at last found Comanches, though not of their own band, hunting with some of the Kiowas. Even a few of the Cheyennes and Arapahoes were along, compounding the confusion of many languages. The talk was that all the tribes—on and off the reservation—were restless, looking for a fight. It was said that even the Comanche was to conduct a Sun Dance.

This surprised Gray Horse. The People had never put much credence in the group religious ceremonies so highly regarded by most plains tribes. The Comanche tended to look upon others' group practices with a faint amusement, accepting them as a great show to watch but not to be taken seriously, for the other tribes were notoriously superstitious. The individual Comanche needed none of this, and he needed no priest. He knew very well who his own true spirits were; he conversed with them regularly.

This year, however, a new feeling of urgency had swept the plains like a wind-driven grass fire. Even Indians who distrusted each other pulled together belatedly against the threat of a common enemy whose strength had to be met before it was too late. The Comanche had become—at least for now—tolerant toward the foibles of the neighboring tribes. He wondered if there might be some little substance scattered here and there in their sometimes contradictory rites of worship.

From the first Comanches they encountered, Gray Horse and Limping Boy began hearing of a fiery young Quahadi who had talked with the Sure Enough Father and had been shown a vision of a victory that would drive the white man forever from the plains. In that vision he had been told to gather the Comanches to the Wichita Mountains and conduct there a Sun Dance like those they had often watched among the Kiowa and Cheyenne brothers. From this dance would emerge a powerful medicine that the white man could not defeat. The soldiers and the hunters would be crushed like insects. The buffalo would be replenished, and the land would forever belong to the People.

For his own part, Gray Horse was not convinced, but he could see no harm in the dance. The Comanches' own spirits would understand that the People were not truly proselytized to alien faiths, that they would use them only as a temporary expedient. Still, the dance was too near the reservation for him. He had a deep dread of that place.

"We will watch from afar," he told Limping Boy. "We will see enough."

Even after hours on the trail, Gray Horse periodically felt a chill along his spine as he stared in awe at the immense aggregation of warlike horsemen who rode on either side of him. This was a scene the old men of future years would describe reverently to wide-eyed grandchildren, as Gray Horse in his boyhood had heard his elders tell about the great Comanche raid of another generation which had slashed like a skinning knife all the way to the Gulf of Mexico. He had been too young for the Elm Creek raid of 1864, the largest Comanche warrior gathering in history. But it fired his blood to be part of this force—several hundred mounted warriors riding in an easy trot, spread in a loose and easy formation like a large flight of geese moving to their summer feeding grounds. These warriors rode west to wrest their ancient buffalo range from the invading white men and leave such a trail of blood and destruction that no *teibo* would set foot on that ground for another twenty years. They were Comanches, for the most part, riding lean, carrying little except for weapons. They were resplendent in color, each man's bullhide shield decorated with bright feathers and his own personal designs, reflecting his individual whims or perhaps the type of medicine that gave him his power. Beside the Comanches rode a delegation of their Kiowa allies, and a number of Cheyennes thirsting to avenge themselves on the men who had starved or driven them out of their homeland on the northern plains.

It was a huge and deadly force, surely strong enough, Gray Horse thought, to push to the great blue waters of the Gulf as their fathers and grandfathers had once done. But from the first, a persistent worry had nagged him like a buzzing mosquito. Each time he tried to trace the source of that doubt, his eyes returned to the young rider responsible for this massive war party, the intense and persuasive young man named Isatai, or Hind End of the Wolf. Gray Horse had never decided just what he should think of Isatai, the man many Comanches proclaimed a prophet. Untried as either a warrior or a medicine man, he had risen up out of the frustrations and despair of the reservation people and had proclaimed himself the instrument of their deliverance. Wondrous things had been told of this blistering young orator. Reliable men swore they had seen him bring dead bodies to life. They had seen him cough up a wagonload of cartridges and swallow them again—enough cartridges to kill every white man from the Canadian to the Nueces. He possessed powers like those in the tales from the olden times.

All these miracles had been performed and seen on the reservation, so Gray Horse had not witnessed them for himself. He did not know how much to believe of Isatai. A man proved himself by his deeds, not by his words. So far, Gray Horse had seen no deeds. But he wanted to believe, for Isatai had stirred all the warrior spirits in his blood. The sullen hatred had become a consuming flame in his soul.

Isatai had not done anything about the grasshoppers. The dry summer had brought on the largest hatch Gray Horse had seen since he was a boy. At times, the passage of the huge mass of horses through the short, dry grass raised great clouds of the leaping insects, a maddening plague to man and beast. He irritably brushed them from his legs, from his body. His pony slung its head and switched its tail, fighting them from nostrils to flanks. Still, the hoppers did not seriously slow the Indians.

These fired-up warriors were on their way to obliterate a buffalo-hunter post which had arisen last winter like a festering sore at a place the white men called "Adobe Walls" on the eastern Texas plains. Nearby crumbled the ruins of a mud trading post which William Bent had built in 1843. There, in 1864, a combined force of Comanches and Kiowas had driven off Kit Carson and his federal troops, along with their Apache and Ute allies. There were far fewer of the hunters at Adobe Walls; riding over them would be easy. With fresh scalps and a victory to revitalize their spirits, these warriors could then turn south and cut a swath across Texas that no man, white or red, would ever forget.

That, at least, was Isatai's assurance. But Gray Horse watched him and wondered, for his own loss of power had made him painfully aware of a man's dependence upon the spirits. If for any reason they turned away from him, there seemed little he could do for himself. Should Isatai's powers prove weak, or his spirits become displeased, they might bring disaster upon all in the party. Though powerful, the spirits were sometimes as fickle as a young woman.

The particular claim which plagued Gray Horse more than any other was the prophet's assurance that he could make every fighter immune to the white man's rifles, that his magic would make the bullets fall as harmlessly as the rain. Gray Horse's observation had been that a man was fortunate if he could extend the protection of his personal powers over a few of those nearest to him—his family, perhaps, or a few comrades accompanying him on a horse-gathering trip. He found it hard to believe that one man had enough medicine to shield an army of this size.

The night before the attack, camp was prudently made some distance east of the post so the campfires and the dancing and the singing of war songs would not alert the white men that death was coming for them at sunrise. Gray Horse solemnly painted his face and body and decorated the strong-legged brown horse he had taken in the spring raid on the buffalo hunter camp. The scalp of the brown's former owner dangled from Gray Horse's feather-rimmed shield, along with the old buffalo tail. While other warriors danced and shouted and made their personal preparations, he walked quietly in darkness to a small knoll. He sat on his blanket and smoked his pipe and opened his senses for sign that the spirits had forgiven the unfortunate incident that had dishonored him in their eyes. All he saw or heard was Limping Boy, standing vigil at a respectful distance, guaranteeing him his privacy in case other men might come along seeking a secluded place to commune with their own personal benefactors. Gray

Horse sat through the long hours of the early-summer night, talking silently from his heart to spirits that seemed not to hear. Two hours before sunrise he solemnly folded his blanket and walked back to camp. Limping Boy followed without question.

On the surface, the great army seemed a hopeless mixture of languages and general confusion, but singleness of purpose bound strangers to one another. Breaking camp, they seemed to move in unison without conscious signal, like a great flock of wild birds circling and swooping together. Plodding of the hoofs of seven hundred horses made a low rumble on the short-grass turf.

At first light, they came abruptly into sight of the hide hunters' camp, and the smell of wood smoke touched Gray Horse's nostrils. The Indians quietly formed themselves into a massive line, with Isatai on its right end, his body yellow with the magic paint that no bullet could penetrate. The sun would rise behind their backs and blind any white men who happened to stir from sleep before the bullets and arrows struck or the war clubs fell. Bullhide shields rattled dryly as warriors nervously struck them against bows or rifles or lances. Horses pranced, sensing the excitement building in the men who rode them.

The dim light showed Gray Horse four small sod buildings set in a line, with a large picket corral to the right. He saw no movement. The hunters must still be asleep. For the moment, he felt reassured. All seemed to be as Isatai had promised. These wrathful riders of judgment would swarm out of the dawn like a thunderstorm, and in minutes not a white man would remain alive. He watched Isatai, feeling somehow a little sorry for him, for the prophet was not to ride down in the attack and see his enemies die. It was his duty to remain behind and watch from afar, using his power for all the fighting men.

Gray Horse switched his gaze to the young war chief Quanah, who was to give the Comanche contingent what leadership there was in a band of individualists who recognized no man's authority over another. Quanah, tall and straight, strong and bold, was the son of the well-remembered chief Peta Nocona and a white captive woman named Cynthia Ann Parker, taken as a girl in a devastating raid along the Navasota River back in 1836, the year the *tejanos* had fought and won their war against Mexico. She had been "freed" by Texas Rangers in 1860 but pined away and soon died, white of skin but Comanche at heart, an alien in the white world of her birth. The boy Quanah had grown up as much a Comanche as any man in the Quahadi band, though he was sensitive about his white blood and took frequent sweat baths to rid himself of a white-man smell that his heritage had saddled upon him.

The Kiowas had brought along a bugler, who by the look of him was not Kiowa at all, but probably a Mexican captive along with the tribe. From down the line Gray Horse heard the bugle blast. Suddenly the broad formation was moving. Seven hundred voices raised a blood cry that must have shaken the low hills east and south of the wide meadow. The drumming of hoofs swelled like rolling summer thunder. Breaking through a line of cotton-woods and willows and crossing a narrow creek, the wedge be-came broken and confused as the faster horses pulled ahead. The little string of sod structures seemed to rush at Gray Horse as the leading edge of the rising sun brought them to a flaming or-ange. He rode bareback, with only a horsehair rope tied around the horse's middle so he could hook a toe and drop down on one side, away from enemy fire. He leaned over the horse's withers, trying to aim the big rifle he had taken from the hunter. The front sight bobbed hopelessly up and down, making him con-sider dropping the rifle and using the bow.

Then something went suddenly and drastically wrong. Isatai had promised that the hunters would be caught in their blankets and die with the sleep in their frightened eyes. But red flashes of gunfire blossomed behind the white men's walls. The large Sharps slugs snarled like hornets. Horses screamed and fell threshing while the wide line of yelling warriors was still two hundred yards away.

Gray Horse was among the first to go down. He heard the dull thud as a slug drove into his horse's chest. The mortally wounded animal broke stride. The ground rushed up. Gray Horse went rolling, directly under another man's running pony. A hoof struck him across the back. Stunned, he saw other riders charge by, missing him by inches, while his own horse kicked helplessly in its dying. He pushed to hands and knees, blinded by the dust that burned like ashes in his eyes but listening to the rapid gunfire, the rolling of hoofbeats, the shouts that changed tenor as the charging Indians realized they had met an unexpected and determined resistance. He pushed to his feet, wiping a forearm across his eyes, trying to look through the dust which drifted like a heavy fog. He felt a sudden fear for Limping Boy but was unable to pick him out of that shifting, surging mass, the heavy smoke.

The momentum of the charge slammed some Indians against the buildings like a wall of floodwater breaking upon a bend in an arroyo. But the majority pulled up short, stunned and uncertain over the resistance. The ferocity of the gunfire from inside the buildings seemed to indicate that a hundred men were forted up, though scouts had said there were fewer than thirty.

Fewer than thirty, yet they withstood a charge by seven hundred. The first assault broke up and fell back in disorder and frustration and anger. Gray Horse stared, not quite believing. All across that big open meadow he saw downed horses and downed men. Some moved, some did not. Against all of Isatai's promises, against all of his magic, the white man's bullets had proven deadly. Gray Horse turned half around and peered through the dust at the yellow-painted prophet who had remained behind. He wondered what Isatai was thinking now.

The doubt that had plagued Gray Horse from the beginning became dark and numbing. It was bad enough to have had good medicine and lost it. It was worse to have had false medicine from the beginning.

Death glazed the eyes of the brown by the time the first bewildered warriors straggled back, looking over their shoulders in disbelief as the white men's bullets kept snarling past them, bringing down a horse here, a rider there. Gray Horse saw two horsemen carrying a limp Comanche between them, getting him away from the fire. Even before they eased him to the ground, he knew the man was dead. One of the riders carrying him had been Limping Boy. He rode to his cousin with concern in his eyes. "Brother, are you badly hurt?"

Gray Horse felt a throbbing where the hoof had struck, and a tickling sensation indicated that blood was running down his back. A warrior was meant to die from an enemy's bullet or arrow, not from the hoof of a brother's horse.

"I am all right," he said, "but I am afoot." He looked over his shoulder again, his voice edged with resentment. "I could take Isatai's horse. He does not intend to use it."

Limping Boy's startled expression showed that he feared sacrilege. He said quickly, "We took many horses. I will get one for you." Almost as soon as Gray Horse had retrieved his bridle and hair rope from the dead horse, his cousin returned, leading a dappled gray which had belonged to the white men. "It fits your name," he said.

The horse snorted and rolled its eyes in fear at the strange smell of the Indians. By strength and will, Gray Horse managed to get his bridle on it and tie the horsehair rope around the skittish animal. Limping Boy gripped the bridle and held the gray's head tight against his leg while Gray Horse sprang onto its back.

The Kiowas' bugler sounded another call, and again the Indians massed a charge toward the sod buildings. They shouted and fired their rifles long before they were within good range. Again gray puffs of smoke belched from the windows, and horses went rolling, screaming. Long before he reached the sod walls, Gray Horse knew there was little chance this charge would breach them. The fire was too intense.

Much of the heart was gone from the warriors. Many pulled up short and turned back. Gray Horse was convinced that had all held to their purpose and been willing to pay the cost, they could have overwhelmed the hunters by the force of their numbers, swarming over them like ants over a grasshopper. But the wave broke and fell away, and only a handful of men carried the rush to the very walls. He felt a slug sear his ribs like a heated iron, but it did little more than tear the skin. Then he was against a wooden door, hammering on it with the butt of the buffalo rifle, trying to break it in. The stock splintered in his hands; the door was solidly blocked. He shoved the muzzle through an open window and jerked the trigger. The recoil tore the rifle from his hands. He burned his fingers grabbing at the barrel and let the smoking gun fall. The horse shuddered. Its legs buckled as a hunter shot it from under him.

He found himself trapped, his back against the rough sod wall. He tried to reach the broken rifle, but a gun blast went off almost in his face. Breathing hard, sweat burning his eyes, Gray Horse flattened himself against the wall.

In front of him, downed warriors crawled through the grass. One by one they were picked off by defenders inside the buildings. Wounded horses limped aimlessly across the open field of battle. Others stood on braced legs, heads down, slowly bleeding to death. A few which had belonged to the hunters made their slow and painful way toward the buildings, instinctively seeking aid from trapped men unable to help them.

Cautiously, hugging the wall, Gray Horse worked his way around the corner. A short distance to the rear he saw dried buffalo hides stacked high. Taking a deep breath and touching the medicine bag that hung loosely around his neck, he sprinted, cutting from left to right and back again, trying to be a poor target. Just as he reached the stack, a bullet plunked into the stiff hides and raised a puff of dust.

Safe, he dropped to his knees to catch his breath. The stench of the hides was overpowering. Behind the pile he found a prostrate Kiowa warrior struggling to breathe. Blood pumped spasmodically through a blackish hole in his chest. The wounded man tried to speak but made only a gurgling sound. Gray Horse dropped to one knee, gripping the dying man's hand to assure him they were brothers. The Kiowa gestured. Gray Horse saw that in his struggles he had lost his leather medicine bag. It lay in the grass behind him, in a long trail of drying blood beyond the hide stack. The man was afraid of dying without the protection of his medicine. Taking another deep breath, Gray Horse ran out into the hoof-beaten grass. He scooped up the bag as a rifle roared. The slug ripped grass where the bag had been.

The Kiowa hugged the bag against the bleeding wound as if expecting it to draw death away. It did not. His fingers stiffened forever around the amulet of his faith.

The Kiowa had died with eyes open, and Gray Horse left him

that way so he could see the path as his spirits led him to a better land.

For a time the firing lessened. Gray Horse imagined the consternation and doubt that must be chipping away at his comrades' faith, for nothing was as promised. Most had come into this battle convinced that not one man would die.

Eventually the desultory firing turned rapid, and from a distance he heard that Kiowa bugle. He stood up, knowing that another assault had been mounted. He heard hoofs. Shortly several riders swept past the buildings, frustrated in their attempt to smother its occupants. With them trotted a riderless Indian pony —Comanche by the paint and the gotched ears. Gray Horse shouted and waved his arms. A Kiowa recognized his predicament. He caught the loose horse's reins and loped up to the stack. The Kiowa's eyes narrowed in outrage as he saw the body of a brother. Gray Horse, who had nothing left but his medicine bag and his shield, picked up the dead Kiowa's fallen rifle and shot pouch. He sprang onto the paint pony, then with his hands told his rescuer that together they should pick up the fallen warrior and carry him away to a more worthy place. Each man leaned down and grabbed an arm, taking care not to let the dead warrior's shield be lost; in the hands of an enemy it might give adverse power over the dead. They rode away with the body between them.

Running, Gray Horse saw that all the white men's horses had been run off or shot, including some in the big picket corral. Dead and dying horses by the dozens littered the open meadow between the buildings and the little creek. There were dead men, too—more than plenty. He saw horsemen cutting back and forth across the bloody ground. Most of their attention was devoted not to annihilating the white men but to recovering the bodies of their own. At some distance, Gray Horse and the Kiowa reined up, gently easing the dead man to the ground between them. Gray Horse turned the paint around. He tried in vain to see Limping Boy amid that surging, shuffling, confused aggregation. A chill touched him as he pondered the possibility that he might find his cousin among those who had died.

Angry voices turned his head. He saw a furious old Cheyenne haranguing the frozen-faced Isatai, challenging him in Cheyenne tongue and hand signs to go with him and recover the body of his son, fallen in front of the walls, victim to a bullet Isatai had promised could not kill. Isatai, sweat running down his painted torso, could only stare ahead and try not to see or hear.

Some in the party charged at the walls several more times before the angry sun climbed to its noon peak and bore down with an accusing heat. But an increasing number held back, no longer willing to pay the price. So far as they knew for certain, they had killed but two white men, caught asleep in a wagon on the north side of the corral, unable to reach the safety of the buildings before the first wave overrode them.

A Comanche was never compelled to go into battle against his will. If his signs were not proper, if he felt his medicine was wrong, it was his privilege to draw aside without prejudice or shame. Gray Horse had feared bad medicine after the first charge. He had made the second against his better judgment, still caught up in a patriotic fever even when his heart told him the battle had soured. But he made no more charges. He withdrew, as did many others, to watch from the timber along the creek.

A cold wind seemed to touch him, but when he looked to the trees he saw no movement in the leaves. He shivered in the warm sun.

Occasionally, though the range was long, he fired the Kiowa's rifle at the windows, hoping the man's spirit might guide the bullets in. By early afternoon the shot pouch was empty, and he laid the rifle down, cursing it for its failures. A rifle was an alien thing without warmth or soul, a tool of the white man—and possibly the white man had put a magic upon it to make it useless in the hands of others. Gray Horse quietly resolved that in the future he would use only the bow, for it was born of the earth, a natural thing of wood or bone and buffalo sinew. It lived and breathed and had a spirit of its own, where the rifle was cold and hard and prone to treachery, ofttimes killing its owner or his friends instead of his enemies.

Fear weighting his heart, Gray Horse mounted the paint and rode slowly from the north end of the Indians' position toward

the south, searching for Limping Boy. From cluster of Comanche to group of Kiowa to scattering of Cheyenne, he moved
in a walk, calling. At last, near the base of a flat-topped knoll
where Isatai had retreated with a nucleus of his friends and stubborn supporters, he found his cousin lying in the shade of his
pony. His chest was partially stained by dried blood. A wound
that had shattered two ribs was covered by horse dung to draw
out the poison and the fever.

A smile broke across Limping Boy's sweat-streaked face at the
sight of Gray Horse, and he tried painfully to rise. Gray Horse
motioned for him to hold still. He dismounted from the paint
and squatted to grip his cousin's arm. "How many times did you
go against the walls, brother?"

"Three," Limping Boy said weakly. "The last time, I received
this." He motioned toward the wound. "My pony brought me
out."

"I should have been there beside you to bring you out." Gray
Horse added with pride, "You were braver than I was. I went
only twice."

Limping Boy looked at the paint, his eyes confused. "That is
not the horse I caught for you."

"That one died at the walls. He was not much good."

"Then you had two horses shot from under you. That is
enough glory for one day."

"I think we have all had enough glory at this place. We should
go. We cannot fight prairie dogs in their holes."

He turned his back on the fighting and remained beside his
cousin to see after him when the fever came.

Three days the Indians remained, but the fight was gone from
them. From a distance they watched white men venture out of
the buildings, cautiously at first, then boldly. Afoot, their horses
taken or killed, the hunters used buffalo hides to drag dead
horses away from their doors and reduce the stench the heat
brought. Gray Horse grimaced as he saw them pitch warriors'
swelling bodies onto the stiff hides and drag them out upon the
prairie, to be eaten by wolves or to rot if not recovered by their
friends.

Some of Isatai's supporters were obliged to protect the

prophet from Cheyennes inclined to quirt him to death. Isatai recalled defensively that a Cheyenne warrior had killed a skunk on the way to this place, against his specific advice. That infraction in itself had been serious enough to spoil their medicine. Isatai declared that if anyone was to blame for this mission's failure, it was the reckless Cheyennes, who did not know enough to respect another tribe's magic.

So, though not forgiven, Isatai was pardoned, for the Cheyennes and the Kiowas knew he would live the rest of his life in disgrace as a false prophet, a punishment perhaps worse than death. His name was no longer Hind End of the Wolf. He was Coyote Droppings, and would be until he died.

The second day, two wagon trains arrived, bringing support to the white men at the post. Some sniping was done from afar, but no effective action was taken against them.

The third day, Isatai and a few of his remaining friends rode up onto the butte, nearly a mile from the post, to survey the field of battle and talk uselessly about another attack. A puff of smoke arose from one of the windows. A moment later, one of the Indians pitched headlong from his horse.

That convinced the last of the holdouts that this battle was finished. The white men's medicine was too much. Their long-range buffalo guns could shoot today and kill tomorrow. Many of the dispirited ones rode droop-shouldered toward the reservation, dreading the necessity of carrying the black news home to the elders and the women. Others, the bitterness and hatred still burning hot and quenchable only by blood, scattered into small parties to roam the plains and wreak vengeance wherever the opportunity might arise.

Only three white people had been killed by Indians at Adobe Walls, but nearly two hundred were fated to die that summer and fall. Angry remnants of the Adobe Walls attack force scattered like tracking dogs across the upper reaches of Texas, into New Mexico and Colorado, and northward into Kansas where the shattered Medicine Lodge Treaty had been signed in solemn council seven years before. They extracted a steep price in blood for that blood spilled by the buffalo hunters.

As Limping Boy had done the previous winter for him, Gray

Horse undertook the care of Limping Boy. He fashioned a travois and struck a westward course up the sandy Canadian River, moving slowly and stopping often. He searched out the many breaks and tributaries until one day he found a small camp of the unrepentant, kindred spirits to himself. They were of a band other than his own, but that fact carried no importance anymore; they were of the People. They welcomed him as a brother. They had women who would tend to Limping Boy, giving him the honor and attention due a warrior bloodied in battle.

The wound was slow to heal, for a piece of the slug had stayed in his chest. Though weak, he was ready to ride by fall and helped modestly in the buffalo hunt that would provide the People with meat through the coming winter. By the time the little group of Comanches joined other holdout remnants and drifted down to the grand winter encampment in Palo Duro Canyon, Limping Boy's wound had covered over with a magnificent scar, one that a warrior could carry with pride into his years as an elder and show often to admiring grandchildren.

Seventeen

In a way, Gideon Ledbetter hated to see the Comanche women and children leave. Sometimes of an evening, when he had nothing to do, he would walk down to the stockade and watch them over the fence in much the same spirit that people in Saint Angela watched a captured black bear chained behind a picket dramshop.

Of them all, he most enjoyed watching the young woman with the large eyes, for they reminded him vaguely of Hannah's. He saw no other resemblance. Week by week he watched her dark-skinned baby grow plump on the milk of her breasts, enriched by government rations. All the women and children fattened through the winter and well into the spring. The government's purpose, Gideon was given to understand, was not necessarily charity. It was hoped that word of this generous treatment would find its way to the holdout parties which army patrols had been unable to ferret out of their hidden creek-bottom and cedar-brake encampments from the Double Mountain Fork to the upper tributaries of the Red.

At times, watching the gentleness of the Comanche women with their children, Gideon could almost put aside the notion that they were wild people, savages, no more than a step above the prairie animals upon which they depended for life.

Jimbo was the only person with whom he felt free to talk. "I wonder if they're really much different than the folks *we* come from, our granddaddies across the water? Old Colonel used to tell me how lucky I was that I didn't get born a savage like my people a way back yonder."

Jimbo shrugged. "I wouldn't know nothin' about that. I never did know who my people was."

Gideon smiled, remembering. "Big Ella, she used to tell me mine was warrior kings. But she didn't really know; she just made that up."

Jimbo frowned, looking toward the Indians. "These don't look like they come from no warrior kings."

"They got a proud way of carryin' theirselves."

"I'd be proud, too, if I'd been livin' on prairie-dog meat and all of a sudden they went to feedin' me on government beef. They been feedin' them Indians better than us. I don't see me and you gettin' fat."

The Indians remained strange, yet compelling to Gideon even to the spring day they were loaded into tarp-covered wagons and started on the long journey toward Fort Sill.

If the army's good treatment was designed to reduce hostilities, that part of the plan was a failure. Hostilities continued at a level as strong as at any time since the war.

Gideon was sent on his share of the patrols, sometimes finding dead ashes but never a campfire, occasionally making a chase but never a catch. Whatever its frustrations, the trail was preferable to the garrison's dull routine, the rifle drill with empty chambers, the saber drill with blades never used otherwise. The trail and its deprivations were also to be preferred over the manual labor of post construction. The army continued its refusal to expend adequate funds for professional builders on its frontier posts, forcing its Indian-fighting troops to develop more proficiency with pick and shovel than with the antiquated wartime Spencer rifles still considered good enough for the black troops at Concho.

Chaplain Badger still conducted services in a stained tent near the hospital; after six years the army had not yet sanctioned a regular chapel on the post. One Sunday he preached a sermon on wars and rumors of wars. Gideon considered it an appropriate subject, for the post buzzed all spring and summer with stories of Indian battles, of buffalo hunter camps raided, of horse herds run off, of travelers waylaid and killed. Even at the private-soldier level, several times removed from the written dispatches which reached the commanding officer, enough facts survived the filtering-down process to make it clear that casual scouting parties, company-sized and smaller, would not bring the plains warriors to heel. Gideon was not surprised when rumors began that a great army offensive was to be set in motion. What form it might take he had no idea, and it was not the army's concern to have him know. Strategy was rarely explained to the man in the saddle. Most that he learned, he had to learn for himself.

The white woman -Adeline Rutledge-was a case in point. It took Gideon some time to find out about her.

Early in the summer, he began to notice that Lieutenant Hollander seemed less eager about going out on the trail, or about staying out once he got there. Always before, he had seemed to seek excuses to stretch a patrol, remaining off the post while rations lasted, the horses were reasonably strong and orders did not compel his return by a specified date. The sameness of days at Concho had always made the lieutenant restless. Like most officers, he was often obliged to sit up past taps, writing by lamplight the many and detailed reports which the army required and which few black enlisted men were qualified to do for them. Gideon continued to study reading and writing with Chaplain Badger when duty permitted, as did some other soldiers, but progress was slow and his proficiencies not up to army standards.

Hollander's problems in this regard were a source of satisfaction to Gideon. So long as the lieutenant sat hunched over a writing table, he was too busy to bother some hapless laundry girl.

It came as a surprise to Gideon when Hollander ordered a forced march on the return from an unproductive sign-hunting trip west to the Pecos River. Forced marches were not unusual in pursuit, but they were rare on the homeward leg. His first inkling about the cause came when he heard the civilian Maloney ask Hollander, "How's that thick-blooded Yankee gal from the snow country takin' to the Texas summer heat?"

Gideon had never taken much interest in post gossip except when it might have implications for himself, but he knew Jimbo's love of gossip was second only to his love for horses. Few things happened around the post that Jimbo did not hear of, usually in several broadly differing versions. Gideon asked Jimbo who Maloney was talking about.

Jimbo shrugged as if he thought Gideon should already know. "You're bound to've seen her. She's that red-headed gal that come to visit Captain Macklin and his missus."

Gideon shook his head. He hadn't paid much attention to the officers' women. Except for their varying degrees of age, flesh and hair coloration, he had a hard time telling them apart.

"She's a sister to Captain Macklin's wife," Jimbo explained. Macklin had come in to replace Captain Newton when Newton transferred to the privations of Fort McKavett. "Supposed to go back East in the fall and teach school someplace. But she said out loud, real plain, that she didn't figure on teachin' no school. She taken one cup of tea with Lieutenant Hollander and set her cap for him. Says she's goin' to have him in the chapel before the leaves fall or put herself in a convent for the rest of her life." He looked uncertainly at Gideon. "What's a convent? Is that somethin' the white women wear?"

"I don't know. It might be."

"Anyway, it don't look like she's goin' to have to put it on. Lieutenant spends so much time over to the captain's house that they're talkin' about chargin' him rent." Jimbo smiled, confident in his judgment. "You watch, pretty soon now the lieutenant'll be jumpin' over the broomstick, and he'll have another boss besides the army."

Gideon demanded distrustfully, "How come you to know so much about officers' business?"

"I been walkin' of an evenin' with Melinda, the gal that cooks and sweeps out for the colonel's missus now. She's a sister to that no-account woodchopper that hauls stovewood to the officers' houses. He been keepin' company with the servant gal of Captain Macklin and his missus. Shameful, how nosy that gal is."

Though Gideon took it as a point of personal pride not to listen to trooper gossip about which officers were drinking and which were gambling and which were fighting with their wives, he noticed Hollander spending a lot of time looking in the direction of the Macklin house while trying to appear busy at constructive things. Most evenings the lieutenant walked the southern perimeter of the parade ground arm-in-arm with Adeline Rutledge until near time for taps. Then, because he had fallen behind in his paper work, a lamp would burn extra hours into the night in the window of his bachelor quarters on the hospital's second floor.

Sergeant Nettles walked with a noticeable limp, though pride would not allow him the use of a cane. Pain sometimes closed his eyes, and his orders were even more curt and cutting than in the past. Some of the older soldiers, who remembered, said it had been that way with Colonel Mackenzie when he had commanded black troops before he was given command of the white Fourth Cavalry. Mackenzie, brilliant in handling soldiers and fighting Indians, was in constant pain from poorly healed wounds suffered in the war. They made him irritable, highly sensitive to every man's shortcomings and constantly attentive to their correction. It made for a sharp and efficient command, though a nervous one.

Two things seemed to melt the ice from Nettles' black eyes. One was the girl Susie. She would run halfway across the parade ground to meet him, sometimes dogging his steps even when he was drilling troops. Because no relatives had been found, she had been annexed cheerfully to the considerable brood of Captain and Mrs. Ferguson on the optimistic theory that one more, added to so many, would be no burden.

Nettles might hold his ground against a dozen rushing Indians, but against one little girl he was defenseless. Only Mrs. Larrabee raised a fuss about the impropriety of affection between a little white girl and an aging black soldier. Because she was always raising a fuss about one thing or another, hardly anyone paid attention to her except Lieutenant Larrabee.

The other sight which seemed to ease Nettles' pain was that of Hollander and Adeline Rutledge walking arm-in-arm. Nettles would limp out of his way to present the lieutenant a smart salute and Miss Rutledge a smile, and to receive a smile from her in return. Gideon grimaced, unable to reconcile this deviation with the norm.

It seemed to Gideon that the woman had taken this post without a shot . . . all of it, perhaps, except himself and a few other recalcitrants, most of whom had been in the guardhouse and had not seen her.

At mess one night, the lieutenant unexpectedly walked into the barracks. Nettles quickly called the men to attention. Hollander returned the sergeant's salute. He seemed uncertain, laughing and worried both at the same time. "At ease, men. Go on with your supper. I've come to ask a little favor. It's not in the line of duty."

Nettles fetched him a cup. "Coffee, sir?"

Hollander smiled nervously. "Thank you, Sergeant. I'm much obliged." Sipping the coffee seemed to steady his hands. "Men, there's a certain young lady across the way who likes music. I'm not much for music, but I am partial to the young lady. I have a question I would like to ask her tonight, and I think a little music beforehand might help make her more receptive to it. If you men could see your way clear to serenade her for me after a while, I'd see to it that a couple of bottles of good whisky were waiting for you at the sutler's."

Nettles said, "The men don't need no whisky, sir. They'd be tickled to do it and come home sober."

"I know that, but the whisky will be there nevertheless. If she says yes, I may be by later and join you for a drink. If she says no, I'll probably be there anyway."

Nettles broke forth with another rare smile. "Sir, she ain't goin' to tell you no. She's put in too much time on you."

When the lieutenant left, the men slicked themselves up—all but Gideon. He watched with sadness and a touch of resentment. Jimbo went out to sit on the barracks porch, watching across the parade ground for the lieutenant to start walking down officers' row. At dusk he returned. "He's on his way. Let's everybody go."

They all did, except Gideon. The men were arguing good-naturedly over what they should sing as they filed out the door. Songs they had learned over the river seemed hardly appropriate.

Gideon sat on the edge of his bunk, running a finger along lines in a reader the chaplain had given him for study. Jimbo stopped at the door. "Come on, Gid. We're goin'."

"I ain't. You go on."

Jimbo went out the door, hesitated a moment and came back, worrying. "He'll miss you if you ain't there."

"I'm off duty."

Jimbo gave up and trotted after the other men, already stringing across the parade ground, laughing and singing. Gideon clenched his teeth and tried to go on with his reading in the flickering light of a lamp. The lines on the page seemed to fall into a fit of dancing, without music.

He realized he was not alone. Sergeant Nettles stood at the foot of the bunk, staring critically. "I swear, Ledbetter, you do hold a grudge."

Gideon pretended not to know what he meant. "I don't sing good."

"Neither does any of them others. But they'll sound fine because they got the spirit. Of late, you ain't had much spirit."

Gideon's bitterness boiled up. "You reckon that red-headed woman knows about him and Hannah York?"

Nettles frowned. "I expect she knows. Leastways she knows there's been women like her. It's in every man's nature. She won't hold it agin him. You oughtn't to, either."

"I can't help it."

"Seems to me like you could be man enough to set on your pride . . . go wish him well with that good little woman."

Gideon closed his eyes to shut off the burning. Lamp was smoking, seemed like. "He didn't wish me well with mine. He taken the whole thing for a joke."

"Not after he knowed your true feelin's."

"He used her for sport, and then he ordered her off of the post. I lost my woman. Don't seem fair now for him to get his."

Nettles limped to the door and left without a glance behind him. Gideon felt an impulse to shout for him to wait, to go with him because Nettles wanted him to. But everyone would mistake it for a show of respect for Hollander. He had little tolerance for false pretenses.

He picked up the reader and again let his fingers run slowly along the lines. He read the words but not their meanings, for he was listening. In a while the soft summer wind brought him distant voices raised in the old song "Lorena."

> The years creep slowly by, Lorena,
>   The snow is on the grass again,
> The sun's low down the sky, Lorena,
>   The frost gleams where the flowers have been.
> We loved each other then, Lorena,
>   More than we ever dared to tell;
> And what we might have been, Lorena,
>   Had but our lovings prospered well.

Gideon closed the book and laid it on the bunk and let his head and shoulders slump as his mind ran back to a tall young girl with big dark eyes and a voice like tinkling bells. A tear started down his cheek. He moved as if to wipe it away, but lowered his arm and let it run.

Discreetly, because there was enough moonlight for people to see, and certain people along officers' row would surely be looking, Frank Hollander put down his natural impulse to squeeze Adeline Rutledge until she struggled for breath. Time enough for that later, when they walked beyond the last house on the row and casually moved into the black patch of shadow where a low fence marked the western end of the parade. The waiting would make that moment all the sweeter. For now, he could only hold her arm.

She said, "I love your soldiers, especially that old sergeant with the autocratic manner. I think he is cute."

Hollander smiled. "Cute" in no way described the Esau Nettles he knew. "Don't ever let him hear you say that, especially around anyone else. He has more pride than most white men I know. He could stand a dozen Indian wounds better than he could abide being shamed in front of his men."

"I didn't mean to sound condescending. I am sure he is a splendid soldier. I am sure they all are."

He said ruefully, "Not all." His mind ran to little Finley, and to a couple of others who had never quite learned the difference between the left foot and the right one. "But I suppose I have as good a company as you'll find anywhere, among black troops."

She stopped, and he almost stumbled over his own foot. She asked, "Frank, are you ashamed because your men are Negroes?"

"Why should I be?"

"You seem to be apologizing for them a great deal."

"I don't have to apologize for my men. They do their job." He realized he was protesting too much, or appeared to be. He resumed walking. "This has usually been a mixed post, some white troops and a lot of black. Naturally there is competition, and my boys fall short in some areas. Almost every one of them was a slave. You can't expect . . ."

Damn it, he was apologizing again. Stubbornly he said, "I volunteered for this regiment. I came into it with my eyes open."

"Then don't be defensive with me, Frank Hollander. I have never asked you for that." The tone of censure faded quickly. "I loved the music. They have to respect you a lot to come over and serenade us that way."

"I bribed them with a promise of whisky at the sutler's."

"The respect is there, just the same. I could see it."

"With most of them, I suppose." He felt again the disappointment that had touched him when he saw that Gideon Ledbetter was not with the group.

She asked, "Are you so concerned over the one lost sheep that you cannot rejoice for the ninety and nine?"

He glanced at her in surprise. "How did you know about him?"

"This is not a large post. Gossip needs no telegraph." She gave his arm a gentle touch that said she understood.

He felt better for that, but regret came into his voice. "He has the potential to be the best soldier in the company, except for

Esau Nettles. Ordinarily I wouldn't be bothered over one soldier, but I did this man a wrong. Everything I do contrives to compound it. I owe him a debt I can't seem to pay."

"You did him no conscious wrong, Frank. Someday he'll see that."

Shame washed over him, for he sensed that she knew it all. "I'm sorry you had to hear it from post gossip first. I was going to tell you myself, and I wasn't going to lie. I wanted you to know the bad side of me along with the rest."

"All you did was to be human. I can see how the isolation and loneliness of a place like this could lead a man to a liaison with an attractive woman. Even a woman of that sort."

"It was worse than you realize. She *wasn't* really the sort you think—not by intention. In her mind she was still a slave, with no right of choice. I took advantage of that situation, and of her."

"So, I gather, did many others."

"Guilt is not diminished by being shared. All I can do is ask you to forgive me."

"There is nothing for me to forgive. That happened before I knew you. It will never happen again after we are married."

He was constantly being surprised by Adeline Rutledge. "Married? I haven't asked you yet."

"You were going to, weren't you? That was the reason behind the serenade, or so I surmised."

"You see through me like a pane of window glass. You haven't known me long enough for that."

"I've known you for years, in my mind. That's how I recognized you as soon as I saw you. I've lived in sin with you since I was sixteen, in my imagination. There's no reason for you to ask my forgiveness. I'm shameless myself."

"Shameless enough to marry a man who has so little pride that he willingly commands a company of nigger soldiers?" He let sarcasm creep unbidden into his voice.

She hauled him up short and faced him around. "I am not that other woman, Frank—the one who turned you away. I am not that foolish. I know who you are and what you are. What other people think is of no consequence to me."

"That's easy to say now, but what about the years to come, when you're on a mixed post and the other women look down on you because of me and my soldiers? They'll be subtle. They won't say it in words, but they'll let you know."

"You're apologizing again. It doesn't matter a whit to me that you command black troops. All that matters to me is that you make them the best black troops in this army. You'll have nothing to be ashamed of, and neither will I."

He didn't care if anybody *was* watching. He put his hands on her cheeks and pressed them tenderly. "It won't be an easy life, being married to a soldier, moving from one post to another, and every one more primitive than the last. Being bumped down in quarters every time a higher-ranking officer moves in. Being left alone for weeks every time a few restless Indians decide to steal some spavined horses."

"My sister is married to a soldier. She wouldn't trade places with Mrs. Grant."

"I am not Ulysses S. Grant."

"For which I shall be ever grateful. I could never share a bed with a man who wore a beard like that."

Gideon Ledbetter stood in the stone corral brushing the brown horse when a shadow fell across his shoulder. A woman's voice spoke behind him. "Private Ledbetter?"

Startled, he turned, holding the brush in both hands. "Yes, ma'am?" His mouth sagged open. He knew she was Adeline Rutledge, though he had never seen her except at a distance. Her hair was not actually red, as he had assumed from descriptions. What he saw tumbling in long curls beneath her white bonnet was more auburn, just red on the edges where the sun lightly touched it. What he saw most of all were unblinking blue eyes and her smile, friendly yet a little shy. He removed his gray fatigue hat.

Jimbo moved toward them, eager to speak to the woman, but out of the corner of his eye Gideon saw Sergeant Nettles stop him and pull him away. Whatever the woman was up to, Nettles was implicated.

She said, "I have sought you out, Mr. Ledbetter, for a purpose. I am Adeline Rutledge."

"Yes, ma'am," he said again, defensively. "I know."

"Something you may *not* know is that Lieutenant Hollander has asked me to marry him."

"Yes, ma'am." He had heard little else last night, after the men had staggered in from the sutler's.

"Frank—Lieutenant Hollander—has spoken to me of you. I am given to understand that but for your quick action, he would probably not be alive today. I would not be looking forward to this happy event."

Gideon's face warmed. He had an uncomfortable feeling that those steady blue eyes could read him to the core, that no secret was safe.

She said, "The company serenaded us. You were not among them."

"I was busy, ma'am," he lied, knowing she knew he lied.

"I shall speak frankly, Mr. Ledbetter. I know of the strain between you and the lieutenant. I know its causes. All of them." Her eyes were ungiving. He had to look away. "I am very happy, Mr. Ledbetter, and I want Lieutenant Hollander to be happy. It would help if he knew he had the respect of all the men in his company. Including yourself."

"That ought not to be no worry to you, ma'am. I ain't nothin' but a soldier." He pondered a moment, then added, "A nigger soldier."

"You're a *man*, sir, and a good one. When the happy day comes, I would like to have your blessing."

"Anything you want to do, it's all right with me."

"When we have the wedding, we plan to invite all of the company to be in attendance. I hope you will be there."

In the unyielding gaze of those disquieting eyes and the warmth of her smile, he felt as helpless as a rabbit caught in a snare. But he found the strength not to surrender completely. "I'll study on it."

She reached forward and shook his hand, which was perhaps as much surprise to him as her first appearance. "Mr. Ledbetter, I would ask no more of you than that."

He felt compelled to watch as she made her self-confident way among the loose horses in the corral. Jimbo rushed to open the gate for her, his hat in his hand. Gideon walked to the fence and kept her in sight while she passed the laundress shacks on her way back to the parade ground. She spoke to a couple of the washwomen, who paused in their hot work over the boiling black pots. Officers' women rarely ventured to this part of the post. Even rarer were the occasions when they smiled at and spoke to the laundresses.

Gideon heard Nettles' stern voice behind him. "I hope you let the lady go away with a satisfied mind. It taken a lot for her to come here and talk to you."

The old stubbornness came first and most naturally. "I didn't ask her to."

Then Gideon relented a little. "I told her I'd think on it."

Wedding plans were a social matter, and social matters on a military post bowed always to the needs of war. Chaplain Badger and the smiling couple set the date, only to be forced to call it off. Patrols were ordered in, and personal affairs were brushed aside upon official notification that Colonel Ranald Slidell Mackenzie was marching north from the Rio Grande to mount the southern phase of a military offensive designed to envelope and crush the hostiles on the Texas plains. Other columns under other commanders would move west out of Fort Sill, southwesterly from Camp Supply, northwestward from Fort Griffin, eastward from Fort Union. Between them they were to harry and chase the Comanches, the Kiowas, the Cheyennes, bouncing them off one another, squeezing them in an ever-tightening vise of power and steel.

Gideon saw frustration in Hollander's nervous manner as the lieutenant moved ceaselessly from the details raking out the stables to those whitewashing the hospital walls and those chopping weeds from the parade ground and walkways in preparation for the Mackenzie visit. Gideon felt no sympathy. Deprivation was good for a man's soul.

The post had not been so thoroughly raked and scrubbed and painted since the last time Mackenzie had been on it. Gideon

judged that had the same manpower and determination gone into
the Indian campaign, the Comanches would already be on the
reservation.

The arrival of the Mackenzie column was a wondrous thing.
Never had Gideon seen so many men, so many horses, so many
wagons drawn together at one time and place. They would have
swamped the fort and its limited facilities, still far short of the
army's frequently mentioned long-range construction plans, so
Mackenzie chose to camp his force on the river, just off of the
post.

In his honor the Concho soldiers brushed their blues and
polished their brass to a shine seldom seen and put on a full-dress
parade. That gave Gideon his only good look at the Indian-
fighting colonel, a gaunt, haunted man with pain in his eyes and
Sheffield steel in his voice. Mackenzie watched the parade solemnly, reluctantly, living up to the demands of military protocol though his mind was clearly on the campaign ahead.

Off duty, Gideon and Jimbo walked down to the grand encampment. They ignored the racial jibes and catcalls that came
from a few white soldiers. They stared in wonder at the strange
and fierce-looking Seminole-Negro scouts, faces black like their
own, but language alien and dress more Indian than military.
Gideon noticed that the white soldiers gave them no sass. If anything, they seemed afraid of them. That was a concept he found
hard to accept—white men fearing blacks. He mustered the
courage to speak to a black man who wore a headdress made of
buffalo hide and horns. The man gave him only a glance, and no
answer at all. Gideon never knew whether he could not understand or simply chose not to.

Oddly, though the scouts were black, Gideon felt no racial
kinship to them. It was as if they had come from some world a
million miles from his own. He had more in common with the
white soldiers. This concept, too, he found hard to accept.

Jimbo had the same feeling but was not in the least disturbed
by it. "I seen a white nigger onct, when I hauled cotton to the
gin for Old Colonel. Had a face like milk, but he was still a
nigger. Same with them scouts. They got black faces, but they
still just Indians."

All of the Concho garrison expected to be sent with Mackenzie, but none of it was. The colonel had his own command,
mostly white. When he finished the tiresome amenities of military pageantry and had the necessary repairs made to his wagons,
he raised a great pall of dust over the northward trail. And left
the Concho complement intact.

There was, at first, a feeling of letdown, of anticlimax.

Chaplain Badger decided it would be a shame to waste all that
polished brass, so he quickly rescheduled the wedding of Lieutenant Frank Hollander to Miss Adeline Rutledge of Cleveland,
Ohio. His chapel tent was too small and much too spartan for an
occasion of such importance. He proposed—and the concerned
parties quickly accepted—that the ceremony be conducted on
the front porch of the Macklin house. That way even the black
soldiers could attend without actually being admitted en masse
into an officer's home.

It was a foregone conclusion that all of Hollander's company
would be there, or nearly all. One man was in the hospital,
fighting off a debilitating siege of the summer chills. Little Finley
was in the guardhouse, paying the penalty for a brawl that had
followed a white infantryman's accusation of thievery. When
anything was stolen on or about the base, it was customary to
blame it on the blacks. In Finley's case, Gideon figured, the
charge was probably true.

After Sunday noon mess, the men rebrushed their uniforms,
rubbing brass buttons already ashine from the tribute to Mackenzie. Jimbo had never complained about the spit-and-polish aspect
of barracks life. He was in his earthly glory when he could wear
his dress blues. Gideon stood in the doorway, leaning against the
jamb, looking solemnly across what he could see of the parade
ground. Jimbo said impatiently, "Gid, it ain't long till time."

Gideon's thoughts reached beyond the parade ground to the
lieutenant, probably trembling by now and dropping everything
he picked up. He thought of Adeline Rutledge and the hope he
had seen in her unblinking blue eyes.

Behind him, Esau Nettles said evenly, "There ain't nobody
goin' to order you to do nothin', Ledbetter. You just listen to
your conscience."

Gideon stared a little longer, flexing his fists. His mind ran back to Hannah York.

The other men filed out of the room, looking shiny enough to parade for Ulysses S. Grant. Jimbo waited impatiently, edging toward the door. "You comin', ain't you, Gid?"

Gideon avoided his eyes. "Don't wait for me."

Esau Nettles watched silently from the door to his room. Gideon sat down heavily on his bunk, his shoulders slumped. He heard Nettles' footsteps but did not look up.

Nettles said, "Your conscience must not be talkin' very loud."

Gideon shook his head. Every word carried pain. "If I was to go out there now it'd be like sayin' what he done didn't matter no more, that everything was all right. But it *does* matter. It still hurts, and I can't be no hypocrite about it. I ain't one of them bowin' and scrapin' niggers that grins to a white man's face and wishes he could kill him."

Nettles frowned. "If you want to transfer to another company, I expect I can fix it."

"You think I ought to?"

"When a man's troubles are all in his head, he generally carries them along wherever he goes to."

Nettles left. Presently Gideon began to catch the distant sound of a piano, the music floating to him on the faint breeze from the south. He got up and walked outside. Leaning against the corner of the building, beneath the portico, he could see a crowd gathered at the Macklin house, a few guests seated on the shaded porch, many officers and their wives standing just in front of the house. Nettles had marched the Hollander company across to the south edge of the parade ground. There they stood, part of the service, yet subtly apart from it.

The little girl Susie stood at attention beside Esau Nettles.

The bride in white and the lieutenant in his blues stood in front of the chaplain. Gideon could hear the sound of voices but not the words.

He looked down, his throat so tight it pained him, his fists clenched. Choking off a crying sound that started deep inside, he rushed back into the barracks and put on his blues. He trotted across the parade ground and fell in at the end of the line just as the chaplain pronounced the couple man and wife.

The two turned. Gideon could not bring himself to look at Hollander, but his gaze touched Adeline Rutledge a moment, and she was smiling at him.

Lieutenant Frank Hollander was given a wedding leave, but not much of one. He took his bride for a camping trip twenty miles south to the springs which gave birth to the South Concho River. Four days later he was back on duty, leading Gideon and the others on a patrol north to the big spring and west to the five wells, making sure no hostiles slipped around behind Mackenzie's force and struck southward.

Eighteen

MYTH HAS CREDITED the Indian with animal instincts approaching omniscience. It has presented him as able to see one bent blade of grass on a broad plain, to follow the track left by a crow's shadow, to sense where his enemy is at all times and know what he will do next. This, of course, is false. Like every other human, the Indian could wander and become lost in unfamiliar country. He was often given to doubt about his own wisdom and that of his leaders. Worst of all, history records that his enemies frequently took him by surprise.

Colonel Mackenzie's great column, ponderous though it was, came unseen upon the western rim of Palo Duro Canyon at dawn the morning of September 28, 1874, and looked in amazement down the steep walls at an Indian encampment stretching for miles beside the creek that snaked along the canyon floor. Here, it appeared at first, must be all the hostiles on the southern plains—Comanche, Kiowa, Cheyenne, Arapaho. And they were still asleep.

The appearance of the cavalry should not have been a surprise, but unaccountably it was. After several skirmishes over the preceding few days as the column had plodded northward across the plains, both Indians and military had lost track of one another. Indian scouts sent to watch the soldiers had missed seeing them break camp in the cold, dark hours after midnight. Now, as the eastern rim of the canyon turned rose and orange, Sergeant John B. Charlton and two Tonkawa scouts found a narrow game trail that zigzagged dangerously down the steep and treacherous wall.

The command dismounted quietly, and at Mackenzie's signal, Captain Eugene B. Beaumont started A Troop moving in single file, leading their horses. They reached the canyon floor beside an encampment of the Kiowas. A family camp chief named Red Warbonnet was the first to see and fire upon them, to no particular effect. As the shots echoed up the canyon, other Indians turned over in their buffalo robes, assuming that some lucky hunter would have venison for breakfast. By the time alarm spread up and down the creek, it was too late. Too many of the soldiers were in the canyon. Instead of a concerted defense, there was panic. Instead of coordination and tactics, there was chaos. Like flushed quail, the Indians scattered in every direction, up and down the canyon floor and up the steep canyon walls.

Gray Horse had been unable to find any of his own band among the people who had come in rapidly growing numbers to Palo Duro Creek, bringing their camp goods on pack animals and by travois, seeking shelter from winter's savage winds beneath the high walls of the canyon. He found no one who could give him news of his uncle-father, his mother, his sisters. All he knew for certain was that soldiers were spread across the plains like packs of wolves, driving the scattered bands out of their hiding places in the arroyos and canyons that previously had been their sanctuary, pushing them mercilessly toward the reservation at Fort Sill. He hesitated even to speak the names of his kin, for they might by now be among the dead. If they still lived, they were probably huddled in misery on that cold and bleak reservation. That was almost the same as dead.

Limping Boy's wound, though still angry around the edges, had largely healed through the summer and into the fall, but he had not yet regained his strength. He could ride horseback but a short distance before his eyes pinched in pain and his shoulders slumped in weariness. Gray Horse's instincts were akin to those of the wolf; had he been able to choose freely, he would have stayed out the winter in some small and secret camp with just a few others of the People, or even alone. But he feared that Limping Boy might not live to see the grass turn green and the summer birds come north. For his cousin's sake, he elected to join the great encampment.

He was striking his flint and steel to build a fire in the center of the cold tepee when he heard the shots from far down the canyon. His first thought was that it would be a foolish deer which came to drink out of a creek where so many tepees stood. Some fortunate family would eat better today than he and Limping Boy. But as the firing intensified, he threw a blanket over his shoulders and grabbed his quiver and bow.

"Limping Boy, get up," he shouted. "Something is wrong with the Kiowas." He did not wait to see his cousin throw his robe aside. He rushed through the flap, untethered his horse and leaped upon it bareback. He heard Limping Boy behind him, shouting for him to wait, but he could not; a dark foreboding enveloped him, and his skin tingled with the need to be moving.

Galloping toward the Kiowas, where the firing had begun, he saw many people rushing out of their tepees . . . men, women, children. Some of the men did as Gray Horse had done, leaped onto their mounts and ran to the sound of the battle. But many milled in confusion, shouting orders to women and children who cried too loudly to hear. Pack animals and war ponies, boogered by the running and shouting, strained at their tethers. Some broke loose and stampeded blindly, adding to the melee. Gray Horse found himself running into a shrieking, wild-eyed throng of people—Comanche, Kiowa—in headlong flight. He was forced to slow—at times almost to stop—to keep from running over a woman or child or even, he was ashamed to see, a grown man.

Ahead of him the firing had quickened. It was suddenly much nearer. The ground trembled with the sound of running horses. Through a haze of dust he saw blue-clad troopers at the gallop, driving before them a tremendous herd of loose horses and mules, most bareback, some pitching wildly with saddles or packs turned under their bellies. He loosed an arrow at a soldier who passed near him like a whirlwind, but he knew he missed.

Ahead he could see that many of the Kiowa warriors had taken positions in the rocks along the canyon wall and were firing down upon the soldiers. But the range was long for rifles and much too long for his arrows. That dark foreboding came on him even more heavily. Reason told him there were far more warriors in this canyon than soldiers, but they were much too scattered, and too many had already sought safety in flight. Those who had gained the walls might delay the soldiers, might give their families time to escape, but there was no way they could retake the canyon.

He looked behind him for his cousin in the dust and turmoil and the flurry of hysterical humanity. "Limping Boy!" he called, and called again. Through the rush of colors he saw him, afoot. He put his horse into a run, reining up as he reached his kin. Limping Boy, dusty and bleeding, took his arm and swung up behind him.

Gasping for breath, Limping Boy told him a terrified woman had run into him on a mare, knocking his pony down. Limping Boy had been trampled in the moment of pandemonium, and his pony had run away with the others. He had held on to his bow, his quiver and his shield, but he had lost his blanket and everything else.

Gray Horse thought first about going back to their tepee and retrieving what they could, but he saw a blur of blue color in that direction. The soldiers were there. Firing continued, but it was random and scattered, more desperation than defense. Gray Horse felt cold all through.

"The battle is lost," he said disconsolately. "We had just as well go away from this place."

He crossed the creek, for he saw few soldiers on that side. Limping Boy clung to the pony with his knees. In the timber that fringed the creek they came upon a horse which had tangled its tether in the brush. Its markings were Kiowa, but Gray Horse saw no Kiowa laying claim. If one ever did, they could give it back. Limping Boy slipped to the ground, untangled the rawhide rope and formed it quickly into a makeshift bridle. He looked regretfully back down the canyon.

"It is not good to run away from a fight."

Gray Horse frowned. "The hornets are out of the nest and buzzing all around us. There is no way of fighting hornets."

He led the way, and they went on up the canyon.

It took some time for either the Indians or the military to realize the immensity of what Mackenzie had done. Audacity and luck had given him the greatest victory the army had ever scored against the Indians on the plains. His cavalrymen managed to capture most of the canyon's horse and mule herd, leaving a majority of the fleeing Indians afoot. In their escape they left behind them virtually everything except what they wore or carried on their backs. Tepees, robes, blankets, meat supplies, camp equipage . . . all of it was captured and put to the flame. The great herd of horses and mules was taken up the west rim of the canyon. After the soldiers and the Tonkawa and Seminole-Negro scouts had selected the animals they needed for their own use, more than a thousand head were shot so they could never again fall into Indian hands. That stark, bleaching pile of animal bones lay for years as a grim marker of the last grand encampment of the free plains Indians.

It was the climactic crushing blow, leaving only the continued wholesale slaughter of the buffalo to finish the tribes' defeat. Yet it was accomplished with little loss of life. Though grimly determined in his mission, Mackenzie did not kill for the love of blood. Beneath the iron demands of duty, he had a respect for the Indian as a worthy enemy and did not kill him when there was no need. The only army casualty in Palo Duro Canyon was a bugler, shot in the stomach, but back on duty in weeks. No more than a handful of Indians were killed.

Though life survived, a way of life did not. Over the next few years there would be spasms of hostility, last futile threshings of a dying giant; but the heart was gone, the soul smothered.

In the weeks that followed the canyon rout, the soldiers seemed to be everywhere, searching out the draws, the creeks, the canyons, flushing the huddled remnants and hazing them relentlessly eastward toward the reservation. Afoot for the most part, hungry, usually wet and cold, the dispossessed people of the plains straggled along in misery of body and soul, given no choice but eventual surrender and what amounted to imprisonment in a country much different from their own.

Gray Horse tried as hard as any to escape. He attempted first to skirt the long canyon and return to the Double Mountain region he knew so well, but from every promontory upon which he rode he saw sign of the soldiers. They were not hornets now, they were flies; pestering, biting but not killing. Moving away from contact with one patrol or scouting company, he would ride into another. At times they gave chase, and he and Limping Boy had to run. At other times they simply pressed after the fugitives in their own dogged and deliberate pace, giving them little rest.

Hunger was a constant companion. Winter had driven most of the game into cover. Now and then Gray Horse was lucky and killed something large enough to satisfy two appetites, but more often he did well to share a rabbit with the steadily weakening Limping Boy. They huddled miserably in their thin blankets wherever they could find a night's shelter from the wind, and most often they slept without enough food in their bellies to help warm them. They passed many a night wet and cold and sleeping not at all. As Gray Horse feared, his cousin's debilitated condition left him easy prey to the winter chills and fever. Gray Horse took him into a shallow, water-hollowed cave in the red clay and gypsum banks of an ice-fringed creek and built a small fire at the opening's mouth, where the wind would pull the little bit of smoke away. He dared not build it large enough to warm the cave as he would have wanted it to be, for the bigger smoke might draw the soldiers.

For two days he did not know if Limping Boy would survive. The waiting gave him far too much time to think, to remember. Always, though he tried not to dwell upon it, he came back to the fact that he had known nothing but misfortune from the day he and the others had struck those *tejano* settlers and their picket cabin on the Colorado, the day the bleeding woman had touched him and had died with his medicine bag clutched in her contaminating hand. He could not remember that one good thing had happened to him since, or to any of the People around him. The loss of the horses, the rout of his raiding party had followed that misfortune. He had found his camp hungry, and in his absence to hunt for fresh meat, the buffalo soldiers had fallen upon his people and murdered every one. Even as he had sought revenge, a wolf—which should have protected him as a brother—betrayed him and let him be shot. He had lived, but only to endure one defeat after another, the collapse of the Adobe Walls attack, the disaster in Palo Duro. Now Limping Boy hovered between two worlds, and the distant one seemed better than the one where he was.

In the darkness of the long, cold night, the fire allowed to go out because its flame might be seen, Limping Boy worsened. Gray Horse confronted the most terrible possibility of all, one which had lurked around him for months like a hungry wolf at the edge of camp.

Could all this be punishment for the spoiling of his medicine? Could all the People be paying the penalty because he had gone against his medicine in allowing Bear to disregard Coyote's clear message? Could the bleeding woman have been placed there by the spirits to test him? Could the chastisement suffered by all those around him be part of a scourge set loose by spirits angry over his failure to them?

The weight of this guilt was almost too much for him to carry. He cried out to the spirits to do their worst to him but to leave the People in peace.

For answer, he heard only the howling of an evil north wind.

Limping Boy's fever broke, finally, but he was almost too weak to sit on a horse. It would take little to make him sick again —this time probably worse than before. Gray Horse hunted hard and finally managed to find a thin old buffalo bull alone in a sheltered hollow. It reminded him of the one he had watched the wolves pull down at the bottom of the Double Mountains.

Just when he thought his luck was turning, two soldiers rode up on a hill barely three hundred yards away. He had time to slice away only a little of the hump, then jump on his horse and ride away quickly. The soldiers pursued him, and he spent the rest of the day making a roundabout return to the cave where he had left Limping Boy. He built a small fire, but they ate the meat more raw than roasted. He watched his cousin wolf down the first decent meal in two or three weeks, and he knew there was no longer any alternative.

For himself, he had rather die than go to the reservation. But he could not think of himself alone. If his recklessness had put Limping Boy in this condition, it was up to him to make the sacrifice, to save this young cousin who had so long been a brother to him.

He did not go like a slave, in surrender and chains. He went like a thief in the night, riding in the timber, keeping to the rough country, avoiding the soldiers who were like the greenflies that infested a buffalo-killing ground. Tales heard from other Indians encountered along the way indicated that whenever a band surrendered, their horses and their weapons were confiscated. Many of the men were torn away from their families and imprisoned until the authorities could determine which had been guilty of crimes against the white people and the soldiers. Gray Horse had no intention of undergoing this humiliation. He took to riding at night, when the soldiers could not see. He sought out the reservation camps and inquired after his own band. He found many tribes gathered here in sad and weary clusters . . . Kiowa, Cheyenne, Arapaho, Comanche . . . living in their tepees, as of old; but nothing else was as it had been. They were beaten, shamed, on the verge of despair. Always, when he asked after his own, he was pointed somewhere else—and always the information proved wrong. Though he would not speak of it to Limping Boy, he saw the same fear in his cousin's fever-sunken eyes. Perhaps their band had been destroyed. Perhaps they two were the last survivors, like the lone calf of his recurring buffalo dream, searching vainly in a field of bones.

Then, one bitter night when snow lay heavy on the ground and flakes of it stuck cold against his face, he rode toward a blaze he could see flickering on and off like a firefly as the falling snow thickened and thinned. He made out the familiar form of buffalo-skin tepees set in a rough circle as had so often been the custom among his band when the camp terrain permitted. He and Limping Boy rode between the lodges and approached the fire. Like a wraith out of the night, an old man stepped into the dancing light and bid them welcome. He told them if they were hungry, there was meat.

A terrible chill took possession of Gray Horse. He knew that voice. It was Black Robe, the uncle he called father. He tried twice before his own trembling voice took hold.

"Father! Do you not know me?"

Sliding down from his horse, he threw aside the blanket that had covered him, and he stepped closer to the fire.

The old man began to weep without shame and threw his arms around Gray Horse. "My son!" he cried. "We had long since mourned you for dead."

"I have been like dead for a long time," Gray Horse said weakly. "I would not be here now, but Limping Boy is sick."

The old man had a strange smell on his breath. Gray Horse thought it was the white man's whisky.

Black Robe hugged Limping Boy and called him son, though he was not, and pointed to a lodge which glowed faintly from the light of the fire inside. "You will find your mother there, son. She has been ill, but you will make her well."

Limping Boy hesitated a moment, staring at Gray Horse. He gripped his cousin's shoulder, then turned and led his Kiowa pony toward the tepee which Black Robe had shown him.

His voice still husky, Gray Horse asked, "And *my* mother? How is she?"

"She lives. She is not happy, but she lives. She will be happier when she sees you."

Gray Horse held his arms around his adopted father a minute, somehow dreading to go to his mother, to be reminded afresh of how much he had lost.

Black Robe asked, "Do you not want to know about your wife, and your son?"

Gray Horse cringed, for seeing his father had already brought back pain along with the joy. "I know what happened to them, Father. The soldiers killed them."

The old man stood back, astonished. "No, my son, they were

not killed. The soldiers took Green Willow and some of the others prisoner and held them a long time at the big soldier village. Your son was born there."

Gray Horse was staggered. "My son? Then I *do* have a son?"

"Yes. Not as healthy as I would want him to be, but this is not a healthy place."

Gray Horse trembled. "Where are they?"

"In their . . . in *your* lodge." He pointed. Gray Horse stood a moment as if frozen to the snow, staring toward the tepee.

Black Robe said quietly, "It is better that you wait until later to see your mother anyway. She is not young. She might die of the surprise. I will tell her and get her ready. Go first to your own."

Gray Horse started walking, leading the horse, slowly at first, then faster. By the time he reached the flap he was almost running. He did not take time to tie the horse but simply dropped the reins in the snow. He raised the flap, bent and went in, letting it drop shut behind him to close out the cold.

On the other side, across the fire, a wide-eyed woman sat wrapped in a blanket, her eyes going even wider at the sight of a ghost. She stood up slowly, shakily, letting the blanket fall away. In its folds sat a boy of a year, thin-faced but as wide-eyed as his mother.

Gray Horse took two long strides as the woman screamed his name and rushed to him. They clasped each other with all the strength they had.

The frightened baby began to wail.

The spirits had put Gray Horse through his punishment. Now, he knew, they had at last relented.

Nineteen

It often seemed to officers and men that some malevolent spirit guided the army in the timing of its calls upon those who wore its yellow and blue, and those who waited for their return. Captain Macklin had been detailed upon a routine scout to Horsehead Crossing and back by a roundabout circuit that led to the big spring, watching for Indian sign that never materialized. There seemed little reason to expect any, for hostile activity had been sporadic and small since Mackenzie's devastating fall and winter campaign had forced nearly all the unhorsed and hungry holdouts to the reservation. But duty is duty, and routine is often the most difficult duty of all. The captain was obliged to leave the post without a proper farewell to his wife, the sister of Adeline Rutledge Hollander, for she had taken to her bed with a fever. When he returned, it was the sorrowful duty of Adeline to lead him to a fresh grave in the white section of the post cemetery.

As always, disease and privation killed more people of Fort Concho than the Indians ever had, and to this constant danger the civilian population who marked time at home were as vulnerable as the men who took the field.

Now it was Frank Hollander who must leave, to continue earning the captain's bars which finally had come to him after his years of waiting for the slow wheels of army procedure and seniority to turn. Adeline's baby was due any day. A job was to be done, and there were not enough officers on the post to do it properly. A party of discontented Comanches had bolted the reservation and roamed loose upon the plains, striking at buffalo hunter camps, killing those they could, setting others afoot and running off with their horses and mules. The orders came from General E. O. C. Ord himself and were passed on to Frank Hollander as the most available officer. He was to ride north, set up a base camp in an appropriate place of his own choice, then search the plains until the hostiles were found and driven back to the forgiving and protecting arms of the Quaker agents at Sill.

He formed his company after breakfast the morning of July 10, sixty soldiers, more or less, and a newly assigned lieutenant named Judson who had come down from Sill with Colonel Grierson when the Tenth Cavalry headquarters was transferred to Fort Concho.

Gideon Ledbetter knew it was likely to be a long scout, for they had with them four well-loaded wagons drawn by six-mule teams, there being no pack mules available. He felt like a pack mule himself, so burdened was he with extra ammunition for his old Spencer.

Private Lonnie Bowes had tried to feign sickness that morning so he would not have to go, but Esau Nettles rolled him out of his bunk and made him walk a straight line across the floor of the barracks. He declared him well enough to ride to hell and back.

Said Bowes, "That's where it's liable to be. I tell you, Sergeant, I heered a hoot owl up behind the window for the last two nights. Them's bad omens."

"A hoot owl ain't goin' to hurt you, but *I* might. You want a bad omen? Look at me, because I'm as bad a one as you'll ever see. Now, daddammit, git your britches on."

At Hollander's nod, the new lieutenant gave a curt order to Nettles, and Nettles formed the horsemen into a column of twos to take their leave of the post. As they passed Hollander's stone house, Adeline came awkwardly down the steps and out the newly painted white gate in the picket fence finally put up to set off the parade ground from the houses of officers' row. Gideon thought irreverently of a remark attributed to Colonel Grierson that Mrs. Hollander "carried her whole future in front of her."

It had seemed amusing at the time, but Gideon did not smile now, for he saw the white handkerchief clutched in her hand. Though he mustered no real sympathy for Frank Hollander, he had only compassion for this woman.

Hollander looked first at his wife, then back to Nettles. "Carry on, Sergeant. I'll catch up."

Properly the order should have been passed through Lieutenant Judson, but Hollander had long been accustomed to relying on Nettles. The lieutenant betrayed no chagrin over being left out of protocol.

Gideon watched the captain throw his arms around the young woman, and he saw tears shining on her face. Unbidden, regret came over him. He remembered times he had left Hannah without even the chance to tell her good-bye.

The sergeant became aware that everyone was watching. Stiffly he ordered, "Eyes . . . *front!*" and, riding beside the young lieutenant, led them away.

Soon Hollander overtook them in a long trot. Gray-faced, he passed the lumbering wagons, then the column without looking either to right or left. He took his place at the head of it.

Gideon heard Nettles ask, "Where'll we pick up Mr. Maloney at, sir?"

"We won't," Hollander replied in a brittle voice. "His wife is about to have a baby, and he is staying with her at Ben Ficklin."

Unspoken, but plain as if he had said it aloud, was the implication that a civilian had personal choices denied to the soldier.

Nettles said, "She's army, sir."

Hollander nodded grimly. "Sometimes that's a hell of a thing to be."

They made twenty miles that day, following the North Concho. If Hollander spoke twenty words, Gideon did not hear them. The captain's restless eyes studied the heat-shimmering terrain on either side of the line of march, as alert as if they were already in Indian country. There had been a time it was, but no more. Mackenzie had finished that. From the few facts the men had been told by their officers, and the many rumors that had floated to them on the air, Gideon surmised that the trouble area lay several days' ride to the north.

They continued following the river the second day, the July

sun bearing down as if in anger, to the point that one of the un-
seasoned new recruits swayed and fell from his saddle at midafternoon. Sergeant Nettles dismounted and shook him none too
gently. "Git up from there and be a soldier!" But the man was
not malingering.

"Sunstroke," Hollander declared. "Let's carry him over into
the shade of those pecan trees." He made a broad waving motion. "All you men shade up. Rest yourselves and your horses
awhile. Drink a little water, but not too much."

The trooper was revived after a time by wet cloths placed on
his forehead and water sparingly given him. Hollander said
something to Nettles. Nettles said, "Jimbo, Ledbetter . . . you-
all ride along with him and keep a watch. If he shows sign of
blowin' out his light again, holler."

Trooper Nash managed to stay in the saddle the rest of the afternoon, though he hunched over and seemed disoriented most
of the time. When evening camp was made, Gideon and Jimbo
got his uniform off of him and led him into the edge of the river
to lie down in the cool water. Nettles remarked that the man was
dried out from the skin to the core and needed to soak up all the
water he could. Jimbo went off to see about their horses while
Gideon sat at the edge of the water to make sure Nash did not
fall unconscious again and drown.

Eventually the recruit recovered enough to eat a small supper
of hardtack and bacon, washing it down with black coffee bitter
as sin but carrying the authority of a two-star general.

Some of the men sat around during mess and complained
about the length of the day's ride and the punishment of the July
sun. Sergeant Nettles waited until Hollander had gone out to
scout the points where he would want to post a guard, then he
walked into the middle of the company and declared menac-
ingly, "Now, you-all listen to me, and you listen real good. I
don't want to hear no man grumble when the captain's around.
He got enough to worry his mind without him puttin' up with
no bitchin' soldiers. You got somethin' to say, you come say it to
me. *I'll* decide whether to fix the trouble or to kick your butt."

Lieutenant Judson sat on a tarpaulin-wrapped pack, sipping
coffee and smiling faintly. Gideon figured it would tickle him

considerably to watch Nettles kick a few butts. There had not been much excitement around Concho since his arrival.

The heat-suffering young Nash was newly come out of St. Louis. He had been at the post just long enough to ride on a couple of scouting trips that had turned up nothing more than a few stray buffalo that had not drifted north in the spring. He nudged Jimbo, who seemed to attract new recruits in the same way he had of drawing dogs or quieting horses. To a half-scared young trooper just coming onto a strange post, Jimbo's ready grin was like a lantern in a window at home. "Jimbo, you reckon this time we're liable to really fight Indians?"

Jimbo shook his head confidently. "Indians is smarter than a bunch of soldiers. They wouldn't ride around in heat like this."

That was a lie, but it was told in a good cause. Gideon left it alone.

It would be merciful, he thought hopefully, to send Nash back to Concho. He could read the notion in Hollander's face more than once during the evening as the captain stared silently at the recruit. But Gideon guessed that a countering thought also was running through his mind. Nash could not be sent alone; he might not make it all the way. The command would be short two men rather than one. Hollander gambled on losing none at all. Nash was still with the company when the men hitched mules to the wagons and saddled the horses the third morning.

The young soldier made it through the day without anyone having to hold him on his horse, and Gideon saw nobody else showing serious symptoms. Hollander held to a slower pace and camped early in the evening beside springs at the head of the river. By then Nash was fit enough to care for his own horse and to stand a tour of guard duty. Tough, Gideon reflected. But it took tough men to come into western Texas from less strenuous climes in the middle of the summer and stay on their feet. He had seen men faint away on the parade ground.

The fourth day's ride was longer than expected. Hollander had intended to camp at the White Springs but found them dry. A dark look passed between the captain and Esau Nettles. At length Hollander said, "We'll have to make the big spring, then. It's never been dry yet."

Three more days they traveled, to Wild Horse Springs, to the upper Colorado River. Hollander began searching for a suitable place to set up his base camp. Moving northeasterly, they headed toward Bull Creek. Suddenly Hollander reined to a stop, staring across the prairie. Squinting against the glare, Gideon saw a horseman coming in a long trot. He dropped his hand to his carbine. At the distance the rider could have been an Indian, though Gideon could think of no reason a lone Indian would move directly toward a company of cavalry except ignorance. He had seen no sign of any that ignorant.

The rider was a white civilian. A hundred yards out, he raised his hand in peace, which to Gideon seemed unnecessary. He was hardly likely to open hostilities on a column of troops.

"By George," the dark-bearded man declared when he was within easy hearing, "we're sure glad to see you soldier boys."

Hollander took off his hat and wiped his sleeve across his forehead. The heat had robbed him of humor. "I don't believe, sir, that you will find a boy in this company."

"No offense meant, Captain. I'm an old soldier boy myself. Maybe I don't look it now, but I was."

"Which army?" Hollander asked dubiously.

"Union, of course. Do I look like a Johnny Reb?"

Hollander frowned. "Without the uniform, I find it increasingly difficult to tell."

The man shrugged. "You'll find some old Rebs in our outfit up yonder." He half turned in the saddle and pointed his chin in the general direction of a low, flat-topped mountain that lay to the northwest. "Yankees, too. Old enemies pull together when a new one appears."

"I suppose," Hollander nodded. "I was told to be on the lookout for a group of buffalo hunters who have banded together against the breakaway Indians."

"That's us. We gave up hunting buffalo. We've hunted Indians instead."

"My orders were, if I found you, to see if we can work together. You show us the Indians, and we'll fight them."

The hunter rough-counted the troopers in dry amusement. "Captain, I believe there are more than enough to go around for

all of us. Those Indians killed a couple of men and then ran off
the whole horse herd from Rath's trading camp on the Double
Mountain Fork late in the winter. Even since then we've chased
them awhile, and then they've chased us."

The hunter rode alongside the captain, telling him of the frustrations his group had suffered in their efforts to kill buffalo
against Indian resistance. Gideon caught it in pieces, enough to
learn that close to a hundred hunters had banded together originally. In ever-diminishing numbers they had been playing tag
with the Indians back and forth across the plains all spring and
into the summer, winning a scrap here, losing one there. By ones
and twos and threes, the disheartened had given up the struggle
and retreated to Kansas.

"We're down now to twenty-three men and a Mexican guide.
Of late we've gone to calling ourselves the Forlorn Hope. That's
what it is if our luck doesn't switch around pretty soon."

Hollander seemed to know much about their situation already.
Gideon took it for granted that officers were privy to much information that failed to find its way down to the common soldier.

The column came presently to a small creek, where a group of
men were camped in the welcome shade of scrub timber.
Gideon's mouth was dry, and he could almost taste the cool
water, just looking at it. But he had to wait for orders.

Several men walked out to meet the column. With few excep-
tions they were bearded and shaggy, for the social graces were
without consequence in this environment, and whiskers helped
protect the face from blistering sun and scorching wind. The
man who appeared to be the party's leader shook hands with
Hollander as the captain dismounted. He gave the troops a quick
and not totally favorable appraisal.

"Darkies," he said. "I had hoped they'd be white men."

Hollander replied firmly, "I doubt that the Indians will know
the difference, or care."

The captain gave orders for the company to make camp.
Gideon was too busy for a while to pay much attention to the
buffalo hunters. As a class they were of only passing interest to
him; he had seen many in Saint Angela and found them inclined

to be loud talking and high smelling. These, however, were of more interest simply because they were here.

Hollander walked out among the hunters and ordered them to fall in. They just looked at one another, then back at the captain, none moving. Hollander's face took on a flush of embarrassment as he realized belatedly that he was talking to civilians. He made an apology of sorts, at which the hunters grinned.

Gideon chuckled at the captain's discomfort. Jimbo was not smiling. His loyalties were clear. "Captain don't hardly see nobody but soldiers. He forgets how to talk to other people."

"Bet he don't talk like that to his red-headed wife," Gideon said.

Esau Nettles had eyes in the back of his head. "Ledbetter, you got nothin' better to do, you go help water them mules."

The mules, still in harness, drank eagerly and took a long time to fill up. Standing there, Gideon watched while the captain read a paper to the hunters, who had drawn into an informal circle around him, subtly reminding him they were civilians. The words were lost in the mules' splashing. When the captain finished reading, some of the hunters gestured toward the northwest. That, Gideon guessed, was where the Indians were.

The lieutenant had been busy supervising the making of camp. On his return Hollander briefed him on the conference. These hunters were no blundering, stumbling, leaderless adventurers. Largely veterans of the war, they had formed a military-style company with a chain of command and individual members' responsibilities clearly designated. They were limited only by their numbers and their supplies.

"Hunting buffalo or hunting Indians, they have been back and forth over this country enough that they know most of it. They agree to join us for the mutual good."

"Do you think it will work, mixing military with civilians?"

"The war was fought mostly by civilians, Lieutenant. They put on a uniform, but at heart they were always civilians."

"But one side lost."

Hollander decided the creek was suitable for his base camp. He spent much of the following day setting it up, unloading the wagons. Cutting the teams from six mules to four, he dispatched the empty wagons back to Fort Concho for additional rations and forage. The other eight mules he kept to carry packs.

The men welcomed the rest, though it was not for their benefit. The hunters did not want to move until their Mexican guide and a couple of men with him returned from scouting to the west and northwest. The men bathed and washed the crusted sweat from their clothes. They brushed their horses and fed them grain to give them strength they would not get from the half-cured grass which bordered either side of the narrow creek. There had not been a lot of grass on the trip. This had been another dry year.

Gideon noticed that Hollander seemed to study his silver pocket watch a lot when he was not busy supervising establishment of the camp. Jimbo disclosed that his wife's picture was on the inside of the case.

In the afternoon a buffalo hunter loped into camp and slid his horse to a stop, spraying sand. "Indians coming yonder."

The camp was instantly aroused, and Hollander posted guards along the perimeter to make a defense. From where Gideon stood, carbine clutched in a sweaty hand, he gradually began to make out five horseback riders through the swimming waves of heat that melded prairie and sky together. He could see a patch of something white, which eventually took form as a flag.

Lieutenant Judson said, "Truce. Do you suppose the Indians have decided to give up to us?"

Hollander was studying them through his binoculars. "More likely they are going to invite us to give up to them."

It was not a war party, Gideon decided, for two of the Indians proved to be women, two others mature men past their warring prime. Only the leader was young, a tall, strikingly muscular man wearing little more than breechclout. He carried a white cloth tied to a rifle barrel.

There were about eighty rifles or carbines in camp, almost every one of them pointed at him. He was slow and deliberate in his movements, making it clear he was not a belligerent. "Peace!" he shouted. "Peace." He raised his free hand.

Hollander took a few steps forward. "Peace."

The two women, trailing the three men, looked frightened.

The men were grave but made a strong effort to betray no anxiety. The leader tapped himself on the chest. "Quanah. Quanah."

Gideon blinked. He had heard that name somewhere.

The Indian reached slowly into a deerskin bag tied behind him. He brought out a large envelope that bore some kind of seal. Cautiously Hollander took a few more steps and accepted the envelope from the outstretched hand. The captain read a moment, then turned to the hunters who had crowded closer. "Gentlemen, no doubt some of you have seen this man from afar —perhaps over the sights of your rifles. I doubt that you have ever seen him this close before. This is the chief Quanah, of the Quahadi Comanches."

Gideon glanced at Jimbo, his mouth dropping open.

One of the hunters said gruffly, "I've seen him, Captain, and shot at him, too. If you'll step a little to the left, I'll be tickled to try again."

Hollander shook his head grimly. "This is a letter from Colonel Mackenzie at Fort Sill. It gives Quanah permission to come out onto the plains in search of his straying brethren and take them back to the reservation. It says no one is to molest him."

The hunter demanded, "You have any idea how many white men this Quanah has killed? And white women, too, for that matter?"

"I am sure it would come to a considerable sum, but the orders are clear. We have to let him go on his way."

Quanah seemed to know only a few words of English, but he did better in Spanish, a result of trading with the Comanchero cartmen out of New Mexico. He conveyed the idea that he believed his wayward tribesmen to be somewhere to the southwest, where water and grass were plentiful.

The leader of the buffalo hunters, a tall man named Thompson, said, "I believe he means the Mustang Springs, Captain. And I also believe he means to deceive us."

"How?"

"Everything points to the Indians being yonderway, northwest. I think he wants us to follow him on a wild-goose chase while his red brothers cut around us and get back to the reservation."

"That's what everybody wants—to get them back to the reservation."

"Not with all the stock they stole from us. Once they make the reservation, nobody ever gets back a hoof. It's sanctuary, like a church."

Hollander weighed the hunter's opinion and agreed. He folded the paper and handed the envelope back to Quanah, motioning for him to be on his way. Quanah held back, making signs to indicate that he and his party were hungry. Hollander gave them rations and watched uneasily while the Indians ate. They filled their waterskins and proceeded southwestward.

Gideon kept watching them as long as they were in sight. More than once, Quanah looked back to see if someone followed. If what the hunter said was right, the Indians were probably disappointed.

After supper the tall Thompson came back to sit awhile with the captain, smoking his pipe and sharing reminiscences. The hunter had been in the war and afterward had been a field officer under Mackenzie for several years on the frontier before some Eastern review board decided his services were no longer required by an army that needed to cut personnel and pare expenses to the heartwood.

The hunter lighted his pipe with a splinter of dry wood ignited beneath the captain's blackened coffeepot. "I take no pleasure in killing Indians, Captain. I wouldn't say this to just anybody, but there are times I almost sympathize with them. When I can forget the friends of mine they've killed . . . when I can forget the sight of men I rode with butchered like a beef . . . I can see why the Comanches and the Kiowas and all those others keep running off from the reservation. They still figure this to be their country. They never had a government before to tell them where they could go and where they couldn't. They did what they wanted and went anywhere they were strong enough. This land fed them, gave them clothes and shelter. They were part of it like all the other wild animals, like the wolf and the buffalo. If I were them, I'd fight, too."

"But you're not them."

"No, I'm white, and white men need this land now. A man has

to side with his own. I doubt that the Comanches were the first Indians here. There were others before them, and the Comanches drove them off. Likely as not those others drove off somebody who was here before *them*. That's the way of the world. The strong take and the weak yield. It's the white man's turn to take. Destiny never backs down for sentiment. Neither does nature."

Hollander frowned. "And who will come along someday to take it away from *us?*"

"Nobody, Captain—at least not from you and me, because we won't stay to claim it. The soldier never gets to keep what he wins. He wins it for someone else and then moves on. We hunters won't stay either, most of us. When the buffalo are gone, the land will be ready for the farmer, the stock raiser. We are tools of destiny, Captain, you and me and your darkies here. We'll do our bit and drift away with nothing to show for it."

When Thompson returned to his own camp, Lieutenant Judson moved closer to the captain. "Couldn't we find some way to live with the Indians?"

Hollander poured a fresh cup of coffee. "The Indians—these plains tribes, anyway—are too different from us. They don't see life in our terms, and we can't see it in theirs. The white man gains respect by his work, by what he builds, by what he accumulates and keeps. These things mean nothing to the Indians. They are warriors. A warrior gains respect by his feats in battle. Put an Indian where he can no longer fight, and how is he to live? What is he to live *for?* Where is he to earn respect?" Hollander shook his head. "Try to put us together and the white man will always covet the Indian's land. The Indian will always be looking for a fight so he can win honor. We're incompatible. Somebody has to yield altogether, and that somebody has to be the Indian."

The lieutenant stared into the red embers beneath the coffeepot. "When you think about it, it's sad."

The captain gazed a long time across the rolling prairie, toward the distant blue hills where the Indians were likely to be. "You're a soldier, Lieutenant. A soldier learns not to think about it."

The Mexican scout returned the third day. If he had a last

name, Gideon never heard it. All he heard was "José." He saw little to set the dark-skinned, black-eyed little man apart from countrymen in and around Saint Angela. He seemed to regard the black soldiers with disdain, which Gideon found funny, in a dark way, for the white people treated both Mexican and Negro as inferiors. The two darker peoples should have considered themselves kindred spirits, but did not. José seemed to speak no English; he talked to Hollander through one of the hunters who had a smattering of Spanish. Gideon heard Hollander say the guide was a former Comanchero Indian trader who had switched his allegiances at one end of a rope with Mackenzie tugging at the other end—figuratively if not literally. A good trader learned to know the winners from the losers. There was no question who was to lose, in the long run.

Gideon guessed the Mexican told the captain about Indian sign, for Hollander left twenty troopers and two buffalo hunters to guard the supply camp while forty troopers and the rest of the hunters set out with a string of pack mules and several days' rations. The sun bore down like a demon aroused, and Gideon found he was by no means the only one who looked back regretfully at the tree-lined creek and its shade. His mouth was dry before his horse had gone two miles. The company rode many more before making dry camp.

The name of Double Lakes kept drifting back along the column on the next day's hot, dry march. Gideon began to build visions of clear blue water, the kind he had seen a few times on the lower plains when summer and fall rains filled the natural playa basins. They were a sight he and fellow soldiers had shared with few men other than the Indians, for he had seen their banks teeming with great herds of buffalo, of antelope, of wild mustangs running, tossing their manes, their long tails almost dragging the ground. He had seen birds by thousands—birds he could not name because he had never seen them before or since.

Gideon's disappointment was keen when the column finally topped a gentle rise in the sun-browned prairie and came in sight of the so-called lakes, their dry bottoms cracked, their powdered alkali skin shining fiercely in the sun.

He heard Hollander curse quietly but acknowledge that the

Mexican had promised nothing better. The column rode down to the edge of what had been a lake. A thin line of rotting debris showed last year's high-water mark. Dried, dead weeds testified that once there had been moisture enough for them to make their crop of seed, which lay dormant now beneath the curled and brittle litter, waiting for nature's next erratic demonstration of its dedication to the survival of all things.

"The shovels, Sergeant," the captain said.

Gideon and Jimbo happened to be nearby, and Nettles' eyes lighted upon them first. They untied shovels from one of the pack mules and walked out upon the dry lake bed, the captain beside them. "Dig here," he said.

Dry as the lake appeared on the surface, Gideon was surprised to find mud just inches beneath. "Keep digging," Hollander said. "The water down there may not be pretty, but it will be wet. Fish sometimes survive in that mud. When it rains and fills up the lake, you'll find them."

Gideon was not looking for fish; he just wanted a good drink of water. What gradually seeped into the first hole he dug seemed more mud than anything else, but while he was digging additional holes, he noted some clearing in the first one. Hollander waited a little, then dipped water in a collapsible cup. He smelled of it, touched it tentatively to his lips, frowned deeply and took a good swallow.

Grimacing, he wiped his sleeve across his mouth. "The Comanches have a strong prejudice against digging holes in the ground. Something about some evil spirit they are afraid of setting loose. I believe that prejudice may be justified."

Much digging and much patience produced enough water to satisfy the horses and mules, to fill the canteens and the coffeepots for supper. The coffee was made strong enough to mask the water's flavor. Gideon would not have asked a dog to drink such water under ordinary circumstances, but now he drank it himself gratefully. He reflected at length upon the inconsistency of personal standards.

Far to the west, dancing under the sun, lay a line of sand hills that were a glaring white most of the day, turning blue as the sun began to descend to the west of them and threw their eastern face into shadow. Somewhere yonder, the buffalo hunters insisted, they would find the Indians. Gideon stared at this miserable lake which so grudgingly yielded up its sorry water and wondered if those sand hills held any water at all.

The company made camp at the edge of the lake while José and several hunters scouted westward toward that elusive line of distant sand. Toward noon the following day, two vague dark forms began to show through the quivering heat waves and materialized into hunters on sweat-streaked, foam-flecked horses. Thompson rode out to meet them and brought them to Holander.

"Indian sign, Captain. José sends word he's found the tracks of thirty or forty hostiles west of Dry Lake." He pointed westward. "It's fresh sign, or was when these men left him. He'll keep following and let us catch up to him."

The bugler sounded the call. The horses were saddled, the mules quickly packed, leaving nothing and no one at the Double Lakes camp. The midafternoon sun was as heavy as some hot, giant hand pressing down on Gideon's head. It seemed to strike the parched ground and bounce back up into his face. The light breeze brought little comfort; it, too, carried the breath of a blacksmith's forge. The plodding feet of the column's horses powdered the dead short grass and mixed it into the rising cloud of light-colored dust. After a while Gideon lifted his canteen and took a couple of swallows of the water he had hated yesterday. Today it was as sweet as mother's milk.

His action was infectious. Jimbo, licking dry lips, untied his own canteen. Gideon listened to its sloshing sound.

"Jimbo, that canteen ain't full. Didn't you fill it up before we left the lake?"

Jimbo shook his head. "I was too busy helpin' pack the mules. It's half full. Didn't you hear them say we was headed for another lake?"

Presently Sergeant Nettles dropped out at the head of the line and sat on black Napoleon by the trail, warning the troopers as they rode by him to be sparing with their water. "Liable to be awhile before we fill them canteens again."

He could have saved his breath. As the men felt thirsty, they

drank. When the column reached the rim of Dry Lake a while
before sundown, most of the canteens were empty. Hollander
sent Gideon and Jimbo forward to try the small pool of shallow
water they could see shining red in the tired but hostile sun, far
into the middle of an otherwise dusty, crusted lake bed.

Gideon never tasted the water; he didn't have to. The thirsty
Jimbo pushed the dust-colored skim aside with the flat of his
hand and scooped up a palmful of water. He brought it to his
lips and spat involuntarily. "Great Goddlemighty!"

They carried the bad news to Hollander, but he and the
troopers already knew from watching Jimbo. Hollander said
loudly so everybody could hear, "Spare your water, men. We'll
get none here."

The order was late in coming. Most of the troopers had no
water.

While they were at the edge of the lake, discussing their disappointment, the Mexican guide and the rest of his hunter party
rode in from the west. José pointed northwesterly; the Indians
were moving that way.

Hollander said to the hunter-interpreter, "Ask him if there is
water along the route."

The scout replied that there should be, though Gideon studied
him with narrowed and doubting eyes, feeling that he lacked assurance. The scout seemed more concerned over the fact that the
Indians might be getting away than over the availability of
water.

Hollander set his jaw firmly. "Take us to them."

In the dusk Gideon saw that Jimbo's lips were gray with dust,
that he licked them often without apparent effect. His friend's
eyes were glazed. Gideon shook his canteen to see how much
water might be left, than handed it quietly to Jimbo. He did not
dare look at the other men like Finley or young Nash; he did not
have water enough for them all.

Jimbo took the canteen regretfully. "This ain't goin' to run
you short?" The question was one of courtesy and form; Jimbo
could tell Gideon's water was nearly gone.

"There'll be some more along the way," Gideon assured him.

The captain ordered a halt at dark. The company made a dry camp. For the most part, the men were grimly silent, eating little because they had no water to wash it down. A few argued with those who still saved a little water and were unwilling to share their last sips. Finley came to Gideon, begging for his canteen. Gideon handed it to him, rather than try to convince him it was dry. Finley turned it up and held it a long time. When he lowered it, his eyes were angry. "One drop," he exclaimed bitterly. "One little old tyntsy drop." Finley tossed the canteen at him. "I bet them white men got water."

Gideon doubted it. The hunters seemed to be suffering too. "You go tryin' to steal any, they'll kill you like a Comanche."

If Finley heard, he made no sign of it. Gideon made up his mind not to worry about him. He lay awake much of the night, his mouth painfully dry. He had to struggle to work up saliva and ease the hurt. When he swallowed, there was never enough to coat his throat, and the sensation was like the sharp edge of a knife scraping his windpipe. Dawn found him awake and miserable. He was up before the call came.

Breakfast was a hollow ritual, most of the men eating only a little, choking it down with considerable effort. Gideon glanced into the hunters' camp and saw no one making coffee. It was just as well. The smell of it might set off a minor mutiny.

José impatiently set out on the trail ahead of the others, and they had to push their horses to keep up. Gideon noticed Jimbo was sitting stiffly in the saddle, rather than his usual casual, even slouchy manner. "You all right, Jimbo?"

Jimbo nodded and mumbled. His lower lip had cracked, showing a rusty-colored patch of dried blood he had not been able to lick away.

The morning sun blazed down angrily upon their backs, then on their shoulders, sometimes the right, sometimes the left. Gideon rode woodenly, his eyes set on the riders in front of him. It took him awhile to realize they were shifting direction every so often across the dry prairie and across the patches of hot sand where a low variety of oak grew, most of it reaching no higher than the horses' knees.

The Indians knew about them, he reasoned, and they were starting to zigzag to confuse the pursuers. It did not occur to him they might have a stronger and grimmer purpose.

The hurting in his throat grew worse. It was as if he had swallowed a hoof rasp, and it had scraped away the throat lining all the way down. Every now and again a choking sensation compelled him to try to swallow, bringing a pain that doubled him over. His head throbbed, and he found it hard to see past the captain at the front of the column. Some of the men swayed in their saddles. Little Finley was hunched, staring at the ground as if in a trance.

The guide stayed out in front, watching the plainly beaten trail. The buffalo hunter-interpreter stayed with him. Periodically one or more of the other hunters moved forward awhile, inevitably slowing later until the main column came up. Several times Hollander sent the lieutenant or Esau Nettles forward to ask the guide about the water he had promised, and always the answer came back that it had not been where José had expected.

The Comanche trail gradually became less pronounced, for individually, or in small groups, the Indians had dropped away from the main party and angled off at tangents. It was a pattern Gideon remembered well, and he was not surprised that José sometimes agonized over which trail to follow. He always chose the heavier one, but Gideon could see frustration in the way he looked back over his shoulder at the smaller trail he had to abandon.

What surprised Gideon even more was the scout's continued ability to devote himself to the tracks with the determination of a bloodhound. Even granting that he was to a degree a native of this punishing land, he was still human. Around him, Gideon could see men sun-cooked almost to the point of falling unconscious. Once he had to dismount—a strong effort in itself—and help the fallen Finley back into the saddle. Finley groaned a protest and tried weakly to swing a fist at him. Even with Jimbo's help, lifting Finley was almost too much effort. Gideon's head reeled. The strain fired a reddish glare in his eyes.

The recruit Nash fell. Gideon stopped the plodding brown horse and looked back, waiting to see if someone else would make the effort. Sergeant Waters did, his eyes wide with alarm. It occurred to Gideon that no one was talking. His own tongue was dry and felt as if it were swelling.

José's extra riding took its toll of his horse, if not of the man. The sun was directly overhead, bearing down without mercy, when the Mexican stopped, his horse dropping its head and trembling. Earlier it had sweated, but now even the sweat was gone, dried and leaving a crust of clotted dust where saddle or reins had not rubbed it away.

Gideon's eyes began playing tricks on him. It was as if he were looking down a vaguely defined tunnel, everything out of focus except squarely in the center. It was all he could do to see the men who rode before him. He felt crazily imprisoned in a blanket of heat that wrapped itself around him.

The captain stopped as he came up to José, and Nettles did likewise. The next man behind seemed not to see and bumped his horse into the sergeant's. The same thing happened to the second man back. Nettles rubbed a dusty sleeve across his mouth and tried vainly to spit. "Daddammit, you-all watch!" The voice seemed not quite his own.

The halt broke Gideon out of his tormented trance. The troopers' horses were hanging their heads, many bracing their legs and trembling. One collapsed, almost knocking down the horse next to it. The trooper spilled out of the saddle and scrambled away, avoiding being pinned. Hollander looked, more resigned than surprised.

The interpreter had some trouble getting his message into words. "José's horse has given out. Can't trail any further without another horse."

It took the captain a few minutes to get started, and his voice was angry. "Where's the water? He promised us water."

José seemed to understand the question and began answering before the interpreter was through. He did some shrugging, some pointing.

The hunter explained, "He says we should've found it. Says this has been a bad year, and lots of the old waterholes have failed."

The captain pointed at the tracks. They were far fewer than

earlier in the day. "I think the Indians have tricked us . . . *him.* They've led us back and forth across these sands—these dry flats —keeping us away from water."

José said that sooner or later the Indians had to go to water themselves.

The captain studied the men and horses of his command. Three troopers had dismounted and lay on the ground in the shadows of their horses. Little Finley was one, groaning as if in anticipation of death. Most of the rest were hunched in the saddles, their eyes closed against the relentless sun, their lips dried and cracking from the sun and the hot, searching wind.

"What if we forget about the Indians for now?" Hollander demanded. "What if we strike out for the nearest water? How far would it be?"

The guide's words were definite, but his manner was not. Hollander turned to the lieutenant. "He's lost. He got so absorbed in following the Indians that he forgot to keep track of landmarks."

José understood more English than he could speak, for he began to argue before the interpreter told him what the officer was saying. He kept pointing in a westerly direction. The interpreter said, "Six or seven miles. He says there's water in six or seven miles. He just needs a fresher horse to find it."

Hollander pondered, his eyes on his suffering men. Finally he said to Nettles, "Get him my big bay." The captain had brought one of his private horses, tied behind a pack mule. José slipped the saddle from his exhausted mount and put it on the bay. Mounting, he told the captain and Thompson of the hunters to follow him; he knew he could find water.

The interpreter did not try to stay up with him. His own horse was too far gone. The bay, though it had had no more water than the other horses, had an advantage in not having carried a load. José set a pace the company could not match, and soon he disappeared into the false blue mirage lakes that shimmered treacherously in the sterile sands.

Woodenly, mutely, the command straggled along in his tracks. Gideon kept watching Jimbo. When his friend seemed in danger of falling from the saddle, Gideon reached out and gripped his arm. "Jimbo, you take ahold of yourself."

Jimbo had not been far short of unconsciousness. "I'm all right," he mumbled. "Just got sleepy."

José had ridden almost due west awhile. At a dried-out waterhole he had suddenly changed direction back to the northeast. It was not quite a hundred-and-eighty-degree turn. Gideon heard Hollander and Thompson arguing over whether the Mexican knew where he was going.

The buffalo hunter grunted impatiently. "I don't know this country like he does. But if we stay here, we'll starve for water."

Lieutenant Judson listened silently, his head down. He was almost out of it.

The two men talked awhile, their voices rising in anger. Gideon sensed that the anger was directed not so much toward each other as toward the streak of bad luck which had brought them to this difficult point. In a few minutes they agreed upon the only course open to them from the start. They had to follow the guide.

"He may still be lost," Hollander said.

"We know *we* are."

Jimbo seemed to have pulled himself together after almost falling. He was looking around more. Together he and Gideon steadied the young Nash when he showed signs of letting go. Behind him Gideon heard a dull thump as another trooper fell and began trembling convulsively on the ground.

Sergeant Waters, who brought up the rear, shook the soldier violently. He looked frightened at the lack of response. Gideon dismounted and walked back. He caught Waters' wrist. "That won't help him. What he needs is a drink."

A soldier in the column began to whimper. Waters looked around quickly, shaking. He tried to speak, but his dry, swollen lips betrayed him. He finally managed, "Ain't no water left."

A buffalo hunter quartered his horse into the cavalry company and dismounted slowly, heavily, canteen in his hand. It sloshed a little. "Saved this for myself," he said thickly. But he unscrewed the cap and let the water trickle slowly across the trooper's dry lips, catching drops with his finger when they were about to run away, forcing them back into the delirious man's mouth.

Captain Hollander sat quietly on his horse, watching the men work with the fallen trooper. His eyes searched the rest of the company, the thought painfully clear. Which man was likely to fall next? Almost immediately, one did.

Hollander bowed his head. Gideon could not tell whether he was praying or simply hiding his eyes from the relentless sun. When Hollander looked up again, he sought out Jimbo. "Come here to me." The captain got to the ground carefully, painfully. "How do you feel, Jimbo? And how is your horse making it?"

Jimbo replied with more confidence than Gideon thought was justified, "Fine, Captain, sir. We both fine."

"Jimbo, if anybody can keep a horse going, you're the man. For the moment, consider yourself a corporal. I'm going to detail you some men whose horses still look as if they'll make it. You're going to take canteens and follow the trail left by that Mexican. Think you can do that?"

Jimbo had seldom lacked for confidence. "Sure, Captain, sir. Want us to go and fetch back water for the rest of you?"

Gideon felt a clutch of fear. This was more responsibility than Jimbo had ever been given. What if they lost José's trail and fell to wandering? What if Indians came upon them in their helplessness?

"Captain, sir," Gideon spoke up, "Jimbo's apt to need help. I want to go with him."

Hollander cut his eyes to Gideon. He shook his head. "Ledbetter, I'll need all the steady old hands I can keep. You'll stay here, in reserve."

Gideon wanted to argue but realized it was useless. He watched in helpless silence while Hollander picked seven more men to go with Jimbo. Gideon studied his friend's face and found no apprehension or doubt. Jimbo did not comprehend the risk. Maybe that was just as well. Gideon said, "Jimbo, you ain't never been away from me before, hardly. You watch out now."

Jimbo came as near smiling as his swollen and bleeding lips would allow. "Old Colonel, he didn't raise no idiots."

As the men tied empty canteens to their saddles, Hollander

gave his orders slowly, repeating every point. "You watch that trail closely. For God's sake, don't lose it. When José finds water, give your horses a drink, rest them a little while, then backtrail to meet us with those canteens. You understand, Jimbo?"

Jimbo nodded. Hollander said, "Then go, and good luck." Jimbo saluted and led the men out, following the guide's tracks in the hot sand.

Gideon's fear would not let go. "Captain, what if that Mexican *don't* find water?"

Hollander did not answer him in words, but his eyes gave the answer Gideon dreaded. He watched Jimbo and the others disappear into that shimmering veil and was surprised he still had water enough in his system to produce a tear.

The fallen men were revived and lifted back onto their horses. Gideon wondered how the horses found strength to carry them. Moving slower now, soldiers and buffalo hunters trudged along the trail beaten by the guide and by the canteen carriers. Gideon felt his brown horse Judas breaking down, his steps labored. He dismounted and began to walk, leading the horse. Around him, other men did the same. A common fear ran through the command. Every soldier had been told and drilled and told again that losing his horse on these open plains was tantamount to suicide. A man afoot was a man soon dead.

One of the horses which had dropped back almost to the rear of the column fell to its knees, then lay over on its side, kicking convulsively, making a harsh and agonized sound in its fight to breathe. Its rider pleaded with the animal to get up. He tugged in vain at the horse's head. At Captain Hollander's command, a couple of soldiers managed to work the trooper's saddle free and slip the bridle off. The saddle was added to a pack mule's burden. The captain's pistol cracked, and the weeping soldier fell in behind the others, walking.

After a while, two men were down and showing no signs of getting up. No water was left anywhere in the command. The buffalo hunters had exhausted the last of their own, on themselves or on sunstruck soldiers. Hollander held his hand before his eyes and squinted toward the lowering sun.

"The column can't waste the daylight that's left," he said. "We can't wait on these men. Sergeant Waters, you still look strong. Stay with them until they can get to their feet, then bring them on."

Waters had never argued with white officers. But he came near it now. Gideon saw raw fear in the man's white-rimmed eyes. "Captain, you hear them men a-groanin'? You leave them here, they'll die. We'll all die."

"Sergeant, when you accepted those stripes you accepted responsibility. Now do what I tell you or by God I'll be forced to do to you what I did to that horse back there."

Nettles moved up. "Captain, I'll talk to him." While Hollander pressed on, Nettles sternly told Waters to get hold of himself and be a soldier, a man. Walking away, he caught the question in Gideon's eyes; Gideon had never seen Waters so frightened. Nettles said, "It was their groanin' got to him thataway. He's heard many a one groan before."

Gideon looked back once and saw Waters standing alone with three horses, two men lying on the ground. He realized that as long as he had known Waters, the man had always seemed alone. Half a mile farther on, atop a small rise, Gideon looked back once more. Nothing had changed. Waters remained where he had been. The heat waves dissolved him and removed him from view.

It seemed forever before the sun sank beneath a cloudless western horizon, tempering the terrible heat. But dusk was far from cool. Gideon tried not to look behind him anymore, for he would be dismayed to see how little distance they had actually traveled. He did not want to look forward, either, to be reminded how far they still had to go. But anxiety compelled him to look eastward every now and again. Somewhere up there were Jimbo and the canteen carriers. Any minute now, God willing, they might show up on the trail ahead, bringing back water and salvation.

Gideon could see nothing in the gathering dusk except a round hill dead ahead of them, rising a little higher than the plain around it. By now he was having to walk along beside the young Nash and hold him in the saddle. Ahead of him, Sergeant Esau

Nettles was leading Napoleon and holding on to little Finley. Nettles' own feet were dragging. His limp was pronounced. If they walked much farther, someone would have to help the sergeant.

Hollander, his face blistered by the sun, kept riding back along the stretched-out line to make sure no one stumbled and was left behind. His short growth of whiskers had taken on a coating of alkali dust and blow-sand. His lips, like everyone else's, were swelling and breaking.

He pointed. "The hill," he said hoarsely. "The top of the hill. We can see and be seen."

The grade was modest. At another time, the hill would have been no climb. But Gideon labored, each step harder than the last. Esau Nettles fell. Gideon moved forward and took hold of him. Leaning heavily on Gideon, the sergeant pushed to his feet. Little Finley's horse had gone on. Nettles tried to catch up with him, to resume his support of Finley. Gideon said, "Let him go. Time Finley taken care of hisself. You better ride Napoleon the rest of the way, Sergeant."

"I don't want to kill my horse," Nettles murmured.

"Druther kill yourself?"

He helped Nettles get his left foot into the stirrup, then gave him a boost into the saddle. Nettles could not hold back a quick cry of pain as his left leg slid heavily over the horse's rump. His hand went to his hip, where the Comanche arrow had struck him long ago.

Before good dark, they were on the hilltop. Unsaddling was slow and clumsy. Unpacking the mules was worse because of the weight. When its pack was removed, one of the mules stretched to urinate. Little Finley held out his cup and caught it full while Gideon watched in disbelief.

"Man," Gideon managed finally, "you're crazy," and tried to take the cup from him. Finley found the strength to pull out of his reach. He turned away to protect himself from interference and raised the cup to his lips. He choked and spat and went to his knees. He tried again and managed to swallow some of the hot, sharp urine. He doubled over, retching.

Gideon saw that other men were watching, some in disgust,

some in hope. The next time a horse stretched, two men were there with cups. One vomited almost instantly, but the other managed to force most of his cupful and keep it down.

One of the buffalo hunters mumbled through swollen lips, "My God!"

From behind a distant small knoll, two Comanche warriors watched as the cavalrymen and the hunters collapsed on the round-topped hill. Gray Horse grunted his satisfaction to Limping Boy. "They will bother us no more. By tomorrow night, if their medicine is not strong, they will all be dead. And the white chiefs can never say we killed them."

Limping Boy shook his head. "We led them here."

"But it is the land that kills them, not us."

Gray Horse walked back to his tethered pony and took a long drink of water from the deer-paunch bag tied to his rawhide saddle. Watching the soldiers had made him very thirsty.

He swung onto the pony's back. He and Limping Boy started eastward, after those who had ridden on before them. They had many horses and mules to take back to the reservation.

Twenty

THE CAPTAIN WENT through the motions of setting up a guard mount, but it was a futile effort. Most of these suffering men could do little to defend themselves should the Indians choose this time to attack. Gideon's vision was so blurred that he could not have drawn a bead. Sergeant Nettles could no longer control his limp. He kept his eyes on the captain and contrived not to move more than necessary when the captain looked in his direction.

Gideon asked, "Sergeant, why don't you take your rest?"

Nettles' eyes flashed in anger. "You tryin' to tell me what to do, *Private* Ledbetter?"

"No, sir. Just come to me that you had a hard day."

"We all had a hard day. Mine ain't been worse than nobody else's."

"You've rode back and forth, walked back and forth, seein' after the men. You gone twice as far as most of us. You rest, why don't you? Tell me what you want done and I'll do it."

"I want you to leave me alone. Ain't nothin' wrong with me that ain't wrong with everybody here."

"The rest of them got no arrow wound that ain't ever healed up."

The anger in Nettles' eyes turned to sharp concern. "It's all right, and I don't want you talkin' about it." He glanced quickly toward the captain and showed relief to find Hollander's attention focused elsewhere.

Gideon said accusingly, "You been hidin' it from him."

He could not remember that he had ever seen Nettles show fear of anything. But the sergeant was fearful now. He gripped Gideon's arm. "Don't you be tellin' him. Don't be tellin' nobody. Without the army, what could I be? Where could I go?"

"Lots of things. Lots of places."

"You know better than that. In the army I'm a sergeant, a *top* sergeant. I'm somebody, and I can *do* somethin'. Anywhere else, I'm just another nigger."

"Captain'll see for hisself sooner or later."

"Not as long as I can move. Now you git to your own business."

Sometime during the early part of the evening Gideon heard horses walking. He pushed up from the ground, listening, hoping it was Jimbo and the canteen carriers coming back. He was momentarily disoriented—dizzy—but he realized the sound was from the wrong direction to be Jimbo. It was coming from along the column's backtrail, to the west. He thought about Indians, but they wouldn't make that much noise. The clinking and clanking meant cavalry horses.

Captain Hollander figured it out ahead of Gideon. He walked to the edge of camp and did his best to shout. "Waters! Sergeant Waters! Up here!" His voice was weak and broke once.

The horses seemed to stop for a moment. The men—one of them, at least—had heard the captain. Hollander shouted again, his voice hoarser now. After a moment, the horses were moving again. The captain grunted in satisfaction. His good feeling was soon spoiled, for the horses kept walking, right on by the knoll.

"Waters!" Hollander tried again. Gideon took up the shout, and so did several others. The riders continued to move, passing the hill and going on eastward. The captain clenched his fists in anger.

Gideon volunteered, "I'll go, sir. I'll fetch them back." Hollander only grunted, but Gideon took that for approval. He started down the hill, his legs heavy. He shouted every so often for Waters, but he heard no reply. When he stopped to listen he could tell that the horses were getting farther from him. He tried to run but could not bring his legs to move that rapidly. He stumbled over the crown of some dried-up bunchgrass and sprawled on his belly. He invested a strong effort into getting on his feet.

Behind him Hollander called, "Come back, Ledbetter. Let them go."

He wavered on the point of insubordination but found he could barely hear the horses anymore. He had no chance to catch them. Wearily he turned and began the struggle back up the hill. It must have taken him an hour to reach the huddled company and fall to the ground.

Hollander stood over him, against the starlight. "You tried."

When he had the breath, Gideon said, "They just never did hear me."

"They heard you. Waters simply did not choose to stop. He's saving himself, or trying to."

A question burned in his mind, and he came near asking it aloud. *Are we going to save ourselves?* His throat was too dry to bring it out.

Nettles came over after a while to see if he was all right.

Gideon demanded, "What was the matter with Sergeant Waters? I *know* he heard me. I never figured *him* to panic out of his head."

"I seen him when the men commenced to groan. It was the groanin' done it. You ever wonder why he drank so much? It was to drive the groanin' sounds out of his mind."

"I don't understand."

"Old days, Waters was a slave catcher. It was him that kept the hounds, and him the white folks give the whip to when he caught a runaway. He didn't have no choice—they'd of took the whip to *him* if he hadn't done it. Now and again they made him keep whippin' a man till the life and the soul was beat out of him. I reckon them dead people been comin' after Waters ever since, in his mind."

The night breeze turned mercifully cool, but it held no hint of moisture. Gideon woodenly stood his guard duty, knowing he would be helpless if anything challenged him. He heard men groaning. The sound made his skin crawl. He could imagine how it had been with Waters. Across the camp someone babbled crazily, hallucinating. Gideon lapsed into sleep of sorts, or unconsciousness. When he awoke, color brightened the east. His head felt as if someone were pounding it with a hammer. His tongue was dry and swollen, his mouth like leather.

Sergeant Nettles lay on his blanket, his eyes open. Gideon crawled to him on hands and knees. He knew what he wanted to say, but his tongue betrayed him. He brought out only a jumble of sounds. He worked at it a long time before he summoned up a little saliva and forced his tongue to more or less his bidding. "You all right, sir?" he asked.

Nettles nodded and pushed himself slowly from the ground. At the edge of camp, Captain Hollander was moving about, the first man on his feet.

Little effort was made toward fixing breakfast. The men could not eat. They could not swallow without water. The captain started trying to pack the mules. The regular packer had fallen behind yesterday with Waters. Gideon began to help. It was almost more than he could do to lift a pack to the level of a mule's back. Had the mules been fidgety, he could not have managed. But they were too miserable to move around.

He could see a little better this morning, for the rest, and his legs moved easier than last night, but the gain was of only minor degree. A stir among the buffalo hunters attracted his attention. He became conscious that many of their horses and pack mules were gone. They had strayed off during the night, or perhaps Indians had stolen into the edge of camp and quietly made away with them. The hunters staggered around uncertainly, accusing one another mostly by gesture, for they were as hard put as the troopers to convert gestures into understandable words. In a little while hunters and soldiers started a ragged march down the gentle slope and left the round hill behind them.

Grasping at hope wherever he could find it, Gideon told himself that perhaps Jimbo and the others had stopped at darkness for fear of losing the trail, and by now they were on the move again, coming to the rescue.

The morning sun was soon punishingly hot. Miles went by slowly and painfully, and Jimbo did not come. Far up into the morning, after a couple of troopers had slumped to the ground, Hollander called for a rest stop. They had moved into a sandy stretch of ground with low-growing stemmy mesquite trees and small oak growth shin- to knee-high. Many of the men draped blankets over these plants and crawled under them as far as they could go for partial protection against the punishing sun.

Gideon turned to look for Sergeant Nettles. He found him shakily trying to dismount from his black horse Napoleon. Gideon reached to help him. He spread a blanket across a bush and pulled the corner of it over Nettles' head.

Young Nash tried to dismount but fell and lay as he had landed. Little Finley sat hunched, crying but not making tears. He tried to talk, but the words were without form.

Hollander was somehow still able to articulate, though he spoke his words slowly and carefully. He said it was his judgment that José had become lost and was not coming back—not today, not ever. The men who had gone on after him with the canteens must be sharing whatever fate had overtaken José.

Thompson argued sternly that somewhere ahead lay Silver Lake, and that it was no doubt José's goal. It couldn't be more than a few more miles—fifteen or twenty at most, he declared.

Hollander shook his head violently, his face flushed. If water were that near, and José had found it, Jimbo and the others would be back by now. The captain pointed southeastward. He still had his compass. Water anywhere else was a guess, and evidently a bad one. But he *knew* there was water in the Double Lakes. It was time to stop gambling and go for the cinch.

Thompson was aghast. "You know how far it is to the Double Lakes? Those darkies of yours—they're almost dead now. They'll never live for another sixty-seventy miles."

"They'll live. They've *got* to live."

Thompson insisted that water lay much closer, to the northeast.

Hollander countered, "You said that yesterday. How far have we come? How many more men can we afford to lose?"

"Go that way," Thompson insisted, pointing his chin across the sandy hills toward Double Lakes, "and you'll lose them all."

"There is water at Double Lakes. There is only death out here in these sands. Will you go with us?"

Thompson turned and studied his hunters. "No, we're trying for Silver Lake. It's there. I know it's there. I beg you, Captain, come on with us."

But Hollander had made up his mind. "I've already gambled and lost. I'll gamble no more on water that may not exist. Best of luck to you, Thompson."

The buffalo hunter saw the futility of further argument. "God go with you, Frank."

Hollander nodded. "May He walk with us all." Anger stood like a wall between the men, but each managed to thrust a hand forward. The two groups parted, the hunters toward the hope of Silver Lake and a short trail, the soldiers toward the certainty of Double Lakes, a long and terrible distance away.

The last time Gideon glimpsed the hunters, fading out of sight far to his left, four were walking, the rest hunched on their horses. Though he had not become personally acquainted and could not have named any except Thompson, he felt an ache of regret, a sense of loss as they disappeared into the shimmering heat.

He had no feeling for time. His legs were deadweights that he dragged along, one step and another and another. His vision blurred again. He trudged with his head down, following the tracks of the men in front of him. He no longer thought ahead, or even thought much at all. He fell into a merciful state of half consciousness, moving his body by reflex and instinct. His tongue had swollen so that it almost filled his mouth, and at times he felt he would choke on it.

He was conscious of hunger but unable to act upon it. He put hardtack into his mouth but could not work up saliva to soften it. It was like dry gravel against his inflexible tongue. He had to dig the pieces out with his finger.

Rarely did the horses or mules urinate, but when they did,

someone rushed with a cup. The thought was no longer revolting to Gideon. Captain Hollander passed out brown sugar for the men to stir into the urine and increase its palatability. Some was given back to the horses, which at first refused but later accepted it.

By midafternoon, when the heat was at full fury, a horse staggered and went down. Hollander cut its throat to put it out of its misery. Finley came with his cup and caught the gushing blood and drank it, and others took what they could catch before death overtook the animal and the flow stopped. Some of the men became violently ill; the blood was thick and bitter from the horse's dehydration.

Hollander was compelled to call a halt. Men were strung out for half a mile. Orders meant next to nothing. This was no longer a column of soldiers; it was a loose and straggling collection of half-delirious men struggling for individual survival. Gideon saw Nash fall and wanted to go to help him but for a long time could not move his legs. Only when he saw Sergeant Nettles collapse upon the sun-baked sand did he muster the strength to stagger twenty steps and throw blankets over the men's heads to shield them from the sun. He slumped then, too exhausted to do the same for himself. He lapsed into a dreamlike state and seemed to float away like some bodiless spirit, back to the plantation. He heard the happy voice of Big Ella and the others there, and he splashed barefoot into the cool, flowing river.

The heat abated with sundown, and night brought a coolness which broke Gideon's fever. He roused to the point that he could look about him and see the other men lying in grotesque positions, many groaning, half of them suffering from delirium.

He rallied enough to crawl to Sergeant Nettles. At first he could not tell that the man was breathing. He held his hand just above Nettles' mouth and felt that faint but steady warmth of breath. Probably the sergeant was unconscious. Gideon saw no point in trying to bring him out of it. The Lord was being merciful.

Sometime in the night Captain Hollander started trying to get the men on their feet to use the cooler hours for easier miles. Gideon watched him impassively at first, until the man's strong determination began to reach him. Sergeant Nettles arose and began limping from one man to another. Gideon pushed to his feet and helped.

He heard Hollander say thickly, "Good man, Ledbetter. Get them going."

In the moonlight it was apparent that several horses had wandered away. Judas was gone. Gideon could not bring himself to any emotion over that. Half the men were afoot now, their horses strayed or dead. Many of the pack mules were missing. Nettles asked Gideon to count the men, to be sure they left none behind. He found it difficult to hold the figures in his head. His mind kept drifting to other things, other times, other places far better than this one.

Many blankets and packs were left on the ground as the company moved out. A couple of men dropped their carbines, and Gideon forcibly put them back in their hands. A little later he looked back and saw that one of the men was empty-handed again.

He dreaded sunrise, but it came. He sensed that they had walked or ridden many miles in the cool darkness. The heat was blunted the first couple of hours by a thin cover of dry clouds that held no promise of rain. These burned away, after a time, and the men and horses trudged under the full punishment of an unforgiving July sun.

A transient thought flitted through Gideon's mind. He wondered where the Indians were. It struck him as strange that he had gone so long without the Indians intruding on his consciousness. It occurred to him that it had been most of two days since he had heard them mentioned. Odd, that the mission which had brought the soldiers into this blazing hell had been so completely forgotten in the face of a more elemental challenge, simple survival.

A staggering horse brought the procession to a halt. Without waiting for the captain to give an order, one of the troopers cut the animal's throat, and several fought over the gushing blood. Gideon saw Nettles start toward the men to break up the fight, then go to his knees. Gideon took it upon himself to part the fighters, throwing a couple to the ground with more strength than he had realized he still owned. Little Finley's own horse went down on its rump. Finley stared dumbly, making no effort to join the struggle to capture its blood. He lay down on the short, brittle grass and wept silently, his shoulders shuddering.

Through all of it, Nettles sat helplessly. The spirit was still strong in his black eyes, but the flesh had gone as far as it could. Gideon managed to get the men under some semblance of control, making gruff noises deep in his throat because he could not force his tongue to form clear words. He felt the eyes of Hollander and Nettles upon him. Without being formally bidden to do so, he took command upon himself and motioned and coaxed and bullied most of the men into movement. Lieutenant Judson, weaving a little, got on his droop-headed horse and took the lead.

Soon only five men were left, Gideon and Hollander on their feet, the sunstruck Nash and shattered little Finley lying on the ground, Sergeant Nettles sitting up but unable to keep his legs under him.

By signs more than by words, Nettles conveyed his intention of staying with Nash and Finley until they were able to move. Then he would bring them on, following the company's trail to water. Captain Hollander nodded his assent, though Gideon saw sadness in the man's blue eyes. Hollander took the big black hand in both of his own and squeezed it for a moment, silently saying good-bye to an old friend. Hollander turned away quickly, not looking back. Nettles raised his hand again, and Gideon took it.

The sergeant mumbled, but Gideon made out the words he was trying to say. "Take care of them, soldier."

Gideon tried to assure him he would be back as soon as they found water, but the words would not come. He turned back only once, a hundred yards away, and took a final look at the sergeant, still sitting up, holding the reins of big, black Napoleon. For a moment, in spite of the heat, Gideon felt cold.

The column moved until upwards of midday, when the heat brought more horses to their knees, and more of the men. By this time the company was out of control. Now and then a man in delirium struck out on a tangent of his own, away from the main body. At first Gideon tried to bring them back but soon had to give up, for the effort was a drain on whatever strength he still held in reserve. He stopped thinking ahead but concentrated on bringing one foot in front of the other.

When Lieutenant Judson went down, slipping from the saddle and landing limply in the dry grass, the column stopped. The lieutenant's horse braced its legs and stood trembling. It no longer sweated, though a crust of dried mud clung to its hide. Hollander tried to rouse Judson but could not. Hollander gave a little cry and slumped to the ground, covering his face with his hands. By instinct more than reason, Gideon helped him to a small mesquite and threw a blanket over it to shade him, and to shield the captain's emotions from view of the men. The lieutenant's horse, untethered, began wandering off southward, dragging the reins, drawn by instinct in the direction of Concho. Gideon knew he should make some effort to bring it back, but he lacked the willpower to move. He sat with his legs stretched out before him on the ground and watched the horse stumble away to a slow death somewhere out there on the parched prairie.

After a time, Gideon became aware that the captain was trying to call him. Hollander motioned with his hand. Gideon crawled to the officer on hands and knees.

Hollander extended his silver watch, despair in his sunken eyes. Very slowly, very deliberately, he managed a few clear words. "Wife. Give to my wife and baby."

Gideon reached for the watch until the import of the captain's words penetrated his fevered brain. Hollander was giving up. Gideon looked slowly around him at the men sprawled on the ground, covering their heads with blankets if they still had them, hats if they did not.

If Hollander died, these men would die. Hollander might be no better man than they, but his was the leadership. His was the example they had been conditioned to follow, as they had been conditioned all their lives to follow one white man or another. It came to Gideon that if he accepted the watch, that would release the captain to die in peace.

He felt a flare of deep anger. The captain had no right to die! He had brought these men here; he had to live and take them out. Gideon drew back his hand. Shaking his head, he tried to form words first in his mind, then get them out on his dry, swollen tongue.

"No! You'll live. *You* give it to her."

The captain reached out with both hands, the silver chain dangling. His eyes begged, though his cracked lips formed no discernible words.

Gideon almost gave in to pity, but the anger was still hot in his face. Stubbornly he pulled back. The words came clearly in his mind, though he could not get his tongue to speak them.

You got a baby now, more than likely. You owe that woman, and you owe that baby, and you owe us! You goin' to live if I got to kill you!

Only the anger came out, not the words. But the captain seemed to understand that Gideon refused to release him from his responsibilities. Hollander turned his head away, in the shadow beneath the blanket. He clutched the silver watch against his chest, his shoulders heaving.

In a while he was somehow on his feet again. He motioned for Gideon to help him lift the delirious lieutenant onto the captain's own horse. Gideon tied the young officer in the saddle. Hollander struck out again southeastward, his steps slow and deliberate. He was setting a pace, an example. His shoulders had a determined set. Gideon sensed that the captain would not give up again. He might die, but he would not surrender.

Gideon had trouble distinguishing reality from hallucination. His head roared from fever, and it ached with a steady rhythm like a drumbeat. He imagined he could hear the post band playing a parade-ground march, and he tried in vain to bring his feet into step with it. His vision was distorted, the men stretched out of shape, the prairie rolling in waves. Cajoling, threatening, he got the men to their feet one by one and set them to following the captain. Some moved willingly, some fought him, but by and by he had them all on the move.

Stumbling, bringing up the rear so no one could drop out without his knowledge, Gideon moved in a trance. It occurred to him that a couple of the pack mules had strayed off on their own. Only two were left.

Each time a horse staggered and fell, its throat was cut, and the men caught the blood and gagged it down. The captain's horse gave up after a long time, going to its knees. Gideon struggled to untie the lieutenant but could not bring his unresponsive fingers to the task. He cut the rope and tried to ease the officer to the ground. He lacked the strength to hold him. He and the lieutenant fell together in a heap. Gideon looked up at the horse, afraid it might roll over on them. He dragged himself and the lieutenant away before someone cut the animal's throat.

That was the last of the horses.

He lay struggling for breath; the exertion had been severe. The men were like gaunt scarecrow figures out of a nightmare, their uniforms a dusty gray instead of blue, many hanging in strips and ribbons. The faces were stubbled, the beards matted grotesquely with dust and horses' blood as well as some of their own, for their lips were swollen out of shape and had cracked and bled. They no longer looked like soldiers, they looked like madmen—and Gideon feared he was the maddest of them all.

The packs were untied from the mules, and Lieutenant Judson was lifted aboard one of the last two surviving animals. Again Gideon tried to tie him on, but he could not coordinate his hands and gave up the task. Delirious or not, Judson would have to retain instinct enough to hold himself on the mule.

The ragged column plodded and staggered and crawled until far into the afternoon. Hollander motioned for a rest stop in an open plain that lacked even the low-growing dune mesquites over which a blanket could be stretched for shade. Hardly a blanket was left anyway. The men had dropped them one by one, along with everything else they had carried. Troopers sprawled on the ground, faces down to shield them from the sun. Gideon fell into a state more stupor than sleep. After a time, he felt someone shaking his shoulder. Hollander was motioning for him to get up, and to get the other men up. Gideon went about the task woodenly. He helped Hollander and one of the other troopers lift the lieutenant back onto the mule.

Gideon saw that Hollander was studying the other mule, which had remained riderless. The wish was plain in the officer's eyes, but Gideon saw there a reluctance, too. They were no longer officers and men; they were simply men, all in a desperate situation together. Hollander was uncertain about using the advantage that might save his life.

Gideon felt a sudden temptation to take the mule himself. He had the strength to do it. At this moment, he was probably the strongest man in the column. Nobody—not even Hollander—could stop him if he made up his mind.

The thought became action to the point that he laid his hands on the reins, and on the mule's roached mane. He leaned against the mule, trying to summon strength to pull himself up. But he could not, and he realized slowly that it was more than simply a matter of strength. It was also a matter of will. Sergeant Esau Nettles forcibly pushed himself into Gideon's mind. In Nettles' eyes, such a thing would be a dishonor upon Gideon and upon the company.

Gideon cried out for Nettles to leave him alone, but in his mind he could see the sergeant's angry eyes burning like fire, and their heat seemed to touch him and force him back from the mule.

Gideon motioned for Hollander to take the mule. Somehow his tongue managed the words. "Ride him. Sir."

He had not been willing to give Hollander release to die, but now he offered him release to live. Hollander stared at him with remorseful eyes. With Gideon's help, he got onto the mule's back. He reached down and took up the reins to lead the mule on which the lieutenant had been placed.

A momentary wildness widened Hollander's eyes. The thought behind it was too clear to miss: with these mules the white men could leave the black soldiers behind and save themselves.

Reading that temptation, Gideon stared helplessly, his mouth hanging open. He knew he could not fairly blame Hollander, for he had almost yielded to the same temptation. One pleading word shaped itself into voice. "Captain . . ."

The wildness passed. Hollander had put aside the thought. He pointed with his chin and motioned for Gideon and the others to follow. They moved off into the dusk, toward a horizon as barren as the one behind them. But the waning of the day's heat brought a rebirth of strength. Gideon kept bringing his legs forward, one short step at a time.

Darkness came. He knew men had dropped out, but he could do nothing anymore to help them. He followed the sound and the vague shapes of the mules. He had only the cloudiest notion of time, but somewhere, probably past midnight, he heard a cry from Hollander. Fear clutched at him—fear that Hollander was stricken. Gideon forced his legs to move faster, bringing him up to the mules. He stumbled over an unexpected rut in the prairie, and he went heavily to his hands and knees.

Hollander was making a strange sound—half laugh, half cry. He pointed at the ground. "Trail," he managed. "Trail."

Gideon felt around with his hands in soft sand, trying to find solid ground to help him push back to his feet. Slowly he understood what Hollander was trying to say. He had stumbled into a trail—a rut cut by wagon wheels.

"Shafter," Hollander said plainly. "Shafter's trail."

Shafter. Of course. Colonel Shafter had been all over this country the year before, exploring it in a wetter, more amenable season. These ruts had been cut by his long train of supply wagons.

Lieutenant Judson seemed more dead than alive, responding not at all to Hollander's excitement, or to Gideon's.

Hollander pointed down the trail. "Double Lakes. Come on."

Gideon felt as if he were being stabbed by a thousand sharp needles. Strength pumped into his legs. He struggled to his feet and found voice. "Water, boys. Water, yonderway!"

The men quickened their steps, some laughing madly, some crying without tears. Gideon stood at the trail in the bold moonlight, pointing the troopers after the officers and the mules as they passed him, one by one. When the last had gone—the last one he could see—he turned and followed.

The mules moved out farther and farther ahead of the men afoot, and after a long time Gideon thought he heard them strike a trot. It was probably in his mind, for surely they no longer had that much strength. Unless they had smelled water . . .

That was it, the mules knew water lay ahead. His legs moved

faster, easier, because now they were moving toward life, not death.

It might have been one mile or it might have been five. He had walked in a half-world much of the time and had little conception of anything except his revived hope. But suddenly there it was straight in front of him, the broad dust-covered expanse of the dry playa lake, and the moon shining on water that had seeped into the holes the men had dug in another time that seemed as long ago as slavery. The soldiers who had reached there ahead of him lay on their bellies, their heads half buried in the water. Captain Hollander was walking unsteadily around them, using all his strength to pull some men back lest they faint and drown themselves.

"Not too much," he kept saying thickly. "Drink slowly. Drink slowly."

Gideon had no time for reason. He flung himself onto his stomach and dropped his face into the water. The shock was unexpected. He felt his head spinning. He was strangling. Hands grabbed him and dragged him back.

"Easy now. Easy."

He tried to scramble to the water again, even as he choked and gagged, but the hands held him. "Slow, damn it. Slow." The voice was Hollander's.

He lapsed into unconsciousness. It might have lasted a minute, or it could have been much longer. When he came out of it, he was hardly able to raise his head. The terrible thirst returned to him, but this time he realized he had to keep his reason. He pulled himself to the edge of the water and scooped it up in his hands. He realized that if he fell unconscious again it must be on the dry ground, lest he drown before anyone could respond.

The water still had an alkali bite, but that was no longer a detriment. Gideon had never known water so sweet. He rationed himself, drinking a few sips, waiting, then drinking again, always from his cupped hand. He became aware that some men had slid into the water and were splashing around in it with all the joy of unleashed children. That this compromised sanitation never entered his mind; he kept drinking a few swallows at a time. Almost at once, it seemed, his tongue began to shrink. He thought of words, and they began to pass his lips in creditable fashion. "Praise Jesus! Bless the name of Jesus!"

Finally, when he came to a full realization that he would not die, he lay down and wept silently, no tears in his eyes.

There was no guard duty, unless Hollander stood it himself. Occasionally the thirst came upon Gideon with all its furious insistence, and he drank. When finally he came fully awake, the sun was shining warmly in his face. Gradually he heard stirrings, men going to the water or from it. He pushed to his knees, blinking in surprise at a bright sun an hour or more high.

His eyes focused on Captain Hollander, sitting up and staring back. Hollander's face was haggard, his eyes still sunken. But he was an officer again. "Ledbetter, let's see if you can walk."

It took Gideon a minute to get his legs unwound and properly set beneath him. But finally he was standing, swaying. He took a few steps.

"Ledbetter," Hollander said, "I need a noncom. I want you to regard yourself as a corporal."

"And give orders?" Gideon was stunned. "I ain't never led nobody. I been a slave for most of my life."

"So was Sergeant Nettles."

"I sure ain't no Nettles."

"Most of us would still be out there in that hell if it hadn't been for you. Perhaps all of us. Like it or not, you're a corporal." He dismissed further argument. "We left some men behind us. I want you to pick a couple or three of the strongest, fill what canteens we have left and go back. Take a mule." He pointed his chin at Lieutenant Judson. "The lieutenant will ride the other to the base camp and bring up wagons and supplies. I'll send a wagon on after you."

Gideon sought out three men he thought had regained strength enough to walk. Almost everything had been discarded along the way, so they had nothing to eat except a little hardtack. The men drank all the water they could comfortably absorb so they would not have to drain the canteens later. Those would be needed for whatever men they found along the trail.

Looping the canteens over the mule, he set out walking, his step improving as he went along. His mind was reasonably clear, and he began mentally upbraiding himself for not counting the men at the lake before he left. He didn't know, really, how many were still out. His memory of yesterday's ordeal was hazy at best. Men had dropped by the wayside—he could remember that —but he could not remember who or how many.

The rescue party came in time to a Mississippian named Kersey, lying in yesterday's blown-out tracks. It took awhile to revive him, and then he clutched desperately at the canteen, fighting when anyone tried to pull it away for his own good. Gideon asked if he knew who else might be behind him, but the man could only shake his head. He could not speak.

Gideon left one of his three men with Kersey and set out walking again, northwestward. Before long his legs began to tremble, and he knew he was approaching his limit. He and the other two looked at each other and reached silent agreement. They dropped to rest, the sun hot upon their backs.

By night they had found just one more man. Gideon had managed to shoot a couple of rabbits, and the men shared those, half cooked over a small fire before sundown. They smothered the fire and walked on for a time to get away from the glow, in case it might attract Indians.

All day he had watched the unstable horizon, hoping to see Esau Nettles and Nash and Finley riding toward them. Now and again a distant shape would arise, only to prove itself false as the heat waves shifted and the mirages changed. His hopes ebbed with his strength.

Night gave him time to brood about Jimbo. He could visualize Jimbo and the men who had gone with him, following the trail of the lost guide until one by one they fell. Jimbo would have been the last, Gideon fancied, and he probably had not given up hope until he had made the last step that his legs would take.

More men had dropped out than Gideon had found. The others had probably wandered off in one direction or another. Some might find the lakes for themselves. The others . . . He slept fitfully and dreamed a lot, reliving at times his own agony,

seeing at others Jimbo or Esau Nettles, dying alone in that great
waste of sand and burned short grass.

They moved again in the coolness of dawn, but the men had
less of hope now to buoy them along. Though no one spoke his
doubts, they were clear in every man's eyes.

The wagon came as Hollander had promised. The other men
stayed behind to leave the load light. Gideon got aboard as
guide. The driver and his helper had not been on the dry march.
They could only follow the tracks, the trail of abandoned equipment, the swelling bodies of horses that had died one by one
along the way. Riding silently on the spring seat as the wagon
bounced roughly over dry bunchgrass and shinnery, Gideon
drew into a shell, steeling himself for what he had become convinced he would find at the end of the trip.

It was as he had expected, almost. They found little Finley
first. To Gideon's amazement, he was still alive. He fought like a
wildcat for the canteen Gideon held to his ruined lips. Gideon
was unable to keep him from drinking too much at first, and for
a while he thought Finley might die from overfilling with the
alkali-tainted water.

Like a candle flame flickering before it dies, Gideon's hopes revived briefly. Perhaps finding Finley alive was a good omen.

The hopes were soon crushed. They found black Napoleon,
dead. As an act of mercy, Nettles had taken off the saddle and
bridle and turned the horse loose on the chance it could save itself. The gesture came too late. Soon Gideon found Esau Nettles
and the young trooper Nash lying beneath a blanket spread for
shade over a patch of shin oak. Even before he lifted the blanket,
Gideon knew with a shuddering certainty. They were dead. He
dropped in the sand beside them, drew up his knees and covered
his face in his arms.

In the wagon he could hear little Finley whimpering, out of
his head. Anger struck at Gideon, sharp, painful and futile. For a
moment the anger was against Finley, a liar, a sneak thief, a coward. Why should he live when a man like Esau Nettles had died?
For a moment, Gideon's anger turned upon God. Then he realized with dismay that he was railing against the faith drilled into
him since boyhood, a faith he had never questioned in his life.

The anger exhausted itself. Only the sorrow remained, deep and wounding.

The trip back to the Double Lakes was slow and silent. Little Finley regained mind enough to be afraid of the two bodies and to move as far from them as possible without climbing out of the wagon. "They're dead," he mumbled once. "Why don't we leave them?"

Gideon chose not to dignify the question by answering it. His contempt for Finley sank deeper into his soul. He made up his mind that he would do whatever he could to force the little man out of this outfit, if not out of the army. He wanted to blame Finley for Nettles' death, though he knew this was not totally valid. Perhaps Nettles had realized he would never make it to the Double Lakes on that bad hip. Perhaps he had stayed behind with Nash and Finley so someone else later would not have to stay behind with him. The more Gideon pondered that possibility, the more he wanted to believe it; it gave reason to Nettles' death, even nobility.

As the wagon went along, it picked up the men who had stayed behind. Most had walked some distance in the direction of the lakes rather than wait to be hauled all the way. All looked in brooding silence at the blanket-covered bodies. Those exhausted climbed into the wagon beside them. Those who could walk continued to do so. Gideon got down and joined them, for he was feeling stronger. The exertion of walking helped the black mood lift itself from him.

Captain Hollander met the wagon as it pulled up to the edge of the lake. Gideon stared, surprised. The captain had shaved and washed out his uniform. It was wrinkled but passably clean, within the limitations of the gyppy water. Army routine had again prevailed over the challenge of the elements.

Hollander counted the men who walked and who climbed out of the wagon. He asked no unnecessary questions. He seemed to read the answers in Gideon's face. He lifted the blanket and looked at the bodies, his face tightening with a sadness he did not try to put into words. "We had better bury them here. This weather . . ."

The digging was left to men who had come up from the supply camp, for they had the strength. Hollander had brought no Bible to read from, an oversight some might regard as indicative of the reasons for the company's travail. The captain improvised a long prayer asking God's blessings upon these men, these devoted servants of their country and their Lord, and upon any others like them who had met death alone on that hostile prairie, unseen except by God's own messengers come to lead them to a better land.

Three more men had wandered into camp during Gideon's absence, men who had lost the trail but somehow retained enough sense of direction to find the lakes. Toward dusk Gideon heard a stir and looked where some of the men were pointing, northward. He saw horsemen coming. His first thought was Indians. But soon he could tell these were soldiers. And the man in the lead was unmistakable.

Jimbo!

Jimbo spurred into a long trot, and Gideon strode forward to meet him. Jimbo jumped to the ground, and the two men hugged each other, laughing and crying at the same time.

In camp, when all the howdies were said and the reunions had lost their initial glow, Jimbo explained that the guide José had missed the Silver Lake he was trying to find and had come instead, somewhat later than he expected, to a set of springs just off Yellow House Canyon. Jimbo and the soldiers who followed had stayed at the springs long enough to recoup their own strength and that of their horses. Some had remained there with the buffalo hunters who straggled in, but Jimbo and three others had filled canteens and set out along their backtrail to carry water to the column they expected to find somewhere behind them. Hollander's decision to strike out for Double Lakes had thwarted them. They marched much farther than they intended and found no one. Fearing that the rest of the company had died, they had returned heavy-hearted to the springs, rested awhile, then set out to find Double Lakes and the base camp below.

Captain Hollander's face twisted in remorse as he listened. The hunters had been right; if he had followed them his troops

would have reached water sooner than they did. Perhaps Esau
Nettles and Private Nash would not be dead; perhaps others
would not still be missing.

Lieutenant Judson tried to reassure him. "You used your best
judgment based on the facts at hand, Frank. You knew this
water was here. You couldn't know there was water where the
hunters wanted to go. They were just guessing. What if they
had been wrong? You had the responsibility for all these men.
Those hunters could gamble. You could not."

Gideon knew Judson was right, as Hollander had been. But he
could see the doubt settling into the captain's eyes. As long as
Hollander lived, it would be there, the questions coming upon
him suddenly in the darkness of a sleepless night, in the midst of
his pondering upon other decisions he would be called upon to
make in the future. To the end of his life, Hollander would be
haunted by Esau Nettles and the others, and the unanswered
question: did it have to be? Gideon looked at him. It was one of
the few times in his life he had ever genuinely pitied a white
man.

Gideon wrestled awhile with his doubts, then approached the
captain hesitantly. "Sir . . ." He took off his hat and abused it
fearfully in his nervous hands. "Sir, you done right. Old Sergeant, he'd of said so hisself, if he could. He'd of said you *always*
done right."

Hollander stared at the ground a long time before he looked
up at Gideon. "Thank you, Ledbetter. There's not a man I'd
rather hear that from than you . . . and *him*."

Early on the fifth day, having sent out search parties and having given up hope that any stragglers still out would ever turn
up alive, Hollander ordered the company to march southward to
the supply camp. Water there was better, and timber along the
creek would provide shade. The trip was slow and hot and dry,
and Gideon found himself skirting along the edge of fear as terrible memories forced themselves upon him.

Late on the afternoon of the sixth day, a column of mounted
men and two army ambulances broke through a veil of dust out
of the south. A rider loped ahead of the column, pulling up in

the edge of camp. He was the civilian scout Pat Maloney, from the village of Ben Ficklin. He whooped in delight as he saw Captain Hollander and Lieutenant Judson standing beside a wagon.

"Frank Hollander! Dammit, man, we thought you were dead!"

He pumped Hollander's hand excitedly, but that was not enough. The ex-Confederate gripped the Union officer's arms and shook him in a violence of joy. "Tell you the God's truth, Frank, we come to hunt for your body. We thought every man jack of you had died."

His gaze swept the camp. Gideon felt the scout's eyes stop momentarily on him and Jimbo, lighting with pleasure at the sight of them.

Hollander replied gravely, "A few of us *are* dead. The best of us, perhaps."

Maloney looked around a second time, his face going grim as he missed Nettles. "The old sergeant?"

Hollander looked at the ground. "We buried him."

Maloney was silent a moment. "We thought from what we heard that we would have to bury you *all!*" He explained that Sergeant Waters had somehow made it back to Fort Concho, with two others. They had brought a report that Captain Hollander and all his men had been led astray by Indians on that great hostile plain, that they and all those buffalo hunters were dying from heat and thirst. They were certain, Waters reported, that no one except themselves had survived.

Maloney pointed to the approaching column. "You can imagine how that news tore up the post at Concho."

Apprehension struck Hollander. "My wife . . . Adeline. She heard that?"

"Everybody heard it."

"She must be half out of her mind. This, and the baby coming . . . We'll have to send word back right away."

Maloney smiled. "You know I got me a new baby boy, Frank?"

Hollander seemed not quite to hear him. "That's good, Pat. Glad to hear it." But his mind was clearly elsewhere.

Maloney said, "Who knows? He may grow up to marry that

little girl *your* wife had. Join the North and South together again, so to speak."

Hollander's eyes widened. He had heard *that*. "A girl, you say? You've seen it?"

"Went by there last thing before I left the post. She looks like her mother. Damn lucky thing, too, because her papa looks like hell."

The trip back to Fort Concho was made slowly and carefully, for more men were afoot than on horseback, and none had completely regained strength. At times even the civilian Maloney would step down from his horse and walk awhile, letting some tired black trooper ride.

Messengers had carried the news of their approach ahead of them, so that most of the people of Saint Angela were lined up to watch the arrival of men who had come back from the dead. An escort and fresh horses were sent out from the post. Hollander and Judson and Maloney rode at the head of the column. Gideon was behind them, urging the men to sit straight and look like soldiers that Esau Nettles would have wanted to claim.

Ordinarily they would not have ridden down the street, but this was an occasion, and the escort wanted to show them off. Lined along Concho Avenue were civilians of all ages, sizes and colors, white to brown to black. Most cheered the soldiers as they passed, though Gideon looked into some eyes and found there the same hostility he had always seen. Nothing, not even the ordeal the soldiers had been through, had changed that. Nothing ever would.

Two-thirds of the way down to Oakes Street, a seedy, bearded man leaned against a post that held up the narrow porch of a new but already-dingy little saloon. As Hollander came abreast of him the man shouted, "Say, Captain, why didn't you do us all a favor and leave the rest of them damned niggers out there?"

Hollander stiffened. He turned in the saddle, rage bursting into his face. He freed his right foot from the stirrup and started to dismount. Maloney caught his arm. "Frank, you ain't got your strength back."

Maloney swung slowly and casually to the ground, handed his reins to Gideon and walked up to the man with a dry and dan-

gerous smile set like concrete. He crouched, and when his fist
came up it was like a sledge. The man's head snapped back, then
his whole body followed. He slid across the little porch, winding
up half in and half out of the open front door.

Maloney looked first to one side, then the other, challenging
one and all. Nobody took up his challenge. He reached down for
the struggling man.

"Here, friend, let me help you up."

When the man was on his feet, Maloney hit him again, knocking him through the door and into the saloon. With a wink, he
took his reins from Gideon's hand, swung back into the saddle
and gave the silent Hollander a nod.

"You're welcome," he said.

Twenty-one

SITTING ON THE ground, staring at but not really seeing the autumn yellowing of the trees above the lodges close-spaced along the distant creek, Gray Horse listened despondently to the chanting of the medicine man in the tepee behind him. Shaking a gourd rattle, waving a buffalo tail, Comes Down from the Mountain was trying to break the fever of Gray Horse's son. The old man's voice was hoarse and weak, for he had been at it since morning without making a showing that Gray Horse could tell. He did not blame the medicine man; Comes Down had power for many things, but he did not have the power to change this miserable place. It was this reservation which had kept the boy from being strong and that had him struggling now for every breath that entered his body. Summer had been close and oppressive; the wind did not carry away the heat as on the plains. Winter here howled down like an evil old sorcerer who hated all men, and there were not enough canyons and sheltered places to protect all the people from its assault.

The white men had promised much to the Comanches if they would be good Indians and stay on the reservation. Gray Horse wore the red flannel shirt they had given him to replace the buckskins, and over it a coat from which he had torn off the sleeves to leave his arms free. The agency-issue trousers were so large that he considered using them to cover a sweat lodge. Most of the time he wore nothing more than his accustomed breech-clout, which flapped below the tails of the altered coat. The hat he had thrown away. His buffalo-horn cap was to be preferred, though he seldom wore it anymore. That was for a man on the war trail or on the hunt, not a captive sitting idle waiting for the white man to bring rations which might or might not come. Often they did not—or if they did, they were less than promised.

The white chief Mackenzie in the fort was always lecturing the bigger chiefs back East that they were doing one thing after they had said another, but it seemed the big chiefs were too busy with larger worries to listen. They had the Indian where they wanted him, and that was enough. That, at least, was what Gray Horse heard from the elders in council. He supposed they knew. Their knowing did not help, however. Meat was still short, and children frequently cried because their bellies were empty.

The Indian agents had miscalculated. In asking and obtaining appropriations from Congress, the officials had counted on the Indians being able to obtain a substantial part of their meat through supervised hunting of the buffalo. Nobody had foreseen that the vast herds would dissolve before the professional hunters' rifles like snow under a late-March sun. An economy-minded government was not interested now in raising the appropriations to make up the shortfall.

Gray Horse had gone on one of these buffalo hunts, escorted by blue-clad troopers to protect them from the eager guns of the Texas Rangers. The young men had been wildly excited at the start. They had done all the hunting dances and had made big medicine to be sure the spirits pointed them to the herds. But the medicine had failed. Though the hunters went to the ranges where they had found buffalo in olden times, they came home with the pack horses carrying less burden than they had taken out. In fact, they were reduced to eating some of their horses to keep from starving.

Gray Horse had tried some parts of the white man's road. They had given him seeds, and he had planted them against his better judgment. He was ill at ease scratching the face of his mother the earth. She resented it, too, for she ate up the seeds and let nothing grow. The agency had sent some of the People sheep, driven afoot all the way from the New Mexico lands of the band's old friends the Comanchero traders. Their idea had been for the men to raise sheep for meat and the women to learn to weave woolen blankets like the Navajos. But the People cared neither for lamb nor loom, while the coyotes and wolves developed a strong taste for their sheep. In only a while, the woolly flocks had disappeared.

Gray Horse maintained that the agency people could no more turn an Indian into a white man than they could turn a wolf into a dog. But they kept trying.

Because Black Robe had come to the reservation without more than average coercion, the agents wanted to reward him and many of the other peace chiefs with cows. If the Comanches were not to become farmers, or sheepmen, the Quakers declared, they might be taught to raise cattle.

Gray Horse did not qualify because he had not come willingly or early to the reservation, nor had he been an exemplary "good Indian" since his arrival. In fact, he had avoided incarceration and possibly shipment to a Florida prison at the beginning only by always being elsewhere when the agency people or the soldiers came snooping around. He was a shadowy figure to them, like a wolf, and they were a long time even learning his name so they could enter it on the agency roll. When restless young men occasionally broke out and dropped into Texas looking for horses, buffalo or scalps, the soldiers always came around to see if Gray Horse was at home. Once he had not been, though Terrapin had covered up by claiming to be him. The young soldiers did not know one Indian from another. That was the spring and summer Gray Horse and Limping Boy and some of the others had gone back to the Double Mountain and Yellow House country, harassing the buffalo hunters, stealing their stock, leading the buffalo soldiers into the waterless sands and losing them. The agency people had finally taken many of the newly acquired horses and mules away, but they never found Gray Horse's. He kept moving them back and forth, staying ahead of the searchers until they grew weary and went back to the comfort of agency headquarters. For all they ever knew, Gray Horse had never left home.

Home. Home was a white man's concept when it meant one place, a house that never moved, a piece of land where every tree, every blade of grass became as familiar as the scars on a man's hands or the marks on his wife's body. Home to the People was not one place, but a range so large that a horseman could ride from full moon to full moon without reaching the end of it. To Gray Horse it was from the Canadian River to the Conchos, from the western breaks of the Llano Estacado to the edge of the Cross Timbers.

This was not home; it never could be. This place where they had set his people down was hardly large enough to sweat a wind-broken pony. There was hardly a spot a man could go and not smell the camp smoke of some other band. A short ride in almost any direction brought him up against the Kiowa, the Cheyenne. It was said that even the hated Tonkawas were to be brought to this place, though he doubted the agency people, foolish though they were, would long tolerate their smell.

A shadow fell across the ground in front of Gray Horse, and he looked back over his shoulder at the bent form of his uncle-father Black Robe, walking slowly and unsteadily toward him in the rapidly descending autumn sun. He knew from the unevenness of the steps that Black Robe was drunk again. Those of the agency-given cattle which had not been eaten had been traded off for the white man's whisky.

His father tried to squat on his heels but was unable to maintain his balance. He fell back heavily onto his rump and would have hit his head against the foot-packed ground had Gray Horse not caught him and helped him to right himself. He tried to stretch his legs in front of him, but the pain of arthritis kept them bent at the knees. All the older people complained of arthritis here. It was something else Comes Down from the Mountain had been unable to cure.

Gray Horse could not bring himself to look Black Robe in the face—not when he was drunk. He remembered what his uncle-father had been years ago, in his prime, a warrior as brave as any, counting many coups, riding wild horses and lancing the buffalo with the feral exhilaration bequeathed by the numberless generations of warrior-hunters before him. Now he sat blurry-eyed, aged beyond his years, sick of soul and body. By the look of him, he would go to meet his grandfathers in another winter or two.

It was this place that had laid a curse on him. Out on the plains he would still be healthy for a man of his years. He would be looking forward to many more winters, to teaching his grandchildren how to ride horseback and how to place an arrow where they wanted it to go.

The dark suspicion had grown in Gray Horse for a long time. The white men had put the People in this unhealthy place because they wanted them all to die. They would kill with sickness those they had not killed with the soldiers.

From behind the two men, the cracking voice of Comes Down from the Mountain continued his chant. He blew on a bone whistle and shook the gourd.

Black Robe asked, "Is my grandson any better?" His unhappy tone indicated he knew the answer.

"The fever is worse, and the foul air of this place does not want to enter his body."

Black Robe pondered awhile in silence. "I had a good dream last night. I dreamed I crossed back over the rivers with my grandson, and we killed many buffalo. In my dream I showed him how to use the lance, and he killed many more than I did."

"The buffalo are nearly gone, Father. I have seen it all with my own eyes. The *teibo* hunters have killed them."

"They could not," the old man argued. "There are way too many. The buffalo have just gone to hide in a place where the white hunters cannot find them. But *we* can find them. Our medicine is still good."

Gray Horse let the matter rest. One did not argue with his father, and one *could* not argue with a man whose judgment was stolen by whisky.

Gray Horse did not speak of it, but he also had had a dream of late, a recurring one. It always started with the buffalo dream of old, with the red calf alone among the skeletons of its kind. But

it did not end there, as it had so often done before. In this dream
a wolf came trotting out of the shadow of the Double Mountains
and crossed the prairie, among the bones. Now it turned into a
set of warriors painted for battle. Into the dream came the soldiers, and the warriors charged at them and killed them all.
When the scalps were taken, all the bones rose up and became
buffalo again, and the red calf punched its nose eagerly at its
mother's udder. As the dream ended, the warriors turned back
into the wolf and trotted away through the buffalo, which had
grown into as many as they had been before the white man
came.

He had sat many hours smoking his pipe and brooding over
the dream. It had burned itself deeper into his mind each time it
came to him until he was almost certain it was intended as a vision. But a vision needed a meaning.

He had found no meaning.

The whistling and the gourd rattling stopped. Gray Horse
arose as Comes Down from the Mountain left the tepee. The old
shaman was weary, his eyes downcast.

Apologetically he said, "My medicine is not strong enough
here. If we could take him to a place where I have more power
. . ."

Gray Horse thought of the Medicine Mounds. But that was on
the forbidden side of Red River. The soldiers would surely turn
them back. If not the soldiers, the Rangers. The Rangers would
have no mercy, not even on a sick little boy. They would kill
them all.

Comes Down said, "I am going to my sweat lodge. Perhaps
when I am clean again I will have more power."

Gray Horse bowed his head, his hope weak.

Black Robe said, "He will live, my son. I feel it in my bones.
That is not what worries me. But what he will live *for* . . . that
sits heavily on my mind. What chance does he have to become a
man—really a man? The soldier chief says we must never fight
anymore. There will not be any more war. But how is a boy to
become a man? How does he prove his courage except at war?
How does he earn honor?" He let his face twist at the impossi-
bility of it. "Without honor, he had just as well die now. There

is no life unless there is honor in it. There is no honor without war. Our boys had just as well be white men." The old man knotted his fists. "We should never have given up so easily to the soldiers. We could have fought them. There was a time we could have turned them back. Now we are too weak unless the spirits help us. I am afraid we have disappointed the spirits too much. They do not hear their People anymore."

The old man pushed unsteadily to his feet. Gray Horse let his father precede him into the lodge, hot and close from the fire Comes Down had kept going and the ceremonial water he had sprinkled into it for steam. Green Willow crouched over the bed where the boy lay, her eyes puffed from crying and lack of sleep. She was still a young woman—little past twenty summers —but in her trouble she looked almost middle-aged. The boy wheezed. Gray Horse could feel the heat rising from his small body before he even touched his son with the flat of his hand.

Black Robe said nothing. He turned abruptly and went back outside. Gray Horse heard him wretching from the whisky and the heat and the steam.

He stared helplessly at the tortured young face, until his heart swelled and seemed ready to burst. He turned away, looking at nothing in particular because tears scalded his eyes. He reached out to steady himself. His hand fell upon the round deerskin bag that he had not opened since that last raid into Texas. He had intended to give it to his son someday, that perhaps it might help him gain the power. He unlaced the cover and slipped it off of his old bullhide shield, letting the feathers that rimmed it fall free with the hunter's scalp and the buffalo tail. He looked at the painted wolf tracks and ran the point of his finger along the edge, feeling for the toothmarks left on it that night the great wolf had come to him on the mountain. They were still there, and as he felt them a tingling began on his skin. He straightened. The tears stopped. In his mind rang an old and demanding call.

Without a word to Green Willow he picked up his blanket and his pipe and a sack of issue tobacco. He hung the shield over his arm. Green Willow watched him but did not ask. She knew by the signs what he intended to do.

He walked to the creek in the dusk and bathed himself thoroughly in its chilling water. Careful not to let the water touch it, he hung his medicine bag around his neck again, picked up the blanket, shield and pipe and waded to the other side. He climbed the hill and spread the blanket in the open spot at the top where the trees did not like to grow. He sang the old chants and lighted the pipe and blew the smoke in the old way. Then he waited for sign that he had been heard, that the spirits no longer held their old anger against him.

The spirits could not be hurried. He sat there until sleep came upon him that night, and he lay down facing the east, the blanket wrapped over his head. Without water or food he sat all the next day, smoking occasionally. A cool wind came up with dusk, promising that winter would not be far behind it. It brought leaden clouds rolling down from the north, and after dark a rumbling of thunder. Gray Horse watched lightning ripple far in the distance, and he felt a stirring of apprehension. Few things had ever truly scared him. Thunder and lightning were probably chief among those few; they represented a power great and mysterious, a force even the strongest of the prairie people had never been able to defy. But he made up his mind to stay.

He sat awake far into the night, waiting patiently. Thirst wrinkled and dried his lips. Hunger clutched at his stomach. Not until long after the thunder had drawn away did he begin to feel drowsy. He lay down and folded the blanket over him, knowing the spirits would awaken him if they came. He was thinking about the buffalo dream when sleep came.

The dream started as always, with the buffalo calf in the red hair of its first months, and the prairie on which the buffalo bones lay scattered. This time he saw more than before. The white hunters passed through the dream, looking for more buffalo to slaughter, and he knew why the bones were there. Then, from the west, from the two buffalo-hump shapes that were the Double Mountains, the great wolf came trotting with vengeance in its amber eyes. As Gray Horse watched, the wolf suddenly was not a wolf at all but a band of warriors, and he himself rode at their head, carrying that wolf-track shield with the mark of the lightning. They overtook and slew the hunters to a man. The soldiers appeared on a hill, and he led the warriors

to the attack, waving the shield that once again was invincible to
their bullets. The soldiers fell before them like dead trees before
the flood. The warriors took their scalps and shouted the news of
their victory. And, as in the dreams before, the bones took shape
and became buffalo. And the red calf filled its belly while the
numbers of buffalo grew and grew until the prairie was black
with them. The warriors rode away until only one was left, and
that one was Gray Horse. He raised the wolf shield over his
head, and he became the great wolf. Then he, too, turned away,
back to his home on the Double Mountains.

The meaning of the vision was clear now. The spirits had
given Gray Horse back his power. They wanted him to lead
warriors out to the plains, kill the hunters and defeat the soldiers.
When that was done, the buffalo would come back, and the People could return to the land that had been theirs—that would always be theirs.

"But I cannot go," Gray Horse cried. "My son is sick. I cannot leave him."

A clap of thunder sounded like a gunshot in his ears, bringing
him suddenly awake. A bolt of lightning flashed and struck
somewhere very near him, searing his eyes and blinding him for
a minute. He was aware of a chill wind buffeting him, picking at
the edges of the blanket, rolling his shield across the hilltop.

When he could see, he got to his feet and searched anxiously
for the shield. He found it lodged against some cured bunchgrass
and picked it up quickly before the wind could take it again.
The rain began to pound him, but the greatest chill came from
within. He gathered his things and descended the hill and crossed
the creek.

Walking toward his lodge he heard the wailing of women, and
he knew what awaited him before he stepped through the opening. His heart sank, heavy and cold. He let the half-soaked blanket fall to the ground.

Black Robe stood with his back turned, bracing himself against
a lodge pole. Gray Horse's mother and his sisters huddled together, crying. Green Willow was on her knees beside the little
bed, chanting while the tears flowed. Her black hair had been
hacked short, and handfuls lay scattered before her. She had cut

away the top of her deerskin dress. As Gray Horse watched, she dug the point of the knife deeply into the skin, crying out as she cut a swiftly widening red line across her breastbone, then across both breasts. She jabbed the blade into her arm and slashed.

He raised the buffalo shield to his chest and lowered his head to rest against its rim, hiding the anguish in his face.

The spirits had known. They had set him a task, and they had known he would be free to go.

Twenty-two

SERGEANT GIDEON LEDBETTER hunched over a bare wooden table in the silent company mess and laboriously scrawled troopers' names on the daily report. A flickering oil lamp made the words dance. He wondered if Captain Hollander would be able to read them. Writing had been the hardest part of the continuing lessons Gideon had taken from the post chaplain. Reading had come easier. Though he still stumbled over some of the long words, he could handle newspapers reasonably well now, when he could lay hands on one. The captain frequently left books or magazines he thought Gideon should read.

There were times when he almost wished he had not learned, for often he came across articles that troubled him. He knew agitation had been raised in Washington to disband all four black regiments and declare the whole concept of the Negro soldier a failure. On the other hand, he knew that a young Negro named Henry O. Flipper had been graduated from West Point, the first army officer of his race.

Gideon had read part of the Flipper account aloud to the company. Jimbo had scoffed at the notion. Jimbo didn't believe enough things really happened in the whole world to fill a newspaper. He was convinced somebody just made up most of that stuff.

Though Jimbo refused to accept the news about Flipper, he was willing to believe every dark rumor that drifted his way about the future of the Tenth, and of the fort. Rumors gathered to Jimbo as animals gathered to salt.

Gideon did not want to believe the army would seriously consider disbanding the black regiments. He knew their campaign record was substantial—on a par with most white units stationed in the West. He knew their desertion rate averaged the lowest in the army. Not enough black soldiers left the frontier posts even to give the quartermasters a chance to explain away their shortages. Gideon hadn't read the desertion figures in any of the newspapers which found their way to the post library, however. Even Eastern papers seldom mentioned the black regiments except in ridicule, or occasionally in sharp criticism after racial incidents in some army-post town. But Gideon had taken heart from a favorable report in a military journal the captain had left behind on one of his nocturnal visits to share coffee with the men.

The old stiffness between Gideon and Hollander had largely dissolved after that disaster on the plains, their eighty-six hours without water in the fury of a July sun. Each had taken the measure of the other and was satisfied. Their manner remained proper and respectful, as befitted military protocol, but beyond it had grown a degree of mutual trust like the one Gideon had sensed between Hollander and Esau Nettles. Each man had tested his limits in the presence of the other and had managed to reach beyond them.

Nettles. The old sergeant tracked relentlessly through Gideon's mind, appearing unbidden, unexpected, at odd moments when Gideon was called upon to exercise leadership. Nettles stood in silent judgment like some tall measuring post, and Gideon always found himself looking up. He wore Nettles' stripes now, but he doubted he could ever stretch himself quite as tall.

Suppressed like some nagging pain was a deep dread of real crisis, a fear that he could not ever stand again as he had stood on that hot, dry plain. At times, overreached by Nettles' remembered shadow, he felt almost an impostor.

Hearing footsteps at the door, he looked up over the report. Captain Hollander walked into the messroom carrying his red-haired little daughter on his hip. Gideon stood up quickly. The captain set the girl's feet on the rough wooden floor and said, "At ease, Sergeant. I trust you have the coffee hot?"

Hollander kept a marked cup in the company mess for those evenings when his auburn-haired wife entertained other ladies of the post and had no comfortable place to shelve her husband out of sight and mind. Hollander was not one to frequent the sutler's much, and even less to while away his evenings risking life and fortune over the river in Saint Angela.

The girl toddled toward Gideon on bowed legs. Grinning broadly, he reached out to catch her in case she stumbled. Some officers' wives considered it disgraceful that Hollander allowed black hands to touch his little daughter. Hollander always told them to mind their own business. Politely, of course, and in better-chosen words.

Gideon played pattycake with the girl while he worked up nerve to ask the question. "Captain, they really goin' to bust up this regiment?"

The captain winced at the outrageous strength of the coffee. "You've been listening to sinkhouse rumors again. Rumors will worry you into an old man ahead of your time."

"But, sir, you reckon they'd really turn us out on the road?" It was an old and deep fear, born of the time he had been put off of the plantation.

"The Tenth is safe, Sergeant. You can sleep well tonight. Colonel Grierson has it on good authority from departmental headquarters."

Gideon breathed easier but tried not to make a show of it. "Glad to hear that, sir. I about come to like it here."

The captain shook his head. "I didn't say we'd be staying *here*. The Apaches are still on the prowl out West. People are crying for help. The colonel has orders to move part of the regiment past the Pecos, out to Fort Davis in the mountains."

Gideon burned to know if this company had been chosen, but

he wouldn't ask. He wished Jimbo were here. Jimbo would ask. That was one reason Gideon wore first sergeant's stripes and Jimbo was a private. Hollander had made Jimbo a corporal for a while, but the stripes came unstuck. Jimbo was happier as a private anyway; his shoulders could bear any weight except constant responsibility.

The captain sensed the unspoken question. "We'll be moving, but not just yet. There's word the Comanches—some of them— have bolted the reservation. If someone else doesn't find them, we may have to."

Gideon's pulse quickened. "Comanches? I thought we'd jugged and stoppered them people for good."

"Not all of them."

Gideon had not thought of Big Dempsey in a long time. Suddenly the angry soldier was stamping through his brain. "We drove them people off of their homeland. We put them in a place where they didn't want to be. I reckon it's in every man to want to go back home."

The captain half-closed his eyes, hiding his feelings. "Do you ever want to go back home, Sergeant?"

Gideon pondered sadly. There *was* no home for him on the plantation. There might have been a home for him somewhere if Hannah York . . . He clenched his teeth and forcefully put the thought away.

"Army's all the home I got anymore, sir. Lately I been worryin' that I might lose it. Reckon that's why I know the way them Indians must be feelin'. Makes me kind of wonder if we done right."

"We did our duty. A soldier does his duty and tries not to think about it."

Gideon mused, "Hard *not* to think about it, sometimes."

The captain frowned over the strong coffee. "We did what we were sent here to do. We made the land safe for civilized people. As long as there was danger from the Indians, we were needed and wanted. Now the danger is gone and we're in the way just as the Comanche was."

Gideon shook his head. "It ain't you that's in the way, Captain, it's *us*." He held out his black hand, studying it. "Them people out West, they want us now. You reckon they'll still want us after we've penned up their Apaches?" He answered his own question, tightening the hand into a fist. "When it's all over the Indian'll still be red, and I'll still be black—but the land'll be white."

Hollander said evenly, "And you'll still be a soldier."

Gideon thought back uneasily to Esau Nettles, knowing Nettles would not have let himself be troubled by such doubts. "Not as good a one as I ought to be."

A shout reached him from outside. Heavy boots thumped into the barracks. "Gid!" a voice insisted. "Where you at?" Trooper Lonnie Bowes trotted through the doorway into the mess, saw the captain and halted, bringing himself stiffly erect and raising his hand in salute. Hollander responded without standing up and told him to be at ease.

Gideon pushed to his feet, darkly wishing the captain hadn't heard the casual use of his given name. No enlisted man had ever called Nettles "Esau."

"What you need, Bowes?" he demanded with military stiffness.

Lonnie pointed excitedly. "You better quick-march over the river, Gid. Jimbo's fixin' to git in trouble with a buffalo hunter."

Gideon grimaced. It wasn't even payday. What was Jimbo doing, messing around in Saint Angela? He probably didn't have three dollars between himself and bankruptcy. He said apologetically, "I better go see, sir."

Hollander's eyes showed concern. Two of his troopers had been murdered on the north bank of the river within the last six months. "If you'll wait till I get Melissa home, I'll go with you."

Lonnie Bowes insisted, "May not be time for waitin'."

Gideon said, "I better go on, sir." He saluted, patted the girl on the head and followed Bowes out of the barracks in a long, anxious trot. He saw a hundred points of lamp and lantern light across the river and felt an old hatred lump in his throat.

Saint Angela was growing. Though the neighboring village of Ben Ficklin down on the South Concho River still had the courthouse, that place appeared to be shriveling on the vine. It no longer retained its earlier monopoly on the "better sort." Ginmills and their gaudy sisters in crime still dominated Concho Avenue, but here and there a respectable store had opened its doors, offering better wares. There was even some talk of building a church. While the upright new businessmen were often in conflict with the rougher order on social affairs and politics, virtually everyone in Saint Angela agreed on one point: it was time to move those nigger soldiers away from Fort Concho.

At best, the blacks had been unpopular from the beginning. To ex-Confederates, a black man in a blue uniform represented misplaced authority, a swaggering symbol of a lost war. To Northerners moving in to seize upon rapidly opening business opportunities, Negroes were a social and economic burden. In a subtle way they also goaded the conscience, a reminder that much of the inspirational wartime talk about freedom and brotherhood and equality had come from the mouth and not from the heart, that to some degree the war had been promoted on a lie.

At worst, soldiers and citizens occasionally faced each other in open hostility that rose to riot proportions. Crimes against Negro soldiers were never prosecuted with vigor. White men had murdered them in cold blood and walked away unmolested, while a black soldier who stole a bottle or a silver dollar was thrown into Saint Angela's log-and-mud jail amid the centipedes and scorpions.

As far as Gideon was concerned, Saint Angela could go to hell. In fact, he was convinced it already had.

Following Bowes's hard pace past the corrals, Gideon demanded to know how Jimbo had gotten himself into trouble. Breathing hard, Bowes answered, "It's over some gal."

"A gal?" Gideon said incredulously. Girls had never been a worry to Jimbo. He bought them as he bought whisky, and with as little attention to selection. If one wasn't available or willing, he simply chose another.

Bowes said, "She's a yeller gal. Jimbo didn't like the way she was sportin' herself around that white hunter. Said she ought to be ashamed and git herself on down the road."

The more Gideon thought about it, the less that sounded like Jimbo. Black prostitutes were a permanent fixture in Saint

Angela, offering themselves indiscriminately to black soldiers or white men, paying heed to no color except that of folding money or coin. Jimbo had never made any issue of it beyond making sure he got his rightful share of the women.

Trotting across the new wooden bridge that spanned the whispering river, Gideon followed Bowes onto Concho Avenue. He saw a cluster of his troopers standing near the door of a raw cedar-picket saloon. They were tensely ready for trouble, but he saw with relief that none had started.

A recruit named Allcorn stepped forward. "Ain't nothin' happened yet, Sergeant. Jimbo and that hunter, they still tryin' to stare one another down."

Gideon glanced across the street. A dozen or so white men— some buffalo hunters, some townspeople—stood grimly in a rough line, waiting. At the first sound of real trouble they would come running. His troopers would meet them in the middle of the street, and some on both sides would have to be carried away. It had happened before.

"You men just stand easy," Gideon ordered. "I'm bringin' Jimbo out of there if I have to pistol-whip him." The tight knot of soldiers split apart to let him through. He stopped in the doorway, his eyes anxiously searching the dimly lighted, smoky little room. He saw only four people: a nervous Mexican bartender, a broad-shouldered, dark-bearded buffalo hunter, Jimbo and a girl who sat at a table, her back to the door. Her thin shoulders were hunched. She brought up a whisky bottle and tilted her head back, her black hair hanging in uncombed strings. Between swallows, she seemed to be weeping quietly.

Jimbo looked at Gideon in surprise and dismay. "What you doin' here? You supposed to be over yonder workin'."

"I come to fetch you out of this place."

Gideon cut his gaze to the buffalo hunter, gauging the threat. The man wore a big pistol in a rough leather holster. It looked like a Navy Colt, powerful enough to do grievous damage at close quarters. The hunter studied Gideon with open belligerence, his large hand moving down to the pistol. Gideon could smell him halfway across the room. The man's voice was heavy with disdain. "Sergeant, are you? Well, it's about time somebody come with a little authority. You git this fool nigger out of here before I have to kill him."

Anger built in Gideon, but he battled it down. A black soldier seldom won a fight on this side of the river. "I come to stop trouble, not to start none. Come on, Jimbo."

To his surprise, Jimbo seemed eager. "All right, Gid. I'll foller you outside."

The girl had not looked at Gideon, but on hearing his name she turned and had to grab the table to keep from falling. "Gid? Who that you callin' 'Gid'?" Her voice was thick. She came slowly around in the chair and tried to focus on him.

The face was puffed and ill, the eyes red around dark pupils, but Gideon knew her. His knees almost buckled.

Hannah York!

She tried to get up from the chair but sank back and took a grip on the edge of it. She stared wildly as if searching for Gideon through a fog. "Gideon? That you, Gideon?"

The words wouldn't come at first. He felt as if he had been shot in the stomach. He managed, "It's me, Hannah."

The white man leaned forward, squeezing one eye nearly shut in menace. "Boy, you stay away from this yeller gal. She's mine."

Gideon stepped closer anyway, then stopped. "My God, Hannah, what you done to yourself?"

She couldn't answer. Tears ran down her smudged cheeks. She cried, "Gideon? Gideon?"

He would have moved to her, but Jimbo stepped in front of him. "She ain't who you think she is, Gid."

"I know who she is. I can see for myself."

"But can't you see *what* she is? Ain't a damn thing you can do for her now. She's too far gone."

"She's alive!"

"Take another look at her face. You call that alive? Ain't no tellin' what all's wrong with her."

Gideon started to move, but Jimbo gripped his shoulders. Jimbo said, "I tried to git her gone from here so you wouldn't never know."

"You had no right. She's my Hannah."

"She's *everybody's* Hannah, and *nobody's*." Jimbo glanced back toward the buffalo hunter. "Mister, you tell him how she come to be here with you."

The hunter growled, torn by a mixture of anger and puzzlement. "I don't have to explain nothin' to no nigger."

"Boss, please."

The hunter turned baleful eyes to the sobbing woman. "I found her over in the Griffin country, bein' passed around from one hide camp to another. If I'd knowed what it costs to keep her in whisky, I'd of left her there."

Gideon couldn't tear his gaze from the wreckage of Hannah's face, from the drunken despair in eyes once big and bright and young. "She used to be with an old granny woman. Where's the granny woman?"

The hunter shrugged indifferently. "Died in Griffin. Fever or somethin'. Gal's been doin' for herself the best way she knows how. And she knows how pretty good, when she ain't dead drunk."

Jimbo tried to push Gideon toward the door. Gideon pushed in return. "Turn a-loose of me, Jimbo."

Jimbo seemed finally to give up. "All right, you wanted to see her. So *look!*" He turned, waving his hand toward Hannah. "This ain't the gal you been carryin' around in you. That gal's gone. This here's all that's left, and it ain't much."

Gideon could not look away from Hannah's eyes. He wanted to cry, but tears would not come. Not since the end of that long ordeal on the blistering plains had he shed a tear. They seemed to have been burned out of him. One dry, painful sound came from deep in his throat, and that was all.

Jimbo gripped his arm again. "You ain't no green youngun now; you're an old soldier, with a sergeant's stripes on."

Gideon stared at Hannah, trying to see her as she used to be when they had loved and dreamed and planned together. But all he could see was this broken shell, with death in her eyes.

The buffalo hunter wearied of the indecision. He shook the woman's shoulder. "Gal, you want them niggers, then you go with them. But remember they ain't got nothin' but a soldier

barracks, and you can't go there. I got food and a bed in my
camp, and whisky. Whichaway's it goin' to be?"

Hannah brought her eyes to Gideon's face. They seemed unable to hold him. In a husky voice, she said accusingly, "You ain't
really my Gideon. My Gideon was a *young* man, and handsome."

Gideon's throat swelled. "No, ma'am. I reckon I ain't the same
man."

With a pain like a sharp knife in his belly, he turned toward
the door. Jimbo took his arm and guided him.

Behind him Hannah whimpered, "Where's my granny at? I
need to talk to my granny."

Gideon stopped in the doorway, gasping the cool night air
into tight, aching lungs. Jimbo said quietly, "Luck dealt you a
mean hand tonight."

Gideon shook his head and looked down at the dirty floor.
"Maybe it was the Lord's doin'. Maybe he wanted me to bury
the dead and study on the livin'."

The soldiers came up to them as they moved out into the
night. The recruit Allcorn volunteered eagerly, "If you want to
go back in there and stomp him, we can hold off them white
men yonder. We can hold off this whole damn town."

Gideon straightened, forcing down the choking in his throat.
He made a sweeping motion with his arm. "You're soldiers. *Act*
like soldiers. Fall in!"

Forming them into two lines, he marched them toward the
new bridge. Badly as he wanted to look back, he held his eyes
forward, and he counted cadence to drown out the sounds of the
town.

Gray Horse and his small party of warriors sat in the cold and
concealing shadow of a red clay hill, watching the slow plodding
of a herd of longhorn cattle moving northwesterly toward the
caprock and the high plains. The fresh wind of September
brought the taste of the stirred dust, the smell of the cattle. Gray
Horse had no system for tallying so many animals as the herd
amounted to, but he counted eight cowboys on horseback and
two wagons up ahead, out of the dust. The riders were not push-

ing the cattle but simply keeping them loosely bunched, letting them pick their own pace and graze as they walked.

Bear That Turns to Fight had seen much to complain about since this party of nine warriors had left the reservation in the dead of a moonless night and had set out searching across their old hunting ground. Though Gray Horse had told him a dozen times, Bear still claimed not to know exactly what they were searching for.

"You told us we would see buffalo. Those are not buffalo, and those men are not buffalo hunters."

As always, Gray Horse thought sourly, Bear was deliberately distorting his words, trying to make a show for the other men. The buffalo, Gray Horse had told them from the first, would come later, after this party had fulfilled the other parts of the dream. Once they found and killed the buffalo hunters, then attacked and destroyed the soldiers, the buffalo would come. Until then there would be only the buffalo bones. Bear could not deny there had been more than an abundance of those.

The cattle herd troubled Gray Horse. He had seen enough of the white man's cattle given to the reservation leaders that he knew a little about how they were raised. This was not a steer herd on its way to provide government contractors' beef-issue requirements for the Indians. This was a cow-and-calf herd, with many bulls. These were breeding cattle to be used for stocking purposes and to increase their numbers. Gray Horse sensed that they were going somewhere to fill a vacuum left by the elimination of the buffalo. If the buffalo came back, as told in his dream, they would have to fight the cattle for the grass.

Beef, Gray Horse thought darkly, was a poor substitute for buffalo meat.

Bear declared, "I see only eight men with the cattle and two more with the wagons. It would be easy to kill them all. We could take the cattle west and trade them to our old friends the Comancheros. We did it often enough in better times."

Gray Horse remembered. He had never liked driving cattle. It was slow, monotonous work without interest or adventure, after the initial taking and the discouragement of pursuit. Cattle were without character, he thought. They were to the buffalo as the dog was to the wolf. He said firmly, "We did not come here to take cattle or to trade with the Comancheros. We came to live out the dream."

Bear argued, "But nothing has been as you said. Your dream was probably brought on by stealing Black Robe's whisky."

Gray Horse stiffened in anger and came close to striking his kinsman with his bow.

Bear knew he would not, and he took advantage. "We have ridden almost this many days." He held up both hands, the fingers spread. The Comanche lacked a satisfactory word for *nine*. It was usually termed "almost ten," or "not quite ten." "We have seen no buffalo, or buffalo hunters, or soldiers. We have not seen anything. I am hungry. My nephews are hungry. I say we take the cattle and kill a few for meat before we trade the rest."

Bear made a motion as if he meant to go ahead. Gray Horse reined his pony around and blocked him. "The cattle and what we might trade them for would last only a little while. If we bring back the buffalo, *they* will last forever."

He cut his eyes sternly from one warrior to another, challenging Bear's growing influence. Gray Horse had been fortunate to have even these eight; he did not want to lose any. He had spent days riding the camps, carrying the red banner of war, seeking out former warriors beknown to him, scattered in misery and idleness on the crowded lands reserved for the Comanche. He had told many people of his dream and of its strong reality. He told them he was certain that the wolf had brought him the dream as a vision, and that the medicine of the wolf was strong enough to see it through. But too many remembered the false prophet Isatai and Adobe Walls. All his persuasion, all his pleading, had brought him only a few old friends who had ridden with him before the Colorado River calamity. Limping Boy was with him, of course. Limping Boy would follow him into the burrow of the cannibal owl. And there was Terrapin, staunch at heart if weak in body. Terrapin had contracted the fever last winter and had never regained his strength as of old. Gray Horse had not wanted Bear at first, and had not asked him. But after his lack of success in finding other men to go, even Bear had seemed acceptable. Now he doubted again. Bear was like the cross-grained buffalo bull that seemed to be in every herd, frustrating the hunters, breaking up the bunch before the killing was done.

Counting himself, Gray Horse actually had only seven real warriors. Bear had brought his untried young nephews, Walks Backward and Beaver Tail. They were fourteen and sixteen, and neither had yet acquired medicine. In an earlier time Gray Horse would not have considered either of them a minute. But he had been grateful, at the last, for anybody.

Now he was no longer proud of his liberality. The boys agreed eagerly and loudly every time Bear expressed an opinion. Now they itched to go kill those cowboys, to take their first scalps and count their first coups.

"We can take those cattle easily," volunteered Walks Backward, the oldest of the pair. "My brother and I can kill the *tejanos* by ourselves."

Bear corrected him. "The three of us."

Gray Horse knew that was empty talk, designed to shame the others into going. "Go then, if you want to, but it will be just you three and no more. The rest of us have important work to do."

He was not all that certain of the others, except Limping Boy and Terrapin, but no one challenged his words. Bear and the two youngsters found no support strong enough to defy Gray Horse.

Bear said scornfully, "Then you sleep again and see if your next dream shows us where those buffalo hunters are."

The Double Mountains stood like two large blue buffalo far to the southwest. Gray Horse and the others had searched that area, but some instinct kept drawing him there again. When dealing with the unseen, he had always found it wise to follow his instincts unquestioningly. Often the spirits' words were meant to be heard by the heart, not by the ear. He pointed toward the mountains. "We will go that way when the cattle are gone."

Bear argued, "We have been there before."

"We will go there again."

When he thought they would no longer be seen by the cowboys, he started. He did not look back for the others, for to do so indicated doubt, and he wanted the men to feel that he did not doubt them. That placed a heavier obligation upon them. After a time, Bear began pulling up beside the other riders by ones and twos, tolling them back to the rear and talking earnestly. Gray Horse could not hear the words, but he knew what the talk must be about. For a man who claimed strength in his own medicine, Bear had little faith in other men's power.

Halfway to the mountains the men stopped to water their mounts in a small creek Gray Horse had known all his life. Its water was better than most in this region; it carried only a trace of gypsum. Bear reined in and let his animal drop its head beside Gray Horse's pony.

"We have decided. We will ride with you as far as the mountains. If you have shown us nothing by then, we go back for the cattle."

"Who has decided?" Gray Horse looked around him at the other men and doubted his cousin. He saw no sign in their faces that any except those two foolish boys supported Bear.

"*We* did," Bear blustered. But he did not carry the argument further. Gray Horse sensed that he was being tested.

"The dream was clear," he said. "When the time comes, we will all be shown."

He kept a strong face as they resumed traveling, but a nagging concern nibbled at his confidence. Even losing those three would cripple them, pulling them down to six. What if some of the others *did* follow Bear?

The raven brought him his answer. He first saw it at some distance, drifting casually. Presently it appeared overhead, cawing. After circling a few times, it flew off almost due west, toward a point north of the two mountains.

Gray Horse's skin turned cold. The raven had long been revered as a finder of buffalo. "He points the way."

Bear reined up, resisting the change in direction. "I promised to go with you to the mountains."

Gray Horse said stiffly, "Then *go* to the mountains. But *we* are following the raven."

He did not look back, but the sound of the horses told him the other men followed. Bear and his nephews held back, then trotted up grudgingly to the others.

The raven dropped from sight, but it had done what the wolf had sent it to do. No more was expected of it than that.

Everywhere, Gray Horse saw the scattered buffalo bones, most of them a year old or older. He had not realized it would be so difficult to find buffalo hunters. He had not foreseen, any more than they, that their own diligence in killing would so quickly eliminate their reason for coming here. Two years ago this land had been infested with them like the buffalo with ticks. The face of the mother earth had been cobwebbed by the tracks of their hide wagons. On the big breakout, the Comanches had raided Rath's large supply camp one night, not far from these two mountains, and had run off every horse and mule on the place. The camp was gone now. The buffalo which had sustained it were used up.

Almost used up. A few survivors remained, here and there, along with a pitiable scattering of those desperate few hunters who had not moved on to other places or other work. Not quite believing the thoroughness of the killing they had already done, these men still grasped at the hope that somewhere must be a hidden valley in which no one had looked, a place where buffalo still swarmed as thick as greenflies and where a hide hunter might yet have a chance to make the fortune that so far had eluded him.

It was just such remnants that Gray Horse and his warriors found, three men scavenging the last small pockets of the once-huge herd. North of the mountains, along a gyppy little creek, these Fort Griffin hide hunters had come upon thirty or forty head that somehow had escaped the greater slaughter, and they had proceeded to annihilate these bewildered survivors in one well-directed stand. Gray Horse rode cautiously around the brow of a flat-topped hill whose protective crown rock sat precariously balanced beyond the red clay base which rains had cut away from under it. The flat rock seemed ready to slide loose and crash down at any time.

Along the creek lay the skinned and swelling buffalo, nakedly streaked white and red, shining eerily in the autumn sun. The men had finished loading the stiffened hides onto a single wagon and were hitching a team for their departure. One man, the hunter of the trio, sat astride a long-legged bay horse. The other two were skinners, of a lower order on the social scale, and had to ride the stinking wagon.

Gray Horse's heart quickened. It was not quite as in the dream; he had seen more hunters. And the creek bank here was littered with spoiling carcasses rather than whitened bones. But they would be bones when nature's scavengers had done their work. At some distance he heard a plaintive bawling sound, and it drew his eyes. Squinting against the sun, Gray Horse made out the form of a buffalo calf, tottering in a clumsy gait among the dead. The hunters had missed it, or had chosen not to take it. Perhaps their hearts had been touched and they had thought to let it live. But it was probably not yet large enough to live on grass alone. Left here without mother's milk, it would slowly starve. The process had already begun.

It troubled Gray Horse that the calf was nearer brown than red. That was also contrary to the vision. However, he thought, the essential requirements had been met. All but one.

"Kill them," he said.

Bear passed him, and the two boys rushed after Bear. When Bear let loose a loud whoop, the boys copied him. Gray Horse held back a little. Perhaps it was just as well to let the youngsters have their chance. Few of their age had it anymore.

The hunters seemed benumbed. It had been so long since they had heard of Indian trouble that they had no longer considered the possibility. The one on the horse finally came to his senses and whipped the bay around. He spurred up the slope and away as hard as he could make the horse run. The two on the wagon knew their peril and screamed at him to wait, to help them. Their pleading seemed only to push him to more speed southward. The wagon horses were frightened by the oncoming Indians and began plunging against the traces. The wagon's brake was set, so they dragged a locked wheel. One of the skinners jumped to the ground and brought a rifle from beneath the wagon seat. The other sat frozen, his eyes grotesquely wide. He seemed unable to defend himself either by fight or flight.

The two boys struck first. They carried war clubs, and it would have been more honorable to have used those at close dis-

tance where the danger to themselves was greater. But they had
trained under Bear, and they chose to kill at the longest possible
range. Both skinners were dead from arrows before the first
clubs ever struck them. The boys beat at them anyway, crushing
their skulls to be sure. Bear came up and took his coup, lauding
the boys for their bravery and efficiency.

"One is getting away," Gray Horse shouted, pointing at the
fleeing hunter skirting a distant knoll.

Bear saw no urgency. "The boys have taken honor enough. If
you want the other one, go after him yourself."

In the dream, none had gotten away. Gray Horse and Limping
Boy gave chase and seemed at first to be catching up to the
panic-stricken hunter. But his horse was stronger and better fed,
while the Indian ponies had roughed out a living of sorts all summer on the limited reservation grass. Gray Horse could see that
the white man was gaining. Only if the horse fell was there any
chance of catching him. He gave up when he looked over his
shoulder and saw the other men dropping behind him, their
horses winded. He reined the pony to a stop and sat awhile in
frustration, watching the white man disappear, still whipping his
bay. Disappointment touched Gray Horse, regret that some
white men thought so little of personal honor. He contrasted
these hunters to the two farmers at the Colorado River crossing.
Those had put up a defense worthy of respect, while these had
been like quail. Perhaps it was to the detriment of the white men
that they kept the Indians penned up and unable to fight, for in
the absence of war, the white men were degenerating as the Indians had.

He turned back to rejoin the others, hoping the party had
done enough to satisfy the spirits, though the details were not
exactly as in the dream. What mattered was the final outcome.

He found the two skinners lying dead beside the wagon, their
scalps taken, their bodies mutilated beyond any necessity of warfare. The boys' doing, he knew, urged on by Bear. It took the
taste of blood to turn a youngster into a warrior, most elders
would agree. Bear had wanted to be certain about his young
kinsmen, and they were eager students. The next thing to have
done, had they wanted to be proper, would have been to cut the

horses loose and set fire to the wagon and its load of hides so no
other white men could come along and profit by them. But Bear
and the boys had not taken time. They had ridden off somewhere.

Grumbling under his breath, Gray Horse rode up on a knoll to
look for them. He heard them whooping before they burst into
sight, chasing the buffalo calf. The boys were in the lead, driving
arrows into the stumbling little animal. Bear loped along behind,
loudly encouraging them.

Gray Horse rode at them, waving his shield, trying to make
them stop. By the time he reached them he was much too late.
The boys had jumped down and cut open the belly of the dying
calf. They and Bear were already dipping their hands into the
steaming stomach, bringing up the curdled milk and eating with
a wild eagerness. Not in years had they enjoyed such a delicacy.

Gray Horse shook with rage. As the other men rode up and
stopped in a semicircle around him he cursed Bear and the boys
as crazy men. "The calf was part of the dream," he shouted.
"You had no right to kill it."

Bear stood licking the congealed milk from his fingers and
palm. A couple of other warriors could not restrain themselves,
for mother's milk from the stomach of a newly slaughtered
buffalo calf was one of the finest foods the earth and its animal
children provided to the People. They leaned over the calf, taking what they could for themselves. A third man cut a slice of
hot liver.

Gray Horse could see how near he was to losing them. They
were all hungry, and fresh meat lay here for the taking. It was
hard to persuade men to listen to dreams when their stomachs
growled. He relented, finally, because there was no remedy now.
The calf was dead. He turned to Limping Boy and Terrapin, still
on their horses.

"Stay here with them. Eat. I am going to the mountain to
smoke, to watch and listen."

Limping Boy asked anxiously, "Don't you want to eat, too?"

"I am not hungry." He was, but he had found long ago that
the spirits spoke more clearly to him when he was tired and hun-

gry and thirsty than when he was full and comfortable and his
body was rested.

"I will go with you," Limping Boy offered.

"No, I need you to stay here and see that the others come
later. You and Terrapin are the only ones who never look back."

He rode toward the easternmost mountain, listening to the
laughter behind him as the men cut into the calf.

He had misgivings. In the dream the calf had still been alive
when the other buffalo came up from the bones. But perhaps it
would not matter; if the others came back to life, so would the
calf.

Visions were seldom exactly like life. And life was almost
never like the visions.

Twenty-three

GIDEON DOUBTED THAT the buffalo hunter's bay horse would ever rise to its feet again. It lay spraddled on its belly, wheezing for breath, its legs buckled. It had been run to the point of exhaustion and beyond. When the hunter had ridden over the hill and almost into the cavalry patrol, he had taken the soldiers for Indians and in blind panic had tried to spur away. The horse, dripping with sweat, had collapsed after two hundred yards.

Captain Hollander had given the hunter a stiff drink from the bottle he kept in his saddlebag. The hunter had recovered to the point that the frightened story spilled out of him in a rush, like water from a turned-over barrel.

"They come on us without warning," he said, breathing hard, his eyes still rolling. "Must've been fifty of them, maybe sixty. We fought. God, what a fight. But my partners didn't have a chance. The Indians was over them like a swarm of hornets. They chased after me, but I managed to fight them off."

Hollander gave Gideon a quick glance with doubting eyes. The dispatches had said the agency was not sure how many had jumped, but there was no indication the number was as great as fifty or sixty. Though the man had already told him, the captain asked, "Where was it you said this attack occurred?"

The man nodded northward toward the distant Double Mountains. "Other side of them hills yonder. We was just fixing to roll towards Griffin when them red devils come amongst us like a cyclone."

Hollander said, "We can provide you a horse if you would like to come with us and show us where you saw them."

Violehtly the hunter shook his head. "I wouldn't go back yonder for all the buffalo hides in Texas, not with no more men than you've got. Soldier, they have you outnumbered by three to one."

Hollander's patrol totaled twenty men. Lieutenant Judson had swung far to the west with another, but he was miles out of reach, over in the caprock country where the high plains broke away. The captain studied the trembling hunter, and compassion slowly overcame his skepticism. "I suppose we can lend you a horse, if you'll turn him in to the post at Griffin and give them this note." He took a piece of paper and pencil from his pocket and began to write. "I want them to know this animal belongs to Fort Concho and to send it home at their first convenience." His brow knitted. "We would hate to have to send a federal marshal after you with a warrant for horse theft."

"I'll turn him in, I promise you that. Unless those savages kill and scalp me between here and there."

"You can come with us if you don't want to go on alone."

The man made a dry laugh with not even a trace of humor in it. "You're paid to fight Indians. I ain't. If ever I get to Griffin alive I'll put Texas behind me and never come back."

Hollander made no comment, but Gideon read the thought in the captain's eyes: it would be a very small loss to Texas.

The captain gave the man another liberal swallow from his bottle and supervised the transfer of his saddle to a brown horse with the US brand highly visible. Should the man encounter another military patrol while riding that animal, he would need Hollander's note. Worriedly the captain watched the hunter on his way.

Hollander mused, "Perhaps I should have kept him with us."

Gideon turned to look back at the men behind him. "Like as

not he'd of throwed some of the men into a panic. We got a bunch of recruits. They ain't been up agin Indians before."

"They'll do what you tell them, Sergeant."

Gideon frowned. He had no such confidence. Drilling them on the post was no great challenge. Holding them together against Indians was a test he had not met.

Hollander seemed to read his doubts. "Old Nettles wouldn't have worried."

"*He* wouldn't of had to."

Hollander stared toward the mountains, his face twisting. "I had hoped all we had to do was to haze the Indians back to the agency. But they've spilled blood now. People will demand blood for blood."

"Same people that been itchin' to get shed of us?"

Hollander nodded darkly.

Gideon said, "The hell with them. Sir."

Hollander showed him a faint smile, but it faded. "I'm afraid we'll have to split the detail. You'll take half the men and circle east of the mountains. I'll take the others and circle west. We'll come back together somewhere on the north."

Gideon frowned again, counting. That was ten men apiece, including the captain and himself. If that buffalo hunter had been even half right . . . He didn't want to think about it.

The captain was ahead of him. "We'll not engage them—not while we're divided. Whichever group finds them first will send word to the other." He looked back at the men. "You'll want Jimbo."

"Yes, sir, if it's all the same to you."

"I never break up a winning hand." The captain picked nine men for himself, leaving the others to Gideon. Gideon noted with satisfaction that Hollander had taken half the recruits. Some officers would take the seasoned men and later blame the black noncoms for any failure.

The captain said, just before leaving, "Remember, Sergeant, don't engage them."

Gideon had no such intention. His stripes wouldn't mean much to a frightened group of recruits under fire. "No, sir." He saluted, but didn't get a salute in return. Hollander had never

been a stickler for the book. Gideon turned in his saddle and surveyed the men left to him. Jimbo, and Lonnie Bowes and Samuel
Cates, good men all, and survivors of the plains ordeal. Solomon
Tucker, transferred from another company after some sort of
ruckus down at Fort McKavett. He knew the inside of the
guardhouse better than Gideon would have liked, but he seemed
steady enough when he was sober. Out here, he was cold sober.
The other five were recruits, only a few months away from the
cotton fields and riverfronts. The hardest stress any of them had
had at Fort Concho was mess duty.

At least he didn't believe he had another Little Finley among
them. Gideon had not been able to pressure Finley out of the
company, but a gaming house fight in Saint Angela had solved
his problem permanently. Five aces on the table had put Finley
in the post cemetery.

Gideon pushed back his misgivings and said, "Let's be a-movin',
or the captain'll be halfway around before we even get started."

His stomach cold, he set out toward the east side of the mountains.

Gray Horse had left his pony tied to a bush at the eastern base
and had climbed to the top of the mountain, carrying his blanket
and his pipe. It seemed easier despite the several years that had
passed since that other time. Perhaps it was that he did not carry
the burdens of youth now, the pressure to prove himself. But he
carried other burdens—much heavier, in their way.

He spread the blanket at the eastern edge, where he could look
southward toward the river. Nearer by he could see the creek
where his band had so often camped. In his memory he could see
the lodges as they had been that morning so long ago when he
had climbed here seeking communion with the great mystery.
He remembered the gray veil of smoke that had risen in the
early-morning hours, to be carried away as the wind arose. He
remembered the faces of that village, so many of them gone
now, and the voices, so many of them stilled. Where once there
had been buffalo beyond counting, he saw only empty prairie,
the grass grown up and matured with autumn, ungrazed, untrod-
den by cloven hoof. Sorrow lay heavily upon his heart, and his

eyes burned; up here he could see this great land in one long, sweeping glance that reminded him forcefully how much the People had truly lost.

He spread the blanket and chanted his songs and lighted the pipe. He talked to the wolf spirit, thanking it for giving him back his power, telling how he had come to fulfill the dream the wolf had given him. He told what he had done so far, and how, though in some ways the reality had not quite followed the dream, the essence of it had been there. He told the spirit he was ready now for the soldiers, the completion of his appointed task. His warriors totaled not quite ten, and he had no idea how many soldiers the army might send against him, but he had faith in the power of the wolf medicine. He told how the People would be joyful in their hearts to look out upon these prairies and see them alive once more with buffalo.

He sat a long time, staring vacantly across the big land, waiting for the answer to come. The wind was cold, but the scrub brush deflected most of it from him, and his body responded to the sun's warmth. He dozed, his chin dropping. He was no longer sure what was reality and what was dream. He saw the land, and he saw the buffalo upon it. He saw himself riding across the prairie on his war pony, among the returned buffalo. Suddenly the pony was riderless, and he saw only a wolf trotting through the grass and small junipers.

He blinked, quickly awake. To the south he saw a movement, not as clear as in the dream, but clear enough that he knew it by its actions. It was a wolf. One lone wolf—the only creature moving across that rolling plain.

The dream, if it had been that, had been short. It came back to him, and he mulled over it and saw it again in his mind's eye. He puzzled, until gradually its meaning came clear to him, and all warmth was gone. He stood up shivering and looked toward the afternoon sun, trying to see beyond it to where the Sure Enough Father lived. But no man could see beyond the sun; it would blind him first.

"Father," he cried out, "is this what you want of me?"

The only answer was the wind talking through the junipers, chilling him with its breath. Gray Horse looked back down across that prairie. He no longer saw the wolf. He saw no rider-less pony, no buffalo. He saw only the browned grass and the green junipers, and the distant line of trees that marked the river.

No, there was something else, way past the river. Something ill-defined, but new. He put his forefingers to the edges of his eyes and stretched the skin to sharpen his vision. The thing sepa-rated into small spots. They could have been anything—antelope, buffalo. But in his heart he knew, for the wolf had told him. These were soldiers. They were the next step in fulfillment of the dream.

He spoke his thanks to the spirit and folded his blanket and started back down the mountain. He could see his warriors approaching, to wait where his pony was tied. His heartbeat quickened as he began planning for the fight. On the bench that stood out from the foot of the mountain, he waved his arms to catch his friends' attention. He made for them the sign that he had seen the enemy. By the time he reached the bottom they were streaking themselves and their horses with paint. Bear had drawn concentric red circles around his old scar. His nephews made liberal use of a yellow paint that reminded Gray Horse un-comfortably of Isatai at Adobe Walls.

He wished he had not remembered.

Gray Horse used black paint to put the lightning on his face and the wolf tracks across his body. He took his shield from its deerskin cover and straightened the feathers cramped from the carrying. He let the old scalp and the buffalo tail hang.

The boys were eager to go, but Gray Horse made them wait. He made them join in the war song, invoking the spirits to smile and give them victory.

"Now," Gray Horse declared, "you will see the rest of my dream. You will see if I lied." He straightened his buffalo-horn headdress, swung onto his war-painted pony and started south to meet the soldiers.

At the distance he had been unable to count them. It did not matter, for the outcome was ordained.

Down here on the prairie the wind was not nearly so cold. The autumn sun was warm and benign in a late-afternoon sky.

Limping Boy pulled up beside him. "It is a good day for a fight, brother. It would even be a good day to die."

"You will not die. It was not in the dream for you to die."

"And you, Gray Horse? What did the dream say about you?"

Gray Horse rode in silence a minute, then pointed. "We will wait for them by the creek where we used to make camp. We can surprise them there."

Rivers had aroused a cautious spirit in Gideon Ledbetter since that first confrontation with Indians on the Colorado. Upon reaching the Double Mountain Fork of the Brazos, he spread the men in a defensive line along its south bank and proceeded to scout the shallow, red-bottomed river himself, new Springfield in his hand. He crossed over on the soft clay and gypsum bottom, exploring the high north bank and beyond before he returned to the brink and waved the patrol across. Though they passed the river in safety, a strong uneasiness continued to trouble him. His itching backside was uncomfortable against the cantle of the McClellan saddle. He found himself standing in the stirrups, straining to see what lay beyond.

Jimbo rode up beside him. He was also turning his head slowly, searching. "You got the same notion I have?"

"They're out there someplace. I feel like I can reach out and touch them."

Jimbo cautioned, "Remember, we ain't supposed to make no fight. Captain told us that mighty clear."

"He didn't tell the Indians."

Gideon looked back at the men behind them, intending to warn them to stay alert, but he saw the admonition was needless. Every face was strained. Every carbine was up and ready. The patrol moved in an easy trot across the gentle rise and fall of the sandy prairie. The tall bunchgrass sometimes rubbed against Gideon's stirrups, for no large animals had grazed it since the buffalo had been removed. The ripened pods, swaying in the wind, kept looking like feathers in front of him. He knew he was supposed to watch the ground for tracks, but he could do no more than glance down at intervals, then up again. He had no intention of riding into an ambush with his head down.

A line of scrub timber ahead told him of a creek. He thought he remembered it from an old scouting trip, a small stream fed by a series of springs and seeps that yielded better water than most. He recognized it for certain as he neared it, recalling that the other time it had shown signs of an abandoned Indian camp. The river caution arose in him again. He slowed to a walk and held up his hand for the men to do likewise. He moved out a little farther in front of them, trying to watch for tracks without looking down for more than a few seconds at a time. As he came to the creek bank, a covey of quail flushed and he whipped the carbine to his shoulder. He stared foolishly at them, when he realized what they were, the tension slowly running down. He glanced back at Jimbo and let a smile break across his face. He found he was sweating despite the chill in the wind. He waited for the men to catch up, which did not take long. There were no stragglers.

As before, he scouted the creek himself, leaving the men sitting their mounts on the south bank. His horse waded quietly across the clear stream and struggled for footing as he challenged the soft north bank. He almost stumbled, and Gideon quickly let up on the reins to give him his head. In the moment that he looked down, the corner of his eye caught a movement.

The Indians came over the bank like an explosion out of the lowering sun, whooping, yipping, firing rifles and loosing arrows. They caught the patrol in midstream. Gideon raised his carbine and made one quick shot into that color-streaked, oncoming mass without taking time to aim. He pulled the horse around and motioned with his hand, urging the troopers back out of the creek.

They turned their mounts. One of the recruits screamed as an arrow thumped into his back. He slid out of the saddle, landing face down in the water. Gideon saw at a glance that he was dead —or would be in a minute.

"Pull back!" Gideon shouted. "We can't stop in this creek!"

The rest of the men were quickly up over the bank. Gideon spurred after them. Jimbo turned and began firing, trying to cover Gideon's retreat. Most of the others were running hard, every man for himself.

"Hold together!" Gideon shouted. "Don't scatter or they'll kill you!"

They weren't listening to him. A cold chill gripped him as he realized his worst fears were about to come to pass. He wasn't soldier enough to hold them.

The Indians' charge wavered. Terrapin jerked as a slug caught him in the chest. He turned half around and tumbled heavily into the water. Gray Horse was in the lead, shouting, loosing arrows at the running troopers as rapidly as he could draw them and fit them to the string. The two young brothers were almost abreast of him, yipping like pups hot after a rabbit. Gray Horse heard a smacking sound. One of the boys cried in agony.

Ahead of him, up on the south bank, Gray Horse saw what appeared to be a solid wall of black smoke, fire cutting through it as the carbines blazed. A horse went down behind him. He felt a blow that almost ripped the shield from his arm. It had turned a bullet.

By the sounds from behind him he sensed that the charge had broken up. He glanced back and saw only Limping Boy, trailing. The rest of the warriors milled in confusion. Bear and Walks Backward were supporting Beaver Tail, holding him on his pony while they took him out of the creek.

Gray Horse shouted and waved his arm. "Come on! We have them!"

No one came except Limping Boy.

Gray Horse realized the futility of making the charge by himself. He turned, motioning for Limping Boy to pull back. Terrapin lay still in the shallow water behind them. Gray Horse and Limping Boy rode on either side, their horses' hoofs stirring a spray of water. They leaned down, each grabbing an arm, and pulled Terrapin up between them. Going up the bank together, they eased Terrapin gently to the ground on the far side of the creek.

Terrapin's eyes were open, but they would never see again.

Gray Horse did not have time for grief. The buffalo soldiers were retreating in confusion. This was the time to strike, to finish the fight before they regained their wits. A black trooper with marks on his sleeve was giving orders. That man must be the chief. If Gray Horse could kill that one, perhaps the rest would fall easily.

He could not give the men time to count their wounds or take counsel with new fears. Beaver Tail was slumped over, holding his hand against his ribs, blood trickling between his fingers.

Gray Horse shouted, "They are running away! They have killed Terrapin and wounded Beaver Tail. Do you want them to escape? Let's go!"

He reined his war pony around but saw hesitation in the men. He demanded, "Are you warriors, or did I bring women?"

He put them to the test by moving into a run, going forward with them or without them. He heard hoofbeats behind him and knew they were coming. They hit the creek and left a wake of muddy water swirling as they climbed the low south bank.

Gideon Ledbetter, riding as a rear guard, saw them coming. "Halt!" he shouted at the running men. "We got to turn and face them. Else they'll ride us down and kill us one at a time."

For a moment it seemed his words went unheeded. But he stopped to set the example, and Jimbo pulled up beside him. One of the recruits reined around and came back. Looking over their shoulders, the others followed one by one. They spread out in a line, Gideon in its center. As the rifle-carrying Indians fired their first shots, the troopers responded.

For a moment, Gray Horse thought he would overrun the soldiers this time. The shield over his left arm, its rim-tied feathers streaming, he screeched the fiercest war challenge that was in him and rode directly toward that rough line of black smoke. He could see the face of the soldier chief, the white-rimmed eyes wide with excitement, and he brought his bow around.

His pony broke stride. The ground rushed up and slammed against Gray Horse's shoulder and then the length of his body, knocking much of the breath from him. Instinctively he scrambled clear of his dying horse, away from those dangerous kicking hoofs.

Limping Boy rode to him through the dust, leaning, reaching

toward him. Gray Horse caught his arm and swung up behind him. Limping Boy reined around and retreated. Gray Horse held his shield over his shoulder to protect his back. To his dismay he saw the other warriors pulling northward, away from the fight. Bear and Clouding for Rain held the boy Walks Backward between them.

Gray Horse called for them to stop. The soldiers were retreating again. It was time to hit them once more. But he fought for breath, and he could not bring out the words as he wanted them to be.

Gideon Ledbetter shuddered. He looked proudly at the line of men who had rallied on either side of him. They had responded to his call; they had followed his orders under fire. But that second charge had come close to overrunning them. The patrol was too much in the open here. He remembered a ravine back a little farther, toward the river. If they could reach it they could set up a stand. All his past experience and all he had heard about Comanche warfare had taught him they almost never knowingly made a frontal assault against a strongly held position.

The last charge had wounded two more men, but the only death had been the recruit Allcorn, still lying yonder in the creek.

"Back!" he ordered. "Hurry! If we can make the ravine we can hold. Maybe Captain will hear the shootin' and come for us."

The men moved out in a body—not in panic, but as soldiers. Jimbo held up to join Gideon as a rear guard. Gideon said, "I'll handle this. You go prod them along. Keep them movin' as fast as they can."

"If them Indians git you cut off out here, they goin' to kill you awful dead!"

"Daddamn you, Jimbo, don't you know an order when you hear it?"

Jimbo hurried after the retreating troopers while Gideon trailed, watching over his shoulder for the next charge.

Gray Horse leaned against Limping Boy's dun horse and fought to put breath back into his lungs. He saw defeat in the men's eyes. The wounded Beaver Tail knelt over the body of his brother, and he cried out in the unrestrained grief of a boy not grown. Bear stood beside him, his arm bleeding. Other men sat slumped on their ponies. One pony bled from a deep gash in its chest where a soldier bullet had slashed through and gone out. It would be dead in a little while.

Gray Horse pointed toward the retreating soldiers. "Their spirit is broken. We can get them this time, and it will all be finished."

Bear's eyes were full of anger. "Look at us, Gray Horse. *We* are finished. My nephew is dead, and Terrapin is dead, and my other nephew has a hole in his side. Half our horses are dead or wounded."

"More reason to kill the soldiers."

"The soldiers! Your dream said the soldiers would fall to us. But you dreamed what you *wanted* to dream. Your medicine is bad."

"The medicine is good." Gray Horse cut his eyes from one man to another, fighting the despair he saw. "Don't you want the buffalo back? Don't you want to reclaim what is ours?"

Bear no longer taunted him, because he knew he spoke for the others. "This is not a good fight. We will go away now and fight again at a better time."

Gray Horse pleaded, "If you run away now you will never fight again."

But in the downcast faces he could see the promise of the dream slipping away. The spirits were strong, but the spirits worked through men. Men were sometimes weak.

The riders turned away, moving back toward the creek.

Gray Horse shouted after them. "I will go by myself if I have to. I will kill them alone!"

But only Limping Boy listened. He sat staring down at Gray Horse from the back of the dun.

Limping Boy said sadly, "Brother, the dream has been spoiled." He patted the horse on the rump. "Get up here with me. We can catch Terrapin's horse." The riderless sorrel had followed the warriors past the creek and stood now watching the other horses, its ears flicking nervously.

Gray Horse looked toward the soldiers, still moving away. He tried to hold down the tears that burned his eyes. "Catch him for me."

He looked toward the sun and sang an old song remembered from his true father, who had sung it before riding off to die in battle. When his cousin returned, Gray Horse swung onto the sorrel. Limping Boy turned north, then stopped, for Gray Horse still faced south, toward the soldiers. "We had better go, brother," Limping Boy said. "The others are far ahead of us."

"Go with them. The spirits told me what I have to do."

Limping Boy's eyes showed alarm. "You cannot kill them by yourself."

"The dream said we would kill them. The wolf would not lie to me."

Limping Boy recognized his determination. "Then there will be two of us against them."

Gray Horse's heart warmed. "You have always been a brother to me, Limping Boy. But the dream did not show you to die today."

"Then I will not die. But I will ride with you."

Gray Horse looked again toward the soldiers, still moving southward. "Let's go."

Gideon had watched the Indians pull away toward the creek. Breath had come easier to him. It was the Comanche way to hit hard, then move off quickly, beyond reach. This meant, more than likely, that the battle was done. The patrol had held its ground and had driven the Indians back.

Esau Nettles would not have done better.

In the confusion and excitement he had never been able to count the attacking force, but he doubted it numbered more than eight or ten, nowhere near the fifty or sixty the frightened hunter had reported. He would take the patrol to the ravine and send for Captain Hollander. With their combined force they should be able to overtake the Indians and either beat them or haze them back to the reservation. In either case, it would be a defeat for the Comanches. Probably they would never try such a thing again.

He felt a warm glow of pride as he looked at the troopers ahead of him. Even old Nettles would have admitted they were men.

He could see the ravine a short way ahead. The foremost of the troopers had nearly reached it.

Jimbo shouted a warning. Gideon turned quickly in the saddle, bringing up the Springfield. Incredulously he watched two Indians race toward him. One, on a sorrel horse, wore a buffalo headdress and carried a bullhide shield from which feathers and a scalp and a buffalo tail streamed in the wind. The other rode a dun horse and trailed slightly behind.

Gideon measured the distance to his patrol and knew he could not catch up. Here he must turn and stand.

The troopers began firing, trying to help him. The dun horse fell headlong, pinning its rider in the grass. But the other horseman did not slow or look back. He came on, the bullhide shield over his left arm, an arrow fitted to his bow. Gideon swung from the saddle and dropped to his knee, bringing up the carbine and looking for an opening around the shield.

Time seemed to stand still. The past came rushing over him. He had a chilling sense of having been here before. In the few seconds while he looked for a vulnerable place to line his sights, he had an uncanny feeling that he had seen that shield with the lightning streak and the wolf tracks, the feathers of many kinds. He thought he had seen that face before, a face streaked with painted lightning.

The Indian was almost upon him. As Gideon found an opening to the painted breast he thought he saw recognition in those desperate eyes, a fleeting moment of hesitation. He squeezed the trigger an instant before a steel-tipped arrow seared into his shoulder. In the drift of burned powder, he saw the Indian grab at the neck of the running horse. He saw a crimson stream of blood. The warrior slipped over the pony's withers and fell loosely to the ground. The sorrel began a wide circle, frightened by the gunfire and black smoke.

Gideon swayed, almost falling backward. He struggled to his feet, staggered a couple of aimless steps and went to his knees. He braced himself with his hands to keep from falling on his face. He stared through a reddish haze at the arrow shaft quivering in his shoulder. Instinctively he reached for it but could not pull it out. He felt the blood flowing hot.

Heavy boots rushed through the grass. Jimbo was at his side with Lonnie Bowes and one of the recruits. They caught Gideon as he was about to slump.

"Come on," Jimbo said urgently, "the rest of them Indians is liable to be on us in a minute. Let's tote him yonder to that ditch."

Gideon felt himself half carried, half dragged to the edge of the ravine. They tried to stretch him on the ground, but he fought against that.

"Hold me up," he demanded.

"You got to lay down," Jimbo argued.

"No I ain't. I'm stayin' on my feet. Got to give my report when the captain comes."

The arrow had driven so deeply through his shoulder that more protruded from his back than showed in front. It was far from the heart, but he knew that shock could kill him. He fought against the gagging nausea, the dizzying pull toward the ground. He thought if he could keep talking, he might resist unconsciousness.

"Promise me, Jimbo, you'll hold me up."

Jimbo blurted, "You hang on now. Don't you go and die on us."

"I won't die if you'll keep me up off of that ground."

Jimbo whittled off the feathered end of the shaft, grasped the head and jerked the arrow on through. Gideon cried out and came near fainting. The men tried again to lay him down in the sand, but he resisted. It would be too easy to give up and die there. A sergeant's place was on his feet.

"You-all just keep proppin' me up. I'm goin' to live to be an *old* soldier. I ain't lettin' them white officers out of payin' me my pension money."

He fought to keep his mind running by trying to figure out how much money that might be. Jimbo and the others plugged the hole at both ends with dirty cloth to stop the blood. Gideon's knees sagged, but the men held him up.

He was going to make it. He knew at that moment he was going to live. He had only to keep his eyes open.

Vision cleared a little. The red haze paled. He could see the wind fluttering the feathers of the warrior's fallen shield. The Comanche did not move.

Something did. Gideon cut his gaze to the fallen dun horse and saw the other Indian pulling himself from under the dead weight. Limping Boy pushed cautiously to his knees, then to his feet. He stood there a moment, expecting to be shot. Slowly he drew the knife from his belt and threw it away so all could see.

Jimbo raised his carbine.

Gideon said, "Wait. I don't see no gun on him."

Jimbo lowered the weapon, but not much.

Gideon said, "Been enough killin'. Don't shoot him if you don't have to."

Limping Boy moved slowly toward the fallen Gray Horse, his anxious eyes sweeping the troopers' position. As his confidence strengthened, so did his steps. He made the last few in long limping strides and dropped to one knee. He placed the flat of his hand over his cousin's heart and felt for life. When he lifted the hand it was bloody, and his eyes were stricken. He bowed his head. Tears streamed down his face.

Gideon had never considered that an Indian warrior could cry.

Limping Boy looked around for the sorrel horse that had been Terrapin's. He started walking toward it.

Jimbo raised the carbine again.

"No," Gideon gritted. "Let him go."

Limping Boy caught the sorrel's reins and led it back where Gray Horse lay. He put his arms under those of his cousin and strained, lifting him up. The horse danced nervously, smelling the blood. Limping Boy tried to hoist his cousin onto the sorrel's back but could not.

The soldiers watched him struggle. Finally Jimbo handed his rifle to Lonnie Bowes and walked out slowly. Limping Boy watched him with fear but did not back away. Jimbo started talking, using the gentle tone that had always calmed horses for him. It seemed to calm the Indian. Jimbo took the reins, near the

sorrel's mouth, then patted the animal on the neck and held it
still.

Limping Boy lifted his cousin onto the sorrel's back, stomach
down. His eyes still distrustful of Jimbo, he knelt and retrieved
the fallen medicine shield.

Jimbo took a few steps backward to reassure him. Limping
Boy laid his hand on his cousin's body. He looked one more time
at Gideon and the other soldiers. His eyes were the saddest
Gideon had ever seen. He walked northward, leading the sorrel.
He did not look back again.

Solomon Tucker raised his carbine to the ready. "Sergeant,
we're lettin' that redskin get away."

Gideon motioned for him to put the weapon down. "It don't
matter. It's over." The nausea was coming upon him again, cold
sweat breaking on his face. But he could still see past the walking
Indian, beyond the creek where the other Comanches were in
retreat. "It's *all* over."

The troopers who had been spread out gathered quietly
around Gideon. He saw respect in their eyes, and relief, for they
could tell he was not going to die. He might take it in his head
never to die. In a raspy voice he told them, "They've cussed us
buffalo soldiers before, and they'll cuss us again. But you boys
done a job of work here. They can't never take that away from
us."

Far ahead of Limping Boy, the rest of the beaten war party
turned eastward toward Fort Sill and the agency, the sinking sun
at their backs. Limping Boy gave them a glance but did not follow. They would live out their lives on the reservation and be
buried there. But Gray Horse was going home—where he had
been free, where now he would always be free. Limping Boy set
his gaze upon the reddening Double Mountains, where Gray
Horse's spirits waited to claim him.

Ahead of him, a gray wolf trotted, its nose held high into the
north wind.

Epilogue

THE NINTH AND TENTH Cavalry regiments continued to see action in the Indian wars, moving to far western Texas, New Mexico and Arizona for the final years of the Apache campaigns. All four of the army's black regiments remained intact far into this century.

Two white officers who commanded black troops of the Tenth became supreme commanders in two of this nation's wars. William R. Shafter led American forces in Cuba during the Spanish-American War. John J. Pershing, commander-in-chief of American forces in France in World War I, was first known derisively as "Nigger Jack" because of his black troops. That nickname was later refined to "Black Jack."

Ben Ficklin town was destroyed by flood in 1882. Its survivors moved to the former whisky village of Saint Angela, which grew in population and respectability to become the city of San Angelo.

Fort Concho outlived the Comanche wars by more than a decade, pulling down its flag for the last retreat on March 27, 1889. Most of its buildings became residences and shops. When restoration efforts began sixty years later, a majority remained in good condition. It is one of the most remarkably well preserved frontier posts in existence today.

The Comanche chief Quanah Parker, a leader of the last resistance against the white man, became the strongest of the Comanche peace chiefs. He helped his people cross the difficult bridge onto the white man's road. He applied to the new life the same strong will he had applied to war. He became an accomplished businessman and oversaw his people's financial dealings with the white man, especially the cattlemen who leased Indian lands to graze their herds. Many of these cattlemen had been fierce enemies of the Comanches in their youth but—largely because of Quanah Parker—became their strongest non-Indian friends in middle age and the gray years. Old Rangers and old warriors would often smoke together and share memories of an open-plains era lost to them all.

Afterword

IN ONE SENSE, Elmer Kelton is an anomaly, for he is a full-time journalist as well as a prolific writer of fiction. In addition to over thirty stories printed between 1947 and 1955 in pulp magazines, Kelton has published twenty-six novels since his first, *Hot Iron*, in 1955. Of these, twenty-one can be termed popular because of the format generally attributed to that form of the Western. Three of these novels he authored as Lee McElroy and one—*Shotgun Settlement* (1969)—as Alex Hawk, a house name for the Paperback Library. Kelton's five big novels—*The Time It Never Rained* (1973), *The Day the Cowboys Quit* (1971), *The Good Old Boys* (1978), *Stand Proud* (1984), and *The Wolf and the Buffalo* (1980), all originally issued in hardback by Doubleday—are definitely not in the popular vein but show more clearly Kelton's penchant for character development, his feel for history and folklore, and his ability to construct meaningful plots set principally in West Texas.

Although Kelton has dealt with a black cowboy in *Wagontongue* (1972) and in some detail with Indian life in *Hanging Judge* (1969), *The Wolf and the Buffalo* marks a departure from his norm. In his other works, he has chosen the cattle kingdom, lawman-outlaw conflicts, and early Texas history as his source material. The characters are usually Anglos and Mexicans, and the racial prejudice typical of the period is recorded in the novels. Not so with *The Wolf and the Buffalo*, where Kelton's principal concern is with black soldiers and Comanche Indians. The genesis of this novel may account for the new focus. The book resulted from a request by editors at Reader's Digest Condensed Books for a novel about the black cavalry in the West. Reader's Digest had published Kelton's *The Good Old Boys* in condensed version in 1978 and was evidently pleased with the results. *The Wolf and the Buffalo* was reissued in condensed form in 1980.

Despite its atypical subject matter, *The Wolf and the Buffalo* fits naturally into Kelton's total body of work because it fills an important place in his overall treatment of the settlement of Texas. This treatment begins with *Massacre at Goliad* (1965) and its sequel, *After the Bugles* (1967), two books dealing with the Buckalew family as they come to Texas from the South to settle in Stephen F. Austin's colony in South Texas, fight through the defeat of the Mexican army at San Jacinto in 1836, and survive the resulting period of adjustment. In *The Time It Never Rained*, perhaps his strongest work, Kelton moves beyond the next hundred years, dealing with the drought that gripped the West Texas ranch land in the 1950s.

In a sense, *The Wolf and the Buffalo* is two novels skillfully interwoven to create a sympathetic picture of two quite different cultures locked in a fight to the death. One of these stories follows a young negro, Gideon Ledbetter, out of slavery in Louisiana after the Civil War ends and into the role of a black cavalryman, one of those the Indians called buffalo soldiers because their black curly hair resembled the shaggy bison or buffalo. Ledbetter serves most of his time in the Tenth U.S. Cavalry stationed at Fort Concho, located in present-day San Angelo. Through him, Kelton depicts the plight of a freed but still socially inferior man with the drive and ability to succeed when given a chance; the cavalry gives him that chance. His fortunes rise, though his life is fraught with conflict and disappointment.

The other story is that of Gray Horse, a young Comanche warrior riding proudly with other members of his tribe across West Texas in that period just after the Civil War when the Comanche still formed a physical barrier to Anglo settlement of the area. Following his vigil on one of the Double Mountains located between Abilene and Lubbock, Gray Horse develops his personal medicine only to see it disappear as his family and tribal way of life against an army patrol, which Ledbetter leads, rather than return to the reservation, where only his distraught wife and the grave of their young son await him.

Kelton describes the two cultures in some detail to emphasize the contrast. Gray Horse is nurtured by his tribal patterns of life—his courtship, his vigil, his associations in the warrior society. All of the rhythms of life support him until the system begins to fall apart with defeat by the buffalo hunters at Adobe Walls and the rout of the Indians from their winter quarters in Palo Duro Canyon; in that rout, the forces of Colonel Ranald Mackenzie effectively ended the threat of the Plains tribes to Anglo settlement. The life of Gideon, however, is far different. The abuse he receives following his freedom from slavery and the hopelessness he shares with his companion, Jimbo, as they find a niche for themselves in the army certainly lack the efficacy of the family life Gray Horse has experienced. The plight of the black enlisted men, cut off from women of their kind and shunned even by the rough element in the village of Saint Angela, is further heightened when Gideon thinks he has found love with Hannah York, a beautiful young negro woman and the ward of an old negress washerwoman. When he discovers that Hannah is really a prostitute for the white soldiers, he is crushed, and when he sees her years later, a ruined alcoholic, his hopes of a family life appear dashed forever. He sees the unfair disparity between his life and that of the white officers who command the otherwise black units, duty most Anglos despise. Despite adversity, Ledbetter learns his craft of soldiering in experiences that range from the dangerous charge of his unruly horse toward the first Indians he encounters to the stern discipline of Sgt. Esau Nettles, another talented black man who is determined to make Ledbetter realize his own potential for soldiering. As the novel closes, Ledbetter has replaced the dogged Sgt. Nettles, now deceased, and commands a patrol out searching for renegade Indians.

The action in the novel—the combat between military and Indian—is the stuff of epic, one of the few episodes in American history offering that possibility. Whether by design or not, Kelton incorporates several epic conventions and qualities into the piece. Among these are a balanced contrast in action and characters that strengthens the underlying tension of the piece by offering a dual viewpoint, causing the reader to feel acutely the ambivalence of the

Kelton uses something like epithets in the Indians' descriptive names and the use of the appellation "Charger" for Gideon Ledbetter. There is a strong emphasis on weapons, fighting, and horses; and the strength and courage of the heroes in battle are important facets of their reputations. Further, the conflict between Gray Horse and Ledbetter resembles that between Achilles and Hector. Intervention or guidance of the gods is seen in the spirit that guides Gray Horse, and the somewhat episodic nature of the work is united through the use of the central figures. Also noticeable is the journey motif, seen especially in the trek of the soldiers in search of the Indians upon the High Plains of Texas. The end of a culture, much like the sack of Troy, is paralleled by the capture of the Indians in Palo Duro Canyon and the slaughter of their horses. The buffalo soldiers fight a war in which they have no vested interest, similar to those Greek warriors on the plain at Troy, many of whom had no personal interest in the war they were engaged in.

The conclusion of the novel is typical of Kelton. The tension that has prompted the action is temporarily resolved—the Indians are defeated and settled on the reservation; the soldiers will go on to fight elsewhere. There is no golden sunset for the surviving protagonist, who must press on to face other challenges. In that sense, Kelton's work is universal; the theme which underlies much of his fiction is the characters' attempt to cope productively with adversity much like that which confronts us all.

Lawrence Clayton
Hardin-Simmons University
Abilene, Texas

About the Author

For more than fifty years, Elmer Kelton, who died on August 22, 2009, was Texas' most respected writer about the American West. Author of more than fifty novels, Kelton wrote both serious historical novels and what he called "powder burners." But whether writing serious fiction or genre fiction, Elmer Kelton's work was marked by careful craftsmanship and serious purpose. He was recognized by his peers as "the Best Western Writer of All Time." He was awarded seven Spur Awards by the Western Writers of America, the Levi Strauss Golden Saddleman Award from WWA, four Wrangler Awards from the National Cowboy & Western Heritage Museum, and the Lon Tinkle Award from the Texas Institute of Letters for Lifetime Achievement. For many years, he combined his work as a novelist with a distinguished career as an agricultural journalist, spending more than twenty years as a columnist and editor with *The Livestock Weekly*. His passing leaves a large gap in Texas letters.